D1363554

ALTHEA

(The Divorce of Adam and Eve)

a novel by J.M. Alonso

FICTION COLLECTIVE  NEW YORK

A portion of this book appeared in
New Boston Review

This publication is supported by a grant from the National
Endowment for the Arts in Washington, D.C., a Federal agency,
and with the support of the New York State Council on the Arts,
Brooklyn College, and Teachers & Writers Collaborative.

First Edition

Typesetting by Fleetwood Graphics, Madison, Wisconsin

Library of Congress Catalog No. 76-2875

ISBN: 0-914590-24-3 (hardcover)

ISBN: 0-914590-25-1 (paperback)

Published by FICTION COLLECTIVE

distributed by George Braziller, Inc.
One Park Avenue
New York, N.Y. 10016

For Jessica

Althea

(The Divorce of Adam and Eve)

MULDOON'S CONFESSION

Here goes:

I HAVE NEVER LIKED WOMEN. AS A MATTER OF FACT, I HAVE USUALLY DISLIKED THEM ACTIVELY. TO ME, WOMEN HAVE BEEN THE OPPOSITE OF PEOPLE. By which I mean human, which people ideally should be.

Well, maybe being Irish Catholic and living with my mother until she died a few years ago didn't help my spiritual development any. Mel would say so, if he didn't think I'd punch him in the nose, so he just thinks it.

Naturally, I always do give his opinion serious consideration, because he's not only my oldest friend and advisor, but a genuine, ordained psychiatrist. I mean, hands have been laid upon Mel's that once had hands laid upon them that had Sigmund Freud's own hands laid upon them. But Mel notwithstanding, I still don't think it's my mother's fault.

So, for the sake of making a good confession, let me describe Bridgid Muldoon, my mother.

Short legged and low to the ground whether walking or sitting, she always looked vigilant, as if poised forward on the edge of a throne, watching for plotters. She was tricky, cold and proud, imperious

1

when she had the chance, and ever ready to sacrifice the well-being of any daughter or daughter-in-law for the sake of her convenience, with no visible remorse. Or invisible.

Really, despite 40 years of service as a domestic, she was very much like a queen. And I mean a real queen, whose one morality was *raison d état*, and as to her ego, it was like General Patton's, at least.

Yet, above all, she always considered herself a humble woman from the Old Country, who "knew her place"—unlike a lot of her neighbors and the people she worked for. And because she "knew her place," she looked down on everybody in this world, including the Pope, since he, after all, was an Italian.

As far as I can tell, she never trusted anyone or anything, deep down. And did not die of a broken heart. As a matter of fact, having learned to drive late in life and unwilling to let anybody else touch the wheel, she took the lives of four others when she went, in a three-vehicle collision involving a gigantic orange MTA bus, in Davis Square, Somerville, where the right of way is usually open to debate.

And yet, I have to admit, I got to like her better than I did most people towards the end, after all was said and done. (And I said "like," not "s and to be with for long," which is a different issue.) It's true she was relentless. God help you if she had the upper hand. To the end, she could only be dealt with gently after being disarmed—some of my sisters would say dismembered—and she would never give you a break in a fight. But at least you could always negotiate with her, so long as you had a position of strength. And once in a while, unlike most, she was capable of generosity, even if never at the slightest expense to her ego.

But, say what you will about Mrs. Muldoon, and this is why I disagree with Mel, she certainly was a person. A person and a half, which is why her ego required more space, I guess. As she used to put it so often (it was really maternal generosity on her part, preparing me for the world), "The more there is of mine, the less there is of yours. Remember that, Jerry."

Maybe Mel does have a point. Who knows, since it's supposed to be subconscious. But I can't buy it. Mostly because sex is supposed to be involved. And it is, when it comes to women, which is why I have my own theory as to why, for me, women and people have tended to be mutually exclusive terms.

What makes much more sense to me is the fact that I grew up with the firm belief that the Devil in Eden worked through Eve, whom I could always associate with sex and femininity much more easily than my mother. It was inculcated in me as a child (with ease, never straining my credulity) that deceitful (and, by definition, false-appearing) Eve, her vain head reeling with the golden vapors of fermented apples, gave in to her foolish climbing ambitions and got poor, honest and straightforward Adam into all that trouble we are paying for to this day. This was something Bridgid Muldoon believed in as firmly as Mel does in the Oedipal complex. Maybe more so.

Now that I think about it, Adam never struck me as the ambitious type, at all. Exactly the opposite, poor guy. As my mother would say, "He knew his place." And I do remember as a kid, seeing those familiar pictures on church walls, and not liking Eve, precisely because she was so treasonous and seductive to poor Adam, who was no match for her, and who was henceforth condemned to work and live from the sweat of his brow.

So, since I'm trying to make the best confession possible, I want to make good and sure to point out that to me Eve was not at all like my mother. After all, my mother "knew her place," she said so herself, all the time, and therefore looked down on foolish snobs like Eve and the women whose houses she cleaned. Unlike dumb old Adam, my mother would have seen right through Eve in one second flat, because she knew Eve's kind. And not being a man, Eve couldn't pull the wool over *her* eyes. No sir. Hence her basic queenly contempt for all males, a "boobish lot," she felt, and dirty, too.

But even more important, I always saw Eve as physically very different from my mother, by which I mean gracefully long legged, slender and pretty (prettier if she wore makeup, which she certainly would now, to hallucinate the helplessly susceptible male psyche).

In other words, I'm trying to say that Eve was like "women" while my mother was not. And I always expected I was going to marry a woman, assuming she would be different (please God!) from my mother.

And in case there's any confusion, I don't mean this the way Italians (Mel assures me) can say, "All women are whores, except for my mother, who is a virgin." No question about it: virginity, purity, and kindred utopian ideals (such as an ultimately desired, gloriously wanton, one-woman harem all my own) have to do with sex. I don't argue with Mel there. What I am saying is that these juicy ideals had

3

no connection whatsoever with the unideal world to which my mother so aggressively belonged, and from which she refused to budge. She was, as I said, very much a person, and therefore unideal to a fault.

So, here is the basic reason, I believe, why I found women the opposite of people, one with which Mel would agree. In a word: Fantasy. Almost at once, like it or not, they reek of it upon being sighted. And like it or not, they always tend at once to become humanly invisible, cloaked in the inevitable jungle steam of men's Oedipal fantasies, cultural or personal, or both, it doesn't matter. And the more ruthless ones haven't wanted to give up this power. They've encouraged the male psyche to lose itself in its own fumes, while the others, even when they wanted to be perceived as people, beyond fantasy, couldn't be, for the same reason. Because the male psyche needs no encouragement anyhow.

And I was never so uppity that I presumed to be above this. How could I, when I could never forget from my childhood how even the best of men—and surely Robin Hood was one of them—could be fooled. And was. I may never get over (more painfully disillusioning to me than Eve, from whom I expected nothing) discovering that sweet Maid Marian ended up working for the Sheriff of Nottingham, bleeding good old Robin to death in the name of some false decency—because all of a sudden (always those social ambitions, I guess) Maid Marian had decided, without telling any of Robin's Merry Men, that she wanted to move along and belong to the righteous Establishment. Incredible, I read. And reread. And reread. But it was so. Always the same. Even as Robin lay dying, growing paler by the hour, he was always glad to see her (that sweet, oval-faced vision of hope!) as she came in the door, and brought the silver bleeding-bowl and the razor to his bedside, with a smile as merciless as it was sweet. It nearly killed me.

Robin never, ever caught on to her. I don't believe he could bear to, of course. Frankly, sad as I was to see him dying, I was glad he died without the pain of knowing, because, to put it simply, if you can't trust Maid Marian, who *can* you trust? The world would have died before him. Withered before his eyes.

Of course, the "smarter" and crueler readers might observe that *they* were never fooled because Maid Marian is simply a variant telling of Eve, with Robin another dumb old Adam in a Sherwood Eden, and that therefore we should not have been surprised. But all

4

I would have said to that was: yes, that may be so, but some things one never gets used to. Not the true-hearted. And as inelegant and unsophisticated as it may be, I believed that a real man, one noble in spirit, was always fooled, by definition, and that, as far as I could see, only scoundrels or defused males, cynical in their poverty, could possibly have seen through Maid Marian's lovely veils and then smiled with thin-lipped, knowing amusement. A true man could only remain blind, or weep inconsolably.

And so I thought because, I confess now, mine was the greatest cynicism about women. If, let's say, my mother had done Robin in, I might not really have been surprised. After all, that would have been just people for you. An unreliable lot, sometimes, yet forgivable, humanly speaking. But what I could not forgive was the behavior of the Maid Marian Impersonators (sadly accepting that there were no real Maid Marians) who suckered me every damn time. And anyway, say what you might about Bridgid Muldoon, who might have been, perhaps, capable of slaughtering a generation if she'd seen the need, she'd never come at you with any hallucinating nonsense any more than Little John or Friar Tuck would. As she held the bowl and razor before you, you'd know the executioner at once. There'd be no ethereal glitter there. No sweet illusion. No false hope. And the same if she was actually trying to cure you.

Which is why any Robin, I'm certain, even knowing secretly that Maid Marian meant his death, and that Bridgid was a genuine medical attempt to rescue him, would pick Maid Marian every time. But that's precisely the trouble, of course. What man wants to live with a real Bridgid, when he can die with a false Marian? All that is required is that he, Robin, never perceive Marian as people. Only as his most childish illusion. And that is easy. Even inevitable.

But anyway, to finish my confession, which I never expected to cover me with glory: whosoever fault it was, my mother's or my culture's, it always turned out the same. To me, women were consistently the opposite of people. Less than human, by definition.

And, if they did metamorphose into people, which of course happened very often, then they ceased to be Women for me.

I'll even go so far as to admit that sex with women has always been enormously attractive to me, satisfying and quickly mythic. In other words: sex. However, the notion of sex with *people*, even female people, always struck me edging distastefully toward perversion, thoroughly un-mythic, and possibly admissible *only* if there were no

5

women available. And even then, not expected to be very appetizing. Because, of course, my real appetite was for myth. Colors. Perfume. Incredible hair I could see only with my eyes closed. That is to say, theater. The eternal. The archetypal.

To which women, for both good and ill, tended, as far as I could see, as if answering some innate and implacable natural law. Maybe being closer to Nature at that, they only resembled the human the way archetypes do.

Which is, of course, why I needed so much help from the Unseen and Mysterious Forces. To navigate not only through the blinding hallucinations of the materialistic modern world but through the biological ones filtered up through my own male fantasy. Otherwise, I would never have seen that Light in all its quintessential human clarity, nor perceived Althea as the most unarchetypal, people person I would ever know, poor thing.

For which my own inner Light, obviously, needed considerable development.

THE FIRST TIME

But let me go back to the first time I saw the Light.

It happened after two days of icy October rains and gale force winds, when I was visiting Dr. Mel at McLeod's.

It was about an hour before sunset. The dark rains has stopped some time ago, and the light was now coming through the sagging gray sky much like a dawn.

Almost sleepily, I was staring out of Mel's office window without really looking, half imagining I was not only seeing a dawn, but spring, too. Despite the nearness of winter, the air close to the ground had warmed up, and the softened, wet earth looked yielding enough to let my mind conjure up a few crocuses coming up through the flowerless, mustard colored grass. Everything looked near at hand and deceptively possible under the intimacy of that sagging gray sky, so peculiarly full of light and chilly water, bright and dark at the same time.

In the far distance (not that I was paying attention) at the edge of the golf course where the woods begin, a brown haired, slender man was running in his faded Exeter Academy sweat suit.

He had a way of circling the course and then disappearing into the same spot in the distant woods for a while, only to suddenly come busting out into the clearing again, kicking high, fast and frenzied, as if running for his life. And alarming anybody who saw him do it for the first time, too, because his face turned bright red, as if he were escaping something back in those woods, some cruel creature that had just tried to capture him and maybe, from the look of things, tried to rip out his dearly held, red and palpitating heart. And the explosive burst of adrenaline never let him slow down, it seemed, until he was hundreds of yards out of the woods, either. Whereupon, regaining his calm, he would begin to jog lightly again, circling the course and heading magnetically for the same aperture in the woods he'd just escaped from.

I was disregarding him because I'd seen him do it before. Just about every sunset I'd been there, at least lately. Mel had informed me he did it at dawn too, adding that in his medical opinion the man was progressing splendidly, with his enthusiasm for physical fitness standing him in good stead. And for all I knew, that was so. But somehow I couldn't think so (when I'd thought about it) because, even though he wasn't really doing it, every time he busted out of the woods, looking terrified and kicking at high speeds, I couldn't help but imagine him cupping his hands over his groin, as if racing out of the range of some mysterious Diana-like creature he'd imagined in there. It might have been just Time, of course, which was what usually made other men I knew run hard, trying to protect some terrified and retracting treasure, also in sweat suits, every morning, before work.

Anyway, now I know I should have paid more attention to him. But I didn't then. He was just part of the ordinary landscape to me, and that afternoon the labial softness of the ground called me much more. It was much more appealing, as well as unusual, especially in that dawn-dusk light, at that time of year. It was letting me feel, all through my body, a strange combination of the intimate pleasure of both waking up and going to sleep. And then, just as my mind was coming up with two or three beautiful crocuses, I noticed her. Althea.

She was all wrapped up in her faintly purplish, woolen clothes, looking as if she herself were full of darkened light and chilly water, like the sky.

She was standing upright, still as a statue on the mustard colored hill, directly beneath the two gigantic, gray old apple trees that normally block the view of the abandoned golf course. They weren't blocking the view now. After the ferocious two-day storm, there were no apples and very few leaves left up on their far-reaching branches. They were all over the ground now, making the area look run-down and exhausted, as if Eden had become a slum. And the giant trees, which looked especially bald, struck me in their poverty as what the Tree of Life and the Tree of Knowledge would probably look like today, if we happened to come across them. They certainly didn't look as if they had much by way of magical fruit with which to tempt us anymore. More than anything, they had the singularly unmagical look of very old and very stationary captive elephants standing around at the zoo, chained by one back leg, incapable of going anywhere significant, even if they were free to move.

I say I noticed her, but at the time I didn't think I was noticing *her*, specifically. Not at first, because she was just one among a flock of other, round-backed patients that were peacefully browsing over the mustard colored hill, quietly picking up apples on all fours.

She stood out because she was the only one upright, and the only one not picking up apples. But other than that, she seemed to fit as part of a whole, even though her only occupation in that whole seemed to be just to stand there, rigidly holding out her gathered skirts as the wind occasionally flapped her sleeves and hair.

She was so stiff she looked as if she couldn't bend, as if she were made of one unyielding piece. And as for the other round-backed patients, they were the opposite, because they looked as if they couldn't possibly straighten up and walk on two legs, somehow. They only seemed capable of rearing up on their hindquarters just enough to deposit the little brown and red apples into her gathered-up skirts before dropping themselves softly back down on the ground, to go get more apples.

I couldn't see her profile (I didn't know I was trying), much less her eyes, because the wind had moved her long, heavy, dark brown hair across her face and kept it there. In her veiled stillness, and because of the purple hue to her clothes, she reminded me of a draped Lenten statue in a Catholic church. And she also reminded me of some tough, tenacious purplish flowers that turn up through the New England soil in the fall that wouldn't look beautiful anywhere else.

Meantime, Mel (who was already Hospital Director while I was still an aging graduate student in English, getting nowhere) was placidly occupied at his desk with some confidential papers no doubt

9

having to do with the pastoral scene outside, around Althea.

McLeod's was, as Mel liked to put it when in his Captain Horatio Hornblower mood (complete with arms folded behind his back), "his first ship." He only acted like that, of course, in the privacy of our company.

So, considering everything at face value, I would have thought everything was serene, especially inside me. But I must have sounded some strange alarm when I said, "Hey, Mel. What's going on out there?" because he suddenly jerked his placid head up as if a firecracker had gone off under his chair, and in nothing flat he was standing next to me at the window, barking, "Where! Where!" his ears pricked up, his eyes gleaming with alertness and intelligence as he checked out his flock.

He was acting, of course. Exaggerating, but genuinely alarmed, which was his way. If one were to wake him up in the middle of the night, yelling "Fire!", truly terrified, he would also have put on a broad performance of a man wakened in the middle of the night by cries of, "Fire!" In fact, the more he overdid his responses, the more there was in him to overdo.

But nothing was out of order, as far as he could see. The pastoral tableau was just as arcadian as before, so he let off a somewhat monstrous sigh as he relaxed, and said, "Sorry about that, X.J., . . . for a second there, I thought all my good work had gone to pieces."

"Hey, I never saw you move like *that*, before," I said, "What did you think I was looking at out there, a ritual execution?"

Most soberly (he was on top of the world, those days) he arched an eyebrow in a way that did not eliminate the possibility, and pronounced, "Anything can happen at Preserve Time . . . which happens to be right now, when all the apples are on the ground. It is a time, I'm afraid, for constant vigilance. Constant!" he added, looking at me most severely. Which meant to me he wasn't going back to his paperwork, and wanted to play.

"No kidding . . . ," I said.

"None, X.J. Until my arrival, Preserve Time was always living hell around here. Extremely problematic, what with people slithering up those trees and eating themselves sick enough to fall . . . to say nothing of snipers, of course."

"I'm impressed," I said.

"Oh? Well, *you* can make light of it, but let me tell you what else

10

might impress you, should you wander around down there unattended. Getting smacked off the head with an apple. Most infuriating, believe me. Especially when you are not expecting it . . . *Not*, mind you," he added and smiled his most imperious Captain Hornblower smile, "that they've *dared* against my person that way. However, when somebody does get popped you can expect an apple war down there that can last for hours and polarize this whole institution. The last time, for example, it took my staff over an hour, by my office clock, before order was restored. And *then*, of course, we had hours and hours of fixing up busted noses and broken front teeth . . . to say nothing of the time spent trying to calm the hysterical rage among some of the losers."

"What happened, did your goon squad get too repressive or something?" I said, and he laughed, "The hell they did! You know I'm the softest Liberal in the world. It was a bunch of overzealous patients, as usual, that's what it was. They caught a distinguished member of the Harvard faculty up in one of those trees, and they ordered him down, with no ifs or buts about it. Climbing is against a set of rules we've agreed on *collectively*, I'll have you know, in order to preserve our apple supply for Preserve Time, so, when they told him to get his ass down, he started pretending to be hard of hearing, which made them yell all the louder and get closer and closer, and madder and madder of course, because they knew damn well he could hear them, which was exactly what he wanted, of course, so he could skonk them, which he did with fantastic accuracy." And then Mel began scrutinizing the hill from his window, until finally he said, "Ah . . . there!" breaking into surprisingly fond and indulgent tones as he pointed out the wrongdoer, "*There* he is!"

What I saw was a perfectly bald, large-bodied man with skinny arms and legs around his sagging hulk, and quite as docile looking as any of the other round-backed patients. When he came up to the girl with the gathered-up skirts (she wasn't Althea to me yet), he reared up gently on his hindquarters just enough for me to see his mustachioed face—and suddenly, I recognized him: Professor Ford Law! His behavior was different from that of the others only in that he tried to gather up more apples at one time than anybody else, which meant he had trouble negotiating the half dozen or so that kept rolling off his forearms. But other than that, Professor Law, in whom I too had known a fearsome individuality at another time, seemed a perfectly adjusted and forgettably standard member of the orthodoxy on the hill. "I know him," I said. "I just had trouble recognizing him on all fours. He certainly looks peaceful," I said, smiling, but frankly, it saddened me.

"Doesn't he, though?" Mel said, "Well, *that* is the model quadruped who factionalized this whole place. I'll have you know that even my staff, which has orders to remain absolutely neutral—no matter what—got caught in the middle with no other choice than to join the zealots against the dozen or so patients who suddenly decided the rules could go fuck themselves because they'd found a hero in Professor Ford Law. I'm afraid, X.J., it left a very bad taste. When the official party threw in with the extreme Right Wing, it turned the rebels into the sentimental favorites . . . as you might expect."

"Sorry to hear that, Mel," I said. "I sure hope your staff has regained its neutral image."

Mel put out his lower lip and tilted his head to think good thoughts. "Well . . . *I'd* like to think so. Although memories in these places can be unnaturally long. There's a kind of institutional collective unconscious, you know. There really is. You can spend tens of thousands to refurbish a whole place, make a new start, and then, one day, the paint cracks or something, and the eeriest things come seeping through the walls. Stuff no present patients could possibly have been here to see, like . . . say, the rash of suicide hangings at dawn back in '31 . . . from those apple trees, down there . . . ," and then, interrupting himself cheerfully, he said, "By the way, would you like a bargain in cider?"

"No thanks," I said, unable to check a grimace. "It probably tastes funny." And Mel broke out laughing at my ingenuousness.

"What a barbaric reaction!" he said, shaking his head. "You're so retrograde it's almost refreshing. Really, you *must* try to overcome your Catholic past and stop connecting the mentally ill with souls possessed by the Devil," and he laughed again. "Besides . . . ," he said, "believe me, it's the best cider in the world. And the *hard* cider," he said, "that's even better! It's unique, really. You could drink it forever, because it never gets cloying, and it gives you a drunk you wouldn't believe. Honest to God, I don't know what the secret is either. Maybe there's a McLeod's method, handed down from generation to generation, like the Benedictine formula for brandy," and he half smiled and shrugged. "Or . . . I don't know . . . maybe it's these specific trees . . . All I know is that it's

12

fantastic."

I wasn't sure whether he was serious about his peculiar cider or not, but I had stopped paying attention to him because—just over his shoulder—the scene on the hill had suddenly become illuminated by quite another light. It was becoming completely transvalued. The same things were going on as before, but what I was seeing was different, and not so peaceful, either.

Of course, I didn't believe what I was seeing. But I was seeing it just the same. Not that I understood it, because the Unseen and Mysterious Forces were having at me.

I stood there resisting, trying hard to pretend to both Mel and myself that I was still watching what he'd described: the harmonious peace of Preserve Time, the communal gathering of apples, Mel's triumph as a social engineer.

But, unhappily, it just was not true.

In the revelation of the new Light, the real focus of the action wasn't the gathering of apples at all. It was the tall, upright girl with the gathered-up skirts. What really seemed to be going on out there, as a matter of fact, was the girl's painful indoctrination into becoming round-backed and docile like the others, who relentlessly continued to bring her more and more apples, dropping them into her gathered-up skirts, which were obviously getting heavier and heavier by the moment. It struck me, with brutal clarity, that they were all actually trying to make her bow forward from the accumulating weight, which she was mutely resisting with a peculiar, blind kind of obstinacy.

I felt myself getting miserably anxious, almost sensing physically in myself the strain of how painfully heavy her skirts were becoming as they started to bulge and heap. But despite the growing weight, somehow she still managed to keep her back homosapiently erect, her arms unnaturally, heroically parallel to the ground. Her face and neck remained covered by her hair, but the strain which I couldn't help sensing began showing on my own jaw and neck, which I tried to hide. Fortunately, Mel wasn't looking at me, but to add to my discomfort as I continued trying not to believe what I was seeing so clearly, Mel was off again about his cider. "You won't believe this, but I've had experts taste it, and *they* simply can't get over it! For ethical reasons, of course, I've resisted entering the cider in any contests. But boy! Have I been tempted! Look down there . . . ," Mel said, distressingly pleased with his world and obviously finding it good, and not at all as I was seeing it. "Look at all those apples! More cider soon! You'll just have to taste it!"

". . . I don't think I want to . . . ," I managed to say, permitting myself to reveal no more. After all, maybe it would soon shift back again to what I'd been seeing before. But it gave no sign of doing so, as the others kept heaping apples on the silent, obstinate girl, and I couldn't possibly understand what was holding her up. All I could think of was that I'd heard that sometimes the mad have the strength of ten.

"No . . . ?" Mel said, a bit disappointed. So, to change the subject and to try to take my mind off what I continued seeing on the hill, I said, "No thanks, really . . . Do you vampires make anything else I might like?"

He laughed, good-humoredly. Absolutely relaxed. "As a matter of fact," he said, easily stepping in front of me, facing me, as the scene on the hill persisted behind him, "we do. Or did, I should say. Unfortunately, I recently lost a marvelously talented lady whose great gift was making apple butter. Truly incredible apple butter."

"Lost?" I said, unsettled by the word, turning to look at him by forcing my eyes away from the hill. When Mel said "lost," it usually meant by suicide, which I believe infuriated him because he hated to lose anything.

But his eyes twinkled pleasantly at my having said "lost," and he said, "No, no . . . sorry to mislead you. I only meant lost by becoming an outpatient. And you know, the funniest thing is that she swears she can't make it on the outside to save her life? She thinks she only has her apple butter knack when she's here . . . I think it's the local apples, of course. I almost wish her a relapse, her apple butter's so good," he said, and grinned, adding modestly, "I'm only joking, of course."

For the moment, Mel's talking about the non-suicidal woman with the mysterious apple butter knack had nearly managed to get my mind off the scene in back of him. But then, out of the corner of my eye, I picked up the start of a strangely feverish and then frenzied activity among the round-backed patients that were now bubbling all around her on the hill.

It was as if everything were speeding up, faster and faster, remarkably like the fury of water rising to a boil, as all of a sudden I saw first a few and then several more go spilling over, tumbling and rolling down the hillside, angrily chasing after the brown and red apples that were now streaming down by the dozens.

When they came back up, they were obviously furious, gripping the apples, which they then tried to deposit in her gathered-up skirts again, as if *that* were where they rightfully belonged.

But then I realized she'd dropped her skirts. They just weren't gathered up anymore. And I was sure *that* was true.

She was standing just as upright as ever, and her face was still covered over by her hair, but her arms were down by her sides now, as limp as her clothing, and the limpness seemed to frustrate and enrage all the others all the more. A couple of them even tried to prop her arms up for her, stuffing the cloth of her skirts into her hands, trying to make her hold them up like before. But she'd just let everything drop inertly again, and what few apples had just been put there went tumbling down the hillside, whereupon more round-backed patients immediately went grimacing, rolling and tumbling down after them.

"Oh, dear . . . ," Mel said, seeing what I was seeing too. "I'd better get out there quick. Althea's being difficult again," and he hurried out of the room, leaving me looking out the window.

I still couldn't see her face because of her hair, but now I was sure, absolutely sure, she was smiling as she kept her arms inert, victoriously useless at her sides, while the other patients kept shaking them and mobbing around her.

In a moment, Mel reappeared before me, but much smaller now, on the other side of the window pane.

(On that hill, underneath the trees, next to Althea, he was down to scale. I didn't understand, of course, that the Unseen and Mysterious Forces were planting the image in my soul, and that the day would come when it would burst forth in a vision I hope never to undergo again.)

Because of the window and the distance, I couldn't hear what was being said.

But I could see they were all still extremely agitated as the boiling mood knitted itself tightly around her, and around Mel, too, who was now in their midst as they jabbered away, appealing to him, indignantly shaking apples from their crouching positions as if the apples were proof of something or other.

Mel listened patiently, gently holding her left arm, protecting her while she stood as motionless, even more motionless than the trees, whose branches moved slightly in the wind. And motionless as could

15

possibly be, she seemed as indifferent to Mel as to the whole jab-
bering mob and their furiously shaking apples.

Then, finally, Mel began saying something. Calmly. And the
boiling began easing down as they listened, with more and more of
the patients tending to crouch down, sit on their heels or on the
ground, until all their motion simmered to a calm surface too.

Soon they all looked as motionless as Althea, except for Mel, who,
ever holding her arm, talked gently on and on, as if he were keeping
the waters flat with the gentle breeze of his sermon. And very obviously, though I couldn't hear it, a sermon it was. Undoubtedly
about living with one another.

And for a long time after that day, all that remained concretely
with me was the final picture of Mel holding her limp arm, on the
hill, under the huge, denuded, gray trees, addressing that congre-
gation of momentarily obedient but unsympathetic patients who
only moments before had seemed ready to lynch her.

I can't say I "thought" about it often.

But still, this picture had a way of popping up in my mind
regularly, with all the enigmatic air of self-importance that events
can have in dreams, with the difference that this was a still picture.
Like an *ex-voto* painting on glass. The figures were little. The perspective, with Althea at the center, primitive. And the colors garish.
All illuminated by the sudden strength of that Light coming off her.

And the picture also had a way of dissolving almost as quickly as it
presented itself. As if, having had its mysterious say, it preferred to
leave before I could ask any questions.

But other than that, for a long time the Unseen and Mysterious
Forces didn't do anything else to me.

I even began to accept being visited by her image. I mean, it was
regular, even stable. And it wasn't hard on me because apparently it
wasn't getting any worse, so I didn't worry too much more about my
mental balance. I certainly continued to see the rest of life in the
usual ways.

If those sudden apparitions made me feel anything, it wasn't about
her, really, but about a great sense of distance, which carried an odd,
helpless sadness with it. I even began interpreting the visitations
strictly in terms of that melancholy sense of distance, because the

girl on the hill felt as far from me as any object could possibly be, or any planet even. And that is how I came to accept it. With comfort.

But that sense of comfort was not to last. The Unseen and Mysterious Forces had other plans. It turns out their intention was to move me closer and closer to the Light.

They worked a step at a time, and I never knew when they'd have me take the next step. I'd just be walking along one day, moving in a direction I thought I had chosen, when all of a sudden I'd find myself striding right for the Light, on a path I'd never imagined.

Like the second time.

THE SECOND TIME

It was eleven a.m. I couldn't have been less prepared.

My soul had not yet completed its reentry into my body after its long night out, alley-catting God knows where, when I found myself fully dressed and chugging along like an automaton, doing my best to keep up with Mel along the McLeod Hospital corridors.

Mel, of course, had already been up for hours, and from what I gathered, with great success, as usual. Back then, just to show me the difference between us, he used to tell me he was sharp as a tack from the moment he opened his eyes in the morning. And I used to tell him that this was only because his soul was so disgustingly domesticated for the purposes of work that it never strayed much further away from his body than where he hung his clothes up at night, all so he could get both of them on real quick in the morning to proceed with his career. For which, I assured him, he would pay in Hell, because Jesus Christ died for us underachievers. At which explanation, with the customary cockiness of the unbeliever, he only smiled and said, "You wish . . . "

Anyway, that morning, our mission seemed simple enough. First we were to go to his office to get our squash rackets, and then we would proceed to the Hospital's court, where Mel had now decided he was established enough to exercise a *droit du seigneur* "for therapeutic reasons." Since courts were in short supply around Boston, this meant a breakthrough for us, so as we hurried along he kept assuring me, "Don't worry. We'll get that court. I'll chase *anybody* out of there when I want to play. Lodges, Cabots, *Anybody!* It's my duty! You see, I've concluded it teaches limits. Limits, X.J.! That's where we *all* have to start, isn't it?"

Having trouble keeping up, I disregarded his self-congratulatory manner as his pre-squash war dance (little did I know he was setting me up for bigger game), figuring he was showing off like that to irritate me a little, or just to pretend to want to irritate me a little, as was his great pleasure when the biological impulse to joy overtook him. When that happened, he dearly loved to clown and strut his stuff in the privacy of our company. And I stress that: in the privacy of our company, because he had not yet chosen to play the likes of Captain Hornblower in front of everybody, or any of his other Big Daddy versions, for that matter. No matter how manic he might become when we were alone, we both knew full well what a timid, ingratiating and bespectacled type he could instantly revert to, especially in front of two particular groups: attractive women and the aristocratic rich.

So, as everything along the corridor walls rushed back past me in a blur, including his prattle about himself, I hadn't yet noticed that there was something different about the morning itself. As I kept lurching along, only dimly did I sense with each forward falling step that the world around me wasn't quite the same as yesterday. And furthermore, that all this movement I was caught up in now seemed to be occurring on some other pleasant planet, which was being fed by a different sun.

Even Mel, I began to half notice, was a little different too, somehow, coming through as more "cultural" looking than usual.

His thinning hair had gotten a bit longish of late, and now it was draping infinitesimally, but gracefully, over the back of his shirt collar. This was not the fashion with professionals back in the '50s that it would later become, which put Mel, unknown to everybody, ahead of his time. But that wasn't the only change. Even his thin, elastic figure seemed to be moving as if responding to the mysterious new sun. And as he raced half a step ahead of me, he emitted the vibrant, calisthenic cheerfulness I've always associated with younger symphony conductors.

What can I say, except that in that optimistic morning light, everything about him was managing to suggest less and less the ordinary psychiatrist and more and more the successful artist of some elegant, managerial sort. I wouldn't care to say what an ordinary psychiatrist looks like, of course, but it certainly was getting harder and harder to take him for one of them, which I knew would not have displeased him, now that he was established as one.

What this really meant was that Mel was at last getting brazen enough to go public with his once private disguises—for this was the first day in the history of Mankind that Mel Fish could easily be mistaken for Leonard Bernstein, at least from the side, except for his glasses.

But it still hadn't hit me with its full force.

Not until he led me around the next corner, as if into an ambush, whereupon the transfiguration which had surely started months before, subtly and unannounced, exploded into full bloom. Then, it was complete and undeniable.

With that corner turned, the new Mel came to a full stop, triumphant as an exclamation mark, and he beamed at me, his teeth in perfect condition. As if by a miracle, his elastic, cheerful elegance had become *all* symphonic optimism at last, and there was absolutely nothing sordidly medical left about his personal aura at all.

For a moment I had trouble adjusting my eyes. I simply couldn't account for the transformation, so complete it even included a new brilliance around him so dazzling that I couldn't do anything except come to a full stop myself.

And then I realized what the source of both his pride and his brilliance was: the corridor he'd led me into, opening up before me, which was also transformed. Absolutely resplendent. Flamboyantly decked out with the brightly colored art work of his patients fluttering all over the place, afloat in a magnificent sunlight flooding down from the tall windows that would have done credit to any Summer Arts Festival pavilion. Which meant that hospital corridor or not, there was nothing sordidly medical looking about Mel's place of business, either.

And in the foreground of all this, the new Mel stood, smiling and awaiting my response, until, tired of waiting, he came out with, "Well . . . don't just stand there, man. What do you think?"

I squinted at him, then looked past him down the corridor again. My bad side was taking over. I could feel it. He was foolishly asking

21

for my congratulations after blowing his own horn, and I hadn't had breakfast yet.

"Terrific idea . . . ," I said, nodding and looking down the hall. "Now the place looks like a kindergarten room for when the parents come to visit."

"Oh . . . ," he said, a bit dimmed, so I added with fake innocence, "That's what you wanted, isn't it? I mean, you wanted to get rid of the House of the Living Dead atmosphere, right?"

"Yeah . . . well," he said. "But . . . to tell the truth, we were kind of hoping it would look like a real, grownup art gallery."

"Not with those paintings, Mel."

"You don't like them?"

"Well . . . they're so . . . childish . . . I mean . . . well, I'll grant there's none of the usual dreary steamboats kids like to draw, you know the kind, with the one curl of smoke coming out of the rectangular smokestack, but I still get this sense of . . . "

"Of what?" he asked, a shade testily, pretending no longer to be so interested in my reaction, and wanting to move along, now that I'd been tried and found wanting.

"I don't know. I just keep getting this sense that whoever did one of those things is about to stand up and say, 'I'm little Henry Jones, age thirty-two, Violent Ward, Home Room Five'. Do you know what I'm talking about? Honest, Mel, I'd like to encourage you. And I'm sure this stuff is a smash boffo, medically speaking, but as something pretending to art, it kind of gives me a pain in the ass. Especially coming from grownups. I don't know, maybe it's the signatures . . . You know, the stuff's so bad, and they're so prominent, do you see what I mean?".

But Mel, instead of folding in pain and dropping dead, suddenly laughed, brightening up again. "Indeed! So they are, now that you mention it. And you'll be sorry to know that despite your negative reaction, further proof, may I say, of your spiritual poverty, you have just justified this entire enterprise, as far as I'm concerned."

"How come?"

"Because the basic idea behind this entire exercise, my boy, is to get *in* there and *sti-mu-late* those egos, so they can come back healthy and strong."

"Like . . . gums?"

"Precisely, schmuck. And furthermore, I don't care *what* you think, *I* happen to find these pictures very interesting as art, too. As

22

do many other genuinely cultured people, by the way. So there. Not surprising, of course. As a matter of fact, I've *always* found people in here becoming much more artistic than they ever were before."

"Really?"

"Oh, it's absolutely *notorious!*" he said, defensively arrogant and airy, "Not that I attribute it to myself alone, you understand. Personally, I think it's because in here they find themselves, shall we say, suddenly closer to the wellsprings of inspiration?"

"I hate to break it to you, Mel," I said firmly, "But not . . . from the crap I see on those walls they haven't."

He looked at me with as much aggressive compassion as he could muster, sighed and shook his head, "O.K. Muldoon, so you're *not* very sensitive. Now I won't even tell you about the big art gallery down on Newbury Street that wants to show this stuff. It would only humiliate you. Shall we proceed now to something you *can* understand?"

"Sure!" I said, and so, unsuspecting of what lay ahead, off we went striding manfully down Mel's transformed corridor, with Mel, wanting to seem undaunted, smiling more pointedly than ever, and more than ever, I had to admit, looking like a successful arts impresario. I was on the verge of complimenting him on this, to make up for his other disappointment, but I didn't, as we very quickly went hurrying between the rows and rows of brightly colored, hand-waving pictures, all saying somehow: "Look at me! Look at me!" and managing to raise up a kind of mute, infantile babble of little egos along the corridor walls which was much like the din of a schoolyard.

I felt myself continually bombarded as we moved by the predominance of the fluttering reds and yellows and pinks and greens. No matter what Mel wanted to believe, despite how adultly the pictures were dressed up in expensive frames for this occasion (I still thought of it as Mel's show for when parents came to visit), I couldn't possibly take them seriously as pictures. To me, it was highly ignorable, childish stuff which at its lowest was devoid of skill and at its highest, "cute," and the less attention I paid to it all, the faster we seemed to be walking.

But then, it started.

Bouncing along as we were, there was something I simply couldn't ignore. I tried hard, too. But I just couldn't. Even though I immediately forced myself to keep looking straight ahead, the corners

23

of my eyes were suddenly being accosted by the wild, strange, cavorting motions of the individual signatures.

Suddenly, it was as if the signatures had started moving around restlessly within their framed cages, getting more and more excited, like dogs at the pound going crazy at the sight of a visitor, sometimes leaping up, barking, yelping, even wagging their tails desperately. But all of it inaudible to the rationalist ear, of course, as if contained beyond human hearing by impregnable hospital glass.

Naturally, I kept my mouth shut about it.

But I slowed down (still looking straight ahead, just to be on the safe side). And as I slowed down, their activity lessened proportionately. Then, as I turned to look right at them, to see what was really going on, they all played dead.

But I didn't trust them, sensing it was temporary.

So, trying to sound casual, I said to Mel, "Listen . . . maybe I was too quick to censure. You know how I hate to give any credit, as a matter of principle. Do you mind if I look around a little?"

"Please *do*," Mel said, pleasantly surprised. "You know, to be honest, I never did say they were *great* art, but . . . I do think they've got a *little* something."

I nodded at him, and cautiously began my inspection.

Now that they weren't acting like dogs going crazy at the pound, I started noticing other things about them. Odd things. And not all of them had been calling attention to themselves, either. I'd only thought so, reacting to the aggressive, hysterical types. Actually, a lot of them just seemed to lie there at the bottom of the frame, depressed and curled up, as if only waiting despondently for the metal door behind them to be pulled open by a hairy wrist in a uniformed sleeve which would grab them up by the collar and haul them off to their doom.

I thought I'd seen quite enough, so I turned around to go back to Mel, when my eye was caught by one particular signature across the way.

Mel, misunderstanding the whole thing, smiled and stepped aside, and then drew back.

But I held still. I was too far to read it, but even at my distance, what stood out as its most important characteristic was that it looked very easily readable. Too easily readable. And without knowing why, this bothered me. Even saddened me, with an edge of anxiety I couldn't account for.

24

The script was a sort of petticoated, Palmer method type, the prim and proper kind, like a schoolgirl's. More suitable for filling out a form legibly than for asserting individuality. And the mute thought: God, it would be so easy to forge! passed through my head.

Standing very still, right where I was, I began to get the strong sense that the signature was someone's trace left on life, like an indifferently done dance step. A box step. Learned at a banal ball room dancing class in a suburb. Which made me remember kissing parties. And her kisses, I imagined, were like that too, just like that indifferently done box step, even in her adulthood . . . like her voice, and her opinions . . . or what she repeated as "her" opinions. Confirmed by banal women's magazines. With recipes like her kisses. From the labels of cans.

That palely feminine signature, I was certain now, came from some moist dishrag of a depressed young wife. One who'd been much too docile as a child, almost completely lacking in fire, and much too intimidated a conformist to develop a mind of her own.

And then I finally understood why it was such a terrible failing that her signature could be so easily forged. It meant she could be neatly replaced by some other girl just like her, some other precooked product. Which she well understood. And if she were replaced, it wouldn't make much difference. She could die, and nobody would miss her. Because "her", the unique one, did not exist. There was no "her". "Her" wasn't hers, but "theirs", and they could easily—did so all the time—produce others just like her.

The idea came back to me, stronger: SHE COULD DIE, AND NO ONE WOULD MISS HER, BECAUSE SHE DIDN'T MATTER.

And suddenly, wishing it weren't so, but feeling something like a painful embarrassment because it *was* so, I could sense all too well she knew it. Perfectly. Of course she did. She wasn't that much of a fool. And could not be sweet-talked out of it, either. I could sense she knew it, and that it made her suffer.

Her docile signature with its rounded, prim script was sick-unto-death with bitterness as it followed along the prescribed line to its last, neat letter, beyond which there was no more to be said.

I felt awful, and had to lower my eyes.

I felt awful, too, for having been flip with Mel for his ego-stimulation business, when he was actually trying to help. As I said, to me, women were the opposite of people and this pathetic, depressed goody-goody of a dishrag wife would do nothing to change that prejudice. But what was getting me was that she never had a chance to become a people, for Christ's sake!

And I looked at her again. There she was. Filled with a justified self-loathing, stinking of it, in fact. Staring out and silently breathing her futile, sick-unto-death bitterness after having been picked up and tossed into this hamper of a hospital for ... attempting suicide ... (I couldn't help now sensing the suicide), and I could almost feel on my own face the look of those inconsolably cynical eyes of hers above her prim mouth. We both knew the truth about her, she seemed to be saying. Yes, she wasn't much of a person, she knew that. And it embarrassed me to the point where I wanted to avert my eyes. As to her suicide attempt ... I couldn't escape imagining it now, with all its confused, hate-filled, self-pitying rebellion.

It even made me admire her. Made me think, in my cowardly embarrassment, that she was tougher than I, because it must have taken all the courage that her hatred for everyone and everything could have produced. One last gasp, one last assertion of an almost non-existent self. Sleeping pills, what else?

But now, I thought, after *all* that, here she is. Awake again. In her cage at the hospital. She must have been terribly bitter to find herself alive again. After all that. After the incredible act of getting up enough nerve—for someone who never had any—to take all those pills! Now, kept alive, against her only asserted will. A will she probably will never have the courage to assert again.

And now, here she was, looking at me as she waited for the further humiliation of being "adjusted" to her pathetic dishrag's lot. Even being made to like it—the final humiliation—after being picked up, dried and pressed so she could be put back neatly on the kitchen rack.

I wondered, *could* Mel help her ego grow? God, I hoped so, but ... would she ever trust life enough to develop a nice, rosy, healthy one? Should she?

I was suddenly tempted to openly apologize to Mel.

But I didn't. The impulse, instead, perverted itself to consider asking him if I'd been right about guessing her suicide. But fortunately I had the decency not to do that, either. It wasn't my business. Her suffering, I decided, was not to be used as an occasion for my self-congratulation on my insightfulness.

So, once more I kept my mouth shut as far as Mel was concerned.

But I was more ashamed than ever at my snobbery, at my not having been attracted to her for being the demoralized, cynical dishrag she was, poor thing, and I prepared, timidly, to step closer to the painting.

Maybe to touch it.

I swear, if I'd been drunk and alone, and if it had been at night, I would have been tempted to even more. To kiss it, to lie desperately and tell her she could *not* be replaced in life as easily as all that, to tell her she was unique and irreplaceable, just like any other of God's little souls . . . and if she then looked at me cynically, too cynically and too right for me to bear, that I loved her and wanted to marry her.

But I was neither drunk, nor alone, nor was it late at night.

Instead, I was sober and increasingly aware that I was being observed in the plain light of day by a smiling Mel Fish.

So, considering the situation, I veiled my feelings with the virile hypocrisy of a smirk, and said to Mel, "Interesting."

He nodded, and I all but swaggered up to the painting.

This revealed that the signer's name was James Brownell.

I believe I recoiled, hopefully imperceptibly. But I must have made a face because Mel, damn him, immediately piped up with, "What's the matter?"

"Nothing . . . ," I said, checking the compulsion to wipe my lips with the back of my hand. Now I was also annoyed by the way Mel kept looking at me, smiling.

For a moment, I stared indignantly at Mr. Brownell's tight, self-pleased and prim script sitting neatly on the lower right-hand corner of the canvas, and damn it all, I could sense the man all too well—feet together, hands folded over one another, his mouth clasped small and tight like a pocketbook in a superior, "discreet", little smile. Meant for me! As if looking at me, he was sitting there like a smug, faggotty gargoyle on a cathedral cornice, a dwarf, priestly defender of his cruel Lord's temple. I loathed him.

Then suddenly, to my growing outrage (at having wasted pity on him, not because he was a male, I assured myself), I began to understand what that wet little sneer of his was all about: the nasty little bastard was *presuming* to *share* some unspoken values with *me*! He was taking me, the onlooker, for adult, monarchist authority, that's what he was doing. And furthermore, silently telling me that *he*—the kind of little fink who "knows better"—looked down on the blustery, antisocial types in the cages next to him. Types like *S*-(Desperate *S*, flapping his wings, how I sympathized with him!), the kind that all up and down the hall were flinging and spattering the letters of their names at the visitors like outraged monkeys at the zoo, spitting pestilent fluids, throwing peanut shells and worse.

But not Brownell, that disgustingly authoritarian little gargoyle who continued to sit there in his sphinctered perfection, hands folded, smiling "discreetly" at me.

Well, if he thought he'd found a soul mate, he had the wrong boy in X.J. Muldoon, so, contemptuously, I cut off eye contact with him, and I looked up at his picture. An Aztec pyramid. Grandly geometric. Obscenely geometric. Its thick outlines throbbed with the painter's loving admiration for its inhuman and merciless grandeur.

The massive, vibrant Aztec pyramid sat there like the cupola of a temple big as the whole cruel world beneath it.

Now that I was understanding his picture, Brownell infuriated me more than ever for his little, wet, knowing smile. Because someone like him, I was thinking, *especially* someone like him, should know about the need for compassion, goddamn him, instead of glorying in the implacable opposite, the way he was doing! Obviously, having suffered himself (he didn't get that twisted smirk for nothing), he was the horrible kind of little victim-priest that submits to the rules of his unfair gods and enjoys their cruel power as if it were his own.

Now I was absolutely certain he was cruel. Maybe even a librarian.

(For once, I was right. Brownell *was* a librarian. A very high ranking one. And furthermore, the man in the faded Exeter Academy sweat suit who did all that escape-type of running out of the woods and into the golf course.)

I'd had enough. I turned my back on him and his picture of the world. And then, on a dark hunch, I said to Mel, "Tell me something . . . do you have any patients here who smile with obscene pleasure when you give them electric shock?"

"Electric shock?" said Mel, raising a dubious eyebrow at me. "What do you think this place is, Muldoon, some *Catholic* hospital? We don't try to beat the Devil out of the possessed here, you know. We try to talk him into leaving." And then, after a thoughtful pause, he added with a smile, "Except, of course, on very rare occasions".

I smiled too, and then said, pretending to casually change the subject, "You know, Mel . . . these signatures. They're very interesting, don't you think?"

28

"So . . . ," he said, "you've been psychoanalyzing the signatures, have you?"

Immediately, I felt embarrassed, "Well, I don't presume to be a doctor . . . but . . . "

"But . . . ?" he said, raising the dubious eyebrow again.

"Well . . . can you tell . . . how people's egos are doing," I felt my cheeks flush a bit as I sensed I was exposing myself more and more each moment, " . . . by their signatures?"

"My good man," he pronounced firmly. "Handwriting analysis happens to be, aside from shock therapy, the *other* practice I object to most in the world."

"But Mel . . . ," I said, helpless at finding myself pleading with him for the caged souls, "can't you practically hear them?" And quickly, I tried to retreat with, "I mean, don't those signatures tell you anything?"

"Not very scientific, I'm afraid," he said, dismissing me blithely, and smiling as his back got straighter and his chin went up with authority. He was clowning, of course. Again.

But clowning or not, he just wasn't looking like a cheerfully fraudulent Leonard Bernstein anymore, ready to explain classical music to the eagerest of suburban children. Instead—and I wasn't liking him for it—he seemed pleased to be looking like the prophet of a very ordinary, mean, little god, proud of his insensitivity, with an invisible set of laws under one arm which he revered above all else, and with neither the power nor the inclination to work miracles for the suffering. "As a matter of fact," he said, "I make it a point to ignore that kind of stuff. Shall we go?"

I'd never seen him like that before (nor did I realize that this image of Mel as tableted prophet would be returning in a vision I'd never forget). Now I was glad I hadn't apologized to him for making jokes about his loony art show, back when I was responding to the suicidal dishrag wife.

Such an apology would have been wasted on him. That was obvious. I could tell I'd get nowhere with him, that there was nothing to be done, so I just tried to be satisfied with the knowledge that *he'd* been the insensitive bastard, after all, and not me, so I shrugged. And, to my own surprise, sighed, which made him look quizzically at me, maybe suspecting for the first time that something else might have been going on inside me than what was publicly admitted. I started walking. So did he.

Naturally, as soon as we started into motion down the corridor, so did the signatures, jumping around, calling me.

As we left them behind they were so wildly active in their desperation that I couldn't believe Mel didn't notice them. It seemed impossible. But he certainly gave no sign of it, especially as he smiled in the silent din of the signatures and said, most cheerfully, "You know, if you were working for me I'd fire you just for *mentioning* handwriting analysis. But since you don't, I'll just have to crush your ego at the courts, as is my custom."

Normally I might have said something about his delusions of grandeur as an athlete. But that wasn't what was on my mind, which was why I grunted and tried to ignore both Mel clowning as the cruel prophet and the desperate signatures we passed, and I awaited what I was sure was the inevitable time when this Peculiar Perception would be forgotten (though God knows I still hadn't forgotten the girl on the hill).

And pretty soon I started thinking I was doing quite well, too, in my efforts to be oblivious, or at least insensitive, when suddenly I had to stop again—as abruptly as if I'd bumped into a wall or a person.

Dead in front of me, only a few yards away from Mel's office door, there was a painting.

But it wasn't the painting that had stopped me, because I hadn't even particularly seen it yet. It was a strange, warm Light which had reached me first, emanating towards me in what felt like soft, warm waves followed by more soft, warm waves, unmistakably human somehow. And yet, it was precisely its clear, human quality which made it so strange, so otherworldly even, out of keeping with the world we were in. Stopped in my tracks, I could sense the Light (which had apparently reached out as far as it could, and now floated ahead of me, just out of my reach), like the presence of a speaking voice, talking quietly. I didn't know if to me, or to itself, or both. But it was in a language so clear and yet still so incomprehensible that it suddenly pained me that I did not know it.

Mel stopped too, of course. But distinctly annoyed, scuffling his feet as he did so, while I just held myself very still, letting myself feel that voicelike Light I was sure he couldn't hear any more than he had noticed the signatures, not that I was concerning myself with him at that moment.

Then I heard Mel's voice say, "You *would* have to stop . . . in front of *this* picture."

I looked over at him quickly, practically having to tear my attention away, and half grinned before going back to the Light which I now found I both knew, and didn't know, and I said, not caring how stupid I sounded, "Oh, yeah . . . the picture."

Then I heard him grumble behind me, "I'm afraid I'm going to have to revise my position on electric shock." He knew, of course, that he and I were no longer in the same conversation.

There was going to be trouble ahead. I could sense it in Mel's tone. But now that the Light had showed up for the second time, I found somehow I couldn't possibly care about that.

MEL BEHAVES STRANGELY.
ME TOO.

This picture, I'd soon find out (I already knew it), was like an exposed nerve with Mel.

But the odd truth was that I didn't care about the picture yet, any more than I did about Mel. All I wanted to do, as if my entire body were dehydrated and thirsting for it, was to stay right where I was and keep in contact with that voicelike Light which continued flowing toward me, never quite reaching me.

"Well?" he said sourly. "Any comments?" and I felt he was trying to pull me away, to get between me and the Light, which I was not about to let him do.

Anxiously my eyes glanced at the bottom of the picture and I heard myself protest quickly, "Look at that, Mel! Just look at *that!*" with a stridency that surprised me. I was stalling, of course. Faking. Seizing on the excuse of the signatures to stay where I was. "I mean, Jesus, Mel. How many people signed that thing? One or two? Because it sure looks like one person with two signatures to me."

Simple-mindedly, I was delighted with my quick thinking.

And then I realized I'd just done something I'd never done before:

I'd just put myself in open competition with Mel, and in his own business, which I normally couldn't imagine doing, even if I really believed what I was saying. But suddenly I found myself ready to argue the point to the death. Only dimly did I wonder, why was I competing with him? What for? The answers to which both Mel and I knew, deep down, I think. But so deep down it did us no good whatsoever.

"Let me guess . . . ," he said, his voice so loaded with acid it was starting to spill well over our usual limits. "Let me guess now. You have diagnosed . . . schizophrenia . . . trained as you are in my field by your readings of *Dr. Jekyll and Mr. Hyde.*"

The tension was getting nastier, so I hedged with a bland, "Well . . . ," trying to de-escalate the open competition. After all, I *was* in contact with the Light. That *was* all I wanted. But Mel, aroused, would have it no other way, pushing it up a step further, saying, "No, no . . . since you are so obviously very sensitive to what apparently escapes *me* . . . a vulgar medical man . . . I want you to go right up to the picture and have a good hard look at it. Really, I could use your help, because this is a very special case to me".

I didn't know where all this was leading, nor (I pretended to both of us) why in the world we were flaring up over something apparently so insignificant. But step up I did, and felt a curious excitement at coming even nearer the source of the Light, while Mel stood behind me saying, "This is going to surprise you, Muldoon, because despite my being a doctor, I really am quite sensitive to human suffering. And I mean, I *actually* care about it more than I do about either status or money. Odd, isn't it? So, if you will be so good as to form the words with your lips as you read, you will quickly discover that what you thought were two signatures is actually just the title. One single title, which happens to be *Heloise and Abelard*".

He was, as it happened, correct. Not that it really bothered me, since I'd only talked about the signatures to temporize. So, I acknowledged his being right with a nod and maintained my dignity by disregarding his unpleasant tone. Which was easy. The Light felt stronger as I got closer. It was almost like a breath now, giving off warmth like skin. I was glad he'd made me move closer. I didn't feel like a fool at all.

But now I looked at the picture, which was itself as childish as the rest I'd seen. In its details and techniques, I mean. It consisted of a fallen giraffe, light purple in color, lying broken on an African plain and being consumed at the neck by a banana-yellow, brown-spotted rhinoceros with a kind of contented, tufted sort of lion's tail switching over its massive, armor-plated head.

The broken giraffe's eyes were large, upturned and glazed with a timeless resignation as it entered the formlessness of death.

The rhino's eyes were small, concentrated, but upturned too, and just as glazed as the giraffe's as, lost in ecstasy, he consumed the giraffe's neck. But the rhino's eyes were ecstatic only if looked at in themselves. Actually, they were identical to the dying giraffe's, the only difference being that the rhino's were smaller, hard and concentrated, while the giraffe's were expanded. But the truth was that there really was no difference, because both, in their way, were orgasmic and lost, blind and floating in the taste of an oceanic feeling, all blood and salt and sun-warm as the giraffe's life gently and inevitably escaped the limits of form in the form of the rhino's triumphant jaws.

And the more I looked, the more I realized that both figures were animated by one single and strangely feminine light that united them. The very same Light I'd been sensing, speaking that language I didn't know, which also suffused the whole of the African plain and the sky above. In fact, the shapes of both creatures rose up out of the energy of that one fundamental Light, and the Light was really the only *thing* in the whole picture. All the other forms, such as the plain and the sky and the giraffe and the rhino locked into living and dying were of less than secondary importance, just manifestations of that voicelike Light, which was pure consciousness, it seemed, and could vanish (I suddenly felt with apprehension) in an instant, and make the whole picture blind, and dead.

I must have moved even closer, maybe out of my sudden anxiety about its possibly vanishing. Maybe, too, out of habit trying to touch, as if touching it were truly making contact with a living source, when I found I'd accidentally stepped on the foot of a woman patient who'd been sitting there under the canvas all along. Quickly, I looked down and said, "Excuse me . . . ," but the inanimate woman didn't respond at all. Because she was well past caring about anybody stepping on her toes by now. I didn't wonder I hadn't noticed her. My affront could not compare with the impact of her heavy pregnancy, which all but squashed her like a pile of rocks.

The woman was so drab she was faceless. She was reduced by madness to looking as anonymous as a corpse in a crowd of corpses.

With her mouth parted slightly, her expression was as dramatic as a vacated canary cage. To me, she looked as if the ballooning embryo had driven her soul out of her body, and as if her face was not even going to try to come back into this world until the new shape inside had grown enough of a face of its own to leave her. So, since she was not exactly "there", as they say, I went back to the indisputably more human presence I could feel emanating from the picture, and to feeling myself in uninterrupted privacy with it.

And then, the entire sunlit corridor fell silent behind me, as if swallowed up by the afternoon. Mel was all but forgotten, too, somewhere behind my left shoulder, in another, much more abstract planet than the one where the voicelike Light and I now lived.

And as the silence deepened, it began to seem as if the Light was trying to gather up all its human heat, all its energy, and was finally about to speak to me openly, comprehensibly, as if it had been waiting there for this moment, for me and me alone to receive its quintessentially sentient message—when Mel (damn him) butted in with, "Well? What do your ingenious theories tell you now, old boy? I mean, about concrete human pain?"

I winced, trying to ignore him, waiting for what the voice in the Light was going to say.

But I could feel him and his anger gathering strength too, impinging on me. He was mad as hell, quite aware that I thought of him as the intruder, as he said, "And I mean *concrete* pain, you see. Experienced hurt, and not any facile, fancy-ass intellectual abstractions about it. Well? Which is Heloise and which is Abelard? Can you tell me that? I know what it looks like, but can you tell me *for sure*? Because I could find it *concretely* useful if you could . . . ." Mel was practically vibrating with fury, and the energy of his anger was such that—I'm sure it was his fault—it broke off my contact with the Light.

I could still feel its presence, but it was useless. Now it was not going to say anything to me. Maybe it had changed its mind. Maybe it couldn't yet. After all.

Even so, I stayed right where I was a little longer. But it was too late. The Light was gone, as gone as if it had never been there, and I finally gave up hope, and playing the innocent, as if I'd been in a daydream all this time; I turned to the furious Mel, saying, "Huh . . . what?" with a foolish half grin.

But he wasn't buying any. "Well?" he demanded into my face, his own getting quite tense. "*Can* you tell me which is which?" But then, instead of continuing to blast into my face (which was making me blink), Mel turned to the woman I'd bumped into, and, with a completely surprising tenderness in his suddenly softened voice, he asked her, "Which is it, Althea? I'd love to know . . . ," and he smiled a pained petitioner's smile.

(Looking at the two of them, with me the one left out now, it even occurred to me that I might know the answer, at that. Maybe there was no real division. Just the Light. Which maybe was why the title—which I'd pretended to take for two signatures—had been written out as one single long word, with barely a space splitting Heloise and Abelard at either side of the "and". But I didn't quite dare say it. Neither dare, nor really want to.)

The woman addressed (I still didn't connect her with anyone I'd ever seen before) had been holding her inanimate face as still as a blank mask. But in response to her name, her eyes took on a bit of life and she moved them over to Mel, who now held his pained and pleading smile, waiting on her.

And then, as if by a miracle, all the dead and anonymous dough of her blank face took shape around the sudden trace of an incredible smile, filled with absolute condescension for him.

(I *knew* I'd seen that smile before. Seen it, and also *not* seen it. And this nasty sense of *deja vu* made it hard for my mind to stay in the present, as the smile I'd both seen and not seen before began to float bodilessly and uncrushably shaped in my memory. Now, of course, I know what the secret was: I was remembering Althea's unseen smile, veiled by her hair, when she'd dropped her arms and made all the other patients go tumbling down the hillside after the apples.)

Her smiling, his waiting, was a strange, painful and enigmatic moment. Painful for Mel, obviously, and even for me because I couldn't help but sympathize with him, to the point of embarrassment.

But enigmatic as it was, this much was clear: the queenly rictus animating her face meant to say she did not care to say. And Mel stood there transfixed by her defiance, absolutely put, as my mother would say, "in his place".

As for me, feeling more and more that all this had happened before (and maybe would again), I was increasingly overcome with the edgy discomforts that always seem to accompany the *deja vu*

37

experience.

Meanwhile, the smile stayed suspended on her face for another moment. And then, like an arrogant visitor from the spirit world, it dematerialized, and was absolutely gone, leaving the absent, blank woman in front of us again. And again, though I didn't think of her as dead, I was reminded of the soulless anonymity of naked corpses.

Now that the smile had vanished, both Mel and I could only feel summarily dismissed. As if a palace door had been shut in our faces.

Mel just stood there for another moment, reduced to a pained, self-conscious, biped *non sequitur*. He licked his lips, clenched his fists and then unclenched them. Coughed. And finally tried to grin at me as best he could, our quarrel now forgotten in the fraternity of the dismissed. For a moment, I felt like patting him on the shoulder, but I thought better of it.

Then, with one sudden, huffy stride, Mel started us off for his office in a rush. And once inside he let the door slam behind us much harder than I felt was decorous within his medical objectivity. He almost broke the glass.

"Do you think she heard us . . . ?" I said quietly.

"You bet your ass she did!" he yelled. I was sure she could have heard him then, too, and that he wanted her to. "And mind your own fucking business, by the way."

Talking like that, that is to say, unmedically and like his idea of a Boston Irishman in his wild state, was not at all Mel's usual manner. He only did so when in an extraordinarily bad mood, so I decided to let the matter drop.

How well I remember now the sight of Mel sitting at the edge of his desk. Smouldering. Unapproachable.

Lucky for me I hadn't solved the riddle of which was Heloise and which was Abelard, back when he asked me. Because if I had, I could see he would have had trouble restraining himself from parting my skull in an uncontrollable frenzy.

And if he had managed to stop himself, and let me live, he would never have forgiven me. Because it was quite obvious that *he* wanted to solve that particular riddle, that *he* wanted to be the one and only possible Prince to wake the sleeping Princess from her long dream after biting that poisoned apple. Return her soul to her body, make her a whole living person again. Maybe for the first time, for all I knew.

And watching him (I'd never quite seen him like that before), I smiled, but really, I couldn't help but sympathize with him all over again. And even more deeply, for his childishness.

I could sense all too well that he felt, in the full rage of his megalomania, that she belonged to him, like his fate. And that he had even come to secretly believe that her long, poisoned sleep was a Divine trick on his behalf, a courtesy of Destiny to buy him time until he was potent enough to wake her. And I also knew in my bones that he had imagined, a thousand times at least, that marvelous moment when she would wake, at last. Responding to him (as to no one else), she would stir, then open her eyes . . . and whom would she see first of all? Who, but her shy, bespectacled Prince at whom she would smile, opening like a blooming flower, etc. All this, of course, from the very same, rational Mel, who would one day smile indulgently at me when I foolishly let him know about the Unseen and Mysterious Forces that were in control of my life.

But that was later.

At that moment, I couldn't be annoyed at him.

I remember, also, feeling two things most clearly as I watched him.

First, that comradely compassion I mentioned, like a fellow shepherd wanting to console someone suffering from Pastoral love. puzzling as his choice of shepherdess was to me, since God knows she seemed devoid of either charm or sex appeal.

And second, the sudden, clear and perverse urge to beat him to her, which was also puzzling, considering the prize, since I still did not really connect her with the Light.

Immediately ashamed (considering him, and her), I banished it from my mind, ascribing it to my bad side.

Now, of course, I realize I was only responding to another mechanism implanted in me by the UMFs, meant to keep me moving toward the Light.

Also, of this second time the Light showed up, when, strangely enough, *her* face wasn't present, I can report that the smile she gave Mel moved me along to the Light, too.

Even after I went home that day, I kept thinking: where had I seen that smile before?

In a way, it was odd, because Althea herself had not stayed in my mind. Just the smile. Even before I'd walked ten steps past her into Mel's office, I knew I wouldn't be able to pick her out of a crowd of women in the street, or even out of a bunch of women patients if she showed up among them around the next corner.

If the physical Althea was notable at that point in my spiritual development, it was because she was absolutely nothing more than female flesh and hair to me. Downright generic and perfectly forgettable.

But not that smile, which kept holding its shape and irritating my memory like a piece of metal. That smile, I would know anywhere again, which takes me to Norma. And her smile.

NORMA, AND THE INNER
CHEESE OF LIFE

Before I begin to tell about how Norma led me to the Light, I feel I should say right away that she felt absolutely helpless before the fact that that *was* her name: Norma.

"I suppose it could have been worse," she told me one day with her usual half grin. "I mean, my parents could have decided to call me Vulga. So . . . ," she added with a stoic, adjusted resolve, raising her brow, "here I am, Norma Normalling. Wife, mother and college graduate, at your service. AND the community's, may I add."

Normalling, of course, wasn't her married name. It was Brown, as a matter of fact. But Norma did happen to be her first name. It isn't any more. She has long since decided she does not feel helpless before that or any number of other facts of life. She changed it, and a lot more, when she went off to New York to become something of a ferocious success as a writer, and even a cult figure. But I'm getting way ahead of myself, because that was after our affair. That transformed, later Norma, or, as she since called it herself, that "non-Norma", was unimaginable then.

The Norma I knew, I have to admit, looked an awful lot like most other thirty-year-old, college graduate and faithful wives did back then, in the '50s.

She was thin, with a bit of give to her lower abdomen, from the children, I guessed, with longish, straight brown hair and red lipstick on her pale face. Her fingernails were short, bitten, I assumed, but usually painted red, too, what there was of them.

Back in '53, in what now seems the innocent dawn of Time, Norma could be sighted most any Saturday morning going in and out of Harvard Square stores, carrying packages and books and plants —she was forever buying plants—with a kid or two along. And she always looked a shade overtired, though smilingly so. (Actually, she smiled continually because she was terribly short-sighted, and was afraid of missing people she was supposed to know, who might be just out of her range, greeting her.)

According to her later self, that benign first Norma I knew looked like that because she was just another domestic plant herself, almost entirely dependent on the surrogate and insufficient suns of light bulbs and central heating. "You zee," a later non-Norma was to tell me one day, knitting her brows doctorally and underscoring her point with a peripatetic right forefinger in the air as she launched into her favorite "Herr Doktor" Viennese accent, "Zzzat is *egg-zzactly* how close I vass to zzee *rrreal* inner cheese (meaning energies) of Life!" And then she added with her small half grin that barely retained any of her Viennese professor imitation, "Vvich izz *not* ffffery close, vven you zzzink about it, izz it, zzzere, in my liddle pott!"

When she told me that, of course, she was asking me to understand her having left all that earlier Norma Normalling behind, children, plants, and husband included. All of it, except for the continuum of that half grin and her "Herr Doktor" imitation, which she still used to cover her shyness when being especially serious, and which she would one day tell me she used compulsively only because she had never developed a suitable voice of her own.

But that wasn't how I thought of her when I first knew her, because she looked far from the unhappy creature she would describe to me one day. And back then, she didn't talk about herself that way, either.

To me, she was basically somebody else's model wife, and that's how she seemed to think of herself, too, or at least, seemed to want to.

True, she moved over the streets of Cambridge slowly and exhaustedly, but definitely giving off the gently smiling aura of someone who had willingly agreed to play a woman's secondary role in life. Secondary, that is, to her husband and her children. "In zzatt order ! And zzatt *iss* an *order*, boobie, because zzee zzeeorrie izz zzatt you *cannot* (right forefinger in the air) be an adzequatt mothzer . . . unless you are first an adzequatt *vviffe!*" (Right forefinger *further* up in the air.)

And I'm absolutely sure this is what she tried to do, too, with lots of good cheer, in spite of having an education superior to that of most men in responsible positions, and in spite of having shown far greater promise and talent as an undergraduate than either her husband, or me, just to give two examples.

Before getting married, she'd been a demon graduate student in something called psycholinguistics. But, she told me (while still the model wife, that is), "I liked it *too* much, and something terrible was happening to my femininity. It was being devoured. So I ran out and married Ralph (who was of Swedish extraction, massive, and well over six feet tall). And now," she went on, "by God, Muldoon! Now, I am house proud and child proud! Yes sir! A fulfilled woman, and I'll punch any man in the nose who challenges my femininity!" This was, of course, long before our affair, when it turned out, at the time anyway, she didn't think of herself as a fulfilled woman, after all.

In fact, she told me that before I could even imagine such a thing as an affair between us. Not between me and somebody else's model wife.

Not that I was conditioned to look for them, but about the only signs of discontent with the "woman's lot" I would even have guessed at were a surprisingly cynical sense of humor she would show once in a while, accompanied by what might be called a "wry smile", a continuation of her half grin which was capable of suddenly surfacing on her face looking millions of years old.

And when this smile showed up, I must admit, it looked like the total negation of all her smiling young mother's lipsticked modernity. Frankly, it was unsettling. And thank goodness it didn't come up often. But when it did, it not only looked immemorial, but also as alive as it ever could have been when it shaped the faces of the earliest humans. I can't say it was mirthful. Maybe dinosaurs smiled like that (I remember thinking when I saw it once), when they were dying off as the world's weather was changing, and they knew it.

But if I'd thought they were signs of discontent, I'd have been wrong. Instead of rebellion, the cynical humor and the wry smile at that time (I think) were really gestures of submission and conscious, even ironic, consent to a Life Plan which, alas (a word she used a lot), had put her in "zzecond place", which, according to her, could be worse. "Like, for egz-ample, beink *no* place." And this, of course, in a reality where, in the end, she saw no real first place, anyway.

So, what can I say, except that Norma, on top of being somebody else's model wife to me, seemed to be a credit to our Civilization. If somebody had pressed me on it, I would have even been forced to call her a "nice girl", and hope it never got back to her, since I'm sure it would have offended her.

But thank God I never had to bring Norma home to Mother, because Bridgid Muldoon, God rest her soul, would never have understood how Norma really was "a nice girl". All my mother would have needed was the slightest inkling of Norma's advanced views, of her remarkable interest in sex manuals and pornography, for example, and she would have sized up Norma with small indicting eyes, surely making her feel (for hers was a much more fragile spirit than my mother's) like an absolute degenerate. I mean, my mother wouldn't have understood how Norma was transferring the scientific frenzy she once devoted to psycholinguistics to the technology of the female orgasm because Norma considered it the cornerstone of the home, and an integral part of scientific motherhood.

If I had brought these two fine women together, I would have suffered, I know. But despite my mother's fundamentally Victorian view (from the bottom of society, since she'd been a domestic, but Victorian nonetheless), I could never think of Norma as "dirty", as my mother surely would, and as furthering the decay of Western Civilization.

To be sure, I could see—only too well—how a group of women like my mother, upon hearing Norma's usual loud defense of female masturbation, might have stoned her in a public place, as an example to all similar bitches who "don't know their place". But let me put it this way: in Cambridge, Norma was "a nice girl". She really was, and that was what I liked best about her.

And I even mean "nice" just the way my mother would have understood it, which is sexually. I'd known her to talk to on the street and at parties for a couple of years before our affair began—(to my great surprise)—and I never thought of her erotically. Never.

44

In fact, quite the contrary. And because she was both "a nice girl" and somebody else's model wife, she was a restful oasis for me in terms of sexual tensions. I believe I could have taken her to a baseball game, for example, and enjoyed the game. And when I did run into her, she was one of the few people I was instantly gladdened to see. At first I thought it was because of her good nature and conversation. I knew it wasn't, as they say, "physical". But now I have to admit it was because of her eyes, which were a very clear gray, with a kind and intelligent light in them. They weren't the first thing I noticed about her (it was the same each time I saw her) because they were neither large nor emphasized by make-up (that I could tell). But frankly, once I did notice them, they were beautiful. The rest of her was not. And her walk, which she called her Radcliffe Forward Lurch, was far from graceful. But, once I noticed her eyes, the rest of her physical presence disappeared unimportantly behind them, and then Norma became an absolutely beautiful woman to me. Every time. An oasis of "niceness", and I always took away that memory of Norma with me. Only meeting her again could dissipate it, until I noticed her eyes again, which were always finally, absolutely, limpidly beautiful, and a million light years away from eroticism.

Which is why, after our affair started, I felt a sharp sense of loss.

Now I can see that this loss was an important step in my spiritual development. The Unseen Forces had to put me through it.

Nevertheless, I didn't like it. The sense of loss, I mean. And I'm still not sure I do, as advanced as I've become.

But, on to our affair.

NORMA SURPRISES

On that fateful, sloppy February Tuesday, I wasn't thinking of Norma one way or another. I was too busy being a wretched and paralyzed graduate student who never finished his thesis.

And to make things worse, the Unseen and Mysterious Forces had chosen to make it impossible for me to think of anything but my troubles by planting me across the street from Widener Library, the Monstrous Widener God, according to a friend of mine, who also claimed it was a Unitarian icon.

I didn't want to be there. In fact, I'd been consciously avoiding the place for months and months, so the UMFs must have had to strain themselves to get me there.

But there I was, with my back to Widener, pretending I was looking in Schoenhof's bookstore's plate glass window and hoping I was inconspicuous.

Actually, I was surreptitiously watching the comings and goings just beyond Harvard Yard's wrought-iron gates behind me, which were reflected very clearly on Schoenhof's plate glass.

These enormous iron gates, with the ancient Harvard cop sitting tiny at the lower left, handsomely frame the vast and uninteresting backside of the Widener God.

The front is another story, of course. It is imposing in a patrician way, something like the Lincoln Memorial, with great gradations of steps leading up to olympic pillars. It is most suitable for Harvard Glee Club concerts, which have a way of degenerating into Gilbert and Sullivan ("Bow, bow, ye lower middle classes!") and ideal for Harvard Commencement speeches given by ex-Secretaries of State about the Role of the University in our free society.

But that patrician, Harvard Corporation front of Widener had nothing to do with my reality. I was involved with the back of the Widener God, which is about as interesting to look at as a 1900's factory wall. The only focal point is at the bottom center, right between the huge wrought-iron gates, where there is a kind of cyclopic, rectangular glass mouth that opens and closes discreetly, through which pass Harvard's hardest working scholars, a group that as a rule has very little resemblance to bank presidents and ex-Secretaries of State.

However, I wasn't hanging around there to reflect on the sociological and spiritual differences between the Intellectual Harvard at the back and the patrician Harvard of the Lincoln Memorial front. That I could do at home.

I was caught there, frankly, because Widener has the only accessible men's room in that part of Cambridge, and I'd been walking along with Ben Vartoonian, a fellow graduate student, who suddenly claimed he felt the need to use it, just as we passed Schoenhof's.

"Come in with me," he said with a little sly smile.

"The hell I will," I said, not because I thought he was a pervert, but because I was avoiding my thesis advisor. As a matter of fact, I lived in fear of running into him because I hadn't done a thing for over a year.

I guess I must have stiffened up a lot as I said, "The hell I will," to Ben's suggestion because he gave me another little smile, even smaller than the first, and said, "O.K. . . . O.K. Just wait right here and I'll be back in a second". And off he went, even before I could protest or make another arrangement.

So there I was, unknowingly positioned by the UMF's in a most humiliating position before the Widener God, with my back turned, my face averted, practically cowering and reduced to cursing Ben (who, incidentally, *was* a pervert) for leaving me there.

Though not daring to look at the living Temple directly, I could feel the Widener God's life behind me with all its massive silent vibrations of obscene mental electricity. Sparking from books to minds and back again. All contained in the shadows of the stacks within the infinite creases, in the darkness deep beyond the cyclopic, glassed mouth behind me. More than ever Widener looked like an eyeless cyclops to me, with that low, dark, square mouth.

So, to protect myself, to undeify the living Temple, I tried thinking of the Widener God as just one more Harvard Corporation-owned factory, meshing stacks and stacks of minds with rows and rows of books. After all, professors author books which themselves author professors, and the Widener Factory God was in the business of producing both, which were sometimes barely distinguishable entities. Come to think of it, I knew *many* books that were far more perceptibly human, both in their affects and contents, than many a professor who had turned himself through his life's work into a walking thesis with hat and shoes.

Yes sir, I told myself, it's only the dedicated scholars who are in a state of perfect Communion with the Widener God. That's who. And I estimated disdainfully that 99% of all scholarly work was really produced to certify a lot of people as professors by generating great numbers of books and articles which answered questions that had never been asked in the first place.

I realized, of course, I was thinking all these things because I too wanted to be certified as a professor, to make a living now that I was unemployable for any other trade. And this was not going to happen unless I could get myself into the darkness beyond the Widener God's mouth and start processing myself, with my thesis, right into a state of grace.

And talking about professors, damn Ben Vartoonian still wasn't back (who knows what he might have found in there?) and my dreaded advisor could show up any second and devastate me by asking me something unanswerable, like, Oh, "Hello, Muldoon. How are you?" And, painfully, I realized I was standing in the worst place at the worst time of day if I wanted to deep ducking him: at 5 p.m., just when the professors and the deserving grinds are knocking off from another day at the "life of the mind".

Maybe my advisor wasn't looking forward to seeing me, either. Maybe he didn't start each day by opening his eyes in bed and thinking: "Is Muldoon writing his thesis? Will he come to my office today?" But I was too lost in the superstitious darkness of my guilts to think otherwise. Which meant that each time the Widener God's

49

ghastly rectangle of a mouth opened up—and Ben Vartoonian still didn't show up—I died a thousand deaths, tried to get small, quickly, and hid my face pretending to be looking hard into Schoenhof's plate glass window.

Then, very slowly, the Widener mouth began to open again. But sententiously now, as if about to state some finality in a measured University accent.

I held my breath, cowering, waiting for the announcement. Waiting to see what would come out. And, to the complete distress of my central nervous system, the Widener mouth uttered: PROFESSOR PERRY MILLER. Him! My dreaded thesis advisor . . . who had no place on earth to look at as he came out except straight ahead, across the street, right at me!

Almost as soon as I saw him I started practicing in my mind how I would say: "Oh . . . lucky I caught up with you, sir. I was just on my way in to see you," when Professor Miller, without a single sign of recognition altering his expression, wheeled fluidly to his right and walked on down to Harvard Square on the opposite side of the street.

Maybe, I hoped madly, just maybe he didn't see me! It was possible, wasn't it? I mean he *could* have been thinking about something else, like buying pretzels and peanuts for a cocktail party that night.

Then, stilling my heart, reflected right there on the plate glass, I watched it begin to open again, only this time even more slowly.

Between me and it, behind me, the traffic on Mass. Ave had just mysteriously decreased to the point where it seemed about to evaporate altogether. The sidewalks seemed suddenly emptier, too, as if making room for what would emerge, and even the air became clearer, as if a veil were being lifted. It was one of those strange moments in city streets when everything seems to fall silent at once. The whole Universe, as if prepared, now seemed to be waiting for the great, definitive Widenerian pronouncement.

In the paranoid marrow of my bones, where it's dark and juicy all the time, I was sure it was going to be about me. A final judgment. And it would come out obliquely, without looking at me, because the Widener God never looked. It only had a mouth.

And then, out of that mouth, quickly, rhythmically, popped a series of stately utterances: Prof. Sydney Baldwin, Prof. Henry Hudacheck, Prof. Elias Sarnaki. One after the other, these notions became flesh in the Cambridge afternoon, and, just like Prof. Miller before, walked on down the street to Harvard Square like perfectly reasonable Widenerian utterances.

But I knew it wasn't over. I could sense, even though there was a pause, that the Widener God was building up to a final statement. And I waited, shamed because the Widener God had already made it clear that the base matter called *Muldunius Vulgaris* would never be transmuted into one of its distinguished concepts.

And then, to my total incomprehension, it came, as the Widener God opened its University mouth one more time, held it open, and finally said: *NORMA.*

There she was, Norma Normalling, every inch the college graduate wife and mother, an ideological concept, a thesis made flesh herself. Widener's door closed behind her, and the world resumed its motion, starting with the Mass. Ave. traffic.

Having watched the whole epiphany on Schoenhof's plate glass window, I didn't turn to look at her reality, as it were. I couldn't possibly think about what the Widener God could have meant. I just thought, what's she doing here? And she wasn't outside Widener's door for a moment but she saw me right away, brought her feet together and came to a halt like a sandpiper spotting something.

Shit, I thought. That means Miller saw me too. No question about it now. And I winced, squinting at her reflection with a fatal fascination. Norma, from the starting position of her feet together, strode right for me with the peculiar, top heavy decisiveness of her Radcliffe Forward Lurch, obviously thinking I hadn't seen her.

I closed my eyes. I wasn't hiding from her, but from Miller's phantom, when my back was being tapped. And there was something funny about the way Norma tapped me, too, but I couldn't pay much attention to it at the moment. I simply gave in to the awful, sinking feeling of having been picked out by a catlike Fate for execution, just when I thought I was invisible because I'd kept my eyes closed.

"Yoohoo!" came her voice. "Don't pretend you don't see me!"

And so, slowly and with my head bowed sacrificially, I turned around, and lifting my eyes as if asking for mercy, I said, "Hi, Norma . . . ," only to find her smiling down on me broadly, in fact, rather vibrantly. As if she had just happened upon a delightful chance of some sort. In my weakened condition, she looked like an exposed canary's view of the family cat, especially as she said, "Hi . . . to you . . . ," without trying to repress the predatory cat smile at the corners of her mouth. Her clear gray eyes were especially

51

large, I thought, and her black pupils seemed to be dilating.

For a second I didn't say anything. I was busy trying to reassemble my perceptions and get everything back to normal again, and I guess I took too long because she moved her face forward, looking suddenly more catlike than ever, peering in at the open cage, and she said, "What's the matter? Cat got your tongue?"

Quickly as I could, I resisted thinking she was an agent from a supernatural power, out to test me. I took a deep breath, and sighed.

"You don't seem glad to see me," Norma said with soft encouragement, and then added, to my complete surprise, ". . . Jerome." And when she hit me with Jerome—for the first time in her life—I suddenly felt as if she'd taken possession of my small and naked inner person with her fingers.

And she kept right on smiling, it wasn't my imagination now. She *knew* she had me off balance. Her smile was saying: "Yes, I said Jerome. That *is* your name, isn't it?" Well, yes it is. But even my mother called me X.J. for the last twenty years of her life. Jerome was one of my secrets, almost as secret as Xavier, so secret I'd almost forgotten it myself, until she reminded me.

But she said it with amusement, as if she felt I shouldn't be ashamed of my dirty secret, because she found it, in her womanly tolerance of such intimate things, rather cute.

"Sure . . . I'm glad to see you," I said, and she kept on looking at me with a peculiarly knowing amusement at the corners of her mouth, and looking so directly at me that I found myself lowering my eyes as I explained. "It's just that I was very surprised to find you here." And then, rallying, I looked up and added, "What were you doing in Widener? Using the ladies room?"

"Now Jerome. Is that kind? It just so happens I'm taking a creative writing course which meets in there. I decided to take it because I want to get out and do more things on my own." And now she looked at me to see how I was taking this information, her mouth parted slightly. I didn't understand anything. Her eyes were like silver dollars, now, about to shatter with laughter, and I still didn't understand anything.

And then suddenly I got weak in the limbs, because it came into my head that maybe she was trying to excite me sexually, which was unprecedented. Which could not possibly be true. I told myself to look out for thoughts like that. After all, in my psyche's constellation, Norma was *the* "nice girl", *the* somebody-else's-model-

52

wife. That was for sure. Which surely meant I was imagining things, because maybe "nice girls" do have dirty thoughts, but they don't act on them. Not with me. . . . I mean, I was in a panic about my life as it was already, without thinking about getting involved with a married woman. And especially with her. Because since she was a "nice girl", it would have to be "love", and anyway her husband was enormous, on top of everything.

"Well . . . ?" she said, and kept right on smiling at me in that catlike, knowing way.

"Yes . . . ?"

"Well . . . aren't you going to have the decency to ask to read what I wrote?" she said, "Or do I have to take you by force?"

And I laughed, with great relief. Suddenly I could realign all her behavior, thank God. That's it, I told myself. She just wants somebody to read what she wrote. Thank God I didn't get so fouled up with guilts and what have you that I ended up thinking it was incumbent upon me to lunge at her. Jesus, what a misunderstanding *that* would have been!

"Sure!" I said. "Love to!" I felt like a free man again.

"Well, what a delightfully enthusiastic response!" she said. "Bless you. You see, I just wrote two things, but all I want is for you to read one of them. So you're in luck."

"Oh, I don't mind."

"You're being very nice. And I really appreciate it, Jerome, because part of my deal at home is that I won't burden Ralph with what I write. I *had* to promise, so this places a greater burden on my friends."

"O.K." I said, "But what's with calling me Jerome?"

"Oh, that . . . ," she said, and half grinned, "Well, since it's embarrassing to show anybody else what you've written, . . . I mean, it's a real confidence, you know, I thought I'd let you know I knew something embarrassing about you, too. Does that make sense?"

"Not a lot, but I'll accept it. I'd even accept reading both stories."

"Thanks, that's sweet . . . but not really necessary, dear," and she said "dear" as easily as if she'd said it every day, though she never had. She didn't even seem to know she'd said it, as if it had come out unconsciously. "Besides, I'm only interested in your reaction to one of them. The other one is about how my daughter Garth tried to pee standing up after watching her father. I think she did pretty well, considering, but it wouldn't be particularly poignant . . . I mean,"

53

and she smiled, I would have to say, deferentially, "it wouldn't be poignant for somebody like you . . . who just doesn't have to make that most humbling adjustment." And it was so oddly flattering I had to look down again, embarrassed, feeling my cheeks flush.

Actually, talking about penises wasn't at all unusual for her. She talked about them often, and hygienically, because she believed even more doggedly than Mel that the fundamental trauma in a woman's life had to do with penis envy. Therefore, most days, even her referring directly to my own personal penis wouldn't have affected me the way it did. So, ashamed of myself, I decided it had made me blush and look away because at the moment, in my excitable condition after Perry Miller, my heart was not pure.

My excited heart, in fact, had just started thrashing wildly all over again, like some red bird caught behind my flimsy T-shirt, and I didn't know why, but it was acting as if it had not heard that all Norma wanted was my literary opinion. And it didn't seem anything could convince it otherwise, which was why I kept my head bowed.

"Don't look so disappointed," she said, misreading me. "Really, you *can* read it if you want to. It's just that I'm much more interested in hearing what you have to say about the other one." To which I nodded. And then she added, "Shall we go to your apartment?"

Which started a pandemonium inside my T-shirt.

"Well . . . you see, Norma," I said, fearing for myself, "I'm waiting for a friend."

"*I'm* a friend," she said with implacable logic.

"Yes, true. Well . . . by the way," I temporized, "where are your kids today? You've usually got at least one with you."

And looking at me, she smiled her "wry" smile. I didn't know what it meant.

"Look," she said, "I've tried to tell you. I'm out on *my own*. And don't worry. They're with a baby-sitter, and I'm not expected home for a couple of hours, at least. No questions asked."

"Oh . . . couldn't we go to a coffee shop?" I believe I was pleading.

"No. I consider this very confidential, and I don't want us interrupted, if you don't mind. And don't worry, I'm the kind of girl that takes herself home. O.K.?"

I said nothing. Looked at my shoes.

"Besides, you live near here, don't you?" she said, looking me square in the eye now. "Or . . . am I wrong?"

"Yes . . . ," I said, giving in as if it were an inescapable admission that I lived nearby, despite the fact it was not true. I lived a good twenty minutes away.

"Let's go then," she said. I nodded. And for the first time in that encounter where Norma had so dominated me, she demurely lowered her eyes, which made my legs go weak.

As we walked, I couldn't escape the feeling that in her present softness, Norma would resist nothing I might do.

I'd had these feelings about women before, of course. And sometimes they were right, and sometimes wrong, and I simply didn't know which would be worse at the moment.

NORMA'S CONFIDENCE

Pretty soon, the twenty-minute walk to my place on that sloppy February Tuesday started feeling like forty-five. And the more uncommentingly patient Norma was about the increasingly obvious fact that I did *not* live nearby, the more pointed the moral implications, as far as I was concerned.

And in spite of what she said our mission was, I couldn't help thinking: we met at five. She said she didn't have to be home until seven. Or later. "No questions asked." This meant she probably wouldn't be home to feed her kids. Was she (get a grip on yourself, Muldoon) planning to commit adultery at precisely the time her whole family was gathered around the dinner table? I imagined Ralph, her husband, all six-foot-three of him, with enormous hands and that big Scandinavian grin made to express contentment after drinking full oaken buckets, putting up a good front before Timmy and Garth while he filled in for her—but what would the kids be thinking about their mother's absence? Was I, just maybe, a tool in some perverse, vengeful action of hers against the whole bunch of them?

I fought against believing it. Norma wouldn't do that, I told myself. Because if she was going to be adulterous, it would be

57

because of something extraordinary, like being forced into it by some sudden wild craving for somebody. Which would be innocent, in a way. And anyway, surely she wasn't having a sudden wild craving for me.

Was she?

Out of modesty, I tried dismissing the idea. But I was failing. I wasn't even succeeding in dismissing the idea she was using me to get back at her family. O.K., I told myself, then if that's the case, I have it in my power to stop her from destroying her home. Right?

So, before things go too far, I'd better explain to her it's just a passing craving, one which will be unbelievable to her later, and that she'll be grateful to me because, no matter what happened to her with her family, at least she and I could still be friends.

Of course, before I stopped her, I knew I'd better make pretty sure she had started.

And I must admit, it was sure looking as if she had, because we didn't say a word to each other, the whole way to my place, and when I looked over at her, she didn't look back. All yielding silence and softness, she just kept her head bowed a bit, her eyes cast down as she walked, and her face was smooth and expressionless, which created the peculiar effect of a veil. A veil for a woman who did not want to be identified nor make eye contact with anyone.

By the time we got to the front door of the building where I had my third floor walk-up, I was morally exhausted.

I opened the door, and she, veiled in her expressionlessness, and somehow taking up less space that usual, like a cat going through a narrow space, slipped silently in ahead of me, and noiselessly walked up the stairs, without any hesitation, almost as if she'd been there before.

On the way up, we had to pass Mr. Pansky's open door, and there he stood, as usual, leaning against the doorframe, in an old sweater, drinking coffee out of a glass with the spoon still in it.

Norma went by him without a glance. Moving silently. Veiled as ever. Just like when a cat is like a ghost and vice versa.

And I followed, saying a rear guard and rather moronic, "Hi, Mr. Pansky." But he said nothing, except with his still, Middle European eyes, by way of comment on my appearing in a house of decent lodgers with a woman with no identity.

I smiled with an innocence he did not accept, and kept moving up to my door, where she stood now, waiting, with her small back to me.

I had to nudge against her (she yielded weightlessly) as I slid the key in the lock, and now that our faces were close together she gave me a little intimate smile, with no veil, now that it was just the two of us, free from prying, Panskine eyes.

Once inside, she took off her coat and began moving about freely, looking things over, taking command again. "Sit down," she said to me as I half closed the door. "I'll make the coffee." And she handed me the manuscript.

Sit down I did, and looked at the manuscript, titled "The Grammar of Life".

When she came out of the kitchen area, she noticed I'd left the door open, out of secret deference, of course, to the dirty mind of Mr. Pansky. Without a word she walked over, closed it neatly and perfectly, with barely a sound, and then she smiled at me intimately again, exactly as she had when our faces were close together and I was trying to unlock the door.

I smiled too, clearing my throat, and looked back at the title, not so sure I was going to be able to give her story my full attention. But I kept my eyes on the page as I felt her sit down next to me on the narrow couch. I looked at her. "Please do read it," she said quietly. "It's a very *special* confidence." And now that she sat beside me, our thighs were touching slightly, and she smiled with her lips closed, her clear gray eyes full on me.

I nodded, but everything inside me began speeding up in a great swirl. I was sure I was inflating, changing color to beet red as I do when shy or in a rage, and in my agitation I started worrying I just might suddenly fling the whole typescript in the air and take her in my arms with the sheets falling down on us like confetti as we tangled.

Nevertheless, holding on with all the power left in my chaste Catholic manhood, I knitted my brows and concentrated hard on looking as if I was about to read. Maybe I was. Except that I couldn't keep my eyes on the page because they kept jumping like a compass needle over to her.

With another smile, she relaxed her back into her corner of the couch and lit a cigarette. Then she exhaled a long, soft puff which seemed to empty her as she let the cigarette in her languid hand dangle over the side of the couch.

Everything became very silent.

It was as if by letting out all that smoke she'd emptied herself, become a void, creating a vacuum inside her that, in the angle of the couch, made her the center of the room. And she sat with such a peculiarly exciting, quiescent stillness that I thought all the inanimate things in the room were suddenly potentially animate and tending toward her. Sparked by my own bloodstream's swirling agitation (careful, Muldoon, I think she *might* want you to read), they all not only gravitated toward her (as she smiled faintly in the angle of the couch), but wanted at any cost and over any obstacle to get there in a great rush and end up there in a swirling maelstrom, massing and calling everything else in after them.

And there she sat, stiller and stiller. The center of the potential whirlpool.

Any moment now, I was sure she knew it, I was going to lunge and start ripping clothes for all I knew, as all things in the room were decidedly in motion, going where I was going to go flying myself.

Her eyes smiled. Then, as if to stop me, and stopping all the other potential motion in the room, she raised the cigarette back to her lips and took a puff, inhaling, filling her lungs. "Please . . . ," she said, the cigarette near her mouth, " . . . read." And this time I did, much relieved.

I concentrated because Norma, in her story, maybe was going to tell me something that just might prevent my lunge. Or encourage it. Which I hoped not.

THE GRAMMAR OF LIFE
by Norma Brown

Early in the morning of the day Eva was going to crash the car and kill her husband and disfigure herself, she sat fully made-up in front of her mirror with a drink on her dressing table. With her chin up, her painted, hieratic face was as still as a playing card, and almost as blind with her dulled, unfocused gray eyes between her and the rest of the world, which was also herself.

She allowed herself to be aware of light playing off surfaces. Off her drink, off her bracelet, off her brightly colored lips, and she floated among the shining surfaces.

Everything was surfaces and light reflecting.

And beyond that, nothing. Nothing that mattered. What mattered was only the pretty objects shining, and how they shone. And in the cracks, in the lines between the objects and beyond the reflections, she knew there was only darkness, and a great quiet that began with a serpentine hiss, leaking darkly, ready to infiltrate the day and make it night forever.

Eva's husband, Ralph, was talking on the phone. Laughing. "If matter meets anti-matter," he was saying, "what you get is an explosion!" and his voice shattered into laughter, in sudden, jagged black cracks. Yes. Darkness waited in his laughter, too.

Eva thought about the car's rear view mirror shattering with her eyes in it, the sound of matter meeting anti-matter, and how it wouldn't hurt as the hissing darkness flooded in, no longer contained by the shining surface of the mirror. It would start from an infinitesimal point, just like a leak, and then the cracks would jump and branch, and from its whispering beginning the blackness would grow wider, geometrically quieter, drowning all things and sounds, becoming as wide and as black and as quiet as the whole of the whole of everything that doesn't matter. Where she felt at home.

With her face still held up, always held up, Eva lowered her exquisitely blued eyelids until they completely veiled her dulled gray eyes. She listened closely for the waiting blackness, the whispering promise, but the paining daylight in her iridescent lids forced her gray eyes to bloom open again, and there—trapped and shining sharply in the mirror—was her hieratic playing card face again, perfectly still, and still caught in the world of light and noises—Ralph's world—and in the exhausting masculine illusion that things do matter. That what we do matters.

But it doesn't, she knew, just as she knew about the darkness. No. No faith was required. Not when you knew.

Everybody was trying to convince her, to convince themselves, always looking for connections and causes they could believe in because they were afraid they might fall away in the darkness and disappear. And she was the flaw in the mirror. They knew it without knowing it.

They shouldn't be so afraid, Eva thought. Not that she had the energy, or cared enough, to tell them. Where she was frightened was in the light sometimes. Where they all wanted to be. There, she was an utter coward, despite the absolute stillness of her held-up, painted face, and what Ralph called her shallow serenity based on her selfishness.

Ralph didn't nag her about being shallow and selfish anymore.

Not since she'd come back from the hospital three weeks ago. She'd taken an overdose of sleeping pills because they were full of whispering, heavy darkness, like serpents' eggs.

Now that she was back Ralph let the doctor talk, and he held his tongue. Jenny Long, her friend, didn't try talking at her anymore, either. Somebody must have told her to stop, too.

Now it was left up to the doctor with the sensitive and frightened eyes.

He was most discreet. Patient behind his shining glasses and his shining smile, and timid, too. He moved as if he was afraid to shatter the shiny, brittle world. Pretty soon after she was brought in to the hospital, after they had pumped her stomach, they let her stay around the pool by herself. She would get up early, dress and make herself up, and go sit by the shimmering green pool with a book she never read.

She hardly talked much anymore. She still enjoyed her own slimness, and her feet, which were pretty. And taking care of her self, of her face. Not that she thought it really mattered, but those were her pleasures.

They tried to get her to work, of course, as if working at something would convince her that what she did mattered, just because she had invested her work in it.

"At least you won't be bored," said the doctor with the frightened eyes, smiling like a shy would-be boyfriend offering an ice-cream cone.

"I'm not bored," she told him, so they let her be, usually by the pool. She had Ralph bring her things from home.

Of course, they never did really leave her alone. Not really. Everything and everyone was talking at her implicitly, all the time. Always saying the same thing: what you do matters. What you do matters. What you do matters.

Sometimes it was so irritating it made her explode and bark and bitch, "I am sick of everybody, sick to death of all of you!" But sometimes she almost smiled because they were all so afraid. Especially when the doctor with the sensitive, frightened eyes came to her as she sat by the pool, saying, "How are you today?" He could sense what they never admitted in the light: that when he came to her, he had come to the very edge of the darkness, which, in the morning light by the shining green pool, was looking at him through the black pupils of her lovely gray eyes.

Those gray eyes. She remembered focusing them on Ralph the first time they let him see her at the hospital, when he brought her her things. He appeared in the doorway, framed by sunlight in back of him. He was thinner, worried, and when he sat down next to her he avoided her eyes as she watched him, watched him with her black pupils, at the near shore of the blackness. Ralph looked so much older, she could see where his beard stubble was gray, and she just watched him as he said, "Jesus, I'm sorry . . . ," his head going down, his huge blue-veined hands clasping each other, rubbing, feeling one another, forgiving each other masturbatorily, "Jesus, I'm sorry . . . I'll never . . . ," and he was near crying.

Nobody, especially Ralph, could believe she wasn't upset. She'd be upset if he cried, but she didn't say, "Shut Up," she just watched him.

"Can you really forgive me," he said, "I mean, really forgive me? Not just say you do, but really do . . . I don't know if anybody can do that, forgive, I mean but . . . "

"Don't worry about it," she said, cutting him short. She knew he was talking about her having found out he'd been going to bed with her friend Jenny Long. He thought she'd tried to kill herself because of that. But that was because Ralph, like everybody else, looked for reasons that started with himself. Everybody looked for causes, different causes, as if there really were any . . . especially any such little ones that they could handle.

Her mother had died of cancer. Just before she knew she had it, she was going to leave her father, but had to stay, because she was dying. Later her father married the nurse. Sonny, her father's best friend, always tried to kiss her on the mouth and feel her up when he got drunk, which was often. And the nurse—the tall, skinny, dyed blonde nurse . . . had tried to . . . all those things were true. All these things had happened, and the doctor with the frightened eyes wanted to talk about them with her, because he thought they were reasons. Causes.

It was all true, and so were a lot of other things, too. All of them to do with betrayals, and people using other people and frightening her, and she'd talked about them before, with another doctor. Two other doctors. But they really didn't bother her. Not anymore. They had all happened to somebody else, by now. She was not frightened by their shadows because these awful shadows that once hovered over her bed each night had long ago faded away, sucked up by the

Darkness. They had nothing to do with her because she stayed among shining surfaces now, living in the light.

And she usually felt good in the light, especially in the mornings, when she was made up, which was when they wanted to bother her, buzzing around her, all of them, looking for reasons they could believe in. But this time, she only threw a tantrum twice. Usually, when they talked, she just watched them, pregnant with darkness, full of the black quiet that was waiting to spring a leak, to start a hiss that would terrify them if they heard it, but which they never heard because they talked so much.

"You are wrong, Eva," the doctor with the frightened eyes said, the sun glinting off his glasses. "You do matter, to your husband and to your children. And what you do does matter. The question is, do they matter to you?"

She didn't say anything. That morning she was wearing silver sandals and had just done her toenails. She was especially glad she was thin, that morning. She had never had trouble with her weight, except for being too thin sometimes, and in the freshness of that morning she enjoyed her own slenderness more than ever. So she was smiling.

It wasn't the first time the doctor had said something like that. The time before, she'd felt her eyes get hot and ready for a small, warm cry. The doctor, of course, thought the cry was "because" of something, and he was trying to make her cry again. "You really do matter to them."

"I can believe that," Eva said this time, calmly.

And there was more talking after that, which the doctor did gently, which she permitted him to do, because it didn't matter and she didn't mind.

Before that, of course, they gave her electric shock treatments, too. Twice. She remembered the terror, closing her eyes, the expectation while they strapped her down, and the incredible fulfillment of the terror. The lash and the rush and the scrapping tickle of a thousand rats' feet scampering in the darkness, ripping all through her body, rearing in her forehead, and the incredible serpentine hiss of the blackness in her gums and inside her tongue. And the forgetfulness. Until she remembered.

What did remembering tell her? What was there to know? Nothing. Just that everytime you open something up, there's a serpent there, electric and alive, full of blackness, shooting out and hissing, coming out infinitely, on and on, from the first little dot.

After the treatments, Ralph came every day. The kids and Ralph stayed at his mother's. The kids didn't come, and she really didn't care. Nor did she care whether Ralph came or not.

And one day he asked her, "How do you feel?"

"Better," she said that day. It was true. "How are the kids?"

"Fine," he said, "They miss you." His eyes were large and red. She didn't comment.

And not long after that, when she felt stronger, she went home with Ralph. The kids stayed on with his mother, but they came to see her at her house. A little quieter, a little more cautious in how they touched her. Garth, her daughter with black pigtails and her father's eyes—Ralph's eyes—watched her with an odd suspicion. And Timmy, who was older, was already busy secretly wondering about the why of things. She could see it in his eyes, in his new privacy, in his little sense of injustice that would soon make him believe in all kinds of causes and reasons that started with him, just like everybody else.

Like Jenny Long, who thought Eva had cracked up because of her and Ralph. Like Jenny's husband, Frank, who'd followed her upstairs to the empty kids' bedroom, during the last party, where all the guests put their coats. The room was dark, except for the light from the hall. Everybody was downstairs, pretty drunk, and she didn't know exactly why she had gone upstairs, why he was with her, although she could guess that part. He had been touching her downstairs, and now he grabbed her from behind and moved his hands over her as he kissed her neck, "Come on," he whispered.

"I don't feel like it," she said.

"I know you do," Frank said. They had gone together before she'd married Ralph. "You used to be crazy about it with me."

"I'm not crazy about it now," she said, but he kept working over her. And then, after a few minutes, he moved his hand under her skirt, and then he pushed her forward gently onto the bed, and she lay forward on all the guests' coats. And let him.

Afterwards, she didn't know why she'd done it. He was smiling. "Let's go downstairs separately," he said, and she didn't say anything. She still didn't know why she'd done it, or let him do it, except that it didn't matter. In the dark room Frank squinted at her, and started to get annoyed at her silence. "What's the matter with you?" he said.

"Nothing," she said. *Nothing was the matter, except that Frank thought that who slept with whom mattered—no matter what he said—and she knew it didn't. "Jesus, you're a creep," he said. "Didn't you come?" As if that mattered.*

"Yes," she lied. "Go downstairs." And he went, not smiling now and annoyed at her deadness.

And Eva went to her bedroom and turned the light on. She sat down at her make-up mirror, and fixed herself up, though nothing showed on her face, or anywhere, except that she was slightly sore. But that would go away in a little while. She went downstairs, feeling no different than when she had come up.

And now Eva thought about the first time the kids came to see her, when she was just back from the hospital. She hugged them both, both Timmy and Garth at once (Timmy was a little stiff), and she cried. That is, her face cried. A reflex.

Ralph saw her face cry, and he turned around and left the room, his eyes getting red. She knew he would misunderstand. Make too much of it.

The kids did *matter a little, because it would hurt them to know what she knew, and sometimes she wondered if she was the only one who'd heard the hissing of the blackness.*

So, back from the hospital, Mamma Eva put on an apron and made supper for the children and for Ralph, and acted just as if there was no blackness behind and inside everything, acted as if what one did really mattered. She pretended, along with everybody else sitting around the table waiting for the food to come, that there were reasons for things, and implicitly, just by the way she served the meal, that who slept with whom was the most important thing of all, by serving Ralph first, at which he smiled, the idiot. Not that she cared.

Anyway, it was easier to pretend now than not to pretend and she did it mostly for the kids, and because she felt better for it, if that is a real because. There was no point in doing anything else. Not really. It was too much trouble to explain. Choosing to pretend, going along on the shining surfaces on the blackness, was the easiest thing.

But that was not how she felt the morning she was going to crash the car. She insisted on driving, and Ralph let her do anything she insisted on doing now, so she would drive the car on the way to Ralph's mother, where lunch and the kids were ready. Where they would never arrive because she would break into the darkness.

It was eleven-thirty. Nearly time to go. Ralph came by and looked in, thinking she didn't know he was there, and she knew what kind of a disgusted face Ralph was making—or wanted to make—because she was still just where she'd been since breakfast, sitting in front of her mirror with a drink beside her.

He knew she'd be there, fully made-up, all mornings, and that it was about all she did. It gave her a pale kind of unfocused pleasure to go along with the other shining things floating in the light. She'd done it before she tried to kill herself the last time, too, when Ralph also used to drink in the morning. He used to come to the door, furious, and rail at her, "Is that all you can do, you stupid cunt?"

She wouldn't move at all. Not even focus her eyes as he stood there, furious. "Really, I mean . . . are you so goddamn infantile that all that interests you is looking *at yourself? Can't you even look at your kids, for Christ's sake, I mean, unless you think you make a nice picture with them?"*

She stayed as still as ever, not at all tense.

One time, when she just sat as she was sitting now, after Ralph had been railing at her, drunker that usual, suddenly he rushed in and grabbed her from behind, almost ripped her out of her seat and threw her on the bed. She must have made a face, because he leered, "What's the matter? Am I messing you up?" and then he raped her. Or she supposed he raped her. She didn't fight. It didn't hurt, until he started slapping her face, and when he finally raised up over her, panting, his eyes bright red, his face drawn and contorted, he said, "You can't even be raped!" and he moved off her and left the room.

That time, after he'd moved off her, she just lay still on the bed, feeling her face hurt from the slaps, when suddenly he was back next to her, with a drink in his hand, saying, "I can't seduce you and I can't rape you. All I can do is mess you up, so permit me this small pleasure," and he poured his drink all over her face and hair.

It took her a moment to realize what he was doing and when she finally did and started trying to get away from the falling liquid, he laughed, and then he laughed even more at her anger.

She was wild. She tried to scratch his eyes, kick him in the groin, but she missed and started looking for her nail file, anything, and he laughed and laughed, saying "Woweee! Look at that! I always said that your profoundest emotion was arrogance!" He'd said that before, of course, and so she decided to go into the bathroom to clean herself up.

67

But that was another day.

This time, when Ralph looked in and found her at her mirror, he made no comments. Now he didn't dare, not after the hospital. He simply withdrew.

With her eyes still unfocused, she did not acknowledge her triumph or his withdrawal. Just about everything he said about her was true, of course. She had no trouble admitting she was shallow, "almost to a fault," as he said, infantile, narcissistic, and not really capable of caring about other people. Not even her own children. Not really, beyond the feelings of everything being right in its place and pretty as a picture that acting out the role of mother gave her, especially when they played their own parts properly. Which was why she enjoyed sometimes thinking of getting away to a faraway beach place all alone with the kids and Ralph or even Frank Long, when in her fantasy they would all pick shells together, and where she would serve them all supper in the cottage, after a lovely, lovely day. She enjoyed the thought of it so much she'd even tried it a few times, and found it miserable—but still couldn't help thinking that the next time it would be blissful, especially if she excluded Ralph and his acid tongue from the fantasy and replaced him with someone else. Someone obedient to play the role.

It occurred to her that at the present time she could even make Ralph go along with her to the dream cottage, and obediently play his role with no comments, and she almost smiled at the triumph—and would have if she hadn't preferred to keep her face still.

But she didn't want it now. Too bad. Too bad he never understood that he should have been grateful that she was barely a person, that she enjoyed thinking of herself in terms of pretty pictures, acceptable ones really, neat ones where she was a doll or a bride or a pretty young mommy. He used to throw it in her face, saying that if anybody opened up her head they'd find a swimming pool in there and subscriptions to Vogue, *and he used to say she was just prim underneath it all. Too bad he never understood that if she hadn't cared about the pretty pictures, she wouldn't have cared about anything at all, and then the whole world would collapse, beginning with her children. Her infantile narcissism was what had kept her among them, afloat on the surface of the blackness, knowing it was all shallow and false, but playing along, because she knew that the pretty picture was all there was.*

And she didn't like pictures of herself as a divorcee, shopping just for herself and her cat, with everyone seeing the shamefully small amounts in her shopping cart. She could never live among those reflections returning to her from the things around her. They were too drab. And worse, ugly. She would not—could not—tolerate her own being ugly.

Ralph came back, and asked gently, "Are you ready?"

"Yes," she said, standing up and smoothing her skirt, still looking in the mirror. "I want to drive."

He didn't like that, but he said, "O.K. I'll bring the car to the front door."

She knew why he said that. He hoped that once he was in the driver's seat she'd let him drive. But when he pulled up at the front door she said, again, without looking at him, "I want to drive," and he moved over for her.

She fixed the mirror so she could see her face with no trouble, while she drove, and then she drove, looking in the mirror so much that it started to make Ralph nervous, but he still didn't dare say anything.

And she steered, on the way to where they wouldn't ever arrive, thinking now some things she had thought before, as if she were driving into the rear view mirror. She thought again that, when you come right down to it, Ralph really should have been grateful about her because it's all how you think of yourself, how you talk about yourself. When you come down to it, life in Cambridge is just a conversation, isn't it? Because, what is it you really do? You walk, you talk, you eat, you sleep, you fuck (She hated the word terribly. That was the one thing she'd learned at the hospital the last time. She felt she violated herself every time she used that word.) ... just like everybody else. And the work people do, it very seldom matters. Does it ever really matter? Only in terms of how it lets people talk about themselves, that's all that counts. How you can talk about yourself to others, and to yourself, and how they talk about you.

And how people wanted to talk about her, did talk about her, was on the face of the mirror she was looking at as she drove. That's the difference between people and animals, she thought, because animals have no mirrors and don't know that life is passing them by. The animals have no sentences in which to talk. They are not, she thought, sentenced the same way.

Sentences. Her life was a sentence. A life sentence to be what she saw in the mirror, or pretended to be when she was on her best behavior. Neat and prim. What she was, was a "Pretty Eva" sentence, and the period was obvious. An obituary, in black type, if not a white headstone. A sentence that pretends to mean, to utter itself, logically, to be Eva. Eva, which is really not the subject, but the verb, because she was simply a verb, Eva-ing, which presumed a subject, just because of the verb form, and an object too. But it was all a confusion, a lie, because she was only trying to Eva, and whoever she was that was sentenced to Eva she did not know, nor really cared to know—not anymore. She'd only really cared about how to Eva. And now—she was tired of it. Her life was a sentence, and the whole city and the whole country were millions and millions of stupid sentences, crisscrossing in a stupid, meaningless conversation. A conversation or a monologue, what were all those millions and millions of sentences? Who or what do we suppose is doing all that sentencing, chattering away meaninglessly?

As Eva drove into the rear view mirror, waiting for the explosion of blackness, she was not really bitter about being sentenced, nor about having gone along and having been used in the conversation, or the monologue (she was pretty sure it was a monologue), because, although she knew the sentence had taken over her life, she had never really thought about what else she might be, or how else to talk about herself, except as Eva.

She did wonder though, moments before the mirror was going to shatter, just whose sentence she was, because she knew she had never been her own idea. None of her pictures had been. Who had said: "Eva?" Who had taken over her life, which was not hers? Had never been hers? Nor her idea? Who had said: "Eva," and made her Eva, made her want to be Eva, made her think that Eva was what animated her, and what she had to live up to?

Who had used everyone as part of the monologue?

She knew, almost with pride, a strange new pride she had never felt in the light, a moment before the mirror exploded with her gray eyes in it, that the whispering black silence had never said anything and gave no sentences. Never.

The End

70

SHE WASN'T ASKING FOR PITY

It was awful.

All the time I read, naturally, I was constantly aware of her thigh against mine, a living thigh which Norma and Eva were soon beginning to share, to my increasing unhappiness.

And I could feel her gray eyes on me, too, all the time, apparently amused at my troubles as I struggled ineffectually against Norma's changing by degrees—with each page I turned—into somebody called Eva. But no matter how hard I tried resisting the transubstantiation, I just could not overlook a lot of other things they had in common—aside from that very present thigh against mine—such as a husband named Ralph, a couple of kids named Timmy and Garth, and a couple of "smart" friends named Frank and Jenny Long, all of whom I'd met and seen in three living dimensions.

And I remembered now, too, that there was even a lengthy hospital stay. But I'd had no idea it was at a place like McLeod's. She'd mentioned it to me once, in passing, and now it was beginning to make new sense to me, to my regret.

Maybe I should have been overcome with compassion (with her smiling at me, checking to see how I took it, she didn't seem so pathetic), but I just wasn't feeling secure enough in myself for such a luxury.

Instead, the truth was that I was feeling like a naïve boob, an idiot, as I struggled to come to terms with how little I'd really known about Norma in the first place. Come to think of it, I'd probably only seen her ten or twelve times before in my whole life. One half at parties, and the other half running into her accidentally on the street. Therefore, it was becoming embarrassingly obvious to me that, due to the sappy inclinations of my very ordinary psyche, I'd taken what I'd seen at face value so I could imagine for myself a comfortable Norma. Norma the Nice, a storybook character.

And here in my hands, looking right up in my face, was her "confidence", telling me—while she kept smiling at me, damn it—that in reality she was exactly the opposite of what I'd thought. And it was making me scramble emotionally. I didn't like it at all. What I held in front of me was emitting the very cold Light of some dead sort of creature, the living-dead sort, who inhabited an implacably bald Universe where nothing matters, just as she said, starting with fairy tale notions about the real importance of who sleeps with whom, and where the only values are the ones invented by the weak, in their terror.

Her Light seemed post-human, somehow. And then it came to me: Eva was absolutely Lunar, that's what she was. Dead-souled and made of something like cold, gray plasticine instead of warm, luminous, feminine flesh. And I say Lunar because that's exactly how I've always imagined the moon, as existing in a pure, obscene objectivity. A place where subjective human illusions, such as about the importance and meaning of life, could not possibly take root.

Which means that the moon had an identity for me, all right, but a ghastly, passive one, just like Eva's, whose most powerful if not *only* sign of affect I could imagine was being wet. Which may sound odd, but it meant that when Ralph poured a drink on her in the story, his outraged desperation at her spoke to me in the language of the soul. I admit it. For a moment there, I was on his side. And his huge size, which I knew from life, only served to make his futility all the more touching.

But dead and Lunar as Eva was, she was definitely getting much realer for me, much more present on my couch, than Norma the Nice. With each unhappy moment that passed. Of course, Norma hadn't yet vanished for me. I was not tough enough for that. Norma the Nice was as benignly alive as ever, always believing that things do matter, starting with who sleeps with whom, if for no other reason than the sanity of the children. But she'd been forced to remove herself from my couch to some other, more ethereal realm, as Eva took full possession of her worldly body.

Then I thought: no wonder I didn't feel guilty about my lack of pity for poor, alienated Eva, driving off to her death. She *didn't* drive off. That was the fiction part. Hell, she was right there next to me, smiling at me, challenging me.

So, as I kept my head down, trying to cope, I decided that—no matter what—boob that I might be, I did *not*, God protect me, want to play the part of the shocked innocent when I finally looked up to confront her smiling face.

And then, suddenly, something else made Eva even more real, and the Norma I thought I knew more unlikely. Something that I'd never quite understood about Norma the Nice before, though I'd chosen not to dwell on it. This was, simply, how impoverished, harried and overworked Norma always looked, despite having a very successful husband, a big house on Brattle street, and even a couple of fat, pedigreed English sheep dogs.

Ralph had made it big with Frank Long in the late '40s by starting an industrial consultant's firm that had expanded considerably. And yet, for all that financial success, there was benignly suffering Norma, still doing all the cleaning and shopping, baking the bread and even making a couple of jackets for Ralph, as she informed me, always to be seen moving about Cambridge with a couple of kids draped from somewhere on her as she smiled enduringly and pushed aside wisps of hair from her eyes, looking for all the world like a struggling minister's wife. Now that I thought about it, it was as if she and Ralph belonged to two different economic classes.

I never did understand why she hadn't gotten help from, say, Swedish girls, like the Longs did (not without a breath of scandal). They could have helped with the house, or at least refracted some of the heat from the kids' demands. Then she wouldn't have had to exhaust herself, or burn out her nerves about the kids biting into electric cords and the like. And why didn't she shop over the phone from the fancier Cambridge supermarkets and get gypped, and not care, like so many of the other women in her class?

Now I understood.

It was all making sense, thanks to Eva, particularly as I remembered how one time Norma had told me that having domestic help was not only immoral to her as a democratic American, but that it was out of the question because it would deprive her of what she called her "role in life". It wasn't because she was a tightwad. Damn it all: Norma was worn out because she'd *wanted* to be worn out, to lose herself in maternal chores. It was an ideological commitment, for Christ's sake! Sartre and Freud rolled up into the *Ladies' Home Journal*, trying to save her soul.

No wonder she was punishing herself during the day, like a fanatical nun, disciplining herself with pious punishments. From what I'd just read, I could see she was expiating her sins, or, as they called it in her set, "acting things out".

But that was in the past, because now, I gathered from her "confidence", she was telling me she had lost the faith. She was telling me that despite all that pious behavior, she didn't believe any of it. Including Norma. Not any more. And she was smiling as she let me in on it. Challenging me to accept it.

O.K., I thought to myself, so she's telling me. She's telling me she's Eva. But I started getting mad because she'd fooled me so programmatically into thinking she was the exact opposite of what she was: a Norma. I was getting mad because, once again in my life, my intelligence had been insulted successfully.

Dammit, I thought, she's a female impersonator! That's why she fooled me. And the moment I thought that, I felt one of the oldest and strangest sorts of irritations that men feel—I'm sure of it—when they can take exception to the point of violence. And her smile (which I couldn't help sensing all the time) wasn't helping any.

However, being civilized, all I did was think grumpily: shit, I bet she doesn't even *like* her kids, on top of everything else. I bet that when she's being Norma the Nice, she's the kind of creepy, smiling robot that gives her kids good-night kisses out of the medicine cabinet, following her doctor's prescription. I bet she's one of those Mother-Scientists whose every word comes wrapped in medical white and stinks of medicine. God, how obscene.

But, despite having achieved a degree of self-righteousness, I was still too afraid to look at her. The word that comes to mind is: chicken. And she could see, too, that I'd finished reading her story.

So, having to pick up my head, I came up rubbing my eyes with my right thumb and forefinger, not unlike a little kid who hopes that if *he* closes his eyes, *he* won't be seen.

Unfortunately, I was well aware she could see me, and that her face was mooning full in on mine, behind my hand, as she said, "Well . . . ?"

"I'm thinking . . . I'm thinking . . . ," I said, keeping my eyes closed. But I knew it couldn't last. Sooner or later I was going to have to remove my fingers from my eyelids, open them and confront the reality of cold and Lunar Eva, someone who believed nothing really mattered, including life.

But that kind of ultimate realism was just too much for me, still, even though it was waiting to stare me in the face, so my mind took, or tried to take, the more tolerable direction of compassion for her suicide attempt, in spite of all good sense. That is to say, not that I was admitting it, but I was trying to arm myself through morality, to equalize things a little, as I tried to castigate myself with: Jesus, Muldoon. What *is* the matter with you? You're the one who's cold and Lunar. Just because she isn't groveling at your feet, that doesn't mean she doesn't need help. So why don't you try to help her instead of hanging around here being angry with her for being a fallen woman, with all the fury of your tribal prudishness. You *are* a crud, Muldoon. A real prig.

Unfortunately, the escape attempt failed. I just couldn't kid myself into thinking her "confidence" was a call for help, even unconsciously. Not to me it wasn't. Neither for help, nor pity.

It was a challenge, pure and simple. And the Pollyanna moralist in me, who had hoped to out-superior Eva by barking at me, now had to go back into his corner with his tail between his legs. And stay there.

Because he couldn't cut it with Eva. She would have laughed him out of the room if he came at her like a missionary, and me right out with him. And *that*, I couldn't take.

No question about it. To cut it with Eva, to avoid being laughed at, you had to get her message straight. And the part about her lack of interest in life was only incidental.

The real message, straight, was that she belonged to the Elite of Enlightened Fallen, those who know that terrible secret that nothing matters, including who sleeps with whom, and that everybody invents meanings and importances because they can't take it. Therefore, her smiling question to me was: could *I* take it? Or was I like all the Ralphs and the sensitive young doctors with the frightened eyes who were trying to make a good woman out of her, because they were nothing more than pathetic, infant clingers with film-covered eyes who cannot face the reality of her universe?

Naturally, I knew the answer. Yes I was.

But I was not about to admit it. Especially as I felt her cold breath on the back of my hand covering my eyes, smirking in the shape of a smile which I was sure was becoming disdainful now.

Whereupon, as erotically unaroused as I was, I knew I had to make a pass at her.

Maybe who slept with whom didn't matter in one way, but it was certainly demanded that I give it a try with her, under penalty of scorn. And scorn I could do without, as once more in my life I had to wonder how many times people go to bed with each other when they are both sexually aroused, as compared to all the other reasons.

MULDOON REACTS

But the question was how. How to come out ahead. Or at least avoid disaster.

One thing was sure. I wasn't going to play it like Father finishing his pipe in his easy chair, putting his book down and comfortably going upstairs where Mother waited—at 10:15 smiling, with the lights out. Which was pretty much how I'd tended to imagine sex between Ralph and Norma until a very short time ago. That was not what was called for here.

And unfortunately, my own normal style, I was sure, was unacceptable, too. I mean, I'd always imagined myself as the open, sincere kind of lover, and if I played it that way with Eva, I might wind up at McLeod's myself. And I couldn't bear the idea of having Mel tell me anything about my being a flaming adolescent.

And because of bespectacled Mel, I suddenly thought of how the young bespectacled psychiatrist with the frightened eyes, the one she'd said acted like a timid, would-be boyfriend offering her an ice cream cone, would have made love to her. I could see it clear as day, and it revolted me, because I was sure that dreadful little suburban kid with a degree and status *was* in love with her, and desperately wanted to make love to her.

77

What would he be? 26, maybe? An intern, with a fancy sports car? A little older? Whatever. I knew, I was sure, he'd be a slavish, slobbering dog, disgustingly warm and sticky, pleading with her at least to *say* she didn't believe what he so Oedipally couldn't help but believe about the importance of who slept with whom.

And in response to him, and to his desperate ardor, she'd be smiling, aristocratically cold-mouthed, hard-eyed and lubricated through and through with her coldness, which would only resemble moistness, while her implacably lucid mind contemplated Lunar facts that others, especially the likes of him, could not bear. She would be the unmoving center, enormous, and he would be tiny, busy, moving around her, smiling pleadingly and trying desperately to impart some warmth into her chill immobility from the animation of his own desperate hopes. He would be just as passionate as his own terrified and absolute refusal to believe what she believed, and it would no doubt make him sexually tireless, infinitely potent in the shallowest sense of the word, more than he had ever been even as a sixteen-year-old boy, because his potency would have its endless wellsprings in his all-consuming desire to get her to admit that it wasn't *really* true, after all. He would even tell her he loved her enough for the two of them and that he would go on loving her until she learned from his desperation that in the end, it *does* matter, and he would claim he wanted to save her, in the full sincerity of his self-deceit, little mother's boy missionary that he is, unable to bear believing that he might not be his mother's star little boy, or any other mother's, either.

His shining-eyed image was so undignified in my mind that I resented him for embarrassing me as a male.

And then, in my rejection of him, I must report, my *own* transformation began. To my surprise.

Suddenly, my resentment became cool. Detached. Ironic. I stopped identifying with him quite so much, I guess. Because now, thinking about the nauseating, willing-to-please young psychiatrist, the sort I was sure would enjoy wealth from one day writing a best seller on sexual techniques for Golden Agers, I had to agree with Eva. He *was* vulgar. A pathetic clinger, and thoroughly deserving of contempt. Absolutely, the worst sort of Christian. Indeed, he demanded to be squashed, and I could see it so well, from the point of view of the Elite, that I started thinking that maybe she had *not* made a mistake in confiding in me, after all. Maybe I *was* equal to her.

And I smiled thinly, still without looking at her (although now for effect. I was gaining momentum.). And I began considering myself demonically, like my idea of Oscar Wilde.

I decided: I was going to take her on her own terms.

As a fellow member of the Enlightened Fallen, the truest Elite.

And it occurred to me that to gain status in her eyes, I might even get around to suggesting that I was occasionally homosexual (not true, but it might shake her up) and that, in my advanced decadent opinion, the only difference I recognized between skin and skin was light, but that, frankly, only seeing death excited me erotically anymore (just to show her who's tough around here). But then, in my new mood, I knew one thing instinctively: taking her to bed as a fellow member of the Elite of the Enlightened Fallen carried the hazard of becoming pretty sexless and unexciting, pretty quick. After all, if I did it like that, there would be no generic difference between us aristocrats—except for the polarization of master and slave—which I decided I was going to introduce into our relationship at once and surprise the hell out of her.

I was surprising myself a little, too, I must admit, because until that moment I'd never thought I'd understand the secrets of sadomasochism, not ever having liked either giving or receiving pain.

So, with my eyes still veiled, I made my thin smile more perversely aggressive, and then, as if finding the moment to my liking, I finally lifted up my eyes to her, a changed creature myself.

There she was. Her pupils instantly dilated at meeting mine, and she said, "Jerome . . . ?" as if she had suddenly sensed—alarmed and excited—that I too was a denizen of her Eva's Universe of pitiless gray plasticine.

I said nothing, quite aware I had surprised her and had her off balance, that the advantage was momentarily mine. In the inner courts of my soul, a tennis umpire's voice said: "Advantage, Mr. Muldoon".

The room fell absolutely silent. All things became perfectly still. Perfectly inanimate. Now I felt myself like Camus' Caligula as I watched her in our strange Lunar lull, and I smiled like the executioner god who in his dead, perfect and certain universe now pauses sentimentally to contemplate the uncertainty playing in his victim's eyes. The only motion left, and the virgin, imperfect jewel he is after. The last uncertainty. The last virginity.

" . . . Jerome . . . ?" she said again.

But I held absolutely still for this last, sentimental moment, savoring it, and the future too, expecting that after I'd had my way with her I was going to tell her we were indeed as the gods truly are—indifferent, Lunar, unreproductive, and made of cold, gray plasticine.

Soon, I figured, I'd be moving like a monitor lizard hunting among desert rocks, sensing warm blood, flicking out that olfactory tongue the colors of flame as I sensed she wanted me to humiliate her, abuse her, just so she could have—at least for one moment—the illusion of being alive in herself. I sensed she couldn't, wouldn't, have it any other way.

However, despite my new Sadian lucubrations and my thin, cruel smile, it began to dawn on me that I was just sitting there, just like old X.J. Muldoon, not moving a muscle. And I began to suspect that maybe I wasn't going to go any further, either, as suddenly I feared my demonic smile might freeze into idiocy. To my everlasting embarrassment.

But, lucky for me, I must have been squinting most malevolently in my paralysis because she said again, " . . . Jerome?" quite nervously, and half smiled as she added, "What did you think of the story?"

"I think . . . ," I said, deliberately, "you should stand up when you talk to me."

For a puzzled instant, she looked at me, and then, in a blurt, half laughed. But she didn't stand up. Instead, she reached for another cigarette, lit it with nervous fingers, and leaned back, making it clear she would remain seated. So, squinting some more, I said to myself: a further challenge. Good.

Now she looked as if she were trying to control a tremble, and, just as before I'd started reading, everything inside me began speeding up in a great swirl.

The Lunar room became even quieter, increasing the tension, and, blowing some smoke, she said, " . . . are you sure you want to?"

Malevolently, I stared at her, and forced her to look down to her lap.

She inhaled again, very slowly and deeply this time, and then lifted her head, lay back on the angle of the couch and smiled. And then, looking at me, she slowly let out an incredibly long stream of smoke, suddenly unstopping everything in the room, releasing the maelstrom, and I felt myself lunge at her, feeling all things break

80

free.

Her temperature was icy, just as I'd expected Lunar Eva's to be, but she was much softer and weaker than I'd thought she'd feel. She let me kiss her cold mouth for a moment before turning away.

"I insist," I said, or I think I said, and I did, and to my surprise, not only her mouth but her whole body became feverishly hot in just moments, and incredibly I was engaged in taking off her underclothes as she said, "No, please . . . ," a few more times, but responded undeniably.

I don't mean to relate any details here that are without psychological significance, but I must admit that to my further amazement she moaned and yelled spectacularly as I penetrated her, gripping and clawing me, so much so that, as much as I might be lost in the event, I had to begin thinking about Mr. Pansky downstairs hearing all the noise and maybe calling the police because he thought I was killing her. The first moans and yells were wordlessly primordial, but then she took to yelling over and over again, rhythmically, "Jer-ome! Jer-ome!" and I self-consciously started hoping it would all end soon, for fear of Mr. Pansky. But, strangely, I found myself having not only pleasure but a resistance to exhaustion by pleasure worthy of a pagan god, which not only made her go on moaning and yelling, "Jerome! Jerome!" but made her eyes large and unbelieving as she did so, undergoing a series of spectacular spasms and yielding completely to them, until finally she began folding herself around me and returning affection to me in an absolutely loving way. It was so affectionate and encompassing that, I regret to say, she reminded me of how I'd imagined the young psychiatrist with the frightened eyes would have wanted to make love to her. I went on and on (normally it is not so) until my own blood-curdling climax, whereupon she said, once more, "Jerome . . . ," as if my name were a miraculous discovery, making it sound to me as if it were the first time I'd ever heard it myself, making each of its vowels take on a marvelous three-dimensionality, and that was it.

We had committed adultery.

I don't think either of us quite believed it.

SEX WITH RALPH

I have no idea how deeply Norma/Eva slept, but as for me, when I went out, it was as if I went falling down an endless black chasm that first opened up somewhere in my sinuses. More than falling asleep, it was like blacking out, and down I sunk like a bowling ball into an undersea canyon, the one where all other undersea canyons finally led, knowing that when and if (I wasn't too sure) I came back up to the daylight world from those watery depths, I was going to reappear on new terms, as a new man in the daylight world.

Unfortunately, I didn't like that because the New Man to emerge might well be a mate for Lunar Eva, and life on those terms was not really appealing to me, despite my having postured demonically to make a good impression.

But, to my surprise, as I went slipping down into the blackness, leaving above the world of noise and light that existed between the waterline and the sky, I was actually feeling relieved. Not at all afraid. It was the opposite of what I'd expected rationally. I must have been affected by a lot of notions from the Eva story, all having to do with how human life was a sentence, spoken by "Who-knows-what". And I was very happy with the feeling that "Who-knows-what" was waiting for me at the very bottom, feeling myself excused from the fate of "Who-knows-what's" other utterances, which were rising up by me like racing bubbles as I passed them on the way down, to whence they came. I knew that eventually those bubbles that still didn't know themselves would end bursting up through the waterline and erupting unhappily in the light like implacable little god burps, hearing themselves pronounced as such terribly banal fates as "Muldoon", or "Norma", or "Mel Fish".

And then, on my way down, I recognized a "Muldoon" bubble shooting upward, and it amused me that it didn't recognize me, and I kept descending, happier and happier. Not that I knew what that word "Muldoon" really meant, but I appreciated the fact that I was obviously excused from having to "Muldoon". In fact, I was beginning to feel like when the last bell rings on the last day of school, when summer is still infinitely ahead. And I was getting even happier and happier, caring less and less about "Muldooning" up in the light beyond the waterline because I was now sinking so far beneath all noise, and entering the silence and absolute blackness where there are, I knew, no names, no words, no memory, and above all, no judgments. Just freedom in a wild and conscious Darkness.

And I was just about to touch the *fons et origo*, the blackness from where all utterances bubble forth and where "Who-Knows-What" lives, when some unseen fellow creature who was already there and apparently in some angelic status, began announcing joyously to me: "This is the land of Fuckitall! No laws here! No Obligations! No definitions! Just Fuckitall! Fuckitall! Fuckitall!"

At which point, completely blind in the Darkness but completely delighted, I was sure I had arrived, and would enter great bliss. Only to suddenly wake up, bursting like a bubble myself back in the light. And suddenly *very* ashamed of myself for having wanted all that black freedom. Inescapably awake, I felt as if the moralizing light of day had walked in on me and caught me doing something disgraceful. And then I realized, with some sadness, that I had to Muldoon again. And to go on Muldooning.

That was the only moment I was frightened—just as I woke. In my instant dream analysis, I decided I'd had a dream about my own dying, from which I'd escaped in the nick of time. But that analysis was conditioned by my sense of shame and the presence of the daylight. I really wasn't sure I hadn't dreamed the opposite, either.

But wake up I did, back on my own couch, with the head of a naked woman on my T-shirted shoulder. And the moment I awoke, she started stroking my hair very gently, still keeping her head where it was. From the way she was now acting—if it weren't for Eva—I would have guessed that I had absolutely "won" her, that she was mine and was giving her affections to me without reservation, and she seemed pleased about it. Pleased, and relieved, too, which was odd. She was being so openly affectionate to me that I began to feel guilty for not really liking her quite so much anymore, now that she was Eva.

"Did you have a nice nap?" she said, and kissed my cheek in a gentle way that was meant to be pleasing to me. Which it was.

"Yes," I said. "Did you?"

"A little, and *most* delightfully! I feel like an absolutely new woman, thanks to you . . . Jerome." And she pronounced 'J-E-R-O-M-E" in a mock, formal baritone, then smiled and nuzzled me in a most un-baritone, pleased way. "You really shouldn't have, you know. I've never been overpowered like that before in all my life, you beast."

"Well, uh . . . ," I found myself saying with difficulty, which made her pop her cheerful head up to look in my face and say, "Oh, dear . . . you aren't feeling *guilty*, are you?"

"Oh, no . . . ," I said, and she ducked her head back down again, saying, "Good, because you most certainly should not feel guilty. I mean, I *think* you shouldn't have overpowered me, but I must be wrong because it obviously agreed with me. The experience was most amazing, to say the least. Just incredible. Ralph would have been very surprised if he'd seen how I responded, . . . and as a matter of fact, I'm pretty surprised myself. God, it was marvelous! I didn't know I had it in me!"

The mention of Ralph was distressing, but I tried not to show it as I said, "I don't understand. Didn't you think I might try something?"

"Oh, sure, I guess so. I mean, I thought you might try to give me a nervous little kiss or something when we were alone, but I just wanted you to read my story and tell me what you thought about it."

"And you didn't signal me at all?"

"Not that I know of. You did it all on your own, which is what's so refreshing. But judging from my response, I must have *wanted* you to overpower me, *just* the way you did."

"Well . . . it's lucky for me you did. I mean, God, how embarrassing if you hadn't. I mean, really, I wouldn't have presumed if . . . ," but Norma, laughing, interrupted me with, "For God's sake, don't ruin everything by apologizing! You are a beast, and be glad you are. Really, darling, I'm not telling you all this just to get you off the hook from a *faux pas*, you know. *Obviously* you did the right thing. In fact," she now said ceremoniously, beginning to edge into her favored Viennese accent and sounding as if she were conferring a degree upon me, "I hereby declare zzatt you did zee most kkorrect zzeeeng you could half done, and are *beyond* reproach! How's that? Do you feel more comfortable?"

" . . . Yes. Thanks."

"Did you know," she said, "that Ralph thinks I'm frigid?"

"No," I said, genuinely surprised, though I might have expected it from her story.

"Well, he does. He says sex with me is like an old pretzel dunked in flat beer. What do you think of that?"

"I wouldn't have said so . . . "

"Well, me neither!" she said, and hugged me enthusiastically. "Not *now*, I wouldn't. Thanks to you, my sweet, shy rapist! Are you what I've been missing all these years, Jerome?" And now as she hugged me, she shook me with open, girlish joy.

"Uh . . . can I say something, Norma?"

"Sure! Anything! Name it! Overwhelm me!"

"Well . . . I don't know if I'm really comfortable as a rapist. I mean, it's lonely, somehow . . . " at which she looked up at me with her gray eyes and burst out laughing, but quickly stopped herself to spare my feelings, saying, "I *am* sorry, darling. I guess I shouldn't laugh, but you're so sweet, you just don't understand what real, obscene rape is, bless your heart. You really *are* feeling a little beastly, aren't you . . . I mean, guilty for having abused me with your primeval tool and all that . . . ."

"Yeah . . . ," I said, a bit defensively, "I suppose I am."

"Well, love," she said in a soothing tone, not sounding overpowered at all, "don't. Sex with you," she explained, "is as pure as the driven snow, because I wanted you to do it. Don't you see? You made me glad to give in, so you really aren't a rapist, after all. I guess what you can't know is that Ralph is the real, obscene rapist. And thanks to you, now I'm finally beginning to be sure of something I've suspected all along, about Ralph, I mean . . . which is that he's been raping me all these years in the most hateful way imaginable."

"But . . . what does he do that's so bad?"

"No . . . he doesn't whip me," she said, smiling playfully at me for my endearingly foolish reaction, which I didn't care for, adding, "Were you about to defend me?"

"Like hell. Fight your own battles," I said, feeling quite exposed now, and helplessly stupid. I even felt my cheeks stiffen and feared they might be turning a bit red, so I looked away.

What had really ruffled my feathers, of course (which I didn't care to admit), was that now that we'd had intercourse I knew I would feel myself responsible for her for the rest of my life, no matter what I said. And it looked to me like she was playing with my unfortunate Oedipal superstitions. But fortunately, as if maybe catching on, she took a bit more care in her tone now as she explained, "Maybe it *would* be better if he did beat me into things . . . because that way at least he'd leave me something . . . like my not wanting to. But he doesn't, because he's too good a rapist for that. He makes me do things I don't want to do, making me feel guilty all the time for not wanting to, so I *want* to want to, you see. Out of guilt. That's his trick. He makes me *want* to want to, and not be *able* to want to, at the same time. And then it gets worse, because when I really get worked up to be responsive to him, and I desperately want to . . . then he won't let me."

"He won't?"

"Nope. At the slightest hint of my responsiveness, he makes it impossible and turns me right off. He likes it that way."

"But *why*?"

"Because he's only interested in whatever it is that goes against my grain, don't you see? The minute he thinks it doesn't, he loses interest. He's quite disgusting, really."

"I don't get it. I mean, I find it hard to believe," I said.

"So did I, for a long time, until I finally figured it out," she said. "But it's true. And it's real rape, too. The realest. He systematically turns me into an object, a thing for him to use. And that's what he likes. He's one selfish pig, my Ralph is . . . and what's more, a very sensitive selfish pig. I know exactly *how* sensitive, too, because many is the time I've watched him change direction very quickly indeed when he's sensed something in me that might make me into more than an object. Like wanting to join in, for example. He just *will not* let me give, not the way I want to. Because all he wants is to take, you see. That's all. And believe me, I've tricked him lots of times, to prove it to myself. I've pretended to get to like what he thought I was

87

doing against my will, just for the pleasure of seeing him lose interest, and start looking for something else that he could be surer would bother me. All very subtle, of course. Now *that*, my dear, is a purist as a raper, don't you think? I swear he not only keeps me frigid, but he likes it that way, because he likes that disgusting, manipulative distance.

"How long have you felt this way about him?"

"Knowingly, or unknowingly?" she said, and smiled. "That's a better question. I know it's hard for you to believe, but it's all quite true, and he's been killing me that way. I mean it, Jerome. I know he's killing me, and I especially know it right now, darling, because *you* have made me feel so alive . . . " And, having said that, she continued looking at me, smiling, before adding, "And can I say something cornier, which is also true?"

"Go ahead," I said, my cheeks stiffening apprehensively. "Just so long as it's flattering."

And she smiled at my wisecrack in passing, "Well, it is . . . I think I told you once, I quit graduate school to marry Ralph because . . . well, I could feel my femininity getting atrophied. I was too damn good at my work, you see, and it was turning me into a cold, totally dedicated, inhuman, superefficient bitch, just like one of those prize-crazy rats the behaviorists use in their labs. I could see it all coming. I was going to get so hooked on my work, so perverted, I suppose, that I was going to turn into a real castrator as far as men were concerned. Men, and women, too. I was going to bust *everybody's* balls, the way I was going, and I didn't like it . . . well, I didn't like liking it, let's put it that way. Because I desperately wanted to be a real woman, too, the soft kind of person, with a house and kids and a husband, and happy about it, instead of sublimating the whole instinct into my work . . . like some spinster who can't have what she wants, because, dammit, I thought I *could* have it, and I knew enough about my work that I wasn't going to try to kid myself that I could combine the two things, either. What comes first, comes first, and since I knew what should be first, I also knew I wasn't going to be quite so good at my work anymore. So I married Ralph. But you know what happened? That son of a bitch turned out to be just as bad for me as graduate school. Worse, because he was harder to figure out. You see, he too was systematically destroying my femininity, kind of castrating me by never letting me give, not the way I wanted to, goddammit, which is like a woman should, gladly. He's always forced me to give grudgingly, turning me into a bitch type, after all, and I hate him for it. Really I do. I guess I've been hating him for a long time, but I didn't know it for sure until recently . . . I guess I just don't like hating."

"I don't imagine he does, either," I said. But she nodded, "Nope. You're wrong there. He does. He's even told me he hates impersonally, just to keep up his competitive interest in things. But that's not for me. I'm not an aggressive male having to compete with everybody, the way he thinks he has to. And anyway, I really and honestly believe that a woman's life is giving, whether a man's is or not. The whole thing's like giving milk, kind of, if you know what I mean, and he's just been shriveling me up inside, souring me, and just plain unsexing me, that's what he's been doing. Really, he's turning me into some awful kind of eunuch, on the way to killing me. Do you understand what I'm saying, Jerome?"

"Yes," I said, "I guess so."

"Oh . . . dear," she said, "Has this been too much ugly, domestic crap for you? I bet I sound to you like I'm blaming him for everything."

"No, no . . . "

"Of course I do. I guess, to be fair, I'd have to say it's been a symbiotic relationship. I mean, you can't cheat an honest man, and all that. I'll admit he was getting away with raping me because I was raping myself. Part of the trouble was that I thought I was a masochist when I really wasn't. Because each time he got me to do something against my will, not only did I resent it, deep down, but I never forgot it. Each little sacrifice left a little scar, . . . scar, hell, an ulcer, that's what it left, because it turned out I didn't really *like* that filthy kind of giving, after all. So what happened was that I became a horrible envelope for thousands and thousands of secret little grievances that I'm hoarding, you see. Now isn't *that* disgusting? I think it's the part that gets me most. Honest to God, I've taken to hoarding grievances as if they were points for me, which is really how I was drying up inside and turning into a genuine, *bona-fide* hag. What I'm trying to tell you is I'm a bitch all right, but really I don't want to be one, Jerome, I've *never* wanted to be one, . . . only he *wants* me to be that way, can you believe it? He literally wants me bitching and resentful and grudging and too confused to talk about it when he makes me put out against my will . . . It makes him smile, the bastard . . . ," and Norma gave an involuntary hate shudder. But

89

then she smiled, or tried to smile, more sportingly, saying, "But, looking at it from his side . . . I guess that way I'm a conquest for him every time," and she laughed. "You know what he says when I tell him this stuff?"

"What?"

"He says . . . ," and she shook her head and laughed with a trace of pained admiration, "the bastard says he's only trying to keep the romance alive in our marriage!" And then she added, "But don't think for a minute that he's really admitting anything. He never would, you see. That's his main trick, so when he says that, he pretends it's a joke. A tantalizing joke." And then she shrugged, "I am sorry. Really, I don't mean to go on and on about it."

"Oh, that's O.K.," I said. "I guess I'm waiting to hear you say something flattering about me, remember?"

"Oh, yes!" she said, brightening up again. "No wonder you were so patient. I almost forgot, with all my bitching and moaning. What I was just about to tell you is that I don't think I can ever let Ralph touch me again. Not now, when I know I can still be a woman, thanks to you. I mean, it would be absolutely *impure*. Isn't that sufficiently corny and flattering?"

We hugged and kissed after that, of course. And it was, as a matter of fact, flattering to me. But much as I responded to that, I also felt I was getting roped into much more than I had bargained for, until I finally felt myself compelled to say, "Norma . . . ," in a "serious", throat-clearing way. To which she replied good-humoredly with an equally serious sounding, "Yesss," which mimicked me and made me instantly incapable of retaining my posture, so I shrugged and said, "Well . . . It's just that . . . I mean, I guess, like any man, I've always wanted women to regard sex with me as a religious experience . . . ."

"Yeeesss" she said, "Aaaandd?"

"Well . . . please don't be too hard on Ralph. I'm sure he feels the same as me, deep down inside, even if he hasn't been too successful at it . . . I mean, maybe he's terribly shy . . . " And as soon as I'd said it, I expected her to burst out laughing. But she didn't. It was worse. She simply looked at me, and then produced her incredibly "wry" smile, cynical about men's motives beyond anything I could live with. It denuded me, it made me feel like an insect because it was enormous somehow, looking millions of years old, and possibly even pre-human. "What's the matter?" she said, not joking. "Are you trying to get rid of me already?"

"Oh, no . . . really I'm not," I said, laughing, but alarmed, quite unable to accept her smile's picture of the world, even if it were true. But then she smiled much more gently, and said, "I was just joking, dear. I know you really don't want to get rid of me. I guess the idea of Ralph being shy all this time was just too much for me. And do you know *why* I know better than you do that you don't want to get rid of me?"

"No . . . ," I said.

"Because I know you want to take what I want to give. You'll see. So don't worry so much . . . ," and she smiled, so I nodded. "But I'm sorry to have to tell you," she said, "that you are quite wrong about every man wanting women to respond, bless your heart. You *still* think you raped me, don't you? I mean, you even feel some guilt about it, don't you?"

"Well, yeah . . . ," I said. "I was rather flattering myself that I had, kind of. I mean, you did say, yourself, I overpowered you."

"Yes I did, dear. But deep down our wills were in harmony, or I wouldn't have responded the way I did, so you mustn't feel guilty at all. I'm afraid you still have no conception of what real rape is, do you . . . despite my carefully instructing you on it."

"Now you're humiliating me."

"I don't mean to, dear," she said, smiling very nicely at me with her clear gray eyes. "But tell me the truth, do you think that this was a quick dirty fuck?" and having said so, she continued smiling benignly.

Her gaze was so simple, even and direct that I had to lower mine, saying, "I wouldn't care to put it that way . . . ."

And she laughed, rubbing my head. "Well, it wouldn't offend me if you did. Because it really wasn't. Whether you know it yet, or not," and when I looked up I found her smiling at me, congratulatorily, saying, "*I* know it, and that's enough for right now. What you don't quite see yet, I'm afraid, is that my married sex with Ralph is the filthy one, and this is clean," and she glanced at her wrist watch, and said, "And I better get out of here, right now, because I'm going to be late as it is!"

"Oh . . . ?" I said glumly.

Suddenly, with her mentioning being late, I was struck again by the image of her family gathered around the dinner table, waiting for her, while she'd been with me. And once again, as I had before, I wondered if she hadn't planned and timed it exactly this way, for the sake of revenge. Despite what she'd said about not having expected anything. It certainly did seem possible, considering how she felt about Ralph's abusing her. Surely his punishment would include cooking and tending to the kids.

"Goodness," Norma said as she dressed. "You look so demoralized all of a sudden. Anything the matter?" And she stopped, looking at me.

"No, nothing," I said, smiling, and so she continued dressing herself, saying, "By the way, what *did* you think of my story? That really was why I came here, you know."

"Well ...," I said, "I had no idea ... I mean, it must have been terrible for you," and I was laboring so much that she stopped again and looked right at me. "What *are* you talking about?"

"Well, I didn't know you'd had a breakdown or anything," and she laughed. "Breakdown? Oh, God no!" she said.

"No?"

"I've never even been to a shrink. Ralph has, but not me. You *are* a love! Did you think I tried to kill myself, too?"

"Well ... maybe ... "

"The thought has never crossed my mind! My god, I don't know whether I should be touched or offended, now that I think of it. Did you think I was like frigid Eva? After all this?"

"Well ... no," I lied, "but ... "

"My goodness ...," she said, shaking her head at me. "Look, I really do have to run, but what I really want to know is, do you think I can sell it?"

"Sell it?"

"Yes. That's right. Sell it. I want to get good enough at writing stories so I can leave Ralph. That's why I'm taking the writing course."

"Gee ... I never thought about it that way. I was thinking about Eva so much."

"Oh! Eva!" Norma said laughing. "*That* poor thing. She's an obvious case, isn't she? I mean, she just needs to run into somebody like you ... someone marvelously endowed ... to make her come alive. By God, *then* she'd know that who sleeps with whom matters, don't you think?"

"She would ... ?"

"Of course, dear. So let's not talk about her. Let's talk about me.

92

Do you think I have talent?"

"Sure, but . . . "

" 'But,' " she said, mimicking me. " 'But' . . . I guess we'll have to talk about the 'buts' next time, immediately after the next overpowering. I really would like your detailed opinion . . . By the way, had you been thinking dirty thoughts about me for a long time before this?"

And I bowed my head, because I hadn't, and said, " . . . Yes."

Norma was fully dressed now, smiling at me when I picked up my head, and she said, "Good-by, darling. Call me in the morning . . . and thank you for showing me I'm alive." She kissed me very warmly, very happily, and then said, "Now, *there's* something you can feel responsible for, you sweet beast . . . And please, rest assured that I think who sleeps with whom is pretty important. At least to me. I have the proof, you see, and *you're it!*"

And off she went.

With me smiling as she closed the door.

But even before it was finally shut, with her very last smiling words, "You're it!" now quivering inside me like a couple of fresh-stuck arrows, I sunk into an instant depression, already wondering how I was going to get out of it. The relationship, I mean. And doubting I could. Knowing full well, of course, that if she *did* excuse me with ease, I'd feel more than crushed now. I'd feel downright nullified as a male. Especially after she'd spent so much time addicting me to the celebration of my malehood.

Frankly, I was resenting her. Despite all her flattery and charm. Maybe even because of it, too. Because she'd not only mixed her flattery with a lot of open condescension about my naïveté, which I hadn't cared for, but she'd also given every indication of being ready to take advantage of my basic moral cowardice and general passivity and just plain push me around. Enthusiastically.

Which meant to me that I was getting involved with somebody I was already liking an awful lot less than my old illusory acquaintance, Norma the Nice, whom I could never imagine doing such things, to me or to anyone else, for that matter.

Cursing myself, I just *knew* that I was drifting—drifting, hell, I was being pulled—into an affair in which I was sure to protest my love most the less I liked the whole thing. And that it was an affair I wouldn't know how to end, which meant it would probably be done for me one day, to my further discomfort, to put it mildly.

93

On top of which, I still wasn't really sure *who* she was, now that she obviously wasn't the amiably contented wife and mother I had believed I'd known. Because, even though she'd said she wasn't Eva, and that Eva was just fiction, Eva had rung awfully true to me, just the same. And more firmly and convincingly than the Norma who explained herself ideologically to me. Whom I wanted to believe, of course, but which in itself made her a shade suspect.

Life was not looking good to me. And none of this was going to help me concentrate on finishing my thesis, either.

Not that the UMFs cared.

Actually, they were busy adding to my troubles by interspersing more often than usual now those images of Althea on the hill. Going off like flash bulbs. They'd been a part of my life for some time now, and I'd pretty well learned to disregard them. But now they were coming and going so often that they were adding to my disorientation.

This was because the UMFs were setting me up for an unforgettable explosion of Peculiar Perceptions.

MEL AND MARCIA

Not more than an hour later (the images of Althea had subsided some, but they weren't what was bothering me most), as I cooked my tomato soup on one of my hot plate burners and watched the water boil around a frozen green block of spinach on the other, I tried to ignore that my rented rooms had been transformed forever.

Before she came into it, despite fleeting visits by a few other women, my place had been notably without a feminine presence. As aridly womanless as a men's secondhand clothing store. Not that I'd liked it that way, but at least it had been the kind of place in which I could feel objective and reasonable. But now, every piece of Mr. Pansky's furniture, even the wallpaper and the light fixtures, was getting heavier and heavier with her psychic traces by the minute. It was as if the place were being invaded by a lush, equivocal perfume (though there was none) that just did not let me think straight, and I knew I was going to have to get the hell out of there, right after eating, if I wanted to get some breathing room and a little rational perspective on what was happening to my life.

To the outsider, as I stood vigilant over my hot plate, I might have looked in control of the situation. But my nervous system was itself aboil with all kinds of confusing notions about her. About who was to blame for what in her marriage, and all that sort of thing, as I continually felt myself caressed by her joking, affectionate presence, and could still feel her skin on mine. And much as I wanted to believe everything she said was true, Bridgid Muldoon's spirit would not leave me in peace, suggesting such things as, "Is that what she told you, is it? And you believe it, every word, don't you Jerry? All about how special you are. And naturally you think you're the first, of course, come to save the poor girl," after which would come that short, dry snort of hers. But despite my mother's spirit's merciless efforts to protect me, I already knew for sure I was about to be "in love".

Because, not that it flatters me to admit it in the company of men, but I can't give myself physically, not for long, anyway, unless I can also dive in after emotionally. And I knew that the next time she asked me I would of course give myself physically, naturally, which meant I was going to do it emotionally, too, just to conform to the situation. In other words, this all meant that Norma and I were already "engaged", so to speak, as far as my incurably pubescent heart was concerned.

I'd known this thoroughly embarrassing fact about myself for years, of course. And knowing it had always helped keep me out of trouble before, at the edge of love affairs, as it were. And even during those times when the tide took the initiative and came to shore after me, I'd always been able to run away (since my early twenties, anyway) and go sufficiently inland. But now, to my growing outrage, it was somehow already too late as I felt myself being pulled out to sea. Still not absolutely sure how I'd gotten there in the first place, and what is more, to compound the situation as I reflected upon it, erotically aroused again. Standing there, feeling victimized and futile, suddenly I heard myself cry out passionately, "Fuck Mel!" blaming him for everything.

This surprised me, at first, but then I knew I was justified. After all, I desperately needed a close friend to confide in, right now, and he was all I had: somebody who was often smug, a psychiatrist, and who was historically given to putting me down, however jokingly, whenever he had the chance. And this was by no means a time I cared to be joked with, as I thought to myself that this most certainly was a perfect chance to do it, put me down I mean, and resoundingly, the bastard. And from the wisdom afforded him by his "professional" vantage point, no less.

If it weren't for his profession, I thought, I could forgive him all the rest. Maybe even trust him. But damn it, his profession was such an important part of him it was impossible to eliminate it from consideration. It was almost like his soul now. After all, how could he *help* but pompose at me from his goddamn "professional" vantage point, when he'd been trying to get there all his life? I couldn't help remembering how back in college, when everybody else was having a good time and getting behind in his work, Mel was always in the library, working and smiling antlike. And when the library closed, he'd go right back to his room and stay there studying while even the most obscene grinds would be going out for beers, it being after ten at night. But not dedicated, smiling Mel. Captain Pleasure Deferred. He wouldn't go out for beers even then. Only on weekends. All just so one day, when he grew up, he'd be an important fellow, a doctor, and be able to tell me with that antlike smile on his face something or other about my troubles from a "professional" perspective. Suddenly I was sure he'd been looking forward to that day for years, licking his chops, just as I felt the certain intuition that if one put a full grown ant under a grasshopper's microscope, the damn bug would have a smile exactly like Mel's (I mean back in school) and that it would insist on being addressed as "Doctor"—successfully of course—the principal reason why it continued to smile.

But I wanted so badly to talk with somebody that I was even ready to compromise my paranoia about Mel, I guess, because it wavered as I couldn't help wondering, in my weakness, if maybe, just maybe, considering the delicacy of my situation, he might possibly, despite having given up his early life for the sake of a respectable middle age, pass up this chance to put me down? Could he, maybe, talk to me like a pal?

I squinted hard, trying to imagine it, and the answer came back: no, damn his ass. Why the hell should he, especially after all these years of my making light of his life and troubles with Marcia? When he had me over a barrel? Me, who knew him "back when" and who had always made it a point to treat him as such? He'd never show me mercy now.

Bowing my head, I had to admit I had it coming to me. For harassing him all these years. But my repentance passed as I thought, screw Mel anyway! I wouldn't call him, even if he was the last person on earth (which, for all practical purposes, he was) because even if by some miracle, he *did* give me a break, his wife

97

Marcia would pick up the phone. Which was absolutely intolerable. She *always* picked up the phone, to shield the good doctor. She much preferred that Melvin, as she called him, got rid of his no-account chums (mostly me) once and for all, and spent his time as he should, socializing with her and fancier people, now that he was getting to be a real Big Daddy. Therefore, she'd been running a splendid isolationist campaign for years now, being inhospitable to those of Melvin's friends she considered a waste of valuable time, while she drove him deeper into the suburbs toward fanciest Lincoln. As much as the idea of Mel pulling rank on me annoyed me, the prospect of hearing her modulated "adult" voice over the phone grated on me even more. I just didn't feel like going through one of her alienating routines at the moment, thank you, with her either pretending she didn't recognize my voice after all these years, or some other cheap trick that culminated with her intoning, "Oh, yes. One moment, please. Dr. Fish! Telephone!" as if she were dealing with such low life as some desperate suicidal patient who'd had the nerve to interrupt the doctor's dinner with his family, a moment to be treated reverentially by all of humanity, in Marcia's opinion.

Indignation flushed through my system, just at the thought of Marcia. They deserve each other, I told myself.

But thinking about Marcia softened my heart. Poor Mel. It was he who introduced me to the powerful concept of the women in men's lives being portraits of said men's souls—and vice versa, of course. He'd called it the Anima Theory. I even remembered one dark and stormy night, only a year ago in a Porter Square bar, when we were both drunk and he was having troubles at home, as usual. Since he was of neither Catholic nor Protestant stock, he was already drunk over his head as he started explaining his ingenious and implacable theory to some guy, a local Irishman who was himself avoiding going home to his wife for as long as he could. And while the rains came down in the cement night outside the guy listened with sloshed and puzzled interest, perfectly politely, until it suddenly dawned in his murky head that *his* wife, according to what this Fish was saying, was a portrait of *his* soul, and since he was a Catholic and believed he *had* a soul, deeply offended, he cranked up and took a punch at Mel, right there at the bar, and sent Mel sprawling back onto a table.

I remembered the moments leading up to that punch, which the guy never expected he would throw. They came floating into my mind like a slow-motion film clip. Mel talking away, hardly looking at anybody, the guy listening, the rains outside coming down as the moments kept moving forward, frame after frame, implacable, until the guy winced in pain, suddenly understanding what Mel was saying about what his immortal soul was like, as Mel, obsessed, kept on insensitively talking and talking, explaining the terrible revelation while the guy started looking as if he wanted to jump out of his skin, when suddenly, in some kind of last-ditch rebellion against the terrible news he was hearing about himself, the guy cranked up and let Mel have it. And Mel went sprawling off his stool, spread-armed, backwards, to the amazement of all, including the guy who'd belted him.

As soon as he'd done it, the guy hissed unhappily, " . . . Shit!" as if he'd dropped a load of dishes, and then instantly moved forward to check into Mel's physical condition. He was the first one there, trying to help him back on his feet by pulling him up off the middle of the table where three other men had had their drinks spilled and were left to contemplate the damage in stupefaction. "Jesus, I'm sorry, pally," the guy was saying as he held Mel up from under the armpits. "I don't know why I did it. You O.K.?"

And Mel, finally upright, smiled sadly as he straightened himself out and said, "Yeah, I'm O.K.," with true forgiveness. "I'm fine."

"Jesus. Let me buy you a drink, buddy. O.K.? Don't know why I did it, honest."

"Please . . . it's all right," Mel reassured him, grinning sadly like a punched ant as he crawled back up on his stool and regained his position on the mahogany bar. "I understand your feelings. Really I do. I just should have taken more care to explain that very few men are flattered when they see pictures of their souls. Most men are so ashamed they try all their lives to escape them. It's the most human thing imaginable, really, trying to be other than what you are . . . ." something or other about "trying to be other than what you are", of which he was sure he was proud—at which point I quickly took Mel you trying to tell me something, buddy?" apparently catching something or other about "trying to be other than what you are", of which he was sure he was proud—at which point I quickly took Mel under his left arm and turned the direction of his mouth away from further dangers while I said, "Naw, he's not saying anything. Forget it. He's a good guy but he's shitface, and when he gets shitfaced he talks a lot. I'm going to take him home now, anyway," and the guy nodded, excusing Mel for being in a condition he found forgivable. As I eased Mel off his stool and headed out for the rains outside, Mel's legs were wobbly. Suddenly he seemed much, much drunker than before the punch, as if the blow had loosed all the conduits and now the rains flowed inside him, and he knew it. Speaking under his breath as he smiled at the onlookers he passed on his way out, he said to me, "I'm afraid I was incautious, wasn't I?" And as soon as the bar door had closed behind us and we stood under the protection of the doorway, I said to him, "You sure *were* incautious, you asshole! You just can't talk that way to people who believe they have immortal souls."

"Oh, God . . . ," he said, and then giggled, "what if we *do*? . . . I mean, what if they *are* immortal? God almighty, what punishment! Surely that can't be, can it, Muldoon? Surely the Christian rumor is pessimistic? Surely eternal rest means that we are finally rid of our Anima-tors? . . . our Anima-motors?" Then he fell into a silence so glum I knew he had to be thinking about going home to Marcia, stinking of alcohol, rained on and punched in the face, no doubt to hear some comment about men trying to prove their masculinity, etc., etc., etc.

Poor Mel. My heart began softening toward him as I pulled the spinach out of the boiling water with my stolen Hayes-Bickford's fork. Maybe, I started thinking, I'd been much too defensive, because he couldn't really one-up me when it came to women. As a matter of fact, he might even be the humblest of men when it came to that subject, because when he looked at Marcia he thought he was seeing the incarnation of his own banal soul. And I remembered that on the very same dark and rainy night, when he had spoken so incautiously in that North Cambridge bar, he said to me outside, "Tell me, am I animated by a doctor's wife, having long been animated by a doctor's mother?" before adding, "Don't answer that, you latent homosexual!"

"What do you mean?" I said, not at all aroused by his challenge and far more concerned with making a decision on whether to wait for the rains to ease up before going to the car or just brazening it out.

"I said," Mel repeated, "You latent homosexual."

"Oh," I answered, and looked up at a street lamp to see how the rain was doing. I was aware that when Mel got in an especially misogynous mood, he liked to act like his idea of a local Irishman.

100

He liked to get out and get drunk at bars and even tried once in a while to complete his Irish-like behavior by pretending to get pugnacious, so I ignored him. It was just his way of being naughty and playing hooky from life with Marcia and everything she stood for. Of course, since *he* also stood for it, I might have resented it as slumming on his part, with me as the slum. And sometimes I did. But usually, since I didn't really expect him to change his suburban wall-to-wall stripes, I figured I'd either indulge him or drop him, and I didn't want to drop him since I didn't have that many friends in the first place. On the other hand, neither did he, so we were even, which made it all much easier.

However, much as I ignored him as I checked out the sheets and sheets of rain, Mel kept mumbling away beside me, now saying, "I dunno what I mean . . . ," before immediately correcting himself with, "Yes I do! Now I remember! I'll have you know that Marcia says we're both latent homosexuals because if we weren't, I'd be home with her and not out drinking with my old pals. Therefore, you are a latent homosexual."

"I didn't know you were going out with me just for my body," I said, but he was lost thinking about Marcia's accusation, monologuing away with, "You know, she really *did* pull that one on me. On *me*! The master! Can you believe it? She threw Dr. Joyce Brothers in my face with impunity, because deep down she doesn't believe I'm a real head doctor, anyway. Not like somebody on the consulting staff of the *Ladies' Home Journal*."

"Look, Mel, I don't want to hear any more about your troubles, because if you tell me too much and then don't leave home, you're going to hate to look me in the eye later, and then you'll never invite me home for supper."

"I never do anyway."

"True," I said.

"So I'm going to tell you. . . . She's been complaining that after I put in my long days, exploiting anxieties and suffering at the office, I don't come home with the right attitude. I simply don't rush her into the bedroom. And I don't. You probably get laid more often than I do over the course of the year. Isn't it terrible? But she's right. She just doesn't turn me on, and she assures me that it's abnormal, or rather, normal in a latent homosexual, that is to say, an *immature male*."

"Well, I just don't see how talk like that doesn't act like an aphrodisiac on you, Mel."

"True enough. God knows she's trying, but I'm failing. I mean, is she not furious and red in the face most of the day, bitching about every little thing, and has she not gained God knows how many pounds and isn't it true that she no longer fixes herself up much at all? You have noticed, haven't you?"

"I thought she was taking to looking like an artsy Protestant instead of a brassy girl from the Bronx, Mel, which says a lot about your soul having completed a course of studies at the better Eastern Universities."

"Maybe so, but I guess my erotic dream life is still tied up by painted-up, brassy Bronx girls. How can I tell her? Should I be ashamed?"

"Yes, Mel. You should be ashamed. You'll never become a Unitarian head doctor this way. You will always be the kind of sordid sneak that runs off with flashy receptionists with bleached hair, and I've always known it. Unless, of course, Marcia and I can send you to a good analyst to get this stuff out of you."

"You're right. I mustn't be too hard on Marcia, merely because she wants to look like she just got up from a spinning wheel. She *is* my soul, my very soul, Muldoon, and she's ahead of me in trying to purify herself of her earthbound Bronxian dross. I'd bitch either way. She just wants to look like my soul wants to look, which is of course why I look down on her . . . I mean, I'd like to think that at least I am superior to my own soul, even if I'm not."

"And quite rightly."

"Aren't you going to argue with me? Aren't you going to defend me against myself?"

"I can't. Your arguments are crushing," I said. And Mel nodded his head and lamented, "Damn it, Muldoon. How I wish you had an ambulatory portrait of your soul so I could make some observations about you. But I guess I can't, because you probably don't have one. A soul, I mean."

"I'll tell you this much. I'll never bring a girl home for *you* to meet."

"Very wise," he said, and that day I felt superior to him, just as I was beginning to, again.

No wonder I didn't mind Mel's slumming with me, I thought. And no wonder I didn't drop him. I had the responsibility of charity toward him, that's what I had, because of my sense of his solitude.

Without me and a few other no-account friends, Mel was condemned to solitary confinement in his and her idea of adulthood, all the time, every evening, for the rest of his life. Poor Mel. Trapped in something he made himself because he thinks he should like it, and who keeps hoping he *will* like it, when he grows up.

He never had a chance, of course.

I remembered his touching interview with his mother before his marriage, this time concerning another girl not unlike Marcia. According to him, he'd confessed to his mother that he did not love that particular acceptable girl, even though they had been going together for a year, and his mother had impatiently replied: "Why not? She's a nice girl." And because he couldn't think of a good enough answer he almost married that girl. To the stern maternal challenge of: "You're not happy? Is that normal?" he could answer rationally that indeed, it was quite normal not to be happy, but in his ruby heart Mel believed that while it might be normal, just as he said, it was also not *successful* to be unhappy, and he simply could not accept being unsuccessful as normal. Not for him. Which I felt was both his downfall and the difference between us.

So, I told myself as I warmed up to calling him after all, why did I like him, considering he was such a potential fink? Because, bless his ruby heart, try as he might to become a full-time adult, a real doctor inside and out, he always failed. Marrying Marcia hadn't been enough. Going every morning to an analyst to get exorcised hadn't been enough, either, and all for one good, fundamental reason: Mel was incurably silly. He just couldn't resist it. He always ended up flirting with being flamboyantly disreputable, and he did it knowingly and compulsively. Why else would he invent stuff like Preserve Time? Why else would he talk about things like the Anima Theory in public, where he might be overheard at any moment by a member of the American Medical Association? What dark and lovable impulse was it inside Mel that made him "incautious"? And now that I thought about it, why else was he looking less and less like a confidence-inspiring medical man and more and more like Leonard Bernstein, complete with increasingly leonine hair? Because, as the years passed, Mel was trying less and less vigorously to live up to his and Marcia's idea of respectability as he surrendered himself to that other side of him.

Good old Mel, I decided, he *is* disreputable! And he needs his old friends. So, reassured that he could not successfully look down on

103

me, I dialed his number, fully prepared to brave any of Marcia's efforts to alienate me.

"Hullo-o-o . . . ," came her deep, modulated voice.

"Hi, Mrs. Doctor?" I said. "This is Muldoon. How are you?" I meant to make it impossible for her to pretend not to recognize me, but it wasn't necessary because suddenly her voice melted with gratitude, "Oh . . . Muldoon!" and I knew right away Marcia and Mel were having troubles at home. She'd never stoop to being nice to me otherwise, and she sounded as if she'd been crying as she said, "Well, now that you ask, I'm so-so, I guess."

"That's good," I said. Actually, Marcia had already said enough to make me sorry I'd called. I knew her well enough to know that she took having marital troubles as a public humiliation. A good wife has a successful marriage. And her being friendly to me, one of Mel's unwashed companions, was some sort of surrender for which I was not prepared, so, a little embarrassed and pretending not to notice her being upset, I said, "Is the beloved electro-therapist at home, by any chance?"

"No, he is not," she said somewhat bitterly. "I thought he'd be with you."

"Oh . . . well, gee . . . I'm sorry, he's not, Marcia. I guess he'll be in later, though, right? So why don't you just tell him I called about a game of squash tomorrow. O.K.?"

"Sure. I'll tell him," she said, sounding most defeated and friendly. "I'm sure he'll want to play . . . with *you*."

"Oh . . . " I was very embarrassed now, and quite ashamed of having been fresh to old Marcia, now that she was so clearly down. "Well, I guess he ought to want to play with me. He always wins."

"Is that the secret, Muldoon? I was just wondering why it was that he never wants to play with me," and then she changed her tone. "Listen . . . before I forget, I've been meaning to invite you over for dinner. We haven't seen you in an awfully long time. When can you come?"

"Most any night," I said, nearly overwhelmed, and immediately remembered this might no longer be so, now that my social life included Norma.

"Is Thursday O.K., then? That's probably a good time, and I do expect Melvin to be back by Thursday. I hope so anyway."

"Sure. That would be great. And, hey . . . I hope this isn't as messy as it sounds," I said, and I do believe I heard her sneer at me disbelievingly. She fully expected me to be glad she was having troubles with Mel. "Me too," she said, and then added, "You know, I have a great idea. Maybe I'll have several of you fellows over and make a big night out of it. I'm sure Melvin will enjoy that."

"O.K.," I said, "that sounds like fun," and after that we hung up. Though not without my having registered on her phrase "you fellows" as meaning a lot less than "you fellows who are the kind I want my Melvin to play with". But she'd sounded so down that her condescension didn't really bother me. After all, as far as she was concerned, she apparently felt she'd already bowed her head in a gesture of defeat by being friendly and inviting me to dinner, which she obviously wouldn't do if it weren't something that might keep Melvin home. Maybe, I thought, she'll try to build him a replica of the *Land of Odin* bar in Porter Square, put it down in the basement, and then wonder why he never uses it.

Actually, I was starting to feel a bit betrayed by Mel myself. Because he had not called me to go out and get drunk, as he usually did at times like these, with troubles at home. And now I could use his company.

And then came a single, hard knock sounding on my door like a furious and, at the same time, saddened note.

Suddenly, feeling myself unexplainably touched, all I could think of was a frustrated ghost pathetically banging at a seance table where no one is expected to be sitting, reduced to using the material form of the knock on wood like an expletive, cursing with anguished fury at something that must have happened to it in the world of the spirit.

In a way, this intuition was correct.

The Unseen and Mysterious Forces had positioned me where I now stood to receive a most important message about Althea. Frank Long's death at her hands was coming soon, and I was being prepared.

In order to do so, the UMFs were about to detonate such a great fireworks of Peculiar Perceptions in the black firmament of my subconscious that, afterwards, my waking life would never be the same again.

Which was why I was already trembling.

A MESSAGE FROM THE UNSEEN
AND MYSTERIOUS FORCES

Then came another bang, just as passionate as the one before, only harder, as if the frustrated ghost wanted to break right through the material door that was keeping it out of my reality so it could stand before me, right on Mr. Pansky's floor, and tell me something.

And with that second bang, as with the one before, a flurry of flash-bulb-like visions of Althea, static on the hill, standing under the trees, surrounded by the round-backed patients, went off in my head.

Now then, I firmly believe, and I think most sensible people will agree, that it usually takes us years before we finally understand what really happened to us at critical moments in our lives. In fact, the one thing that usually happens is that we miss the point altogether the first time around.

So it was with me.

Really, I had *no* idea that by opening that ordinary wooden door with its drearily shiny, dark finish, I'd be letting into our shallow, daylight reality a most important announcement from an evolving Universal Consciousness in which Man, at his highest, only dimly

107

participates.

I wasn't even sure there *was* such a thing.

However, I am now convinced (a) that I am not crazy (which I will leave for others to judge) and (b) that this is indeed what happened. I am also aware that my credibility is not helped by my talking like this.

So, without further apology, now that I believe I do understand what happened, in order to speak truthfully (even if not credibly) I have to report that when that second bang came, *two* of me jumped to attention.

One of them was the Secret Me who, literally, tried to jump out of my skin. And the other me, of course, was the one whose skin presented the obstacle. That is to say, that more familiar resident of the material world, *Muldunius Vulgaris*, Ph.D candidate and son of Bridgid Muldoon from Brighton, Mass.

Instantly, the startled *Muldunius Vulgaris* stepped up to the door, believing (though not completely now) that he was walking there by himself. Actually, he was being propelled by the Secret Me, who, until that call, had barely known it had been there, itself.

That Secret Me, of course, had been around all along, at least since I was born, but in a seedlike *homeostasis*, waiting (without knowing it) for just such a call to wake it up and make it want to burst through the containing surfaces. I estimate now that it had probably about as much an idea of itself as a jellyfish swimming in the ocean. Before the call, I mean. It had probably only known of itself negatively, that is to say, by maybe trying to escape danger whenever it felt its existence threatened. But other than that, it had just moved along dreamily with the tides, unindividuated almost to a fault, and obediently assuming that all truth lay up there with *Muldunius Vulgaris,* that public me.

However, when that banging came, all that unconsciousness came to an end, because the Secret Me not only woke up, but it went berserk with desire. It wanted that door opened more than anything in the world, *Muldunius Vulgaris* or no *Muldunius Vulgaris*, absolutely *knowing* (without ever having suspected it might know) that once that obstacle door was out of the way, it could both be out of *Muldunius Vulgaris* (himself a material obstacle) and see itself, which was one and the same thing. The Secret Me intuited that the wooden door was an exit out of the shallows of our ordinary, material perceptions, leading to the luminous, spiritual world of a true consciousness, and, at the same time, that the door was a veil to a brilliant, magic mirror that could return my Secret Me's never-before-seen image. Consequently, it was going crazy inside darkest *Muldunius Vulgaris*, making him tremble unexplainably. Unexplainably, if you don't take into account the Secret Me. Naturally, *Muldunius Vulgaris* tried to get a grip on himself as he was moved to the door, trying to ignore all these wild rumors inside himself. He even tried to believe that his hand shook because of a sudden flush of adrenaline that responded to the violence of the unexpected knocks, and certainly not because of anything so preposterous as a Secret Me's excitement at the possibility of seeing itself which, by the way, *Muldunius Vulgaris* could dimly begin to imagine by now, to his increasing discomfort, much as he tried to dismiss it as a malfunction of his rational, daylight mind.

But by the time he put his trembling hand on the doorknob, he was sure that something very serious was going on, because the excited trembling of the Secret Me and his own hand's visible trembling suddenly synchronized perfectly. Bravely, *Muldunius Vulgaris* opened the door. Breathlessly, both waited to see what lay behind it.

There, of all things, stood Mel Fish, transfigured. Hands on hips, head cocked to one side with the defiance of the gallantly wounded. His hair was very disarranged, he wasn't wearing a tie, and his skin was shiny, as if fevered, as he exuded some sort of wild, ego-exploding desperation which he resisted with a slanting smirk.

Upset as he looked, he also looked younger, and, not that I said so, better than he had in years. Painfully younger, to be sure, but it was the pain that seemed to transfigure him, suggesting a most un-Mel-like passionate instability, an explosiveness, as if his soul were suddenly composed of gasoline fumes.

And transfigured Mel, who hadn't smoked for years, produced a nearly empty cigarette pack, lit one defiantly, and said with his slanting smirk, "Can I come in?"

I was so surprised, I stood absolutely still. The sight of Mel had let down both the Secret and the materialist Me as our moods synchronized again. After all, it was Mel with a difference, but it was still just old Mel Fish that had been knocking on my door. So, the Secret Me, watching him puzzled with its newly opened eyes and listening with its barely budding ears, could not possibly understand what was so interesting about this, or how in the world Mel Fish could be its own image returned from the world of the Spirit. And even *Muldunius Vulgaris*, who until just now had been secretly ready for a significant message from the as yet officially unacknowledged UMFs, wondered what kind of a call this could be. At best, a wrong number. And so, disappointedly, the Secret Me began sinking back down into its undividuated, embryonic state, leaving *Muldunius Vulgaris* to himself again.

Mel, who'd been standing in the doorway waiting all this time, announced, "I'm coming in anyway," and he swaggered past me in his new wounded adolescent's way.

"Oh, yeh . . . ," I said, realigning my bearings. "Come in. Come in," and I shut the door behind him, innocently thinking that whatever had been going on was over, and quite unaware that the important announcement from the Unseen and Mysterious Forces had at last penetrated into my world of ordinary perceptions aboard Mel.

Now, all that seemed unusual was Mel's mood. It struck me that to anybody who cared to look at him on his way over to my place, he must have looked youthful and explosive, without giving a damn about it, which was most uncharacteristic of him. In fact, this challenge to the world was in itself puzzling, because at least since back in Junior High School, that is to say, even during his fat puberty, Mel's public style had always reeked of middle-aged stability, being already totally dedicated to convincing the world to take him seriously as a doctor. It had been this, more than anything else, that had gotten him such posts as Chalk Monitor and class valedictorian. And even when he'd fooled around in private, his favorite clowning postures had always been caricatures of men-in-charge. But, at that moment, as he spun to face me and dropped himself into my easy chair in one exhaling motion, it was as if he had just thrown away, in one petulant, frustrated fit, his whole life's collection of future Big Daddy, trust-me-with-the-world-order outfits, revealing an altogether unsuspected adolescent, satanic kind of rebel who now, in his disaffection, wouldn't mind bringing down the whole disappointing world. It was as if, for some reason or other, those earlier disguises had been thrown away because they'd turned out to be of no avail, after all, to God knows what he'd been after all his life. And as he looked up at me from my easy chair, rejecting whatever pity I might offer him, he conveyed to me all the romantic and disorderly unhappiness of a twenty-year-old boy who has just been terminally dismissed by the love of his life.

110

Instinctively, I knew his condition had nothing to do with Marcia. With a half grin on my face, I was just about to say something to make him feel better, when once again, out of the muddy bed of my subconscious, came floating—slowly and singly this time—the bright image of that once nameless girl I'd seen from his window. And again, with its fiercely harsh colors and its hieratic two-dimensionality, it presented itself like a primitive religious painting done on his office window-pane.

But it didn't pop and vanish this time. (I'd known it wouldn't, just from the slow way it rose.) This time it stayed, and static as ever, it grew brighter and brighter in my mind, becoming so commanding it suddenly eclipsed Mel and my easy chair altogether.

Muldunius Vulgaris remained in the world of ordinary perceptions, up there with Mel, moving mechanically, smiling as if he had a soul, as if he weren't an automaton. But he was an empty husk, because now the Secret Me was really where I was.

Now I understand what was happening a little better.

The Light was signalling again. And that returning vision of Althea on the hill was the beginning of the message from the UMFs. It was absolutely necessary that someone perceive that Light, because she'd be killing and butchering Frank Long very soon.

And because of all the barriers of the rationally perceived, material world (including that structure of materialist prejudices, *Muldunius Vulgaris*), the UMFs had chosen to send the suddenly adolescent Mel to the Secret Me so as to project the Light upon him. Because the Light needed something through which to manifest itself, just as ghosts need material things to knock on, to be heard among us.

And now I understand, too, why they chose to do so on the very night—no less—of the day I'd had my first carnal encounter with Norma, a lady who up till then had been my feminine ideal as well as her own. It is important to notice that this is *not* a very high ideal.

At that time (1953), she didn't know any better, of course, and neither did I. Which was *precisely* the point on which the UMFs wanted to enlighten me, and eventually Norma and the rest of us.

In other words, *Norma Vulgaris* of 1953 was indeed the portrait of the soul of *M.V.* of the same period. But souls and skins have a lot in common, and now the UMFs wanted Me to evolve out of that historical Self of 1953, which remained behind with Mel, moving, talking, reacting precisely like the series of social tropisms he'd become, so as to prepare for the life ahead of us.

This is why the UMFs were commanding that Secret and still embryonic Me to crawl out of that moment in history that looked like a man (no one, blinded by ordinary perceptions, would notice) and were magnetically forcing it to sail up closer to Althea's luminous image. It was like an escape window they were offering, so they could be perceived expressing themselves as they preferred to do: in the language of the soul, in the concrete images of dreams. So that one day in the future, wakefulness could be understood.

Althea waited for me far away, encased and embryonic too, as if trapped in Mel's rectangular window, veiled by her stubborn hair and her purple-hued clothing beneath the wind-denuded Trees. And even before I knew it, my Secret Me, commanded, had detached himself and was flying toward her, and became the only Me.

And sailing bodilessly, rising effortlessly, the Secret and Only Me suddenly knew things I never realized I knew. Such things as: that distant window (which I'm passing through now) only seems (seemed) rectangular because it's Mel's window. Mel's medical window.

And as soon as I'd passed through its logical, rectangular frame, I found myself infinitely beyond it and floating prenatally among cloudlike banks and streams of rumors, like

> it must have been a green
> we'll never see again . . .

which hung above the world I was entering, spiced with the pungent scent of the fallen apples I could see below. Some of the rumors kept on saying themselves as repetitively and absently as children's songs

> it must have been a green
> we'll never see again
> swimming those apple-heavy boughs
> no matter how many swords

112

we change into ploughs

while others appeared and disappeared in helplessly alarmed
snatches, saying, almost shouting, things like

and the eyes of both were opened!
and they knew that they were naked!

And as I floated among the shifting rumors, quite cheerful about
my bodiless freedom as if, somehow, I were getting away with
something, I began realizing I already had the sense of smell as well
as of sight and sound, prenatal as I might be. And I could see below
me, too, where there had recently been a savage storm that had left
the world for dead, with the Trees tipped and nearly uprooted.
Fierce dark rains had so riddled the hill that the earth looked soft
and exhausted. And the memory of the storm's violence was still very
much in the air, in the fierce freshness, just as sharp as the pungent
smell of apples, wordless, but as thick and present as the rumors.

I could sense the storm was still nearby, waiting to come again,
swollen and dark inside the sagging charcoal sky. And now I could
sense, too, that the next time it came, it would flood everything with
a dark and chilly sleep, which, suddenly, I didn't know if I feared or
not, because it had a delicious promise of freedom I couldn't understand and for which I felt the trace of an unaccountable shame.

Every now and then the panic in some alarmed rumors shoved me
some and made me briefly change directions, but mostly I continued
hovering in the same place, feeling myself exempt from whatever
had happened before me, and I began concentrating on watching
Althea below me. She looked quite victorious, with the breeze
keeping her obstinate hair across her face, while in contrast, the
Trees looked whipped, bowed, tilting their gray, immemorial shapes.

And I began noticing: their shapes seemed to respond to some very
tired, ancient breathing. And it struck me that the Trees weren't
only Trees. They might change, at any moment, into something like
Temple Elephants, maybe with their next breath.

Suddenly, I was startled by a clear-voiced, angry-sounding

. . . who told thee
that thou was naked?

and an instant later, the same voice demanded

113

what is it that thou
hast done?

But live as it sounded, I had the sense that maybe the voice was just a
floating rumor, too. Nothing new, but a painful memory recalled by
the exhaling Trees, and I recognized the voice when it said

behold!
the man is become as one of us now . . .

as the memory of the Lord God. Which curiously didn't frighten me
at all, as, floating peacefully, I thought: to whom might the Lord
God be speaking? He said "us". Who's "us"? I'd never noticed "us"
in Genesis before. Could there be other Lords, just out of sight?
There must be, I was thinking, when I suddenly went into a spin as
the swelling Trees breathed near bursting, and my bodiless, prenatal
spinning came to a sudden stop as I heard my naked body smacking
nastily against the muddy ground. It hurt, and I didn't feel exempt
anymore.

No sooner had I heard myself thwacking against the mud, I also
heard myself braying away with an uncontainable, red-faced rage,
and found myself, too, trembling on the mud, down on all fours.
Suddenly I was mad as hell, not sure at what, exactly, but also like a
witness to my own anger, outside of it as I looked around while rant-
ing away. And finding I was not alone. To my surprise, I was just
one of many. All around me, there were lots and lots of others, down
on all fours, howling furiously, red-faced and naked just like me,
sore-bottomed and turning so red-cheeked in their total rage that
they looked like nothing but furious, wailing red faces, concentrating all of themselves into their outrage like colicky babies.

And there, right in the middle of that down-on-all-fours, naked
mob, was Althea, the object of our rage. Standing upright. Fully
dressed and silent. Contained to the point that it very much seemed
arrogance, with her face, as always, covered over by her heavy hair.

And she wasn't alone.

Next to her, also upright, unlike the rest of us, and holding her
limp left arm with his right, was a balding, bearded man.

I would say he was naked too, like us, except that he really wasn't,
because his baldness, his beard, and a book he held authoritatively
under his left arm all managed to dress him and give him rank.

114

He looked faintly familiar, but I couldn't identify him, because, all of a sudden as we trembled in the mud and bleated, madder and madder, I realized what we really wanted to do was to tighten the ring around her, mob her, pull her down and rip her apart, clothes, flesh, hair and all.

But the bearded, bald man was keeping us back. By his presence. He and he alone was protecting her.

And his tactics were working. At least for now. Because, held back, we started howling and trembling all the more, the holding back compounding our fury.

But he was so successful that our red-faced noise soon began decreasing, turning into a rather low and nasty grumbling, which was letting me hear him say, "Never forget! When we first opened up our eyes in this abandoned garden, we were just helpless sucklings! Nothing more, I can assure you, than bad smelling, feeble worms without a shell! Impotent! Vulnerable! And giftless!"

Now it struck me that there was something downright superior and offensively didactic about him, even in the way he stood in front of us, holding Althea's left arm with his right.

And then I recognized him: Mel! The Father of Preserve Time!

But the grumbling went on, even if the mob was momentarily checked. If Mel saw me, he chose not to distinguish between me and the rest of the furious mob, which was correct, but which I resented. I resented it terribly.

And then, just as it came to me I'd never seen Mel with a beard before, I noticed that the book he held so authoritatively under his arm had a bearded, bald man on the cover. And bearded Mel was also conveying the impression he too was bald. Just like the man on the book's cover. He did it with something like a pink cap or a prosthetic bald patch on the crown of his head. It was quite official looking at that, the way he wore it. And then I realized he was impersonating the man on the book's cover, for our benefit. And terrified for him, I thought: Jesus, if they ever catch on, they're going to kill him, too. For sure!

But Mel, to my admiration now, showed no trace of anxiety whatsoever.

I could tell (we all could) the book with the bearded man on the cover was a Book of Law, when suddenly I was struck by something else: tableted, bearded Mel was holding Althea's Heart arm! *That's* what her left arm was, and his right one was his Law arm!

Suddenly I was understanding the true meaning of Right and Left as I never had before! I was amazed at its clarity and wondered how I had ever missed such an obvious thing before, because it was clearly obvious to everyone there. It was absolutely common knowledge, and Mel was playing on it to make his point just by the ritualistic way he stood. He was even trying to seem all Right side.

I squinted hard at the Law book he held under his Heart arm, trying to read the large red print on the white cover, seeing something like *Civ* . . . and *Its Dis* . . . when I noticed a heretofore almost invisible stream of electricity coming out of the book and running directly across his chest, all the way to his Law arm, with which he held Althea. The electric stream across his chest, in fact, seemed to be what raised him up on his legs so homosapiently erect as he declared, "I'm telling you! Civilization is our first and most potent tool! And it was built upon the renunciation of our personal instincts, especially our violent ones! And we must sacrifice them again, or perish! So, hold your water!"

Until that moment, Mel had seemed in control. But now I wasn't so sure.

Our constant trembling and grumbling was getting thick around me. Making our pack animal-warm. Momentarily letting us forget the cold, wet mud, making us feel increasingly warmer. And as we started edging in, I knew that very soon we would bunch up around Mel and Althea and explode in a hot, homicidal froth, like a pack of wild dogs. And that I was going to be washed right along with it, no different from anybody else.

But I didn't care. It surprised me. But I still didn't care because as we edged in, I wanted to see Althea's face, and the closer we moved in, the more excited I found myself becoming. We were all very excited now, the whole pack of us, almost gay in a malicious, righteous anticipation of ripping her apart and maybe him, too. Of seeing her face. And suddenly, from behind, I felt myself shoved, and I shoved forward hard when Mel, ever alert, suddenly yelled: "BEWARE OF LARGE SHADOWS!!" with sensational effect.

He stopped us in our tracks. Suddenly, I felt the cold and fear rushing through the pack, disorganizing us. We looked up, and then started scattering yards away from one another, where we stopped, trembling, looking around terrified for the Large Shadows. The grumbling that had massed so dangerously moments ago fractionalized into silence, and instead of the blood-hot group sense, now we were very aware of the distances between one another. And we felt the awesome minimizing caress of a chill around our hairless, puny bodies down on the wet mud.

Isolated now, crouching down as much as we could (as if getting lower would give more protection), we trembled harder and harder, like high-strung rodents. Some of us kept our heads up, very still, watching round-eyed for predators.

We waited, any moment now, for the cold sudden flood of a Large Shadow to swoop down upon us, for the quick scuffling sounds made by the unlucky ones. When that came, that would be our best chance to bolt for safety.

In the terror-filled lull, as we trembled and waited, the silence opened up over our heads. And then, in the silence, the rumors became noticeable again.

> And they heard the voice
> of the Lord God walking
> in the garden
> in the cool of the day

and I understood now, the rumors too were about Large Shadows preying upon us as I heard

> . . . What is it that thou
> hast done?

And the more we waited, the harder and harder got the trembling, making some eyes glassy with resignation.

The tension was too horrible to endure in isolation. We knew our best chance was to be scattered, but bad sense prevailed because, even though we knew better (That's what the Large Shadows want! I thought, to catch more of us at one time!), we started edging together again, with little, shamed, dirty smiles on our faces, as we looked for a shelter in numbers that we knew wasn't there.

And then, timidly at first, the murmuring started up again, asking about Large Shadows. Then it began flushing hot through our ranks like a familiar fever, filling the distances between us, warming our bodies and beginning to make us a cohesive group again. We were whispering now, giddily, all of us, about the Large Shadows, when, as we crowded closer and closer together, I noticed for the first time

117

how very badly we smelled. It was rank. A combination of sweat, and urine and fear, and the warm air where we huddled smelled much like the bottom of a pen.

I badly wanted to stand up, but I didn't dare, superstitiously still believing that keeping low in the crowd protected me. Resentfully, I glanced at Althea (she had never moved), assuming she didn't have our smell, which made her alien. As for Mel (he hadn't moved either), that social climber, I suspected he had washed it off.

Now I wondered if maybe I was the only one, if nobody else was bothered by the stench. Maybe it had been there all the time, right along with the rumors hanging in the air we breathed, constantly present like a shameful memory, and which now were like part of our stench. Like our giddy, fearful whispering seemed to be.

But I wasn't the only one bothered. As I made contact with other apologetic eyes (apologizing for wanting to huddle together even though we all knew better, and for stinking), I realized everybody was just as uncomfortable with the stench as I was.

Like a prelude to fatality, the whispering died down now. There was silence again.

We held still, with nothing to do but wait. Speculation was all done, as we were all both thinking and trying not to think about the Large Shadows.

In the new hush, we stank even harder of all our old fears, and the stench identified us, making a herd smell. We were almost grateful.

But more time passed, and still no Large Shadows.

So now some of us, the braver ones who dared to look, started rearing up on their hindquarters here and there, with heads twitching over shoulders like anxious squirrels, checking the ground, then the immediate horizon, and even giving a quick peek up to the threatening sky before lowering down again. Pretty soon many of the rest of us were doing it too. In fact, we were all doing it, as the tone of the silence changed, became splattered here and there with bits of inquisitive chatter, until finally the inquiring silence began to direct itself at bearded Mel.

It was now being recalled that it was *he* who had alarmed us in the first place, just as we were about to move in on Althea.

Murmuring of the nastier sort started, getting darker and less timid by the moment.

All eyes sharpened on Mel's suspect figure now (as I realized, for the very first time, that his beard was fake, like his bald patch, and I wondered if everybody else knew it too. Because if they did, I was sure it would be further held against him.).

Mel, of course, was not unaware we were all looking at him, so he said, "I bet you are all wondering where the Large Shadows are, aren't you . . . ," and he smiled and shook his head with great good cheer at us. "Well, my friends, I was beginning to think you'd *never* ask!" and he laughed like a high school teacher who enjoys presenting little puzzles to his class. "So-o-o . . . in my capacity as spokesman for the Right side, that is to say, the Civilized side, I'll tell you!" Whereupon he beamed, "That was *no* false alarm, people! Why, I was warning you about the one Large Shadow which lurks nearby all the time, just waiting to devour us all . . . and I bet you *still* don't know what I'm talking about, do you?" And again he shook his head, a bit more seriously, at our obtuseness. I have to admit, much as he might irritate me, watching him there acting as if he had nothing to fear in the world, I became nearly lost in admiration for his *sang-froid*, when he suddenly exclaimed, startling me and everybody else, "TYRANNY!!! That's what I'm talking about! I'm talking about the Large Shadow of Tyranny, which has a wing span as big as all of us put together!"

This was met with signs of growing puzzlement in the crowd, as well as a new freshness in the nasty rumblings quite clearly directed at him.

Nevertheless Mel, ignoring these negative notes, smiled. "You see," he said, "before man was man, he was *forever* following his violent, predatory instincts and plundering those of his own wretched kind who were even more impotent than himself. And believe me, he did it by Brute Force! Tyranny, that's what it was. The most terrifying Large Shadow of them all, projected on our unattractive herd by the cruelest predator of them all . . . by He-Who-Has-The-Chance! But it was Civilization, my friends, our Champion, that stopped that giant winged Tyranny!" and he paused with his face set in a stern (toward tyrants) but compassionate (toward us) expression. "And Tyranny is *not* Civilization, no matter what anybody says!"

And every time Mel mentioned tyranny, my eye was caught by the assenting nod from a strangely familiar, rather bulldoglike, squat older female across the way, directly in back of me. She was just as naked as the rest of us, and not in Mel's class, of course, but more authoritative than the common lot, somehow, though part of it. And she kept right on nodding at me in a most domineering way, with an

119

odd familiarity lighting up her little blue eyes which seemed hard as dice and as square as the rest of her. I could not place her. But whoever she was, she was obviously telling me that whatever Mel was saying now about Tyrants was something she'd been trying to drum into my head for years, with less fancy words.

Mel had no idea he was being backed by her, which was very much to his advantage, as he went on with, "The problem was Impotence! *Immer Impotenz!* And Civilization changed that, people, by changing us from the pathetic, wretched worms of the past into MEN! Powerful, at last! You see, it was the power of Civilization, generated by the collective renunciation of our individual instincts, that we used to force those more powerful worms . . . those Tyrants, to submit to the Collective Will! We had individual power condemned as Brute Force! We invented . . . Justice!!" And to my relief, this declaration was met with a sudden salvo of yips of approval from the older creatures like the square old female (with surprisingly small breasts) who yipped right along with the rest. However, she was not so carried away with enthusiasm that she took her eye off me, still demanding I fall in and yip my Amen.

"Indeed!" Mel cried out almost ecstatically. *"That's* how the power of the brutal . . . that is to say, the power of the Bigger . . . was replaced by the power of the Community! Through Justice! We invented Law, and deemed it Morality! We took the Right arm and called it . . . the Left arm! We turned the blood-red Heart, that wildest of beasts, into *our* beast of burden!!"

And at that resounding declaration, all the older creatures reared up on their haunches almost as one and enthusiastically sent up a bursting and clattering cannonade of hallelujahs by the rapid-fire slapping of their bodies with their weak but insistent arms. It went off overhead like invisible fireworks celebrating a tiny national holiday.

Mel, standing still beneath this rain of public approval, humbly smiled both his personal gratitude and his congratulations to the elders for their show of responsibility, to which they responded anew by making the spirited and slightly fragile cannonade pop and crackle above us with new energies, like a little summer shower kicking up harder just when it seemed to have eased off.

Clearly, the elders meant this display not only as support for Mel's sentiments, but as an example to the young fry as well, and now they took to raising their eyes Biblically up to the sagging gray sky, as if the will of the Lords were expressing itself through their Amen. In fact, they were even managing to act as if their own noises were actually descending magically from the sky, despite the fact that they were making them in the first place.

And now Mel patiently waited for a pause, again speaking through the ritual language of his body stance by holding Althea's limp Heart arm in a new way: as if she were the banner of Civilization, and he, the standard bearer. And when the pause finally came, he smiled and said quietly, "Thank you. Thank you. And now, let's all bow our heads and contemplate that most miraculous notion of all: Justice." And having so spoken, he bowed his own head prayerfully, soon followed by everyone else as all heads went down in quick sequence. Only Althea's remained erect and still as the wind rustled her hair very gently. Contrasted with the rest of us, she looked more arrogant the ever, and I wished she didn't, sure that was how all the trouble had started in the first place.

My head went down too, but instead of the word Justice, all I could think of was Althea's obstinacy and her opaqueness, and my mind began to flood with a chilly darkness, as if she and this darkness were one and the same. It made me nervous, so I peered up to see what was happening.

Something was. The hauntingly familiar older female, four-legged as the rest of us until now—had ceased to conform. She was, to my distress, waddling forward seallike to the inner forefront of the ring and heads everywhere began lifting to look at her. Then, giving up her seallike posture as she came to a stop, she reared back penguinlike and mutely started gyrating her short arms while bobbing her head in a decidedly nasty way.

In no time at all, a revolution was in progress. All the elders were imitating her, silently, following her rhythms, giving them strength, generating some sort of moral electricity. I looked at the startled Mel, and then back at the elders. Something had gone very wrong. I knew it all had to do with the word Justice, on which Mel wanted everyone to meditate. But this militant display of piety was not what Mel had wanted, at all. The situation was getting out of control again.

Now that the older female was upright and just a few feet from Mel, I'd expected her to be nearly as tall as he was, or at least taller than she'd been squatting down. But to my surprise, she wasn't. She seemed to have just one basic height, squatting, sitting or standing, and her familiarity continued to haunt me as she ground on with her silent arm-gyrating and head-bobbing, leading the elders. The apparently hundreds of elders. And then she started shooting commanding glances at me again, ordering me to fall in with her.

I didn't move. She didn't like it. Her glance at me got angrier. She was going to overpower me when she got me alone. I knew it, just as I knew somehow she'd get me alone, for sure, and I figured she must have done it before, in dreams I'd forgotten.

The silent demonstration was getting fiercer and fiercer. The ring closed up a bit, and despite the growing frenzy, like an unpleasant miracle, none of the gyrating arms knocked against one another as the crowd synchronized. At the moment, nobody seemed to have the power of human speech except for Mel, as once more the elders took to looking Biblically up at the sky, and yips started sparking out of the ring here and there, and began multiplying like cries of gulls before a storm, and the righteous eyes that shot up at the sagging sky alternated with shooting at Althea.

In fact, to my amazement, I was also up three-quarters, gyrating my arms and bobbing my head.

Our leader, the older female, hadn't seemed to have the gift of speech any more than the rest of us, but suddenly she yelled out clear as a bell: "Let's get her! Let's teach that fancy bitch her place!" and a ripping flurry of new yips and righteous screeches shot up in approval as my heart froze. Not only because I was afraid for Althea. But because I had identified our Madame DeFarge: Bridgid Muldoon, my own mother!

Of course she knew about injustice and tyrants, and Protestant Tyrants especially! In the Old Country, under the heel of the British Black and Tan, for God's sake, during the Irish Rebellion! She'd told me about it many times, as part of the Old Terrors, before coming to America. That's what she thought Mel meant by Civilization!

Bearded Mel's soft brown eyes restlessly appraised the deteriorating situation. He licked his lips. Then, clenching the book with the bearded man on the cover tightly to his chest, he yelled: "No! Stop! In the name of Civilization!" And to my surprise arms slowly decreased their gyrations, heads became progressively stiller. But it obviously wasn't going to be for long. At any moment now, we would be falling back into the magnetic pull. And when we moved again, next time, he was going to get ripped up for sure, right along with Althea.

"Look here," Mel said quickly. "Civilization was built on the renunciation of instincts, as I told you, and that's the *rule*! We just cannot have the community act like a violent individual any more than we can let anyone else do it! If we let the community act like a Large Shadow, I promise you we'll all be miserable again!"

The conditionally stilled Bridgid Muldoon now sat back on her haunches. A knowing smirk slanted across her face, and I knew what she was thinking as if she were thinking it right in my own head: This bastard's trying to deprive the people of justice, that's what's going on. And it's one of those priests, or doctors, or fancy-ass professors that's doing it, as usual. The Liberal bastards, again. Wouldn't you know it, trying to climb up in the world on our backs, betraying us to the rich with a lot of words.

"Please understand," Mel said, trying to look like the principled sort we should have in charge. "As Father of Preserve Time, I am a *committed* Liberal!" And at the word Liberal, which he obviously felt would be to his advantage, my mother looked over at me and arched an eyebrow.

(Oh, God, I thought, remembering what my mother had told me before going to Harvard. "Look out for those Liberals," she said. "They pretend to side with the people, but they always think they're better than we are. They're all social climbers, every one of them, just trying to get in good with the Big Boys, so watch it, because they'll sell your ass out every time. Every time!"

"Maybe I shouldn't go to Harvard, mother."

"Don't be stupid. You go there and get in with the people that can do you some good, Jerry. That's the only way you'll get anywhere.")

Mel noticed my mother's knowing glance, and he licked his lips nervously again. He'd always been afraid of her, ever since the first day I brought him home for lunch from Junior High School.

"By the way . . . ," she said to him, right out, getting cheeky now, "Why are you standing up, anyway?"

"Oh . . . that!" said Mel forcing a chuckle, looking down as if surprised at his own feet. "It's just a habit, Mrs. Muldoon," and she looked over at me again, making me smile in weak apology for my friend.

Poor Mel, smiling deferentially at my mother, no longer seemed to know how to hold himself upright, for fear of incurring further censure. So, doing his best by hooking one leg around the other one so that he remained standing like a flamingo, he said, "Well . . . I'm not really trying to scare you about Large Shadows now . . . so let's forget that part, O.K.? Let's concentrate on what there is in it for us if we . . . ," whereupon he was interrupted by a male a few feet away from me, who said, "What's in it for you?"

But my mother cut him off, "Let him talk! We'll see about him later."

"Thank you, Mrs. Muldoon," Mel said. There was no doubt at all now that his life was on trial, too, so instead of holding himself formally as he had up to now, with his authoritative beard and book, he started trying to get his stance to be as informal as possible, within his priestly possibilities, and he smiled pleadingly, "Look, everybody . . . I'm talking about *Happiness*! Do you know what I mean, everybody? Happiness?"

And Mel's male tormentor, who'd just interrupted, said in a very weary and unimpressed tone, "Oh . . . Jesus . . . ." Instantly I guessed him to be from my old neighborhood. We always said "Jesus" like that when we didn't believe something.

"Come on now!" Mel protested. "I mean it realistically. I mean avoiding as much unhappiness as we can, too . . . because what *is* Happiness?" and in his new informality he winked at a couple of younger males next to him. "We all know, don't we? *We* don't need this book I'm holding to tell us that the prototype of the experience of Happiness is the sexual experience, do we? You sure don't have to be a Professor to know *that*, right?" and he winked again at the male young fry, who exchanged smirking glances with each other until they realized Bridgid Muldoon was glaring at them. "But that's just the prototype, and what *that* all comes down to, as all the older folks here know, is the old meat and potatoes issue of satisfying a need you're born with, in relative safety . . . safety from unhappiness! Get it? Come on now, everybody . . . isn't the satisfaction of needs in safety the *real* definition of freedom . . . huh . . . ? said Mel, persisting in trying to sound like his idea of a "regular fella" while defending himself pedantically. "Isn't freedom, when you come right down to it, freedom from the sources of our unhappiness . . . huh, gang? I'm talking about the old Pursuit of Happiness, people!" he pleadingly protested. "I'm talking about the *real* purpose of life now. Isn't that what we're really after, each one of us, just to eat our fair share of the pie of life . . . when all is said and done?" And with his head down now, as if to be patted, and his large

124

brown eyes up, he turned to smile toothily at my mother in an intimate and personal appeal, looking for all the world as if he had, at that very moment, a piece of that very pie in his mouth. It was the kind of smile that unthreateningly begged for understanding because, really, we all did that kind of thing in private, too. The smile was also the kind we called in Brighton, Mass., a "shit-eater". "Mrs. Muldoon . . . ?" he said, meekly, tentatively, "Happiness . . . ?"

She didn't buy it. Her eyes narrowed.

Poor Mel never did realize my mother never believed in such a thing as Happiness in the first place. Not the way he did. As a matter of fact, she firmly believed that the prototype of the experience of Happiness was really revenge—not sex—and she'd pass up many another fleeting pleasure to "get even", as she called it, because no other satisfaction could really compare with that one. Not in this world.

And as she continued to stare at him, a most ominous silence followed. I closed my eyes only to hear Mel chirp almost hysterically, "Look everybody! Can you see what I've got on my head?"

The silence continued bearing down, and with my eyes closed, I heard a nasty male voice say in slow, stalking tones, "No . . . we can't see . . . what you've got on your head . . . because you're standing *up* . . . you jerk!"

Nasty, sadistic laughter followed that, the kind of distant thunder that licks its muffled chops in anticipation. I cringed as much as I could and closed my eyes even tighter, trying to wish myself right out of the place. But it was not to be, because I heard Mel say, "Hey! You're right! I *am* standing up, aren't I . . . so, for the sake of our magic show . . . if you'll give me another second here . . . ," and at hearing "magic show", my eyes popped open, and there was Mel, obviously about to play his very last card.

He'd finally let go of Althea's rag of a Heart arm, which dropped indifferently to her side. I guessed he knew by now he couldn't really give her much protection anymore so, smiling all around, he proceeded to reach up on the crown of his head, pull out a pin, and pull off the bald patch he had up there, which he then held up before us, as he announced: "All right, people! Concentrate on this symbol of the Right side and get ready for the magic show!" The object he held before us turned out to be that pink, circular sort of cap which was not unlike a yarmulke. "Hey!" somebody shouted, "I know what that thing is! It's a foreskin!" And there was more nasty rumbling laughter, but Mel quickly countered with, "Correct! A foreskin, in spirit if not in fact! Oh, boy, I can tell this is going to be a *GREAT* magic show! A circumsised foreskin, you see, is just a little piece of yourself you sacrifice to the Law. You might even think of it as a token castration . . . but that would be short-sighted, because it's what makes us Men, and far more powerful than any animal . . . as you'll see if you stick with me," he said, and winking, put the cap back on his head. "And now, people, when I put my head down like this, what does it look like?"

"It looks like . . . a priest's bald spot!"

"Terrific!!" Mel said, as if he couldn't have been more pleased. "Oh, boy, are *we* going to have fun in a minute!" and he smiled over at my mother, feeling on surer ground now that priests were being talked about. Unfortunately, he didn't know she didn't like priests much, either. She regarded them as smooth talking, spoiled parasites that don't like heavy lifting, who go around consuming the best food and drink from the best tables, always through the sweat of the poor. In fact, she believed this so firmly she had once wanted me to become one of them.

("It's a good life, Jerry. Believe me. Very little exertion there."

"Yes, but . . . I wouldn't be able to get married, mother."

"Don't think you'll be missing all that much, Jerry.")

Therefore, from her squatting position, she continued to squint unimpressed, although starting to blink herself, while Mel remained innocent of her true attitude, saying, "You see, people, this little cap is both a sign of my humility and what makes me a *real* man," and he winked again. He was winking an awful lot now, and I was blinking whenever he did, getting a moment of darkness between every image of Mel and his cap. In fact, everybody was blinking now, just like my mother and me, and faster and faster. And I realized, helplessly, he was controlling us all with his blinks, turning the world into a flickering movie while we provided the light energy for his magic show.

Suddenly, his motions jumping wildly between dark pauses, I saw him grab his pink cap from his head and he yelled, "So, out of the renunciation of our instincts: HERE WE GO!" and he flung his cap high in the air.

It floated up luminous, uninterruptable, through both the darkness and the light.

Then, it stopped, and I heard Mel's baritone voice—impersonating the gods—announce

> behold, the man is become
> as one of us now!

Then, quickly, his chirpy tenor came back with

> "Look, everybody! Look!
> That symbol of our humility
> is the true Masculine Spirit!"

The hovering pink cap began to stretch up, constantly swelling, becoming electrically animate, as unpredictable as a snake about to jump, and, as it reached outward, it began to take the shape of something between a naked man and an armored, pinkish monster. And it continued to grow, beginning to turn on itself admiringly, like a priapic sunflower, and as it grew and swelled, brightening each time, the radiating pink light showed the paling hill and the Trees waning each time and even the people were minimized by its growth, as if their life, too, were being sucked up by the growing monster.

"Look at him!" I heard Mel say. "The new Lord in the garden, created out of our little sacrifices, out of our humility! The true Masculine Spirit! Our Right side incarnate, and made Power! And everything becomes his food. Isn't it great? You know, people, all the animal strains become his pets, and even the inanimate mineral world translates itself into energies for his Spirit and Form! *All* through the miracle of Negative Entropy!"

And the new Lord, autonomous and huge, stood in our midst for another moment, always growing and brightening and admiring himself, when suddenly he pricked up his auditory organ, and then took a leap into the darkness to some place an infinite distance away. He moved at an incredible, joyously increasing speed until he disappeared from our darkness, and we, momentarily relieved, all fell silent. Then, in a pleased and intimate tone, Mel said, "The Big Fella must have heard something on another planet." We remained silent.

A few moments later, from an infinite distance in the endless blackness, a tiny vibrant pink dot soared toward us until suddenly, fully formed, the new Lord was standing among us again, in our center, bigger and brighter than ever, radiantly exuding more of his electric narcissism as he floridly continued to evolve out of himself—when suddenly he stopped and fixed his attention on me. Oh, God! I thought, why me? and shut my eyes so as not to see, but it was useless. I could see him no matter what, and cursing Mel and his magic show I saw that the new Lord's crystal eyes were enormous lenses, now filled with my own pathetic little naked image trembling and down on all fours, ready for the picking. The new Lord smiled, unmistakably, and I never felt so vulnerable or so impotent in all my life. I froze, waiting, while Mel from somewhere out of sight said lovingly, "Isn't he *magnificent*! He's our exact opposite, you know. Nothing impotent about him, and that's because he didn't grow out of any rib from our Heart side, but out of our very own invented Right side . . . Needless to say, people, *He* doesn't *smell*!" and he laughed. "We should all try to live in imitation of our new Lord . . . within our possibilities." And Mel sounded very amused.

I, however, could not be, as I kept watching my smallness in his lenses, feeling all too much like his exact opposite while my heart pounded near explosion in my fragile rib cage. "Mel . . . ," I said, suddenly able to speak at last, "what's he going to do with me?"

"Who . . . ?" said Mel, "The Big Fella?" and he chuckled, torturing me as if the new Lord's powers were his own. "Gee, I couldn't tell you off hand, but he'll do *something* with you! I mean, everything, but *Everything* is put to use by the Big Fella, eventually. That's his secret of success, you know. Busy, busy, busy! Nothing gets rest with him around. No sir! Not even the blood of the ancient dinosaurs or whatever else might be trying to hide dead under the ground in the form of oil! Everybody and Everything works for the true Masculine Spirit, by golly! That's real virtue, by the way . . . the root of which," he added in an I-told-you-so tone, "is in the Latin word *virtus*, meaning manhood . . . and not ape," and he chuckled with an obscenely pedantic self-satisfaction.

The new Lord kept me in his geometrically adjusting lenses for another moment, and then he pivoted one hundred and eighty degrees, making my image disappear with his lenses as he illuminated Althea, who suddenly profiled ahead in his throbbing, ultraviolet light. It was her turn and I thrilled with relief as if an avalanche had just missed me, and I trembled with giddiness.

But then, as I looked, in a great silent yawn—millions of years wide—the back of the new Lord's head revealed itself open to my human eyes, and my giddy relief changed to vertigo from the revelation. At first, it was like a crosscut of Widener Library, but instantly its mirror walls showed the new Lord's expanding interior as stacks and stacks and more stacks of books spreading uncontainably in every dimension, always deepening. And everywhere, from book to book, in millions of places, electric sparks and streaks were jumping like intermittent, brilliantly exploding serpents creating more books and more electricity, and revealing more expanding, ever deepening blackness to be filled by the self-generating galaxies of starlike sparks and cometlike streaks which went on and on, always exploding silently in the blackest, deeper and always deepening distances. And as the electric streaks and galaxies swirled and multiplied, they left behind in their wakes batteries and batteries of other serpentine galaxies made up of mute, dark books like streams of eggs ready to explode, to translate memory into serpentine energy.

I lost my sense of up and down, fought against losing my breath, thinking in terror as I felt the absorbing pull of his awesome, expanding interior: "He's going to *use* me! He *is* going to use me!" But it was impossible to keep my breath. My lungs felt like flattened envelopes as the galaxies went on whirling over me and beneath me and around me, and went on and on like a Universe of suddenly living, faceless numbers exploding their secret names orgastically to the will of the new Lord, and became one with his substance and spirit, and power.

Suddenly, I realized where I'd seen a bit of that electricity before: leaping out of Mel's Law book, running across his chest and to his Right arm, keeping him up on two legs while the rest of us were down on all fours.

All of Mel's words, I realized now, had simply been the verbal expression of that electricity from the book he held. He'd been talking that electricity with the gift of tongues from the Masculine Spirit of the new Lord, saying in words what the exploding galaxies were saying in electric numbers, and I heard Mel chant

> I am
> the living song
> of the parted open stones
> become his Power and Glory
> and His and His alone!

Then, thank God, a merciful blackness began in my sinuses and I could breathe again. Though I still watched the new Lord's revealed interior—that endlessly expanding Library night alive with the terrible electricity that was the inner secret of the Universe—my sense of vertigo passed. And I stopped feeling that I was about to be sucked out into the infinite Power and turned into another comet. My life was returning to me with my breath, and that Library night that had opened up before my eyes sealed itself, disappeared from view, and I knew that for now it had passed me by.

And now I was seeing Mel again, for which I was grateful, beard, book and all, with Althea next to him, clothed and veiled as always, with Mel looking distinctly like Moses and Sigmund Freud in three naked dimensions. But he suddenly dissolved, and was replaced by the throbbing, ultraviolet figure of the new Lord, who was now the one holding Althea's arm. Then, with a silent explosion of darkness, Mel reappeared, only to disappear again, instantly, and then reappear, always replaced by the new Lord, all between multiplying explosions of silent darkness which came and went so quickly I soon couldn't tell whether I was seeing Mel or the new Lord, or if there was a difference anymore since Mel seemed to love him so much.

But whoever it was, it was unquestionably the spirit of the new Lord who was starting to give shakes to Althea's rag-limp, Heart arm, like whiplashes, which was what was creating those explosions of darkness coming out of her. And he shook her a little harder each time, maliciously, joyously. Sometimes, it seemed to me that the intermittent Sigmund/Moses/Mel was the one there gently and protectively holding her arm, but that protectiveness became a cruel joke when the new Lord was again revealed, grinning ultraviolet, shaking her harder, thrashing more darkness out of her which, I realized, was coming out in mute, obstinate pain.

She kept on convulsing, her hair jumping in pain, until she looked so limp I didn't think I could see any sign of rebellion left in her. And as I breathed the merciful darkness in my own sinuses, I knew, absolutely, that the new Lord had come to our midst to do something total to Althea. Something beyond rape. That was why he hadn't been interested in me.

I didn't know what he was going to do next. But I dreaded it, because maybe he was going to rip her open with both hands and scrape out whatever darkness might still be hiding inside her, and then turn her inside out, like an animal hide.

Then, as nothing more happened for the moment, I looked down with increasing sadness at her feet and saw that the darkness lay there, in puddles. And I realized it hadn't died there.

It was still alive, but disoriented, without sure form, as it struggled weakly with the mustard colored grass, edging down the hill little by little without getting very far as it dreamily tried to remember its lost profile, the one that had been Althea.

I breathed in my own darkness, ashamed I still had it while hers was gone, and I knew now that mine and hers were the very same, the blood of our souls, and hearing Mel's voice I cringed with hatred as he said, "Isn't this exciting? Now, let us join our voices in joyous, thanksgiving prayer . . . all together now

> . . . and the renunciation
> of our instincts
> is the source of the living song
> of the parted open stone"

and he was indeed joined prayerfully by everyone around me until, suddenly, Althea moaned. Once.

Silenced, all eyes turned to her again, including the beaming new Lord's, as she started shaking rapidly all over again, by herself now, so rapidly I almost expected her to rattle. But she didn't make a sound, shaking wildly away, until at last she moaned again, moaned deep and long and darkly in a horrible surrender, as if the whole dark earth had parted itself open at last. And she collapsed, absolutely, like a rag, and lay inert among the pools of breathing darkness that no longer recognized her.

There was a new deep hush among us now as we watched the glowing, ultraviolet new Lord standing over her, all triumph and future, while the ignored puddles began to move a bit more, still almost imperceptibly, in silent tongues around the obstacle of his feet, as if trying to escape his glow.

And then, yips went up everywhere, along with the peculiar applause of puny arms beating against the sides of naked bodies.

And the applause and yipping began increasing in volume and enthusiasm as we all noticed that Althea's inert body was taking on life again as it lay on its side, and was also starting to glow. It was swelling, too. Becoming round and ultraviolet and obviously solid. She had been impregnated by the new Lord! There was no question: her flesh was becoming his spirit.

131

And then, suddenly, she threw her head back, finally clearing her face of her hair, with a gesture of victory that was unmistakably the new Lord's. And she laughed, like clanging bells announcing the greatest of victories by the strong. Her laugh clanged on and on, and the people cheered.

(But I still didn't believe I was seeing her face, because what she revealed was a roundly symmetrical, grinning, metallic sphere that only *suggested* a face. His.)

"People!!" Mel cried out deliriously happy, "I think that the Big Fella has chosen her as his bride! She's a lucky girl. All's well that ends well. And I do believe she's not one of us any more, not completely anyway."

And then, to my amazement, someone dared throw some sort of missile at her. It missed. Then another one came flipping by me toward her, a little hard apple, which hit her in her swelling center. It, too, clanged, and everyone was delighted. Even the round, metallic symmetries of her face grinned along. Everything about the new Lord was triumphantly grinning too, exactly like her, and delight was everywhere. Except in me.

I looked at the puddles. They hadn't dried yet. Maybe they wouldn't dry up, I thought, if they could only keep moving, even a little. I knew Althea's Light wasn't on her face, which had been transformed into his, and I wondered if her Light was hiding in those dark puddles which now began to slide slowly, blindly, through the grass, unobserved by everyone but me.

I DIDN'T KNOW SHE HAD FIRED HIM

Meanwhile, back up in the shallows of ordinary perceptions we usually call consciousness, the corresponding Muldoon did continue to wonder why Mel had come over. And transformed, too, emanating all that wounded youthfulness and uncharacteristic air of passionate instability which, as I said, rather became him.

Because God knows it was odd to see him like that, so defiantly nihilistic, after a lifetime of his trying to inspire confidence in his leadership. As I said, he did look as if some heartbreaking rejection had caused him to throw away all his Big Daddy disguises (with him wanting the world to know he'd done it, too) because they'd been to no avail to something he'd been after maybe all along. To what, I didn't yet know. (It was to Althea, of course.)

It was clear, however, that he didn't want to discuss it with me, not yet anyway.

So, that night, as we put away nearly a bottle of my bourbon, we deferred to his sorrows, which did appear to be worse than mine, judging from his transformation. And I respectfully limited myself to keeping him company as he drank himself into oblivion, without

133

requiring any further explanations from him. Initially intending, of course, to ask him what the trouble was, if the time seemed right later on. However, reaching oblivion myself, I never did, finally, get around to asking him.

Therefore, my memory of the ordinary events of that evening are very vague; at least, at the waking level.

But I do recall how he managed to break my only two drinking glasses, fairly early, in fact, during one of his more sordid outbursts of self-pity.

He was in the process of telling me (with a sad, sad, melodramatic smile) that after all these years of indefatigable careerism and social climbing on his part, he had come to realize the folly of it all, and that he was only marking time on this earth, waiting for nothing special. And since he was, so were we all.

He was an old friend. Usually he wasn't like this. I didn't expect him to make a practice of public self-indulgence, since he never had (though I did wonder if he might). So I listened.

According to him, we were all like fruit flies, mindlessly engaged in reproducing, vanishing and reappearing, thus creating a constant, noxious cloud on the biosphere of the world, which he called (the hint of a tenor's sob appeared in his voice behind his sad, sad smile) "this fucking flying boulder", which he saw as hurtling through space with us aboard "on its way to nowhere".

And he was saying this all quietly enough, which made my compassion fairly easy, when, having so declared, he suddenly banged on my table with his right fist, very very hard, contorting his face and simultaneously bellowing out a miserable, Satanic cry of pain, filled with all of our God's abandoned bastards' fury and futility before the Absurd, which came out pathetically as: "Balls!" Whereupon my glasses, which had risen at least an inch off the table from the trauma of his blow, bounced off and got busted on the floor.

Startled, I looked up at him, but with his gesture complete, I only found him smiling sadly at me again, rather peacefully now that he'd unburdened himself. But he didn't even say he was sorry about the glasses, which I took to mean he felt sufficiently upset to expect me to indulge him.

So, I cleaned up the mess, with melancholy smiling Mel just sitting there, watching me do it down on the floor. And after watching me at work long enough, he said, "Why bother, X.J.? I mean, why bother doing anything? You know what we're all doing, don't you?

134

We're pounding sand, that's all. Just pounding sand . . . and do you know why it's imperative for us to get to the Asians and the Africans before the Communists do?"

"Why?" I said, looking up from the floor and trying to let him know I was a touch irritated, to which he was completely insensitive as he continued illuminating me with his sad and gentle smile. "So they can pound sand for *our* side. That's the meaning of the Cold War. What politics all comes down to."

"Is that so . . . ," I said, standing up with the broken glass in my cupped hands, and he sighed his confirmation.

Then, as I went off to dump the refuse, he sat back and patiently waited for me to come back to him with something else for us to drink from.

Which I did. But at that point my attitude was that I might continue to indulge him. In fact, I knew I would. But that he'd better not push his luck. And one thing was for sure; I was *not* going to pamper him by trying to coax what the trouble was out of him. If he didn't want to tell me, he could go with those details to his grave. I was not entering into *that* kind of dance with him, since my *own* details interested me a lot more, anyhow. And furthermore, if he got himself so sick he started vomiting, for example, he was going to have to handle those problems *himself*, and leave none to me. Or I'd clobber him, broken heart or no broken heart.

All of which I tried to communicate to Mel by the way I smacked the stolen Hayes-Bickford's cups down on the table in front of him and said, "Now cool it, because this is *it*. Don't break anymore. Got it?" To which he smiled and sighed, as if telling me he would try to do his best but couldn't possibly promise his pain might not suddenly overcome him again, and that he really did appreciate how sweet it was of me to tend to him this way.

So, with my elbow still on the table, I pointed one right index finger in his face, and I said, "I mean it." To which he only smiled and sighed again.

Soon, however, we had consumed enough bourbon for my attitude toward him to have changed again. And become compassionate.

By this time I wasn't asking him what the trouble was not only because, for all I cared, he could stuff it if he didn't want to tell me, but also because (not that I really cared about knowing the details myself) I had the strong sense that whatever the problem was, it was a source of shame as well as grief.

135

My intuition was, as it turned out, correct.

Unknown to me, Mel had been dismissed that very afternoon by his star patient, Althea Stanton. She felt she had better things to do, having fallen in love with Frank Long. (And this was, as history is my witness, very shortly before she killed Long, too, not that *that* would have necessarily saddened Mel, since he was the reason she'd decided to discontinue her daily visits with Mel.) Hence Mel's new disconsolate comments about the pointlessness of life, and his feeling entitled to collapse into narcissistic despair at my place.

However, be this as it may, I forgave Mel his trespasses before long, passing out myself, or I think I did, and when I woke up the next morning, he was gone.

Not that my first thoughts concerned themselves with him, having my own miserably dehydrated condition to contend with. But I was sure, I *assumed*, he would have made it to the Hospital on time, despite his heartfelt remarks about pounding sand. No matter what happened the night before, I knew that in the end Mel was incapable of not answering the call to duty in the morning. He may have looked down on me for not being more of a success, like himself, but he also knew that *I* knew he lacked the moral power to be a screw-off, like me. Therefore, I wasn't surprised to find an ashamed little note from him saying:

> *My imagination has failed me again. I'm off to the*
> *sandworks. Pray for me.*
> *Yours in Christ,*
> *Mel*

Were I not so hung over at the time, I might have been touched, remembering how demoralized he'd been the night before. But that morning, since my body, soul and mind were all baked together into one wretched unit, about all I could do was wish for the gift of death.

I cared about nothing, thought about nothing, and went downstairs to my mailbox, as if the mechanical motion might give me some relief. It did not.

Down in the front hall, the French-Canadian mailman had jammed a huge manila envelope into my box, for which I cursed him with a hatred the size of the Universe, since I'd often asked him to leave such things on the floor.

And I would have left the package there, but I heard Mr. Pansky's door open above me. When I looked up, there he was, leaning on the doorframe, one leg crossed over the other, in an undershirt and sweater, drinking coffee out of a glass with the spoon still in it, and watching me.

He was retired now, so that's all he did, be a full time witness to Decadence (mostly me). His wife Sophie, who still worked, was the Judge he reported to at the end of each day, and everything I did was becoming an offense to her womanly decency, cornerstone of Civilization, which was threatening to make the stairway unnavigable for me, especially when we were both there at one time, Mrs. Pansky and me.

To make my situation worse, it looked like junk mail, but I didn't want to give him the satisfaction of seeing me so hung over that I couldn't cope with my own mailbox.

So, with an acid smile, calling up all my spiritual and physical resources, I struggled (at the expense of a fingernail) until I finally extricated the cursed envelope, put it under my arm unopened, and trudged back upstairs with as much dignity as possible. However, even as I passed him and felt his ever alert Middle European gaze on my back, I knew I'd be reported, and punished by Mrs. Pansky's silent glares, at my very next, "Hi, Mrs. Pansky".

So, when I shut my door behind me, I felt even more miserably dehydrated and anti-Pansky than ever, two things which were blending into one searing passion which was taking over my whole being. Therefore, to interrupt this process, and for the sake of doing something, I opened the envelope. What I pulled out, however, was not junk mail. It was the typescript of a story, and a note. From Norma, whom I'd completely forgotten.

I admit it. I had absolutely forgotten her. And in my wretched condition, marooned up in that meagre desert of Panskys, it was Norma the Nice that came to my mind first.

It was an unexpected delight. Suddenly running into Norma the Nice, model modern wife and ideal acquaintance, was as pleasant and refreshing as meeting her accidentally on the street had ever been for me. More so. It was like a glass of cool, clear water. A reprieve.

At that moment, in my weakened condition, the opaquely white and naked married woman who'd been on my couch the day before (whom I was just beginning to remember) was not part of my emotional landscape. Not yet anyway. No doubt because in my state,

137

I was far happier to hear from good old Norma the Nice than from any new, messy entanglement—up to which I did not feel.

Unfortunately, the note soon changed my peacefully chaste notion by starting out with

Darling:

which hit me with its full force: yes, I was indeed being addressed as "Darling" by a married Cambridge woman who'd picked me up in front of Widener Library, as I recalled, then gone to bed with me—noisily—while her family ate supper. And this lady had a great big rich husband, too, who might not like it. And furthermore, she was following it all up. It was not a one-time thing. I had *not* been excused.

I looked at the note again, and the married woman persisted

> *Darling:*
> *As I'm writing you, I feel myself tingling. I'm hap-*
> *py!*

This here married woman was striking me as the soupily romantic kind, which made me even more uncomfortable.

> *We're having a party Saturday night. Please,* please
> *come. If you don't, I'm afraid I'll lose touch with*
> *the real me. I won't be able to get away for at least*
> *another week, and I don't want to leave that me,*
> *and us, too far behind. Darling, sometimes it*
> *already seems like something that happened to*
> *someone else. Did it?*

It did to me, and I started to feel embarrassed for both of us, and a touch guilty, especially as I read her plaintive:

> *I can't tell you how frightened I am of having it all*
> *become unreal, and of eventually forgetting and*
> *losing it all. Please, love, don't you forget, or the*
> *girl you know will disappear. Then I'll just be left*
> *with that unreal Norma, the moronically smiling*
> *potted plant you used to meet on the street, who is*
> *so hopelessly separate from the inner cheese of life.*

I puzzled over that one: "The inner cheese of life"?—until suddenly, in my head, I heard Norma's favorite Viennese accent, enunciated by Norma the Nice, and I realized it should be read "the energies of life", which brought back some sense of familiar reality to me. But Norma the Nice, after peeping through this aggressively romantic married woman's note, disappeared, as the note said:

All I can promise you Saturday, my sweating beast, is courtly sublimation and maybe a few sordid kisses in the coatroom. But I must have your body near me as soon as possible. As you well know, I don't believe in courtly sublimation (not for me anyway) unless it is absolutely inevitable. So keep up your morale. You shall be amply rewarded.

Would it shock you terribly to know I've been lost in glorious erotic fantasies about you? Please don't look down on me for them. Right now they're my only link with the living Norma. The only thing that pulls me back (must this be my reality? God, I hope not) is when Ralph touches me. It's horrible, really. One moment, I'm alive, sexually responsive, hungry, a woman, and then he absolutely freezes me with his touch. Rapist that he is, I'm sure he enjoys it. He just won't leave me alone. Something in his eyes tells me I've become very interesting prey to him again. I must be radiating. Maybe my pores are more open, more sensitive to the light and air. It's like a seduction in reverse, because he just won't stop until he's deadened me. It's just like I told you. He only likes it if he's convinced I don't, so his unlove making makes sure I don't, with a subtle tactical brilliance and ambiguity he finds delicious, the bastard!

Maybe I'm being paranoid, but I swear that he's subliminally aware that I'm coming alive, and the big horrible predator gets excited and is out to kill the living me. He'll do it, too, if I don't see you again, and soon.

139

I hate him. Really I do. Especially his nasty trium-
phant smirk after . . . well, after. But sometimes I
almost feel sorry for him. It's as if he needed my life
to sustain his own. He's like one of those awful,
cold-blooded snakes scientists are so fond of
keeping in glass cases (right behind the music
stand with Bach and Mozart scores, of course) to
which they feed live, warm-blooded little white
mice.

> *Yours, if you'll save me,*
> *N.*

P.S.
Dear sweating beast. Come after 9. The party, in-
cidentally, includes Ralph's partner, Frank Long,
who is every bit as awful a snake as Ralph, and his
rather Gothic, raven-haired girlfriend of the
moment. His wife isn't in town, not that it would
stop him. Anyway, the girlfriend's name is Althea.
Both she and her name fascinate me. I met her
doing research for a story at a crazy Feminist club
in Boston, which she, incredibly enough, founded.
I'm afraid I introduced her to Frank. I'd like you to
meet her, and to know what you think of her. That
is, if we can tear her away from Frank long enough
for a chat. I'm afraid she's as enraptured as I am.

After reading the note, I didn't feel enraptured. Despite all the
heat she was putting on me, I felt like I was reading somebody else's
mail. More like a spectator, by a long shot, than one of the actors
across the footlights in this married lady's complicated sentimental
life.

And I realized I liked the distance. It gave me a brief feeling of
superiority. But brief it was, because deep down, to my humiliation,
I knew for sure that any second now I was going to be pulled across
those footlights, whether I liked it or not. And then, gone for good
would be any feeling of superiority, because once again I was going
to find out that romantically I was disgustingly like a dog. Feed him,
and he's yours forever, especially if you can keep others from feeding

140

him early in the game. Feed him, and he develops a whole mythology about you, and then a theology. And he doesn't even have to like you, ever, to be yours. As a matter of fact, it crossed my mind that I didn't know many people involved in love affairs who didn't think badly of each other.

Not that I *didn't* like Norma. I certainly did. Maybe more than ever. But that was really Norma the Nice I was still liking, because she was above all easy on the nerves and would *never* presume to take one over and push one around—which was obviously what this new person was about to do to me. Push me all over the place with her enthusiasms. And I couldn't do anything but resent *that*.

In fact, if ever I saw a note written by a woman who promised to be the consumer of entire human beings, liver and all, I believed I was holding it in my right hand.

Which meant that suddenly, right then and there, Norma was becoming a bewildering Cubist monster for me. Simultaneously now, as if on one flat surface, I had to contend with not only this melodramatic (and most pressing) married lady, but with my old un-forgettable acquaintance Norma the Nice as well, right along with the distinctly possible (and well profiled) Norma the vengeful adulteress who manages to get herself entangled in wild and loud embraces on a bachelor's couch at precisely the time her unap-preciative family usually eats supper. A detail that kept bothering me, because my experiences with infidelity had always eventually turned out, somehow, to involve revenge on the part of the lady.

But, distressing as these un-Nice possibilities were, there was still another one that was worse: Norma as Eva, the cold and Lunar creature from her story.

It did little good that the Cambridge wife in search of "the living Norma" had personally assured me that she, unlike Eva, considered who slept with whom to be most important, which was how, she claimed, I'd come to her attention.

Much as I wanted to be persuaded, frankly, I was increasingly leery that at any moment Norma the Cubist monster would suddenly roll up with a great snap, whereupon all two-dimensionality would disappear as Eva burst forth, emerging in three sculptural, classic and archetypal dimensions as the one true and fundamental Norma, after all. With all the other Normas having only been cosmetic masks for the perfectly smooth, post-human and ultimately faceless Eva, whose egglike, Lunar facelessness was nevertheless conveying to

141

me an implacable smile. As implacable as the one Althea had given Mel when she'd sat beneath her painting.

I know it's not to my credit as a sexual liberal, but what kept me leery was one inescapable fact: she'd gone to bed with me, hadn't she? Was that, I couldn't help asking myself, the behavior of a Good Woman? A woman who cared? Would Norma the Nice ever do such a thing? What about the children?

Naturally, I wanted to believe it was, because it flattered me. But why should I, *Muldunius Vulgaris* of Brighton, Mass., have been chosen from among all other males as the object of her affections?

Looking at the note again, it became even harder to believe it was addressed to me, son of Bridgid Muldoon, and written in all sincerity. And then, a curious new perspective came up: I imagined my mother reading the note, and the look she'd give me upon finishing it. Was there any question what *she'd* have thought about it, or about Norma? I could almost hear her say, "Jesus . . . ," and then look at me with utter contempt for the stupidity of males before looking away in disdain—which made me smile. Something I could permit myself because she was no longer present, and I put the note down.

I guess, having thought about my mother's unquestionable opinion, and having smiled, I felt relieved. And, once again, very much like a spectator to a piece of dramatized gossip about a married lady named Norma and an accidental gentleman I impersonated. And then it happened. Imperceptibly, I had crossed the footlights and was now on the other side.

The phrase, "when Ralph touches me", rose out of the text and his enormous figure loomed frighteningly in my imagination like a giant sword-wielding shadow.

Despite all her stories about what a rapist he was and what he was doing to her in general, I nevertheless suddenly felt toward him the yielding weakness that comes from guilt. I felt the sudden urge to plead my case to the great, sword-bearing shadow, explaining how I'd really been the helpless victim of her wiles, due to my relative youth, sir. And if the living Ralph, all 6'3" of him, had then and there appeared in my apartment and without further ado proceeded to pound the crap out of me, I wouldn't have lifted a finger in my defense, since I felt he had both the physical and moral advantage. Maybe her stories about him were true. Maybe he was a rapist. But I felt that though I might not approve, he was possibly even justified, for all I knew. Feeling a new shame now, I badly wanted not to be involved, guessing that maybe both Ralph and I were victims of her wiles, when suddenly Norma's phrase, "he won't leave me alone", popped back into my mind, interrupting both my cowardice and my youthful guilt with an altogether new feeling I didn't like at all: jealousy. I didn't admit it, but my cheeks felt flushed. Secretly I knew all along that "he won't leave me alone" was eventually going to get me, and from her residence in my soul, Bridgid Muldoon communicated to me: "And why do you think she'd bring up that little detail? Especially with that business about his smirk, as she puts it, 'after'?"

Badly, I wanted to think it was protectiveness I was feeling. But it wasn't. It was jealousy. Uncomplicated jealousy, to my mounting irritation. I didn't care whether she objected to his touch or not. I just didn't want him to do it—under any circumstances—and I couldn't help thinking he wouldn't if she didn't invite it in some way. I was furious with her, not with him—for his touching her, for her mentioning it, and for having pulled me across the footlights so completely with her equivocal maneuvering.

All of which meant, of course, that I'd reached a sorry pass, because although I didn't quite know just who Norma really was anymore (except that I was actively disliking her now), I felt possessive as hell about whatever the phenomenon that answered to the name of Norma was.

With dread, I looked at the typescript. What if she'd decided to describe the martyrdom of sex with Ralph, in detail, which was probable? I didn't want to read it, but I knew I was going to. Even though I wasn't rejected, I nevertheless felt like a rejected lover about to peep into his old girlfriend's window. I was going to read the story out of morbid curiosity. And, deep down, because now that I faced a forest of Normas where I was pretty sure to get lost, I guess I also hoped that her story might give me an inkling of her true Light, as it were, which could help me, one way or another. Because, if that Light turned out to be Eva's, I was going to run like hell.

Of course, I also couldn't help hoping that I'd find out from her story that my worst suspicions weren't true, and that Norma's true Light would turn out to be sweetly nurturing and Marianic, after all. That is to say, the Light of my dreams about Norma the Nice.

(Little did I know that the Unseen and Mysterious Forces were about to confront me with quite another Light on those pages. The

143

very same Light that was already signalling me desperately in dreams I hadn't dreamed yet, which was trying to come to terms with my Secret Me.)

(What was happening now was that *Muldunius Vulgaris*, the Public Me, was about to receive the signal up in the daylight world, ordering him to move even closer. All in preparation for the moment when full understanding was at last called for. When body and soul would at last have to come together.)

What I thought I held in my hands, after the first look, was another Eva story, which upset jealous *Muldunius Vulgaris* right away, since this is what he wanted least.

As I recalled from the previous Eva story, Eva had ended up by driving the family car, with Ralph inside, toward a whopping crash with the full intent of killing everybody.

Therefore, the title of the story, "Eva in Limbo," suggested to me that we were following Eva into the next life.

EVA IN LIMBO
by Norma Brown

Within her thick, prenatal darkness, Eva didn't move.

She was waiting. Happy and excited. Not daring to move. Yet feeling more alive than she'd ever felt before, just by waiting to live.

Her life had never been hers before. Now she knew she'd been everything's whore. But it would be different soon, with the freeing of her soul. With her bursting out into the light.

But she knew she mustn't move (not yet), mustn't open her eyes and break the darkness, not until she sensed the precise moment when finally (finally! finally!) a long dark shape came racing, cutting through the depths of the transparent green waters like a great dark fish, gathering speed and strength until finally (finally!!) it exploded up gloriously (so gloriously it made her weak), breaking through the surface of the clear green waters, out of the shadowy depths and into the new and never-before-seen-daylight! . . . And only then should she open her eyes . . . but to see what? A portrait of her own soul, standing before her? Tall and proud, like a Diana with arrows in her quiver? With free, naked feet swift and strong enough to mark out

144

the measure of the Universe with the personal measure of her own strides?

Yes. That's what she waited for in the darkness. Her *soul. Coming to lead away her body. Filled at last with* her *soul. Her true soul, not as it had been, but as it* should *have been. A soul she could love, at last, not like the slavish one she'd hated, that whore's soul, that series of loathsomely conditioned reflexes that had made her believe once she didn't have a soul . . . which had been true, in a way. Because it hadn't been* her *soul she'd had. What else could eternal damnation be, she thought, but an everlasting life for that fake soul which had existed only to prevent the birth of her true one . . . the one she was now waiting to see?*

Of course, she knew it had been her fault too (but had that *been her?) because of her (until now) incurable compulsion to humiliate herself before any authority. No, that must never happen again. She had to save herself, wait, not open her eyes, not until that powerful fish finally came soaring up out of the depths and exploded into the light. She absolutely* had *to keep faith with the fish of darkness . . . or she'd come out too soon, and be captured in the light, made a captive again. A whore again. Dead, again.*

. . . and then, it came. Just as she'd known it would. The temptation. Dancing beyond her darkness. Making her smile.

She began hearing (it had a cruel hook in it, she was certain, but it still made her smile) the lure of an enthusiastic, angelic-sounding voice (it's a false angel, Eva! she told herself, but it still amused her), shining and prancing on the surface, on the other side of the darkness, silvery like a fish fly . . . talking about Heaven, trying to entice her out of the darkness . . .

And then the dancing started soaring, swooping, darting! Becoming more and more angelic and silvery in its flight, making her think of leaping up after it in a great splash, open-mouthed with desire.

But she held fast, eyes closed, even though the silvery bait began to remind her of other angels that had populated her mind: gigantic and adolescent-faced, long-striding, exciting angels (always exciting!) with great, capelike wings that would give them spans more than twice their height when they stretched out against the sky . . . golden haired angels (golden like exploding suns!) with beautifully chiseled features more like Joan of Arc's than any other's.

. . . and thinking about those fantastic, androgynous angels with clear, sometimes wicked-seeming eyes, she knew they weren't human, those lovely angels. They had no egos. And because of that, they seemed nothing but all-consuming, demonic egos. But they weren't.

And as quickly as they materialized in their perfect, seamless splendor, their whole existence would suddenly reveal itself (at any moment! . . . in a sudden flare!) as pure singing, all song and fire, clear burning joy . . . because those angels weren't singers. They were songs in the shape of angels. And if they strode among us on their naked, elastic military feet, she knew, it was only to steal our hearts and breaths, to lead us away by the hand up to the great ascending boulevards of light that lose themselves past the zigzagging horizons in the eternal explosion of the never-ending day beyond this darkness . . . Those angels would come, Eva knew, and lead us by the hand, yes, and then suddenly they would burst into the never-before-seen-light and disappear in luminous joy . . . leaving us alone . . . frightened, trembling and naked before all that limitless light.

And then Eva was afraid again. Because that is how she'd be soon, too, alone, trembling and free. And she became ashamed of her fear. We should not, she reminded herself, expect to have those angelic hands hold ours forever, much as we might love those evil-seeming eyes. Remember, they are only meant to lead us for a while, and then to leave us, so we can finally become what we've never been before: Ourselves. Ours. Alone. Finally new. And if our transparent wings then dare unwrap themselves from around our new bodies . . . then finally, perhaps, we shall become angels, too. Remember always, Eva, they do not come to make us theirs, but ours.

But her shame didn't leave her, because she was not at all sure she was ready yet. She still (Damn me! Damn me!) found it so hard, so very hard, not to fall back and think of herself as anything but someone else's captive . . . .

And nearby (of course) the temptation kept darting and swooping. The silvery voice, merciless, kept tempting, describing with its pretty flight the shape of a Heaven filled with happy captives, with a place for all.

She knew it was a false angel as sure as she knew the Darkness that filled her . . . and yet, the mere suggestion of angels, even falsely pretty ones, made her smile again . . . like a courted whore, she *thought, still smiling, until she thought, Damn me! Damn me! And making another effort to be true to the darkness, she began trying to imagine the moment when her true angel finally came. She tried very hard, as if praying to keep the devil from infiltrating her thoughts, to visualize the moment when at last her true angel, portrait of her soul, was finally standing before her, after having been announced by the long awaited, sudden, flying music of that once dark fish as it came soaring up through the green waters, exploding before her into a full angel! A real angel! Naked feet, clear eyes and all! All truth! For once, Eva, for once . . . Truth. Angel! And the letter "A" (for Angel, she thought) whirled in her mind like a glorious sword, dripping with light, strong with fire! Alive!*

Oh, Eva, she told herself, don't open your eyes too soon. Don't, or you'll lose yourself. Wait. You'll know when!

And Eva knew full well, again, that if this time she did not become like the tall, long-haired creature with the wicked-seeming eyes, she would be allowed to fall back to earth again. Unworthy of truly living. Only worthy of being a slave. And the moment she thought that, the letter "A" burned savage and dark red in the darkness, righteous, unforgiving and warning of death if she did not become, herself nothing but Truth . . .

But then, to her own surprise, she stopped being quite so afraid.

The letter 'A' was so savagely strong that it burned away all her whore's fears, and Eva, finding it so beautiful in its strength, now only loved it, for its fire and promise . . . and the Greek word for it was so lovely: Althea . . . Bright. Dark. Bright. "A" would so, oh so soon be coming, walking with scissoring strides and suddenly turn those incredible clear, purple eyes on Eva . . . and then! Would she, Eva, would Eva? Could Eva . . . please . . . see herself in the vast and transparent purple fields that were those eyes? Would she see her own image appear there, transformed, finally rising up . . . please . . . and walking tall and strong herself, wrapped as if in a loose magic cape, spread her transparent wings, finally free?

It was so frightening, yet so exciting, to think of her Angel, burning with so much Truth, that it was a relief to listen to the nearby angelic voice come closer in all its falseness, buzzing confidently like a golden fat bee, talking on and on about Heaven. A false one, but with no fears. She knew she would not follow the false angel, yet it, too had its charms. It rose athletic and adolescent in the ageless way of male ballet dancers, jumping and pretending to flight with its

147

*silly, pretty little promises, and suddenly the false angel's voice cried
out ecstatically: "I don't care if it's vulgar! I love it! I adore it! And I
can tell you for sure that Heaven's going to be one great, never-
ending Broadway musical with ten foot high Big Mommas like Ethel
Merman helping confused young men in love (because you better
believe Big Momma's been there before!) and she'll be convincing
pretty, dynamic girls from the Midwest, so, so much more dynamic
than the boys, as always . . . that Love and the Boy-Next-Door are
ultimately more important than Success on BROADWAYYYY!!!
And joy will be everywhere! . . . as delightfully materialistic but
good-hearted second lead girls will sing about DIAMONDS ARE A
GIRL'S BEST FRIEND and I ENJOY BEING A GIRL! and entire
Legions of MUSCULAR MARINES will whistle wolf calls at them
(which the girls find sweet, not fresh) as in just moments, out of sheer
enthusiasm, those entire Legions of MARINES in T-Shirts that show
they're real He-Men break into THERE'S NOTHING LIKE A
DAME! Oh, I tell you, everything but EVERYTHING is going to be
like a giant Rose Bowl Parade of Grand Finales presided over by
distant Grand Marshals, Ten Feet High like Big Momma, with Successful Marriages of a Hundred Years, Roy Rogers and Dale Evans,
while the handsomest boy . . . masculine but shy . . . and the prettiest girl are getting together at last, and then, of course, the second
prettiest girl with somebody good enough for her, a schlumpy good
provider from Cedar Rapids back home like maybe Karl Malden, a
doglike businessman who doesn't mind second best, if you know
what I mean, and maybe even an older, distinguished gentleman for
Big Momma herself . . . as Thousands and Thousands of happy
Munchkins dance around, happy asexual little Munchkin-Schmoos
who want nothing for themselves but to cheer and applaud and
whose only joy is bringing joy! Big Momma's little helpers in the only
truly IMPORTANT BUSINESS in Life, which is BRINGING
YOUNG COUPLES TOGETHER IN PROPER HIERARCHICAL
ORDER!! . . . And everything will become THERE'S NO BUSI-
NESS LIKE SHOW BUSINESS and OKLAHOMA, O.K.!! as the
wicked witch is dead and ugly Jed and his dirty fingernails have been
totally destroyed for the sin of having even dared to think that they
might have won the affections of the prettiest cheerleader in all
Minnesota! Ohhh! What a hideous crime against Nature that would
have been! How awful: the Ugly with the Beautiful! No sir! Not in
my Heaven! . . . We don't even allow tall girls to get together with*

short *boys, not in* my *GREAT BIG BEAUTIFUL HEAVEN . . .
from* Sea *to Shining* Sea*!!!"*

*And then, just as the angelic enthusiasm had peaked at its highest,
came the contrapuntal, down-to-earth chuckle of a cracker-barrel
philosopher, "Honest, Brownell . . . you're a real nut." The benign,
fatherly voice addressing Brownell, the running angel who so often
wore an Exeter Academy sweat suit, suggested a white-haired,
twinkly-eyed veteran of many winters and many springs. "D'ye really
think that Heaven is going to be like that?" continued the warm,
chuckling, skeptical voice, and Eva imagined Robert Frost talking to
an angel that descended to his deathbed from New York. She'd
never heard Frost speak, but she imagined him in combination with
some sly, white-haired, old Senator. She imagined a Senator Robert
Frost and a poet Sam Ervin, or maybe Everett Dirksen, all of whom
melted with a Carl Sandburg into a Grand Old Man Winter
smoking a pipe. Chuckling. Twinkly-eyed. Amused.*

*"I certainly do-o-o!" exclaimed the clear and believing voice of the
false angel Brownell, and back came the philosophical chuckle,
saying, "Gosh . . . I sure do hope you're wrong, Brownell, 'cause I
never did care for the theatre that much." At which Brownell's
angelic voice rose up, clear and effortless, and burst into easy
laughter at its peak like a small explosion of birds suddenly going in
all directions, though not very far. "Well, then!!" he said, "your
Heaven's just going to have to be a little different, won't it, Dean. Let
me see . . . let's give you . . . I know! A lovely Campus with a silvery
pond in the middle, still as a compact mirror, with lovely girls
bicycling along the approved paths. And of course, it simply must
have co-ed dormitories, so you won't have all that trouble you've
been having from the children getting neurotic from all that
unnatural separation of the sexes!"*

*But Dean Everett Frost Sandburg protested, chuckling closed
mouthed now, no doubt through a pipe, "That's not* my *idea of
Heaven, either, Brownell! Boy, I'd just move into the nut house
permanently if I had to administer co-ed dorms!" and back came
another low, sensible chuckle, at the very idea, and Eva liked
hearing it. It was so handsomely comfortable, like a fire in a hearth,
with crackling sparks of warm amusement through traditional
strong logs of sanity. Eva could easily imagine that voice saying
something Robert Frosty, along the lines of good fences making
good neighbors. "Believe me, Brownell I've got* plenty *of troubles*

from the girls just as it is . . . ," and as Brownell desisted, laughing angelically at the Dean who had not accepted the idea of Heaven that had just been offered, Eva suddenly felt herself relax. She knew now that Brownell's temptation was not strong enough for her either. It was weak enough so she could enjoy it just for what it was, a temptation, without having to open her eyes. And now that she'd found it so easy not to rise up to the bait of all that false Heaven talk, she was pleased with herself for having been good, and waiting.

Confident now, Eva let the voices talk on with no resistance at all as she felt her expectant, slender body absorb the sun's rays and turn them into exciting darkness inside her—when suddenly came a cool dark pause sliding over her body, like a long dark pair of wings. And Eva lost her breath.

And the voices stopped, too. In the silence, she fought against trembling under the great dark wings of that large shadow that didn't move. Nothing moved anywhere now. Not even the silvery voice of the false angel Brownell.

Oh, God, Eva thought, wondering if this was the moment. But she had to be absolutely sure. Was it now that she had to open her eyes? Was Althea really standing there, tall, dark, clean-limbed, without saying a word? Because if she were, Eva knew, Althea wouldn't speak first. No. If this were the moment (Oh God, is it?), Eva knew Althea would simply appear and look around with those incredible, clear, purple eyes, stilling the whole world. Because her eyes were so clear, so honest and unafraid that they burned away all lies, all fictions, all pretended meanings and struck fear into all the phantoms, and surely into false angels, too. They'd cower before those eyes. They'd flee! And Althea, with her clear and honest eyes, would become the unquestioned ruler of her immediate world, like the strong young morning sun. And then, after looking around, Althea would sit down, near her, Eva knew, as all became Althea.

Yes, they'd talked before, she and Althea. But even so, even though the talks had been deeply personal, truthful as Althea's own incredible gaze, and strangely (no, not strangely at all) liberating of new forces . . . even so . . . Eva knew that when the time came, she would still have to prove herself worthy of those clear and honest eyes. Beyond talk. She herself had to become true as she had never been, ever, in all her life.

Eva, feeling herself growing colder and smaller beneath that large, unmoving shadow, trembled before the test.

And, just as she was about to open her eyes, the shadow passed, making Brownell's voice explode joyously again into hundreds of bits of laughter like a released flock of treed birds that had been momentarily silenced by fear. "Well!" he said, "I'm still confident we can figure out a nice Heaven for you, Dean. A marvelous place where things are as they should be!" And the prancing sassiness of the false angel's voice assured Eva completely now that Althea hadn't come yet. That it had been some other shadow. A lie of some sort, because the false angel Brownell wouldn't have dared to speak in her presence like that.

Which made Eva, relieved at not having opened her eyes, feel closer than ever to Althea now as her blood raced through her chilled body again, like billions of ants, warming her. And she felt closer than ever to her new and future Self, too, for having kept faith. But she didn't feel so strong yet that she dared step out into the daylight by herself. For one simple reason: she was waiting to be born again, and she needed to see Althea to know what her true Self would be. Like a newborn swan, she needed to imprint the true image of her future Self.

And if she opened her eyes without Althea, she knew she'd only find herself back by the Hospital's green shimmering pool, where people were always trying to turn her into something she no longer wanted to be . . . where she could only watch lies that wanted to shape her with their shapes, with their piously pretended meanings . . . where she would be lost in the comings and goings among the deck chairs of people like the young doctor with the frightened eyes, Dr. Fish . . . who went by smiling at people like the skinny Anglophilic Librarian, Brownell the lover of Broadway musicals, and the big, good-natured alcoholic lesbian Dean from some posh girls' college or other . . . who in the daylight did look like a combination Robert Frost-Carl Sandburg-Everett Dirksen with a touch of red lipstick . . . They were all doing well as patients. Very well indeed. You could tell by their Heaven talk.

And she was not. Which was also why she didn't want to open her eyes too soon, because if the young doctor caught hers with his (he was always trying to, waiting for her like she was waiting for Althea), he would look at her pleadingly, peering over his glasses, and his little smile would strain, . . . because he knew she wasn't doing well. Not by his standards, because he wanted to imprint his image in her eyes in this her second birth. And until recently, until Althea, she

151

hadn't been doing well by her own standards, either.

"Hi, Doc," the cracker-barrel voiced Dean said. "What's up? Going to be able to squeeze some squash in today?" And now that Eva had identified the specific shadow, she was gladder than ever not to have opened her eyes.

"Afraid not," said the young doctor. Eva could hear him smiling, pretending to seem leisurely, even casual. But inside he was always in a hurry, ticking like a wrist watch, trying to make good, keeping everybody on schedule, completely incapable of distinguishing between his careerism and virtue.

"You'd better get some relaxation, Doc," said the Dean, like an older administrator to a younger one. "That's how I wound up here in the first place. You're working too hard."

"Well, I'll try to get some in tomorrow."

"That's what I used to say," said the Dean. "Believe me, what we should all do is put up that old 'Gone Fishin' sign on the office door and give in to the Huckleberry Finn inside us more often. But of course, we never do, Doc. I understand, believe me . . . I wish you'd take up golf, though, 'cause then I could play with you."

"I'd like to try it," said the doctor.

"Wish you would, Doc. Then I'd have the best lookin' partner on the fairways," chuckled the Dean, and Dr. Fish gave back his little reflex laugh at the compliment.

Obviously he felt he should keep moving. Ticking along. Seeing how everyone was progressing in his or her adjustment. There was never any time to lose because the world depended on him. But he was dawdling. Sinning, to Eva's amusement. The whole world had to keep ticking, and there he was, stuck. For personal reasons. How long could he permit himself that? Althea had told her his job was to get people back on jobs they hated. Back to families that made them miserable and lonely. Back to places in all the institutions of our society—And he always does the same thing, Althea said. He tries to keep everybody convinced that "your lot" in life isn't so bad, once you get used to it. I mean, listen, nothing's perfect, right? And maturity is learning to give up and expect no more than is reasonable. He's really saying: Let's face it, in the conflict between you and your context, you're all I've got to work with, I mean, you're where it hurts, aren't you? And as far as I'm concerned, your hurting is the trouble. His first commitment, you see, Althea had said, is to keep things going. Why else do you think society finds him so ac-

ceptable, even when they think he's talking about dirty things? He's not for pleasure. He's for ORDER. They know it, and if it tickles nice maybe it helps people stay serenely adjusted to their "lot in life" (never mind who says what their lot is supposed to be), and whistling while they work. You see, there's no more Great Chain of Being with Kings and then God at the top anymore, so it's really all up to the doctor. The enlightened world looks to him, you see, and he's no Conservative, no sir, not according to him, because he believes he has a special compassionate understanding of helpless sinners. All sinners are helpless. Haven't you ever noticed how it usually goes? You want a divorce? Let's talk about it. But first, promise me you'll do nothing without consulting me. Now then, why is the marriage failing? We must admit neither one of you is sufficiently adequate, sufficiently mature. Otherwise the marriage wouldn't fail, would it? It's not perfect, but a sound machine basically, and it really should work. The problem is you, of course, and he wants to fix you up for marriage, not the other way around. He's a social mechanic, a plumber, and he'll make you a better functioning part of that machine, and shame on you if the machine breaks down. You're not letting life be good to you, she laughed. Hasn't he told you that? And it's really infantilism, you know. Pride, the Christians called it. Why, we all have to accept our limitations, he'll tell you, isn't that so? Just like little girls have to accept they don't have a penis. But there's no use grumbling about it. You see, once we can overcome the screaming infant in us, the red-faced, bellowing monster trying to rule the world from his highchair with his porridge spoon in his fist (he's the one, of course, who spends all that time "moralizing" about what should be if 'there were any justice in the world'), then we can really get on with the business of living! Live as best you can within the possible, that's what he'll tell you. And then you'll find even more possible than you ever thought before. But scream about your lot from the highchair, my friend, and you'll never get much of anything, except unhappiness. . . . Believe me, Eva, I've been around here, off and on, since I was fourteen, and it always comes down to Parents and Infants. Authority and Rebellion. No matter how they put it, the Great Chain of Being, new edition. Don't you see it yet? It's always telling you you haven't the right to rebel, just the new version of Adam's sin, for modern, materialist middle-class consumption. Just the Oedipal form of the old theology for maintaining the existing order in the world, believe me. Always telling you your

life isn't yours. And that a mature person accepts this. And duty.
Nobody tells you how duties got assigned, of course. They just im-
pute your motives for not accepting them. They call you childish,
unrealistic, and everything is a duty, a "should". Including how you
should like your sex, when you are mature, Althea had said, and she
laughed.

But the truth is sex should be for you. Yours, Althea said. Pure
pleasure, freedom, an expression of your soul. If there really is a
"should" I care about, Althea said, it's that sex should be what you
want, for you, and not the vulgar socio-political act it usually is,
which keeps everyone bound up and whores for institutions. I hate
whores, Althea said. I want sex without whoredom. Do you un-
derstand me?

Eva understood so well it stung her, and now the thought of not
being a whore, for once, was like a brave, brilliant sword before her.
But a sword that could be hers. Herself. For once, a sword she did
not have to kneel before and love for being everything she was not (as
she once had thought men were), nor pay tribute to its integrity while
at the same time deprecating and humiliating herself, acknowl-
edging both its splendor and her worthlessness by slavishly licking
it with an obeisant smile.

And suddenly Althea laughed again. Was it at her? That stung,
too. But it wasn't, because she was saying, "Really, why do you think
the Romans let our good doctors get so far? (She always called
"them" Romans, except when she called them Christians, which for
her meant the same thing.) All he wants, my dear, is for you to hold
still, and be used, and they'll always tell you it's for your own good,
on which they base their authority. And the message is that if you'll
only realize there's nothing for you to do but hold still and take it,
then you'll get into a comfortable position and get to like it. And
everybody knows how easy that is, my dear, and how whores have
free rides, anyway. Few worries and responsibilities. And you know
what that awful Professor Law says about Christianity . . . and she
laughed again . . . he says it simply asks you to spread the other
cheek!

(Yes, he did say that. Regularly. Because the enormous, thunder-
ing Professor Law wanted to taunt the angelic Brownell, whom he
detested for being a Catholic convert.)

And then Eva felt Dr. Fish's shadow glide over her again and stay
there. He was hanging around much longer than usual. Eva knew

why: he wanted her to open her eyes, so he could catch her. He'd have to make up the time later, of course, ticking all the faster. Usually he kept moving along, trying to avoid patients like Brownell, who were always trying to engage him in conversation, but when Brownell said, "We were just having a discussion, doctor, about co-ed dorms in college," the doctor responded with an eager, "You don't say?" as his shadow stayed on Eva. It was like a knee pressed against hers under a table.

"Yes," said Brownell. "What do you think about them?"

"Well, I . . . ," he said with difficulty, and as much as he wanted to use the excuse of the conversation to stay around, he still didn't give an opinion. Eva now waited for his usual medical 'what do you think about them', and she wondered if she could, just by not opening her eyes, actually lure him into giving an opinion. If she'd been interested in him, she might have played with him. But now she only wanted his shadow to leave.

"I know what I think about them," chuckled the Dean. "And that's nothin' compared to what my Board of Trustees thinks about them."

"Cynthia," said the false angel Brownell, "I think you are a disgusting Puritan, don't you agree, doctor?" Brownell seemed sure he had the doctor on his side.

"Well, I . . . ," fudged the young doctor as Eva felt him move closer.

"Watch it, Brownell!" the Dean laughed, "Don't accuse me of being a moralist. Especially coming from you. I'm just practical, that's all. And I don't think those dorms are very practical."

"Quite the contrary, Cynthia," said Brownell sternly, "I don't think the present unisex dorms are practical at all! They are just plain," he added nastily, "ho-mo-sexual! Don't you agree, doctor?"

"Well . . . ," Dr. Fish said, and Eva, teasing, stirred as if about to wake, but kept her eyes closed.

"I'm quite sure you'll agree," Brownell insisted, "that these unisex dorms increase homosexual tensions, doctor. That's why I'm all for co-ed dorms, and the more the merrier. Provided, of course, that the dorm masters are a young married couple with children," he concluded firmly.

"Now, what does that solve, Brownell?" said the Dean.

"Well, for one thing, it gives the young people a proper model to follow—at a very impressionable age, might I add."

155

*"Is there any other kind?" said the Dean, sounding as if she were
winking at the doctor. Now she was the one who felt confident about
the young doctor's backing.*

And then, unannounced, a new silence came over the group.

*At last, Eva heard the twang of the diving board vibrating in the
sun-filled spaces beyond her darkness. And then a splash. Then,
thrilling her, the strong movement of a powerful dark force cutting
through the clear green water. The great dark fish had come! In
another moment, all the sunlight was gone again. Absolutely gone,
as Eva trembled almost uncontrollably now, because once again she
was under a large shadow.*

*The time had come for her to open her eyes! She was sure it was
safe now. Now! she told herself. Open your eyes!*

*And Eva did, only to find Althea's tall profile blackened by the sun
behind her. The black shape that was Althea standing in the
sunlight was bent over to let her hair fall forward, and then, with
large, powerful hands, she wrung out the translucent water.*

*They were all just looking at Althea now, until finally shy young
Dr. Fish said, "Good morning . . . How are you today?" But
Althea's dark shape didn't answer.*

*(Dr. Fish is furious, Althea had told Eva, because I'm feeling so
much better after my abortion. He resents my insolent good health.
He'd like it much better if I moped about with frustrated
motherhood and felt tortured by guilt. Not that he, or anybody else,
mind you, really cares about the slimy little embryo. He really
wanted me to be saddled with a brat, after a good hard and painful
labor, of course, so I could atone for my sins to his satisfaction. But
since I won't even put on a show, he's taking it personally. He's even
pouting about it, as if he were the deprived father. He'd love to
browbeat me, of course, but he's still too intimidated sociologically,
poor thing. Naturally, if I'd been a middle-class girl, or a
Catholic . . . or at least—she laughed—not so much taller than he
is . . .)*

*Althea finished wringing out her hair, and then raised up her
brow, standing up and profiling her fine, square shoulders against
the sun.*

*"How are you today?" the young doctor repeated as Althea sat
down on the deck chair and leaned back to let the sun dry her, when
suddenly, as if hearing him for the first time, Althea turned to him
and said, "What . . . ? I had water in my ears . . . "*

156

"I was just asking how you were," said Dr. Fish, young, clearly feeling more foolish by the moment, and as if having to raise his voice across a chasm.

She looked at him (and for a moment, his soul seemed suspended, floating on his face), and with a polite smile she said, "Fine, thank you," without a trace of irony. Then she leaned back again on her deck chair, looking at no one.

"You sure look fine, gal!" the Dean piped up, trying to get Althea to look over at her. But Althea didn't. She only half smiled, and the Dean persisted with, "It's hard to believe how far you've come back in such a short time. But that's the blessing of a good Yankee constitution for you . . . ," and chuckling, the Dean looked over at Dr. Fish, who returned a little smile though he was not particularly interested in the Dean at the moment. He looked hurt, thought Eva, and it amused her that despite all his disapproval of Althea's immoral recovery, he now wanted to be forgiven by Althea.

But the false angel Brownell didn't care one bit about being in Althea's good graces. He was just plain annoyed, and pretending to ignore her as if trying to go back to an interrupted conversation only he seemed to remember, he declared, "Yes, I am a moralist, Cynthia. And quite obviously," he went on, trying to lash Althea, "young people must be led to accept their proper roles and responsibilities, or they can easily become thoroughly unnatural monsters. Wouldn't you say so, doctor?" In return, Althea, the unnurturing mother, without turning to look, gave the slightest trace of a smile.

But nobody else was paying attention to Brownell now as Althea, stretched out on the deck chair before them, withdrew into herself by closing her eyes beneath the sun. And Eva knew that Althea had entered the very darkness where she'd been waiting. The secret, whispering darkness beyond all pretended meanings, where they knew they would meet.

Now, as Eva looked on with the rest, Althea was before them as if on an inaccessible altar. None of them could touch her. Not Brownell's disapproval. Not the Dean's appeal to Yankee bonhomie. Not the hurt look on Dr. Fish's frightened and sensitive eyes. She was beyond all of them now, turning even the sun's rays into more darkness, and Dr. Fish looked down at his feet in silence. He seemed to be mourning.

But then, picking up his head, he looked over at Eva as if hoping

157

to find in her eyes what he could not get from Althea's, with a pleading thin little smile that was pretending not to. But Eva felt her own eyes grow dead for him and his puppy dog's request, and he bowed his head again.

Finally, as if coming out of a reverie on her deck chair, Althea stood up, and all looked at her. But Althea, with her clear purple eyes, only looked at Eva. And Eva too rose up. Effortlessly. She stretched out her arms, and now felt strong and sure on her naked feet, as if a new pride had risen up with her. And Althea smiled at her the smile everyone had wanted. Eva, unafraid, smiled back because Althea's handsome, sun-filled smile had made her a peer, and she instantly felt the marvelous pleasure of the prideful, sun-hot darkness that was now flushing through her entire body.

Without a word, like exquisitely paired centaurs, Althea and Eva left the pool side, walking on their fine, straight limbs out toward the golf course, leaving the others helplessly behind.

That afternoon, walking towards the woods across the green fields, even as the purple of dusk came, they talked. They talked so deeply it was more like a song than a conversation, and soon Eva could not really tell who was saying what, since they were in such deep accord as one dark, powerful stream blew like one magical feminine wind through them both. A wind that knew, knew them, itself, everything, as it sailed strong and more beautiful than a Venus smile. It was speaking with Althea's voice, of course, but only at first, teaching her to find her own voice. Eva's own lost voice, which was finally saying now in its flight how she could walk in this world as nobody's whore. And when that happened, the voice was neither hers, nor Althea's anymore, but the voice of Freedom itself, with its always new and timeless wings of a true Angel, sailing like the long-haired master of all the purple fields, the same fields where she now walked with her own free and unencumbered feet, as she held Althea's hand.

THE END

But it was not the end for me.

My brain cage became flooded with the purple translucence of those fields, and my poor psyche kept taking off from where her story ended, with Eva and Althea continuing to walk away from the pool area, hand in hand, barefoot, self-contained, and above all superior.

The rest of us just looked on, minimized. Helpless.

And poor Mel, watching Althea, looked more adolescent and wounded than ever as the traces of an idiotic smile remained on the corners of his unhappy mouth like scar tissue.

Cynthia the Senatorial Dean was quiet and stoic in her rejected condition, as if she'd never seriously expected to be asked to go along with Eva and Althea, in the first place.

The one apparent exception among us was the Papist Librarian Brownell, whose face was slightly twisted to one side, concentrating itself on his nose, as if he were breathing in both his masculine contempt and his Catholic outrage through one disdainful nostril. He seemed to make it a point of not looking at them directly in his disgust, but despite his posture, I knew he felt hurt and minimized too, and that it bothered him not to be included in their elite. Maybe more than it bothered anybody else. In fact, beneath his moralizing he really seemed furious that *anybody* could consider forming an elite without counting him in, regarding him as just another one of the plebeians.

But that's what we were. All of us. Brownell too. Plebeians.

It was dusk, the pool area where we were was darkening first, as the distant fields still reflected a great deal of light, with the most light in the greatest distance, out at the shining hill with the giant apple trees. And we by the darkening pool couldn't think of ourselves as doing anything but playing the idiots. We were the ordinary citizens with the most common of values, while Eva and Althea unquestionably felt themselves the aristocrats in terms of us. We served as contrasts for them. It was our only function. And we could see it.

And then, in the transformations of that late afternoon, everything started looking Greek and timeless. Eva and Althea continued walking hand in hand, with the glancing sunlight sinking and playing off their fine strong limbs with a friezelike effect as they headed out for that brilliant little hill, which was shining like gold now, where the two titanic apple trees stood waiting for them.

159

In that distance, the apples on their branches looked tiny, godly, round, metallic and much too heavy for humans, yet light on the mighty, upraised arms of those beings that now looked like the peers of Olympian gods. They became Trees, living, animate. Not yet metamorphosed into moralizing witnesses of men, like the Tree of Life and the Tree of Knowledge. In their magnificence they were beyond that, as beyond morality as the sea and the sun, but they knew themselves. And as Eva and Althea walked closer, they even seemed to stand out against the livid sky with greater and greater animated relief, as if they had moved forward to welcome them. They even seemed to have moved closer together in their exalted anticipation, their upraised branches trembling hieratically as the glancing light played off them with the same darkening and illuminating effect that it had on Eva's and Althea's shoulders and limbs.

The Trees, trembling in their anticipation, announced that Something was going to happen on that hill when Eva and Althea finally got there. I knew it. And I knew it was not going to be easy on my nerves, nor on any of us watching. Now, everything was threatening to change in that late afternoon light.

And as I watched them walk, instead of getting smaller, Eva and Althea seemed to grow taller as they profiled against the horizon. We were the ones feeling smaller and smaller as they grew and darkened against the livid sky. And it was getting harder all the time for me to tell which was Eva and which was Althea because in the distance their dark moving figures seemed more alike with each step they took. And I was struck by how both pagan and angelic their shoulder length hair looked—just like that of those suspiciously elitist Renaissance angels of Eva's story, uncharitable and un-Christian to a fault. And what they were being elitist and uncharitable about, we all knew, was unmistakably us. And all we could do about it was watch them from our own shrinking, intensifying darkness as they continued walking across those luminous fields, toward the excitedly shimmering hill.

Up ahead, the waiting Trees stood even closer, their priestly branches raised up even higher, as if exhorting, their golden apples trembling. And they weren't thinking about us, we all knew that. We were not worthy. Not as Eva and Althea, who I was sure were thinking of us, and quite pointedly, because everything about their identical, sun-darkened movements was taking on a sense of triumph

160

and pride—pride that they were *not* us. They *knew* themselves now, and gloried in knowing that they were the ones to walk those Arcadian fields with the superior freedom of hunters, while we were the small in spirit, condemned to remain in the darkening, shrinking and rectangular area that they had left behind. I wondered if those sun-darkened faces were smiling with one and the same smile to each other now. Althea's smile.

They came near the hem of the hill, and the waiting Trees began trembling even moving excitedly as they looked down on their approaching figures, and were so close to one another I thought their branches might tangle. Suddenly I had to think back, hard, to figure out which was Eva and which was Althea, because their athletic shapes had become perfectly identical now. And neither was leading. Hand in hand, they were absolutely equals, and I had absolutely no idea which was which any more.

There was a slight indentation at the foot of the hill.

Eva and Althea began their descent into its darkness.

The ancient Trees, at the sight of this, raised up their trembling limbs even higher, as if exhorting them more urgently than ever to keep on coming, to join them, not to disappear now that they were so close.

But as they kept descending, only their heads were visible. And then not even their heads. Above their vanished figures, almost in a panic, the Trees bristled in the waning light.

Now that they were out of sight, my mind raced back to the beginning of Eva's story, when she'd waited with her eyes closed, listening for Althea's dark shape racing through the water, listening expectantly for the sound of Althea's breaking up through the surface, so that at last, she, Eva, could open her eyes to see what she wanted to call her Soul. She'd talked of a great fish of darkness coming for her, and of androgynous angels leading her by the hand out into great boulevards of light, teaching her to become angelic herself, so she could finally and truly live.

And in all the transformations, her story began sounding to me like Narcissus, but in reverse. The desired image now came out of the water to meet Narcissus, Narcissus didn't have to dive in. And Narcissus, possessed by his image, didn't die, but the opposite, became alive. Didn't drown at all, which made Narcissus think of us who expected the drowning, and smile.

But then, as their two heads began emerging at the foot of the hill, and there was no hope at all of my being able to guess anymore which was which, the story of Narcissus didn't seem reversed to me anymore. It too became transformed, as if a veil had lifted. A deceitful veil that misrepresented the true story. Norma had long ago become Eva, who was quickly becoming Althea, or enough like her that I couldn't tell if she was or wasn't Althea.

But now the differences didn't matter any more. As the two figures stepped up the hillside as if ascending great temple steps, in their sun-filled darkness they absolutely glowed with self delight at having become transformed finally into whatever it was they now were.

Somehow, what I was watching taunted the Universe, calling out for punishment that would never come. We might fear the punishment, but the two triumphant figures did not.

Then finally they were both on the hill, and the two Trees stood so close together over them that they were on the verge of becoming one Tree.

Then, beneath the hovering Trees, they faced each other, their identical figures totally dark against the luminous sky. They were exactly the same height as they looked into each other's faces for their triumphant recognition, and their profiles were identical.

And then, they kissed, twining their arms around each other's bodies. They kissed on the lips, savoring each other and themselves in the other. One was not possessing the other. Something else was happening as behind them the Trees finally fused into one giant, exalted Tree that suddenly looked like a titan god made of live silver, celebrating their apotheosis with arms that cried out ecstatically up to the sky.

I knew Eva was kissing herself as she wanted to be, and that Althea was accepting her in her new identity by kissing Eva's mouth. And they twined and twined, consummating like matches burning together at the head, becoming identical, perfectly, with that kiss, when suddenly, on that hill beneath the single, ecstatic Tree, now there was only one single tall, long-haired figure to be seen. The kiss out of which it had been born vanished, and now, facing us, emerged Eva/Althea, at last, surveying the fields from beneath the triumphant branches, and looking for all the world like a barefoot huntress.

She had her left arm behind her back, as if hidden, and I noticed the shape of a quiver filled with arrows on her hip, and then, the bow in her right hand.

Now I understood: she was ready to roam over the fields where she was total master at last, to hunt in total freedom. A freedom *we* could never have. And I also understood, at once, that the huntress on the hill would be supported in her paradise by the creatures that lived in those fields, like the rabbits, and the deer, and the birds that cried and quarreled pointlessly as they passed above.

Wherever they might be, even in the cover of the shadows, into which she could so easily see, all the hunted creatures wished they too were living in a paradise. But with their dull brown eyes they refused to see what they could not bear to believe: that they were living in *her* paradise, not theirs. And it was, unquestionably, hers, because they would not have been victims in their own.

Whereupon, we, in our darkness by the pool, all of us suddenly started howling like babies.

The huntress turned to look at us, directly, and her face became visible in the glancing light. We howled and howled, pitiably, and she smiled Althea's smile, proud and completely uncharitable. Telling us that Eva/Althea, the huntress, was not at all about to nurture us. That she delighted in our suffering. She liked it that way, and it was perfectly clear that in her new beauty, she loved nothing but herself, and that she didn't *want* to love anything else. She stood there as an idealist, and she was her own highest ideal, for only she (we all knew it) was worthy of herself. And though we kept crying for mercy and for forgiving love, we also knew that one thing she was not was Jesus.

From our hatchery darkness, as if still hoping to soften her heart, we howled and howled inconsolably, but Eva/Althea's smile kept coming back, lacerating us while she stood on the distant hill, holding her bow in her right arm, with her left still behind her.

Then, as if grown tired of our brattish noise now and wanting to silence us all, she brought forward her hidden left hand and raised it up, and it held, to our horror, a red and palpitating heart. I never saw such red before, so luminous and brilliant, applelike somehow yet unmistakably human, as the one giant Tree behind her was suddenly shaking in spasms of total ecstasy at her gesture, as if divinely proud of his daughter. So proud, it seemed ready to leave the earth and become absorbed by the heavens now that its successor had come to take its place on the Hill. Whereupon, as the Tree vanished, the sky turned blood red as if touched by the high-held heart in her savage left hand.

We, in our hatchery darkness, stopped howling, and kept very, very quiet.

From then on, it was in what we call "real life" that I found I couldn't hide from her. The cruel smiling huntress with a bow in one hand, holding up a trophy red and palpitating heart in the other, had gripped my waking mind—that is, the mind of *Muldunius Vulgaris*—like a luminous cancer.

This was because I had just received the second part of the message from the Unseen and Mysterious Forces. Not that I realized what was going on.

As to my subconscious, of course, there was no peace there either now, since my poor Secret Me was continually getting mauled down there by visions of Althea as the victim of the new Lord, the monster who'd appeared, to my dread, as bearded Mel's prosthetic delight.

I suppose, therefore, I can say that I was being Mutt-and-Jeffed by the Unseen and Mysterious Forces as they continued to soften me up for the big moment.

But, since I didn't really know what was going on, I thought I was going crazy on my own. Not, after all, something uncommon in over-wrought graduate students.

So, to try to make rational sense out of my fragmenting life, I tried to tell myself that the luminous cancer I was suffering from, that angelic and cruel huntress that now roamed the fields of my psyche at her pleasure, was really only another incarnation of the cruel shepherdesses from the Pastoral literature I must have done too much work on. It sort of made sense. Indeed, I noted, they too depended on ripping out the hearts of their adolescent shepherd lovers, however figuratively, after which they gave them nothing but grief, because they believed that their spectacularly arrogant freedom depended on it. To put it simply, the false shepherdesses (which I figured I was correctly perceiving as huntresses) took the position of "better they than me", assuming it was always *somebody* that ended up suffering.

In other words, I was trying to tell myself that the plumbing of my mind was suffering from a momentary backup and overflow of literary illuminations. Which was why, for example, I was suddenly discovering to my great amazement that our modern day golf courses descended from those Arcadian fields once spotted with wild and desperate young shepherds, crazed with grief and in need of the very best care Mel could give them. No wonder therefore, I started thinking, they saw their whole lives as nothing but pain and were forever on the verge of throwing themselves into those mirror-still ponds which now only serve as water traps. And how fitting it is that McLeod's Hospital should so prominently feature an abandoned one!

I could see it all clearly, too clearly: lovers, ponds, the cries of birds and the sounds of streams mocking the laments of the mortally wounded lovers, while not too far away, roving the fields and hunting for more red hearts, the cruel huntresses smiled Althea's smile, disdaining both the weakness of pity and the chains of love. All of which, by the way, briefly convinced me that the Nietzschean Superman could best be perceived as someone acting like a female lead out of the Pastoral literature which, I suddenly realized, had anticipated him.

However, rational as this explanation of my condition was, I never did convince myself that I was suffering from mere literature.

The day of Norma's party was coming, and suddenly all I knew for sure was that *I* didn't want to be one of those shepherds. Not for Norma, not for anybody.

So I decided not to go.

But the day came, and though my heart pumped and flushed, red and furious, "I don't wanna! I don't wanna!" I found myself going, just the same, and remembered that shepherds don't really have a choice.

Just as all the shepherds before me, I guess, I was reduced to hoping that *my* shepherdess would really *be* a shepherdess, gentle and nurturing, and not a huntress in disguise. Which, now that I think of it, is probably what the sheep always think as they trot along.

WHAT MAKES HUMPHREY BOGART SO SAD?

(at Norma's Pastoral Party)

I wished I had known that the UMFs were stepping up their preparations. It would have been a lot easier on me.

But, in keeping with their custom of never letting me in on anything directly, the UMFs—by the day of Norma's party—had me almost completely deranged.

I suppose it was necessary, but I do think it could have been made a great deal more comfortable for me.

From the day I read Norma's Eva/Althea story, I might start walking down a street all right, seeing Cambridge in its standard black and white, neo-Realismo tones, with everything looking as peacefully de-mythified as the sooty pigeons that rose and fell like ashes over the traffic. But then, with no warning, in whopping and painful flashes, the whole town would suddenly stand revealed in the fierce technicolor of until-then secretly green Pastoral landscapes. Whether I liked it or not, the sudden Cambridge was peopled by

167

prostrated suicidal lovers while cruel, red-laughing huntresses were visible darting in the wooded distance among what used to be buildings, having successfully ripped out their prostrated victims' hearts. I was even periodically confronted with flocks of white, fleecy sheep. They would start out looking like sooty cars, and then, in the revelations of the flashes, they looked as neat and clean as kids going to church, ba-ba-ing away uncomprehendingly in their willing-to-please-mother, Sunday best. They didn't know what their lament (and I) already knew about the inevitable transformations of Spring, in the stockyards of Pastoral graduation exercises, where the final lessons were about the dialectics of the predator heart.

So, the splendor of the technicolor visions notwithstanding, I always held my breath when they came and waited for them to pass. I much preferred to see dreary old, black and white, neo-Realismo Cambridge. Junky as it was, its de-mythified people tended to believe that sex, marriage and Happiness were not mutually exclusive terms, but could all go together and were even one's normal due in this world. But after a while, even when my eyes were taking in ordinary neo-Realismo Cambridge again, the painful technicolor message of the Pastoral dominated, and what I was looking at became a Dostoievskian black and white, no matter how much I resisted believing what he claimed when he saw everything in terms of masters and slaves: that the lover is namely he who willingly submits to being tyrannized by what he loves. And I could forget hoping about masters being lovers, by the way, because *they* had become mutually exclusive terms. The Pastoral message said very unequivocally: you cannot be a master *and* love, which was very bad to hear as far as I was concerned, since I had a pretty good idea of the only place where I would fit in.

Anyway, between the time I got Norma's invitation and the day of the party, the world spun equivocally a number of times between light and darkness, with me trudging along, carefully trying to make my way against the flow through all that intermittently Cantabridgian and Arcadian traffic (which was suffocatingly Arcadian as I walked along deep into Brattle Street); and when 9P.M., Saturday, finally came up at me, confronting me with Norma's door, I did the only thing I could: I rang her bell, and hoped that Eva/Althea wouldn't be the one to open it.

Feeling very much like a sacrificial lamb, I waited on her doorstep, hearing the laughter and conversation inside going around and

168

swelling like a whirlpool of Pastoral noises. No one came, and instead of being glad and taking my opportunity to run away, I found myself ringing again, because I felt ignored. And as soon as I rang, the noises inside whirled around faster and gayer and more loudly, as if trying to override the interruption of my ringing. I began to feel snubbed, miserably excluded.

Muldunius Vulgaris cried out: this is your chance! Beat it! But my feet didn't move, and as if lifted by invisible strings, my Secret Me's hand rang the bell again, for the third time, as *Muldunius Vulgaris*, sensing his doom, said: Shit. Now I realize, of course, what *Muldunius Vulgaris* (who believed in free will) didn't understand but which my Secret Me did: that if I had tried to escape, the Unseen and Mysterious Forces would have brought me back by the ear. So, with a sense of fatalism, I waited until Norma's door opened, and when it did I smiled with gratitude for its finally accepting me.

The moment it opened, I got a direct blast of party noises as Norma appeared at last, laughing pleasantly at something behind her. To my great relief, she looked Cantabridgian instead of Arcadian, and there was no visible Eva about her at all. She had her long hair up on her head rather like a Quaker lady, and she wore a yellow peasant blouse and a long, blue, roomy skirt. Nothing could have looked more maternally encouraging, more nurturing than she did as her large clear eyes beamed fondly at me and she said, "Jerome . . . !" and she brushed away a wisp of troublesome hair from her moist temple with the back of her right wrist. In her left hand, off to the side a bit, she held a long skewer with pieces of lamb, which made me think of a blissfully retired, but still sword-bearing Joan of Arc, busy at a Pastoral barbecue now that the wars were done.

She looked very busy but also very pleased, with a bright glow reddening her cheeks that I attributed to both her kitchen activities and the obvious success of the noisy party behind her.

Once again, Norma looked to me like the living image of somebody else's model wife, and I felt like a snake for all my bad thoughts. A loathsome snake. After all, I was there for immoral purposes, and now I almost felt as if I deserved to be driven off by that bountiful skewer, or to have my reptilian head stepped on. Or at least to be formally forgiven. But it was not going to happen. Evil was not recognized as her eyes became bright and dilating with totally open pleasure at seeing me at her door. It was such a generously uncomplicated, innocent welcome that suddenly I couldn't believe she and I were involved in an adulterous affair, or that the perfectly likeable woman and responsible mother I was looking at could possibly do such a thing—even have me come to her house under her husband's nose—so in my shame, I lowered my eyes, only to find a little, dark-eyed, prepubescent girl with short black pigtails staring suspiciously up at me from behind the right hip of Norma's blue skirt. Maybe Norma didn't, but the little kid seemed to recognize evil all right.

Following my eyes, Norma lifted up her right arm and looked down under her wing, and seeing the little girl, she smiled. "It's all right, dear," she said to the little girl, "I've got it. Go see if anybody wants more dip." The grave-faced, little black-eyed girl checked me over again. She had her father's eyes, and I held as still as if I were being sniffed by a mastiff. Then, off she went, and Norma looked after her fondly. I was glad we weren't introduced. Instinctively, I didn't want that little kid to know my name.

"That's Garth," Norma said, beaming and red-cheeked. "My star daughter." And she smiled, wiping her brow again with the back of her wrist. "She was in one of the stories that I didn't have you read."

"I think I remember," I said, recalling something Norma had told me about the little girl's gallant efforts to urinate from a standing position, in imitation of her father.

"She's a tomboy now," Norma said, "but I don't mind at all. I thoroughly believe they grow up to be the best mothers . . . and the best lovers. Isn't she lovely?"

"Yes," I said, and now that we were momentarily alone I found myself adding, even though I knew I was going to feel like a rutting jackass the moment I opened my mouth, "And so are you."

Norma laughed and brandished her skewer, "Any more talk like that," she said, "and I'll . . . run you right through the heart! Cooks have police powers in *my* house, I'll have you know! . . . Now for heaven's sake, dear, come in! I love to look at you, but I simply cannot stand here at the door all day. I've got my enormous adoptive brood to feed!" and with that she turned happily and I followed her in, closing the door behind me.

I noticed that the back of her yellow peasant blouse was stained, not uninterestingly, with her honest sweat, and I knew she couldn't be aware of its suddenly being erotic to me. So far, she'd treated me pretty much the way she always had before, as a bachelor friend of the playful but still proper lady of the house. Therefore, it started to get hard for me to believe that she and I had actually had sex together at my own place, just a few days ago. It made me think that maybe Norma, the one who'd been with me and called herself the "real" Norma, had actually been only a momentary aberration which had disappeared with a return to the daily and purifying routine of life with her children and enormous Ralph.

That is, I was beginning to think, with both shame and relief, and even disappointment now, that maybe this model wife was the realest Norma, after all. Maybe, during that evening, she was going to pull me aside, have a little explanatory chat with me to let me know we really shouldn't do this sort of thing anymore, to which I would nod my assent, act hurt and rejected but stoic as she tried to soothe my feelings—when suddenly, from beneath her floor-length blue skirt, there emerged a surprising live and naked foot, a touch dirty on the sole as could be expected. For some reason both she and I noticed it at precisely the same instant, and she looked up at me as if it were our own wicked secret, and with her eyes gleaming she dropped her voice, saying huskily to me, "The beginning . . . of further intimacy."

I'm sure I blushed as she added in her low tone, "Now you know . . . ," and then, grinning, she pushed up an offering from her skewer at me. "Have some lamb?"

The results were most disconcerting. I couldn't very well tell her my head was full of Pastoralia, but with that unhappy, sweating piece of lamb staring me in the face and Norma glowing wickedly behind it, with the clearest indication that I was to obediently consummate the ritual of my own destruction by taking it off the skewer with my teeth, I thought I was going to get sick. I must have changed color, because she asked, "What's the matter?" maybe a bit annoyed I was flubbing this bit of play.

"I . . . can't," I said, pleading for mercy from my hostess. "I guess I had too much for supper . . . ?"

She looked at me quizzically, then examined my face as if I weren't there. She couldn't tell by such a superficial examination, of course, what had happened to my usual perception of reality. For example, at that very moment, I was also being made uncomfortable by having her whole party looking as Pastoral as it did. It was looking more and more so by the minute, with all the groups of people sitting around the floor being engaged in discussions of ideal love and the nature of pain, even though in black and white, neo-Realismo they sounded as if they were rehashing gossip and psychoanalytic sessions.

Then, as I felt my usual beet-red coloring return, Norma said again, in a low tone but a bit more seriously this time, "We can't talk tonight . . . Later we can sneak off for a few minutes up-stairs . . . maybe . . . ," and I lowered my head, so she said, "I wish we could talk tonight, dear. But, duty calls, you know." And she added consolingly, "Tell you what. I promise you we'll have a nice heart-to-heart talk, soon. And it will be all about *your* heart," and she looked around to see if we were being observed (we were not) before stepping even closer to me to say, "vvhich I vvant to cradle in my hands . . . and drink . . . because I am a *w*ampire!"

In the Transylvanian silence that followed, she appraised me with an arched eyebrow in a splendidly unrelenting, stone-faced imitation of Bela Lugosi as Count Dracula. I felt my face drain again, until finally I managed to say, "Well . . . ," a bit courtly and apologetic, "if you do . . . please remember that I won't be able to give you seconds . . . no matter how much I might wish I might be able to of-fer them to you."

Absolutely unmoved, eyebrow still arched, she said, "Zzzatts oll right," brushing away my excuses as if I were an inn keeper apologizing about the accommodations for the Count, "I never *drink* . . . seconds. I only *drink* . . . ffirsts!"

Before that stone-faced display of *noblesse oblige* I had to admit she was admirably Transylvanian, and wishing she weren't quite so convincing, I tried to get her to smile (her eyes were dead, because she was really into it), so I said, "Jesus, Norma. You do it *too* well."

"Ssank you," she replied with a brief nod. "I've been possessed by the spirit of Dracula for three days now. I just can't stop talking like him, and it's all because of those movie revivals down at the Brattle. I'm even talking to my kids that way. . . . Of course, I'm hoping to inspire fear."

"Well," I said, "you're a smash as a vampire."

She laughed, "For God's sake, don't encourage me. I can't . . . stop . . . myself," she said slipping into Dracula's lilt again. "See what I mean? . . . Fortunately for the world, they're showing old Bogart movies now, and I can't imitate him at all. Come on," she said, taking me by the hand. "Let's get you that drink. You look as if you need it."

As she led me through the front hall she squeezed my hand. In a way, it was like high school again, except I wished she weren't squeezing my hand. I started getting very nervous about enormous Ralph, my host, who of course appeared at that very moment, almost hitting his head on the doorframe. He had a slight stoop which must have come after years of pain. All I could think of, looking at him with my hand trapped in Norma's as she led me around (I wasn't liking her for it, but I didn't have it in me to resist), was the Green Knight after he's picked up his head from the ground and put it back on his head.

I was a very nervous Sir Gawain as Norma called out to her husband, "Ralph!" implacably not letting go of my hand. He came over and she said to him, "You know Jerome, don't you?"

"Of course I do," he said, smiling down at me. "Help yourself to a drink and we'll bump into each other somewhere along the evening. Glad you could come."

He put out his generous right hand which was both warm and authoritative as well as careful of not squashing mine, and just as I took it, peering from behind his tree-sized legs, back came the suspicious dark eyes of Garth, who was passing by bearing dip and crackers for the guests, grudgingly following her mother's instructions when she obviously felt it was much more important to keep her eye on me. More than ever her eyes looked like her father's, except that his were all gigantic cordiality, while hers were suspiciousness itself.

Letting go of my host's hand, I said, "Thank you," and Norma corrected in Transylvanian, "No. No. It's 'Ssank(!) . . . you'," and she proceeded to lead me away from Ralph to the table where I was to fix myself a drink. "I'm going to have to let go of you soon, dear," she said, "so I think I'll deposit you with a group that already has somebody in it you know, and you can introduce yourself from there. It's everyone for himself in this place."

As we navigated through the rivulet spaces among the circles of people sitting on the floor, with me in tow, Norma continually smiled to the left and to the right, pausing to let up-grasping hands take pieces of lamb from her skewer, repeating, "More soon," to everyone until she had nothing left but the skewer itself, whereupon, no longer in demand, she said to me, "I really had no intention of serving it this way. It's so barbaric, and everybody's fingers get greasy, but they seem much more interested than if it comes in little paper plates with toothpicks. Frankly, I think they'd even rather eat without paper napkins, just so they can rub the grease off on their hair like in the Middle Ages, if I'd let them," and then (we had arrived at the table where I would finally get my drink) she added casually, "By the way, did you know that toilet paper only came into use about a century ago?"

"No . . . ," I said, quite surprised by the information, when at that moment, as I happened to look upon one of the groups on the floor across the room, I had the always disorienting experience of *déjà vu*. It wasn't what Norma had just said about toilet paper but the group I found myself looking at that caused it. Most of them were fancily dressed, and it was composed of some people I was sure I knew, some people I was sure I didn't, and some people I had never met, but whom I was now equally sure were familiar to me. All of them sat on the plush green rug around the enormous figure of Frank Long, who was stretched out on his side, leaning on a hip and an elbow and looking about one and one half times the size of the others.

Frank Long was the one I knew there. His supremely confident laugh suddenly rose up over the other voices at the party, which it did every now and then, cracking out like devastating rifle shots, and he looked exactly like he did when I first met him. He had the same thin-lipped, aggressive smile, his rimless glasses still had one lens slightly cracked and held in place by an heroic piece of tape (presumably from squash) and he had what looked like a scotch and water in one hand and a Havana cigar in the other. Unlike the others in the group he was not formally dressed. He wore a herringbone jacket, light chino pants and white tennis shoes, but despite the formality of the others around him he didn't look out of place. As a matter of fact, it looked like everybody else was visiting *his* place as they paid him homage, looking like the little lords and ladies of the court of Lilliput around Gulliver out in a field.

Again, Long's laugh cracked out (I wondered who was dead) and a split second later, like the echo of a rifle shot, so did Norma's husband's laugh sound off, reporting back from the next room. Even though they were in separate conversations, they sounded like they were laughing at exactly the same thing.

I'd always thought that Ralph imitated Long, at least half-consciously, out of a deep admiration for the ruthlessness which the latter practiced as if to the manner born. After all, I knew that

174

Ralph did not come from a long line of Puritan lawyers, clipper ship captains, United Fruit Trustees and Harvard Overseers as Frank Long did. But then, as I heard Ralph's laugh crack out again in the next room, I realized I was hearing exactly the same laugh I'd heard the night they both explained to me their "mushroom theory" of acquisitions of other companies. "The mushroom theory is quite simple, Muldoon," Ralph had said to me that night as Long quietly puffed on his Havana (Long, of course, was speaking through Ralph). "What you do when you buy another company, you see, is first keep their old management in the dark, and then, in the fullness of time, you *can* them!"

And again, that laugh exploded in the other room, stinking as always of metallic potency and priapic self-pleasure, while before my eyes, Frank Long smiled beneath his rimless glasses as he listened to some deferential lady tell him something or other—and I knew that whatever the particulars of their different conversations might be, the source of pleasure for the laugh I heard and the smile I was looking at were one and the same—the exercise of power, which both of them found deeply pleasing in itself.

Now I thought maybe my sense of *déjà vu* might be due to Long's being at the same party with Ralph, his twin and kindred soul. But as the potent laugh clanged out again from the other room, I was invaded by the image of a gigantic mechanical toy crocodile, thin-lipped in its smile too, just like Long. And instantly, I knew that Long, even if his laugh *had* come into the world before Ralph's, was no more the origin of that playful Leviathan laugh than Ralph, the imitator, was. The original source, which I was now faintly perceiving through the temporal form of Frank Long (ominously bespectacled and grinning thin-lipped over his whiskey glass) wasn't human at all. It was a monstrous, mischievous toy god. I was certain of that (not yet knowing why), just as I was sure that the playful monster toy—which knew only *one* game—could do whatever it wanted to with any and all of us, if it took it into its mechanical head to do so. And with no more remorse about what befell us than a mechanical monster would have, either.

And I realized that, just like me, the group sitting around Long's reclining, crocodile-smiling figure, sensed the power of the Original Form, too. But they weren't afraid. That was because—I could see by their smiling attitudes—they were a repellent bunch of devil worshipers, snobs and Manicheans, every one of them.

As I looked over what I could see of the group, my sense of *déjà vu*, instead of leaving, increased, and I couldn't understand why. I looked at the two women who sat at either end of Long, facing him with parentheses of constant, indulgent smiles on their upheld, parted mouths. They were the two people there I was sure I didn't know. But the other two people I could see, whom I was sure I'd never met, were nevertheless very familiar to me. Very oddly familiar. And the more inexplicably familiar they seemed, the more uncomfortably poignant became my sense of *déjà vu*.

One of them was a massive-backed, tweed-jacketed woman with short gray hair who chuckled manfully at whatever Long said, like a fellow executive. The other was a fortyish, slender man with bangs on his waxy forehead who smiled a lot with pink, pinch-mouthed pleasure, lowering his eyes now and then as he did so. And whenever he looked up, his large eyes showed very blue, kind of cheaply celestial, glittering like junk jewelry. And it was written all over him that he was absolutely blissful about sitting so near Long's feet.

Suddenly, the blue-eyed, pink-mouthed man with the bangs and waxy face threw back his face and laughed in a silvery staccato that instantly—I didn't know why—made me think of an explosion of birds at its peak, released with delight at something naughty permitted of Long. And just as I was telling myself that if Long had been, say, a rising Armenio-American used car dealer, the snob with the bangs wouldn't have been anywhere near as delighted by the utterance, it hit me: Of course I know him! He's the painter of the Aztec pyramid from Mel's loony art show! I was absolutely sure of it because I was getting exactly the same Light from him that I'd once mistaken for the suicidal dishrag with the neat, depressed signature!

And I even knew his name: Brownell. There was just no question about it. I was once again in the presence of the Anglophilic Librarian who surely hated the rabble for taking books from their proper places on the shelves, who was, furthermore, the faggot monarchist, Catholic convert and false angel Brownell, whom I'd once been certain would smile with obscene pleasure when given electric shock treatments.

And now, as I looked back at the tweed-jacketed gray-haired woman, damned if she didn't look like a combination of Robert Frost, Carl Sandburg, Sam Ervin and Everett Dirksen with a touch of red lipstick inside the creases of the almost lipless, administrative mouth. This was Cynthia the Dean, from Norma's story. I would have bet all the money in the world on that, so no wonder I was having *déjà vu* discomforts.

"Hey, Norma," I said, "I bet I know those people over there, don't I?" which made her smile, quite pleased as she asked, "Which ones?"

"Cynthia the Dean and Brownell, right?"

"Hooray! Hooray for Norma the woman of letters!" she said, and then gave a little bow from the waist to her own cheer before smiling at me.

"Are those their real names?"

"Yup."

"But Norma," I protested, "why do you do that? It's really very unsettling." What I was really protesting, of course, was how truly unsettling was the problem of distinguishing fact from fiction between Norma and Eva, who was reentering my mind with the presence of Cynthia and Brownell.

"Oh . . . I dunno. I just feel more comfortable, I guess. I do intend to change them before I send them off to magazines, you know," she said, and then squeezed my hand and laughed. "Come on now, don't be so serious, I thought only women were supposed to be so literal."

"So . . . *they're* real, but Eva is not . . . "

"*That* again!" she said and shook her head. "Really, it's very sweet of you to be such a sucker for everything you're told. I suppose it makes you an ideal reader, but believe me . . . most of the time it's just that I like the names, like . . . oh, Althea's. It *is* beautiful, don't you think? You'll be meeting her later, by the way. She's the fascinating girl I told you about," and with that she started leading me to Frank Long's group, saying, "Come on. I'll sit you down next to Mel, and we'll see if we can sneak off for a minute or two later. I'll signal you . . . ," she said, arching an eyebrow at me once more in the manner of Count Dracula, before adding, " . . . unmistakably."

That, of course, made my blood race, but all I came out with was, "Mel . . . ?" completely surprised. Maybe I said that, of course, because it took my mind off stealing a few kisses from Norma in enormous Ralph's own house. "Where's Mel?" I said, possibly blushing.

"Right in front of you," she said. And so he was. In the very same group I'd been looking at, but directly behind Frank Long, who was about one and a half times Mel's size.

Mel, whose mood had evidently not improved since he showed up

177

at my place, had been sulking in total eclipse back there, ignored as the most minor of moons ringing a much bigger planet. But it wasn't just Long's physical interference that had made me miss him. Actually, I'm sure I didn't spot him because he was not emitting his customary expansive social aura as a doctor and adult pillar of the community, but, quite the contrary, that of an interiorized, brooding adolescent who'd love to knock the pillars down. And just like the last time he'd showed up at my place, with his tie off and disheveled hair, there was something romantically wounded and even criminal about him. Maybe because he wasn't wearing his glasses and was puffing away disaffectedly on a cigarette, always a storm signal with him since he was a non-smoker.

I did not have to look around to know that Marcia was not in attendance. She was probably home right now, I figured, stuffing down tranquilizers and wondering what she could do to "make her marriage work", loaded with all kinds of misinformation as to his whereabouts. No doubt she was thinking he was with me, instead of with her meeting his marital responsibilities, and therefore was cursing my name along with his.

As a matter of fact, it struck me that he was looking *exactly* like he had the last time I saw him: historically, the very night of the day Althea had fired him as her doctor. He seemed to have shaved since then, but I wondered if he'd changed his clothes. I was sure he must have, of course, Mel being an incurably clean sort, but he didn't seem to have, inside, as it were.

On the night he came over, when the UMFs had used him to treat me to that thoroughly unpleasant vision of Lord Civilization, the prosthetic monster who grew out of our collective sublimation, Mel had been acting like the high priest of the cult of the monster in our midst. Mel in the vision, I mean, when the luminous giant had evolved out of Mel's skull cap, which was a rhetorical foreskin, as I recalled, while the rest of us had been down on all fours, naked and demanding Althea's blood, like the Primal Horde.

But the most obvious thing about the Mel I was looking at was that he was not being *anybody's* high priest at the moment, and certainly not Frank Long's, whom he clearly resented as everyone else paid homage to him.

For good reason. Long, I'd discover that evening, was the reason Althea had left Mel (to put it from Mel's point of view), and Mel didn't particularly like my figuring that out, either.

But as they sat (or in Long's case, lay) on that pale green rug, Long knew it and Mel knew it, and that was the situation I was being dropped into—without knowing it—when Norma took me over and deposited me next to Mel, who barely said hello to me. In fact, he didn't, and I instantly knew that whatever the trouble was, he was going to wind up demanding I go barhopping with him later, where there would be heavy drinking, foul language, and the ensuing problem of having to extricate Mel before somebody beat his brains in. Whenever Mel felt sorry for himself, he had a way of challenging the world (which he held responsible for his lost ideals) with a lot of deadpan, cynical jokes, one-liners, usually, which made him difficult to be with. Even dangerous, because the people he irritated naturally lumped one in with him. So, even as I was easing myself down, having appraised the situation, I was already wondering how I was going to manage to get him drunk enough right where we were, so as to avoid further trouble, while Norma was announcing to the group, "This is my dear friend, X.J. Muldoon, people. Now, you *will* behave and introduce each other, won't you? I must go and catch up in the kitchen."

Whereupon Brownell, completely ignoring me, piped up at her with, "Listen to *this*, Norma! It's the most amazing thing I've *ever* heard of! Our psychiatrist friend, of *all* people, is defending frigidity as a civil liberty . . . that *is* what you said, isn't it, doctor? What do you think of that, Norma? I'm on the absolute verge of changing doctors!" and he laughed his exploding, silvery laugh.

"Hmmm . . . ," said Norma, "I *was* going to go to the kitchen, . . . but if you're talking dirty, I think I'll stay a minute."

"Yes, love. Do!" said Frank Long, reaching up loose-armed from the floor and capturing her hand as he grinned liplessly beneath his fearsome, Puritanical and technocratic rimless glasses. With her easy, pleasant smile untroubled, Norma let him hold her hand, but I thought she stiffened as Long added, "We might *all* learn something."

Suddenly, I remembered the first of Norma's stories, where Frank Long had pushed Eva—that is to say, Norma?—down on the coatroom bed during a party, when Eva's only rebellion had been inertness. I couldn't help but feel she was holding still for him again as he said, "I'm afraid no one here can agree with the doctor, so we shall be requiring an outside opinion," and because others were present she smiled, quite well, though I was sure now she wanted to pull her hand away.

Now that Long was the one holding her hand, instead of me, I was finding myself paired off next to Mel down on the rug behind him and confronted with Long's enormous backside after his not having given me so much as a glance. Therefore, I disliked him with a new energy as Norma, through her smile, went into her defensive Viennese accent, "Plisss . . . ," she said, "vvvat iss zzzeee qvestion?"

"Well my dear," said Brownell, who appeared to be the harbinger of Long, "in our rather distressingly clinical discussion of love, our Dr. Fish has declared that many women do not achieve orgasm because they simply do not *want* to, out of *sheer* contrariness. Not even *clitoral* orgasms, mind you! Nothing at all!"

"Let me correct you, Brownell," said Mel, exhaling smoke as if he were already at a mahogany bar, hunched over a bourbon, "All orgasms are cranial." It struck me Mel was already talking as if he thought he was the biggest guy around, and I shuddered at the prospect of going barhopping with him later.

Frank Long, amused, laughed his rifle shot laugh at this remark of Mel's, . . . or he laughed at Mel. Mel thought the latter, because he added, directing himself at Long, "Which does not necessarily mean you have to have what we'd call a mind, you understand, just a brain."

"My dear doctor, of course!" Long said blithely before taking a puff on his Havana. "The point of our disagreement is not about what the ladies lack. I believe we're talking about some other lack, on the part of the gentlemen," and he grinned his crocodile grin right at Mel. Who was accused of lacking.

"Oh, yeah?" said Mel, "I presume you didn't know that the historical Casanova was hung like a mouse . . . Even though he was well over six feet. Like yourself, for example."

"I'm not sure I follow," Norma said, pretending not to notice the tension between Frank and Mel. "But Mel is quite right, I should think. At least about women."

"Yes and no," said Brownell. "The really interesting thing is our doctor's attitude. It seems he is actually in *favor* of women not having orgasms. Isn't it amazing?"

"If . . . ," said Mel, "they don't want to. Lots of times they don't want to, and don't know it, mostly because they are confused by thinking that they *should* want to. I simply try to help my patients find out what it is that they really want, that's all."

"But Mel," Norma protested pleasantly, as if trying to be nice to the ganged-up-upon guest though disagreeing with him nevertheless, "why shouldn't *any* woman want to? It is . . . pleasant . . . isn't it?" and the two ladies with the perpetual flattering smiles for Frank Long at the corners of their lipsticked mouths laughed in feminine agreement.

"It all depends," said Mel, holding on. "All I was saying was that many women think they're frigid, which they consider a state of sin, when they are only being proud, which I usually consider a virtue. What they are resisting isn't really the orgasm, you see, but the coercion. I just happen to sympathize with them and champion their cause."

"But doctor!" said one of the two ladies, the blond one, who was in her late thirties and wore a long, gracious blue dress that lay around her on the rug like a small pool, "what I can't understand is why *anybody* would object to being coerced into *that!*"

And Brownell the librarian laughed delightedly, giving Long a quick, conspiratorial look out of the corner of his eye. "One would think they'd be grateful, the wretches!" and Cynthia the Dean, who'd been saying nothing, chuckled along.

"I can't agree with you either, doctor," the other lady said now, whose long brown hair was also in a bun, like Norma's, making her look a bit as if she'd gotten up from a spinning wheel to come to the party. "I'm sure women like to be coerced. We even complain when we *aren't*, wouldn't you say so, Norma?" And everybody laughed, except of course for Mel, and for Norma. Who nevertheless managed to smile, immediately reminding me of her stories about Ralph's peculiar coercions.

Everyone down on the rug (I don't count myself) seemed quite intent on siding with Long against Mel, but not Norma, who now looked over at Mel with a curious new interest while he said to her, nodding at the group in general, "They're all rapists, sweetheart," at which, still smiling, she lowered her eyes. Mel, without knowing, had struck a responsive chord in her. When she looked back up at him, holding her smile as ever, she said, "Tell me, Mel. I was just wondering. Do you ever get another kind of rape? I mean . . . one where, how shall I put it . . . women are coerced *out* of orgasms?" Instantly, I felt uneasy for her, worrying she was letting too much out of the bag about her life with Ralph, but nobody else seemed to catch on. They took it to be just another academic variant on our subject. Mel, at her question, puffed on his cigarette, like Bogart at a bar table, and then, letting the smoke come out of the corners of his mouth, he said, "Why not, sweetheart? Coercion takes any form it can," which made the brown-haired lady cry out, "Why, doctor! I just thought of something! An intuition, really. I bet you don't like *The Taming of the Shrew*! Am I right?"

Mel shrugged again, "I'm not crazy about it, now that you mention it."

"Oh, dear . . . ," the brown-haired lady went on, lowering her eyelids over her brown eyes, still smiling. "Then you probably think it's the story of a rape. I mean . . . an unpleasant one," and there was a general explosion of laughter.

Norma, sizing up the group on the rug, looked over at Mel and said, "By God, you're right. They *are* all rapists! I'm off to get more food. So, if you all know what's good for you, you'll all confess your sins, or I won't give you any when I get back."

And as she went off, Long laughed. Then, turning in my direction and finally acknowledging my existence, he peered over the can of his chino pants down at me and asked, "And what do you make of all this, Mulcahy? Any opinions on the subject of the feminine orgasm?"

"None from the feminine side," I said, which made the Dean chuckle. But I must admit I suddenly recalled childhood, when my older brothers would tickle me as I laughed and laughed, not at all amused, with the final humiliation of wetting my pants while still laughing helplessly, in my fury. "Can't help you there," I added in a baritone and wondered if it could ever be anything like that for women, assuring myself it couldn't.

Long's huge face was mooning down at me over his can like a Mt. Rushmore monument. I'd never had a chance to look at it so closely before, as it grinned at me, idly having asked me my opinion on the modern subject of the feminine orgasm. In the presence of women. Unquestionably such talk would have offended Bridgid Muldoon, and maybe his own mother, too, unless she'd been some sort of renegade bohemian, out to offend. But here we were, perfectly proper in 20th-century Cambridge, passing the time with speculations about the feminine orgasm as we might have talked about local politics, with me feeling far queasier about it than the obviously confident and sophisticated Long, who probably could discuss it in French, too, and maybe had.

Yet, for all the modernity of our moment, I couldn't help seeing his Mt. Rushmore face as fundamentally that of a 17th-century Puritan's beneath it all. In a way, it was like a colossal Jonathan Winthrop's visage emerging out of the stones of the American landscape. But for all its granite, it was not dead at all, but very much alive. And strangely constant underneath changing anthropological layers like his rimless, Rationalist 18th-century glasses, which on his face soon changed him into the 19th-century spirit that culminated in the wilderness-taming, moralizing and Masonic Teddy Roosevelt (the one forever charging up San Juan Hill baring his teeth and pointing his sword, the one who'd refused to meet Tolstoy, claiming he was a pervert, who'd always looked to me like a psychopathic otter) before evolving into the present, sexually sophisticated and highly technocratic mid-20th century form of that face that now peered down at me over the can of his chino pants. I rather sensed he was even overpoweringly technocratic in sexual matters, too, and confident of results if he wished them.

And then that four-century-old face broke into an extraordinarily engaging smile, showing his teeth. It was so disarmingly engaging it took me a moment to realize he was trying to enlist me against Mel. "You know," he said, "even Freud, old Dr. Joy himself, wasn't sure what the devil women were thinking, anyway, even in his last days. Isn't that so, Dr. Fish?"

"He did wonder," Mel said out of the corner of his mouth. "Could you illuminate us here, Long?"

And Long laughed easily and I had to admit charmingly at the challenge. "Maybe they don't know themselves. I do believe that's the problem, you know. But this is also why I firmly believe that when a situation is in doubt, one should help it resolve itself." And turning to the blond lady, he said, "Wouldn't you say, my dear Mrs. Briggs, that there are times when the lady can even be seriously irritated by being asked to make the decision?"

"I should say so!" the blond Mrs. Briggs laughed, and so did the other lady, who decided to inform me with, "It may sound crazy, but all this was preceded by a learned discussion of Humphrey Bogart in *Casablanca*, of all things!"

"Exactly," Brownell said to me. "We started out wondering just what in the world is it, anyway, that makes Humphrey Bogart so sad. He's always moping around so . . . haven't you noticed, Mulcahy?"

"Muldoon," I corrected him stiffly, "X.J. Muldoon." But what an-

183

noyed me more than his getting my name wrong was having Bogart's name uttered disrespectfully by the likes of Brownell. "Well, I admit I don't know what makes him so sad, but I also admit I've always found him very appealing."

And again Long's laugh cracked out like a rifle shot. I didn't like it, since I was the target. Suddenly what I'd said had made everyone there smile (except for Mel, who was again withdrawn into himself and looking more than ever as if he were hunched over a mahogany bar with a double bourbon in front of him, getting more Bogartian by the moment as he exhaled smoke by raising his upper lip and grimacing a bit). I was flustered, and it must have showed because Long said, "I hope you'll excuse us. It's just that what you said fits in so well with what we were saying before you came. You see, I was contending that men like Bogart much better than women do."

"Maybe it's because he plays a tough guy," I said confidently, only to find it made the blond Mrs. Briggs laugh and say, "Goodness no! We *long* ago eliminated *that* theory. He's a marshmallow, I'm afraid."

"A *marshmallow* . . . ?"

"Completely," said Mrs. Briggs. "He's totally wallowing in alcoholic self-pity, now that he's lost his illusions. Why, he's fully as much a marshmallow as that other big fake, . . . you know, Hemingway, with all *his* tiresome masculine protest."

The unexpected attack on not one, but *two* of my ideals at one time aroused a sense of outrage in me that I knew I'd better not reveal at such a party. "What illusions?" I said. "I thought Bogart was supposed to be beyond them."

"Well, yes . . . ," she said, "*beyond* them, but he's still complaining about having lost them, just like the other one, Hemingway." I guess I looked incredulous and maybe dazed because she said gently, as if taking me by the hand along a difficult spiritual path, "You did see *Casablanca*, didn't you?" and, rallying, I nodded my "of course". "Well then," she said, "then you remember he's in *Casablanca* because he fought against the Fascists in Spain and the Right some other place, and now that he's lost, he's become apathetic because the world is being taken over by the Brutes, isn't that so?"

"He also lost out on Ingrid Bergman," I said, I hoped not without dignity, "who turned out to be the woman of the noble Resistance leader."

"But *exactly!*" Brownell exploded francophilically. "He's always but *always* losing out to more potent male figures, don't you see?" And having said this, Brownell beamed triumphantly at me across Frank Long, who sipped his drink with his back to me.

After contemplating the beaming Brownell for a disagreeable moment I decided to turn to Mel for help. "As a headshrinker, Mel, what do you make of all this?"

Bogartian Mel grimaced to let the smoke out through his teeth, shrugged, and said, "Sweetheart . . . some compete and lose, and then there's others that don't compete at all . . . in *any* fight for love or glory . . . as the old song goes. They're the collaborators, X.J. The list of usual suspects, and their attitude is something like . . . if you can't lick 'em, join 'em. Whereupon, if you will notice, they proceed to lick them. Respectfully and amorously, of course. Wouldn't you say so, Brownell?" he concluded, grimacing again in a most Bogartian fashion as the smoke came out.

I must admit, Mel shocked me, talking like that. After all, Brownell had been, and maybe still was, a patient of his. I was quite sure of that, so I raised an eyebrow at Mel. He wasn't being very medical, to say the least. But Mel merely shrugged and raised another eyebrow right back at me before turning away, wordlessly saying, 'Tough. So I'm not perfect.'

If there was any doubt before, there was none now. Romantically disaffected Mel in his fight for love and glory, to refer to the pertinent song in *Casablanca* (and I could practically hear it: "It's still the same old story/ a fight for love and glory") was on a collision course with the Brutes and their satellites. That is to say, with Long and Brownell. Brownell, however, sniffily tried to disregard Mel's roundabout way of having called him, I'm forced to say, a cocksucker in public, while Frank Long, amused, smiled in crocodile fashion above the rim of his highball.

He knew perfectly well, of course, that he was the real target, not Brownell, and it obviously entertained him that Mel was spoiling to get at him. It seemed to make his drink taste better. And obviously, too, he was enjoying torturing Mel, accomplished by his simply being there, though I still couldn't figure out why this should be so. Or why, for that matter, Mel couldn't resist hanging around to take pot shots at Long and his followers, only to come off the worse for it.

Long turned over a bit, and, giving me his disarmingly friendly smile along with the honor of his full attention, he said, "Let me bring you up to date, Mulcahy," and the smile and his personal attention were so concentrated that I almost didn't mind his getting my name wrong again. "We're contending that Bogart is a kind of surrogate Holden Caulfield for post-adolescent men, and that, as the bested lover, he really appeals to the bested adolescent in us. Furthermore, we think that his tough guy posturing is no different from the prep school boy's. You see, Holden is forever using dirty words, although he's an awful little puritan, when you get right down to it. Actually, you know, Holden admits he wants to erase all the dirty words from walls all over the world so he can protect his little sister, who . . . for all we know, is ten times tougher than he is. But then again, she probably doesn't have the same fears of inadequacy," and he laughed. "What he really wants to protect innocents from, of course, is from life itself, which is much too rough for him."

"*Much* too rough for him," repeated Brownell, smiling at me.

"Yes, you see," said Long, "we've also come to the conclusion that poor Bogie is really the seventeen-year-old hero of *The Sorrows of Young Werther* in very thin disguise, because what is really making him so sad is that Ingrid Bergman, charming as she found him, also found it quite acceptable to leave him for another man. Can you go along with us there?"

His literary synthesizing put me back some. I wanted to feel it was my territory. "Yes . . . I guess so . . . ," I said.

"Of course you can!" said Long cheerfully. "Why, just think back to the *Maltese Falcon*. It's exactly the same thing. The poor fellow is forever being betrayed by the woman he loves. She always turns out to be the murderer in the end, or some such. Isn't that so? Why, it's no different than the Chivalric romances, with the Castle ladies playing games with the young, idealistic knights."

"Yes . . . Pastoral literature is like that, too," I found myself observing, partly because of all the Pastoralia in my head and partly because I badly wanted to cut some sort of figure other than that of a dunce.

"Oh . . . ?" said Long, receiving what I'd said with a smile that could identify me at any moment as a braying pedant, should he choose to. I must admit, his smile was so threatening to me that I felt I had to protect myself. After all, Mel was an ordained psychiatrist, and Long thought nothing of using Freudian theories on him. For all I knew, he was also knowledgeable about Pastoral literature. So, suddenly, as I said, "Sure . . . ," I felt as if I were trying to pass an exam, one on which the acceptance of my manhood depended. "You see, the Pastoral lover is always complaining about how his true love went wrong . . . ," and I smiled, while a pause occurred during which Long continued to scrutinize me, so coward that I am, to curry his favor I instinctively added, "like Bogart . . . " Whereupon Long smiled, and then nodded his acceptance of my gift to him: my pride. I felt shame, knowing I'd sold out to ward off his attack, possibly even his laugh in front of others. And I assumed he knew it too, Long being a man of power who now behaved toward me as if he had given me, the petitioner with the peace offering, a place at his table by brightly welcoming me with, "Well, then! Splendid! You agree, too! Now that you mention it, I *can* see Bogart as one of those kvetching (the word was loaded for Mel with Long's disdainful pronunciation) little Pastoral fellows perfectly well!" and his laugh fired off a salvo at my contribution as he treated me to a moment of near peerdom with the lordly glint of his eyes. Now I felt I couldn't look at Mel, but in my shame I stole a peek, only to find he was puffing away, having paid no attention at all to what I'd said. For which I was grateful.

"Well, *I* don't agree!" said Brownell. "I don't think he's kvetching because he's lost Ingrid Bergman, one *bit*! I think it's because he's found out he's not potent enough to satisfy her, if you want to know the truth. Otherwise, why in the world would she have left him?"

"Wait a minute," protested the blond Mrs. Briggs. "I happen to find him charming. Let's not go *too* far."

"But so did Ingrid, love," said Long. "All the young Werthers are charming, unquestionably, and even deserving of pity, unless the Guineveres are completely hard-hearted bores. But I'm afraid their only function is to be played with by the ladies, like charms on their bracelets, if not like lap dogs, which is why Bogart is yipping, and pretending to bark. Actually, poor Bogie is as jealous as a Sicilian, without the capacity to strike back, of course." Long was looking over at Mel now. "And this is what ultimately makes him so flattering to women, enough to be kept around, something like a page, I think . . . and also what makes the ladies prefer grown men in the end. You know, I believe Bogart is *the perfect* Oedipal young man, the lamb in wolf's clothing, of course. Wouldn't you say so, doctor?"

Mel shrugged, unimpressed, "What else?"

"Yes," I said, trying to rejoin Mel, "isn't it a matter of degree?" Mel, however, gave no sign of gratitude.

"*There*, Mulcahy," said Long, "is where we disagree with Dr.

Fish," and Brownell twinkled at me, raising his eyebrows about the "we". I tried not to show my distaste for him. But it was hard, especially as I was remembering my irritation with his loving Aztec pyramid picture at Mel's loony art show, back when I first detested his smug, faggotty gargoyle of a signature for presuming that I, the onlooker, shared his values. But, of course, I didn't want him to think I disliked him for being a faggot when the truth was that I disliked him for being an Aztec.

"Are you trying to tell me," said Mel with melancholy wryness, "there *is* something else for a young man to be?"

"I sure am!" said Long, and Mrs. Briggs, as the interested Eternal Feminine, leaned forward to say, "What *could* you have in mind?"

"Well," Long grinned "for one thing, my sort of man would never *kvetch* . . . begging your pardon, doctor. And he would definitely recognize the notion of True Love as a maternal conspiracy to keep men under control. A crippling fantasy playing to infantile weakness."

"You mean," observed Mel, "you have in mind . . . a man *not* of woman born, somehow? Otherwise, I don't see how he would escape some vestige of the Oedipal complex."

"I have an idea, doctor!" said Brownell brightly. "Perhaps he could be a product of reverse parthenogenesis! A man born out of man, and therefore *completely* masculine. The ultimate masculine! Perhaps we shall have to wait for the laboratories to give us this ideal."

"Dear me," said Mrs. Briggs, "I don't find this attractive at all."

"Now that you mention it," Mel said, "It does sound kind of repulsive, doesn't it? I mean, it either sounds futuristic, or like some muscle man ideal out of the weight-lifting room at the Y.M.C.A. Kind of the same thing, somehow . . . isn't it? I have to admit, Long's and Brownell's ideal male isn't appealing to me either, Mrs. Briggs, but to each his own." And Long laughed at this sally.

"I don't think a monster is necessary," he said. "Just a young man who thrives on battle more than he does on the peace of the maternal bosom, which is the source of Bogart's lament, isn't it, doctor? My proposed hero's secret, you see, shall be that. Being out of the Oedipal fog, he shall also be totally beyond jealousy, which is an utterly childish thing. And he would also be totally undaunted by the fact that a woman can love any other man, mostly because he would be confident, of course, that he could conquer *any* woman, since it turns out that there are no neo-Platonic reserve clauses that are binding on this earth."

"Oh, really?" said Mrs. Briggs with a trace of annoyance slipping into her tone. "And what, pray tell, is it that makes him so sure of himself?" Beneath her smile, she obviously didn't like Long being so sure of *him*self. I watched her closely now.

"Well, love," Long said airily, "my boy would at least be unusual, wouldn't he? That should give him some sort of special chance with the ladies," and he laughed, which now Mrs. Briggs didn't seem to like either, which raised my curiosity about them some more. "After all," Long said, "the most common garden variety of lover is the sensitive, idealistic youth, whatever his age . . . why, I dare say most ladies would feel naked without one around somewhere. But you will agree, I'm sure . . . that the ladies always leave them, some time or other in their careers, to go off with the bigger boys." And smiling, he looked at her so directly that she seemed forced to lower her eyes. Then, perhaps a bit more quietly than she cared to sound, she said, "But they don't always stay with the bigger boys," and then she looked up again, adding, "They often choose to go back, all by themselves." And she smiled a touch acidly.

But at this defense of the feminine choice, Long only laughed again, and now, from watching her face I was sure that there had been something between them as he said, "Do you call *that* choice?" and he laughed again. "Well, if you like, it's a choice. But it's been my experience . . . hasn't it been yours, love? . . . that they only go back when they think they're being mistreated. Haven't you noticed?" And I noticed that around Mrs. Briggs' smile, her cheeks were stiffening progressively as Long went on with, "You see, it's all because, when all is said and done, the very ladies who are so fond of talking about True Love really know the truth all along. I mean, the truth about True Love . . . even if our Oedipal young men can't face it without, well . . . without sometimes quite going to pieces." And he shrugged at her and smiled. "Which makes the ladies lose even more respect for them."

"I don't think so," said Mrs. Briggs. "I don't think that women lose respect for someone with delicate feelings."

"No?" Long said, and laughed. "Then why is it that after pacifying the shattered youths, they still find themselves so interested in the bigger boys?"

That last, I was certain, was a low blow. Mrs. Briggs looked at him for a moment, still maintaining her smile, as I kept wondering what her history with Long might have been, and how the historical Mr. Briggs must have taken it. And while she kept looking at him, Long said, "They *do* find themselves still interested, don't they?" and finally, breaking into a defeated conceding smile, Mrs. Briggs said, pretending to be amused, "You *are* a wicked person," but then she added, "However, your proposed hero doesn't sound very romantic to me."

"Really, Peg!" Brownell said to Mrs. Briggs, "tell the truth. Who would you rather have for company: an infant who is upset because his mommy doesn't live for him and him alone . . . flattering as that may be, dear, or somebody who can live in this un-Platonic reality of ours without hating you for it?"

Mrs. Briggs gave Brownell a perfunctory little smile of admission that went down a little at the corners of her full mouth. There was a touch of sourness to it, as if she were tasting medicine. Very odd. But next she smiled rather good-naturedly about it, and she said to Brownell, "Must I tell the truth about which I'd prefer? . . . May I not?" and she fell silent.

Then, to my surprise, the other brown-haired lady who'd been going quietly along with everything until now, protested with, "Well, he doesn't sound very romantic to *me*, either," whereupon Long turned on her with all the confidence of his enormous body. Despite his rounding on her as if to put down a minor rebellion, she held her ground by keeping her face up, as he said, "I'm surprised *you* reject it, dear . . . ," and he smiled. "But, 'tis true. He's no more romantic, I suppose, than the fellow who tames the shrew and makes her like it, which is surely the opposite myth of Chivalric or Pastoral literature, right, Mulcahy . . . ?" he said over at me as if I were one of his seconds, like Brownell, while still looking at her. She continued to keep her face up, but seemed to be having difficulty as Long said, "And yet, as I recall, you told our Dr. Fish . . . or you implied it anyway, that you not only found that particular form of rape not only charming but," he added, "rather satisfying?" At which, her eyes darkening, she gave Long a very nasty look, meant only for him to see, which lasted barely an instant. Then she lowered her eyes, and sipped her drink.

There was now a quiet pause on the rug where we all sat circling Long. I wasn't at all sure what was happening. I mean, I was, though I couldn't prove it in court, but I could swear Long had just whipped

190

the women back in line for challenging him and his "ideal young man" notion, and now Brownell was keeping an eye out for Long to see who else moved, and needed knocking down. In our midst, Long was looking into his drink with a half smile, letting Brownell, who had his head up and eyes bright, play the part of one of these African birds that live on the backs of rhinos. Brownell looked thrilled by Long's having disciplined the womenfolk, which didn't seem to include Cynthia the Dean, herself an amused spectator who circumspectly held the silent, cracker-barrel philosopher's chuckle inside the bosom of her tweed jacket for now.

I badly wanted to challenge Long, but I couldn't think how. I hadn't especially liked the two ladies before, but now that they'd apparently been whipped, in my presence, I was furious, and furious at my own silence, because the longer it went on, the more it became a confirmation of Long's lordship of the rug. Long looked to me like the kind of total bastard for whom it is not enough to assert himself over his enemies. He enjoyed ritually humiliating his allies, too, like the two ladies who looked quite chastened now. It was as if he found it necessary to regularly let those who sided with him know they were not his equals. Whatever the two women had had to lump, in public, they'd had to do it with a smile, and quietly.

Brownell, his blue eyes twinkling on his waxy face, kept on looking around. The lookout bird was such a joyous helpmate I didn't think he would have minded even if Long had capriciously decided to give him a public whipping, too. Of course it wasn't about to happen. Like my mother said, he "knew his place", and wasn't about to step out of it. But I was getting more and more annoyed with how much the little bastard enjoyed Long's power. It was lighting up his snobby and cynical pink little smile as he continued to look around to see if anybody else dared take the field against Long, savoring every passing moment that no challenger appeared.

Even though I knew the answer, I kept asking myself how come Brownell felt edified while I felt humiliated, as I began considering emigrating to another rug, grumbling about Long with my tail between my legs because I was sure nobody was going to stand up to him, including, unfortunately, me.

But then, from next to me, up came Mel's voice, sounding miraculously nasal, irritating and wheedling. "Hell, I don't know, Long," said Mel, his voice climbing cantankerously as he took the field. "The more I think about it, the more your ideal sounds to me like a stud fantasy right out of the Y.M.C.A. weight-lifting room. I think Brownell here is right about its being the ultimate masculine. I mean, the whole thing does sound kind of familiar . . . you know, like those beef cake muscle man magazines . . . which women don't buy, of course. They're aimed strictly at men of a certain persuasion. Do you know what I mean . . . ?" Everyone was looking at him now, with disbelief and apprehension, but Mel, looking at nobody, puffed on his cigarette and added, "As a matter of fact, I find the whole thing a distinctly authoritarian and, well . . . a frankly *canine* . . . vision of sex. I mean, like homosexual dog behavior, you know . . . when the bigger one growls the smaller one into holding still." And then, after another puff, he added, "Do you people know what I mean? . . . I suppose boys' boarding schools are like that, too, sometimes . . . although I never went to one myself. But I hear it is from a lot of my patients."

A silence followed.

Brownell, stiffening, looked as if he'd been slapped across the face.

Long, however, tightening his smile, now seemed to welcome the challenge. Then, as if measuring Mel, he said, "One of the things I've noticed about your guild, old boy, is that in the end you always accuse people of some abnormality or other. Usually homosexuality, as a matter of fact . . . ," and he laughed, "which, for all the air of scientific objectivity that exudes from your utterances, leads me to think that you fellows are really purveyors of a very ordinary . . . and very . . . middle-class . . . notion of morality."

Being called middle-class, however, didn't silence Mel, who protested, "Please . . . ," sounding pointedly Yiddish as he raised up the palm of his hand to perish a thought. "*I* should criticize . . . what *you* and *Brownell* consider . . . aristocratic *sensibility?*"

Long grinned at him from behind those rimless glasses and I started wondering what he was going to do or say next to lash Mel into line, ideally with an inaudible whimper, like the two ladies.

Mel, waiting, just sat there, not looking at him or at anybody, puffing away and letting it be known that maybe the ladies showed it when Long let them have it, but his own feelings weren't as tender as all that.

Then, just as it seemed Long was about to speak—and maybe kill—he noticed something over Mel's head that interested him much more, and his laugh cracked out again, triumphant. Mel, still not looking at him, pretended to be impervious, but Long's laugh made him blink, once.

Cheerfully, triumphant, Long now began his six and a half foot rise up from the rug, a humbling spectacle that Mel ignored as Long said, "You will excuse me." He was decidedly acting as if he'd had the last and victorious word with Mel, who clearly sensed it, but who so far seemed unable to figure out what this last word was (any more than I could, yet) and now Long, up on his feet, was looking over everyone's head at the front door. Mel, who continued puffing away as if he couldn't care less what it was that had made Long disregard him as significant, was now having trouble not showing his nervousness.

The two ladies, from their sitting, sidesaddle positions on the rug, had picked up their heads, too, and peering around people's legs, craning their heads, also looked at the door. Then, having seen who was there, they looked mutely at each other before exchanging brief, somewhat wry half smiles over what was removing Long from their company, and then they broke off their eye contact to look down at their feet, or the back of a hand, withdrawing their egos.

I also turned to look, wondering now if Mel had actually known all along what it was that had made Long act so decidedly as if he'd been the winner, the man with the last word and the lord of the field.

Finally, through the motion of people, I saw who the devastating last word was in their contest: Althea. Althea Stanton, tall and pale as some sort of night-blooming white flower, stood at the doorway with her gathered-up black hair framing her face, wearing a white blouse that closed at the neck.

She seemed ghostly anxious, looking for someone, and very like a 19th-century portrait, except that her strikingly still face was as sensual in its anxious excitement as no such portrait I had ever seen.

She was surprisingly beautiful at that moment. Everyone glancing at her responded to it, and then looked away, a bit awkwardly, as if they had not expected to come across such a thing as beauty that evening, and didn't know quite how else to react except through hiding.

I don't think she knew how beautiful, how dramatically blooming she was as she stood there. Maybe she'd never been so before that night, and maybe never would again, and I couldn't tell *why* it was that she was, but I could tell she wasn't anywhere as concerned by her impact upon us as she was by finding whoever she was looking for. Which made her beauty so completely without the self-awareness of narcissism that it seemed almost otherworldly, and I, too, found myself looking away, not because it was rude to stare, but because the fact of her passionate beauty embarrassed me, as it did the rest of us, like a breach of decorum.

So, now that I wasn't looking at her, but at Mel, I noticed he seemed extraordinarily bitter, and I gathered he'd stolen a confirming peek, too.

Across the way, Long was now striding through the room like a titan, but strangely keeping out of her field of vision. And he was smiling, cruising above the heads of others, not going toward her but toward the table where the drinks were fixed, while Althea, staying at the door, continued looking in, trying to find that someone I knew for sure, now, was Long. He was already playing with her, grinning through his rimless glasses as he poured himself a drink, looking over and not calling her as she finally launched into the room, still not in his direction. All of her tall, long-skirted, billowing-sleeved figure emanated an aura of purposeful, feminine and even fated silence as she continued moving without seeing him. I thought she might be wondering if she'd been stood up.

She came to a halt. Then, as she scanned the faces before her, her purple eyes fell upon me, stopping for a moment, her full mouth slightly parted. And I froze.

At that moment, Mel turned around, and when his eyes met hers, he blanched. I could see Long across the room, looking at both of them, grinning. Mel knew he was, too, and this time, Mel not only felt the lash, but showed it as she turned away, because he wasn't Long.

Music started playing in the other large room, and Ralph emerged from it, and went to stand next to Frank. Then he said something to him which made them both smile (not laughing out loud, perhaps because it would have made it easier for Althea to find Frank) and then, with Althea still looking, both of them turned their backs and went into the room where the music was now playing.

I felt a new presence over my left shoulder.

I turned, looked up, and it was Norma, her clear gray eyes a little bigger, a little brighter, like pin wheels given to expanding, as if something about Althea made for contagious excitement. Norma's standing there made me instinctively get ready to get up on my feet, as I wondered if this was the moment when she'd want me to follow

194

her somewhere to be alone, as I virginally hoped it was not. My legs, I discovered, were asleep. But they would have tried to move if Norma signalled, even if I feared disastrous results, such as toppling over on the other people, turning my ankles and screaming in pain.

"That's Althea," she whispered, her eyes dilating more, and she turned to smile most personally at me. "In a little while, I want you to meet her." And then she laughed, "I'm afraid she wouldn't register on anybody right now." And sure enough, Althea began moving across the room, drifting like a ghost magnetically drawn to the room where the music came from, oblivious to everyone she passed, although everyone was far from oblivious to her. It was like a breeze ruffling everyone as the tone of the whole party's voices changed and freshened, like the freshness that comes with the darkening sky before a rainstorm. Norma looked after Althea, and then said to me, "She's a lucky girl," and we were overheard by the two ladies down on the floor who looked up at Norma and agreed, in an unspiteful way. To my surprise, they agreed without seeming jealous, the way men might be, like Mel obviously was. But, instead, in the presence of Althea's phenomenon, the ladies seemed willing to play the part of discreet witnesses, even of helpers if need be.

Then, as Althea vanished into the music room, Norma said, "Oh, well . . . ," and then, speaking to the ladies, "Come on, everybody. There's dancing in the other room, and no more grub is headed this way," and she put her hands down to help the ladies up to their feet. As she pulled them up, I helped Mel up too, and as he rose he finally said what I'd been expecting all along, "Let's you and me go for some drinks after this. What do you say?"

I didn't say anything as Norma was pulling me by the hand, leading our entire group of stragglers single file into the other room. Her hand was very lively, warm, almost twitching like a bird's wings, softly exploring the inside of mine and I held it gently, and when we stepped across the doorway she gave me a very bright look which meant: Soon!

It wasn't flattering to know that the aphrodisiac wasn't my presence, but Althea's, as Norma now seemed to be scouting the situation for our getaway.

In the dim light of the music room, several couples were already dancing, and the rest of the considerable crowd ringed the walls, like sea gulls and seals on rocks, watching the few dancers. Norma caressed my hand. No one, I figured, would miss the busy hostess in that situation, and no one would miss me, either. I didn't think six or seven people knew I was there in the first place.

And then, sliding onto the floor with the other couples, came Long and Althea, getting everyone's attention.

The moment they began dancing, they took on a fluid grace that was striking because neither had it when they walked. She certainly hadn't seemed the ballroom dancing type, nor had Long, who now smiled with total confidence, moving her to the soft lilts and glides of "The Way You Look Tonight." It was strange, almost otherworldly, to see her 19th-century beauty in his arms, her senses so obviously aroused yet so oblivious to everything around her, yet moving so gracefully. I was sure she could only dance so well because she was so docile in his arms. As for him, he was far from oblivious to the crowd, and anything but lost in a dream as he pivoted her and even dipped her slightly in front of Mel. Long, I was sure, was holding her so that Mel could watch her face (and eat his heart out), which had its eyes closed, and once or twice even seemed to drain to a nearly deathly pallor after an almost imperceptible spasm following Long's kissing softly on her long, white neck.

Long, the complete master, after showing off his trophy, moved away, and I saw that from across the room that Ralph was looking on, too, and grinning from two heads above the others around him. But I noticed he didn't keep his eyes on Frank and Althea. Instead, he looked right at Norma, as if she had suddenly caught his predatory interest.

I didn't know whether Norma noticed her new admirer or not as she looked admiringly after Frank and Althea and said to me again, "She *sure* is a lucky girl."

"Why?" I said. "Long's a complete bastard, isn't he?"

But without looking at me, Norma said, "You wouldn't understand." Despite her growing excitement from watching Althea and Long, I thought she was beginning to lose interest in me, maybe because she let go of my hand as she let herself be absorbed by the spectacle. She smiled, completely unselfconscious beside me, as Long kissed Althea's sensitive, white neck again, which she left exposed to him and closed her eyes.

Poor Mel was transfixed next to me, and out of compassion I said, "Want to go to the other room for a drink?"

Mel looked at me and smiled pallidly the way, I'm sure, knights must have smiled when they suddenly wanted to go out and find dragons to kill or be killed by, and then said, "I don't know about the other room, but what about Somerville? Want to go there, for the waters?"

The very idea of going to Somerville, Mass., for the curative waters was more than I could face serenely. Barhopping in Irish North Cambridge was already bad enough, since the chances of getting beaten to a pulp were excellent, especially with Mel being in the mood he was in. But going to the Italian bars of Somerville, where it had a way of getting low-grade Mafioso out, and quickly, was simply out of the question, and I was about to tell Mel to forget it when I caught, out of the corner of my eye, another enormous male dancer gliding around Frank Long and Althea. For an instant, it was as if Long and Althea were moving before a mirror. But then the motions began to vary, as if the race of giants were splitting to multiply, and now, *two* like-sized couples were out there, because it was Ralph out on the floor, with Norma in his arms.

She held him tightly, with her eyes closed as she smiled, pliably, and Ralph bent down and whispered something to her. With a snap, she threw her head back to look up at his grinning face with her eyes wide, her surprised mouth still smiling while her eyes scrutinized him for his intentions. For a moment she seemed fragile and on the point of trembling, and he said something else to her, with his mouth now touching her ear. Then, after she nodded, they separated and walked off the dance floor.

I didn't like the look of it, at all.

The song had ended, another started, and Long and Althea also left the dance floor. He deposited her in a chair, and then walked away, leaving her there, to wait. No one even attempted to talk to her. They simply glanced over at her. She seemed to be in suspended animation, to be resumed when and if Long returned.

So was I.

Anxiously, I started looking around to see if either Ralph or Norma were in the room, but, of course, they were not. Mel gave me a shrug and a half smile, and he said to me, "I do believe our host and hostess are trying to put some purifying obscenity back in their marriage."

I didn't like Mel for saying so, but I kept my mouth shut.

Only ten minutes later, Ralph showed up again, alone. Spotting me, he came my way, smiling with a rather washed-out satisfaction, and when he was next to me, he said, "Oh, yes. Muldoon. Having a

197

good time?"

"Yes," I said.

"*Good*. Can I get you a splash of anything?"

"No thanks," I said, and he patted my shoulder and moved on, after one more hostly smile. I still couldn't figure out if he knew about me and Norma, and whether he was playing with me or not. Mel said, "It wouldn't be the same for them without us, for any of them. I feel used, don't you?"

"I'm going to use your head in a minute," I said, and he grinned. He wanted to fight somebody, I realized, and I began to suspect that if he was going to do it, he figured it was safest to fight a friend.

I kept waiting for Norma, but she didn't reappear for another ten minutes herself. And when she did, her mood was not at all like Ralph's. Her hair was combed in place, she had reapplied powder to her face, and her eyes looked smaller and a touch swollen. One thing was clear: she was no such thing as romantically aroused anymore. In fact, rather than blooming, she looked tight, knotty and angry, despite the quick smile she gave me when she saw me. "*There* you are!" she said, and came at me, once more, with the aggressive Radcliffe Forward Lurch.

"I wondered where you went," I said, and her new smallish eyes gave me a bitter look. Ralph was striding slowly back into the room, on his way to the kitchen, and took the opportunity to give us both a sociable wave. As he passed, Norma held her small, hard smile with a hatred for him so pure it rather frightened me. And as soon as he was gone, she said, "I'm going to call you tomorrow. I've got to be alone with you, soon," and then she smiled in a way that might have been enticing if she hadn't been so bitter the moment before. She now reached up from under, took my hand and squeezed it, and smiled on at me in what I'd havė to call a congratulatory manner for the favors she had determined to grant me in her rage at Ralph. But apparently I didn't respond well enough, because she said, "What's the matter? A little frightened?"

I shrugged and smiled, and she said, "Don't be," and going back into her Count Dracula accent, arched eyebrow and all, she said, "I told you . . . ve vould have a leettle talk . . . about . . . your heart."

I laughed. "Do you promise not to drink it up?"

"A wam-pire promises . . . nothing . . . ," she said, stonefaced and Transylvanian, "except . . . to call." This time, despite my efforts to smile, I must admit I found her nowhere nearly as charming as before. I think she knew it, because she lowered her eyes, acknowledging it hadn't come off. And, still holding my hand, though nowhere nearly as aggressively, she whispered to me, "I can't tell you how I loathe him. He's a pig . . . he takes every opportunity to . . . ," and she didn't finish her sentence. Instead she added in a blurt, "I'll call you," and without looking at me, maybe because she couldn't at the moment, she left me.

Mel, who'd been standing just a few feet away, now looked at me in a way that showed we didn't have many secrets from each other anymore. "Shall we be off?" he said, and I nodded.

We went to get our coats, and found Long was there, next to the closet, with some lady I had not been introduced to. The lady knew Mel, however, and seeing him, she said, "Thank goodness! Doctor . . . do come here and help me with this horrible man."

Stopping in his tracks, as if shot by an arrow, Mel looked at me and I decided to leave him to his fate and get both our coats. If he couldn't extricate himself, I was going to leave without him. From inside the closet I heard the lady say, "This dreadful man, doctor, has the most ghastly definition of love I've ever heard."

"Does he?" said Mel. "I'm not surprised."

"I'm sure the doctor has heard enough of my theories for one night," Long said, excusing Mel, as unaggressive as a boxer sharing a locker room with a defeated adversary.

"No, no," the lady said, "I want you to hear this one. He says that love makes the world go round, because it's wanting something someone else has."

"Offhand," said Mel, "that's not . . . extraordinarily . . . nauseating . . . for him."

"But he says that what we want from the other person is whatever they don't really want to give. Isn't that dreadful?" And the lady laughed. "Aren't you going to chastise him? I mean, he totally refuses to think of love as the desire to give."

"Dear doctor," Long said, "you have my permission not to get involved. I'm not even sure *I* want to be," he added and as I handed Mel his coat, I saw through two doorways, into the living room that Norma was passing Ralph, chest high, without looking at him, while he smiled down at her. It therefore struck me, according to the definition of love I'd just heard, that Ralph had successfully loved Norma, and I instantly felt wildly jealous. I admit it. I admit it. I felt horribly jealous, constricted in the chest and unable to hold still, even though Norma obviously hated Ralph, my smiling host, who now looked at me as I slipped on my coat and treated me to a little nod and a wave of his fingers.

"But doctor!" the lady pressed on, clearly in the early stages of her flirtation with Long, "are you really going to leave me with this monster? He even says that what we want from other people is whatever they consider most important, like their pride . . . or their liver, for all I know. Whatever they value most. Or do you think he's right, doctor?"

"Who knows . . . ," said Mel. "Maybe."

"How horrible!" the lady said, not horrified. "Then you *too* are a Cannibal thats needs Christianizing!" and she laughed.

Mel looked at the lady, smiled and said, "Or . . . maybe, the other way around. Yes. Definitely the other way around, in my case. Now, if you'll excuse us, my friend and I are going some place safe . . . like the uncomplicated Land of Odin Bar and Grille."

Althea killed Frank Long a very few weeks after that party. Yet, when I heard about it over the radio, I admit I wasn't surprised.

As I think back on it, what should have surprised me had to do with the Light. Or rather, its complete absence during the whole party. Even though Althea and I had been brought together under the same roof by the UMFs, I didn't get a single blink all night.

Which was, I now understand, *precisely* the point the UMFs were making. The Light was not on, because of Long.

The UMFs had wanted me to see this, of course, so I would be able to understand what she was to do to Frank a little better. And particularly so that, when the time came and it seemed like all Mankind was rolled up into one outraged and steaming Minotaur bellowing deafly for her upright head, *somebody* would be spiritually evolved enough to fully experience the Light of her soul with his own. Because *someone* had to pick up the full purity of her humanity, or our species would cease to deserve even the optimism of the nomenclature.

But, as I left that party, it was very hard for me to understand that everything—and I mean everything, including my jealousy and my distaste for Norma—had been arranged by the UMFs for the sake of my spiritual evolution, which, deep down and unknown to me, was

200

already pretty far along.

And if you'd asked me about women, I still would have had to confess that as far as I could see, women were the opposite of people—especially when in their manipulative and unreflective cynicism they followed their instincts and acted like women.

Which is to say, as I left the party with Mel, I was lapsing into finding relief for my spiritually parching jealousy by drinking the blackest waters of the most unevolved misogyny imaginable. The kind I've only known in Irishmen and, to tell the truth, in the most radical of Feminists.

(I had no idea my next contact with the Light would come in a week, again through Norma.)

MISOGYNY

Anyway, when we left Norma's party, we really weren't too sure where we were going as Mel did the driving, submarining through the Cambridge night, leaving residential Brattle Street behind.

Not that it had come out in the open yet, but he knew that I was quite aware of his unmedical feelings toward his patient Althea by now, and of course, also of his jealousy.

We'd been silent, tunneling along, when he said, "That Norma friend of yours. She reminds me of Marcia."

"How's that?" I said, calmly assuming that whatever he was going to say about "my friend Norma" was really going to be an act of aggression against me; punishment for knowing about Althea's rejection of him for Long.

"It's her attitude," he said. "I could tell just by looking at her. She's awarding herself to you, isn't she, you lucky fellow. And needless to say, if you don't accept, there's something wrong with you, right?"

"How could you tell . . . ?" He did have a point.

"I can tell. I bet she took modern dancing at summer camp, or maybe got an A in creative writing in college, and that her bastard of a husband doesn't appreciate the fact she sacrificed a great career

203

for him. Am I right?"

"No. Wrong. The story I get is the other way around. She says she quit graduate school to get married because she was getting too good at her work. She felt it was destroying her femininity. That's why she got married."

"I see. But she still turned her back on greatness, right? I mean, she didn't give up becoming just another hack professional like you or me or the rest of us, for example, right?"

"I guess so. But she isn't bitching about that part of it. Her complaint is that Ralph won't let her be a woman, either."

"Sounds familiar. How does it work?"

"Well . . . she says he won't let her . . . give."

"Give? It sounds like horseshit already. I can tell you are quoting accurately though. Please continue."

"Yeah, well . . . her story is that Ralph is making a project out of frustrating her femininity . . . and I happen to believe her, by the way." Which I added to let him know in no uncertain terms where I stood, or at least, thought I should stand.

"And you're supposed to save that femininity. Right?" Mel said, but I didn't answer. "I knew it!" he went on, shaking his head. "It's Marcia all over again. And you can't tell me, either, that if she doesn't get fulfilled this time, it isn't going to be your fault, as a man, I mean. Am I right or am I right?"

I still didn't answer.

But I did wish I could really find Norma as likeable as I used to, once upon a time. At that moment, I would have loved to be able to talk to that first, pleasant Norma, good old Norma the Nice, that oasis from tension, that friend. We would have talked about my troubles with the married woman I was finding myself involved with, and she would have been amusing about the whole thing, made sense, and she would never ever have been overbearing with me, nor taken possession of my life, the way she was now, now that she was no longer a friend, but a lover. That is, someone not immediately associated with freedom.

"You see," Mel was saying, "in all my years as a head shrinker, I've only found one class of people not troubled by having to prove their masculinity. And that's women, X.J. Women. *They* don't have to prove it, you see. Jesus, they're a pain in the ass."

"All of them?"

"Just about. Damn them all, they're all pious by nature, believe me. Always have and always will be. In the old days, they were religious, and now that the new religion is all about proper sexual roles and normalcy, they're pious about that too. And you watch, when the next ideology comes up, they'll be pious as hell about *that* too, even if it's the opposite. All of them, and all at once, as if somebody blew a whistle. It's all exercises in piety. Group piety. They like nothing better than leading everybody to church, whatever the current church happens to be. And in my racket, they get to be like nuns, the way they creep around, kind of whispering their beads. Did you ever *hear* their tone after going through any kind of therapy? Their nunny-medical quiet tone? It makes my skin crawl. Shit, I don't think there's one in ten of them, either, that after getting shrunk doesn't start thinking of herself as part of the medical hierarchy. I'm telling you, getting a little shrunk means more to a middle-class girl than a college degree. From then on, my boy, they think they've got everybody by the short hairs."

Mel's misogynistic outburst, the *cri de coeur* which he permitted himself as we now submarined down Mass. Avenue, made me smile. He was starting to sound like an Irishman. But I didn't say so. Instead, I said in a conciliatory tone, "Don't feel too bad about it, Mel. Somebody told me that if it weren't for women, just about all professionals would starve to death. We *need* them."

"Yeah . . . I've heard that a million times, too," he said a bit more quietly. "They sure are always hanging around priests or doctors or beauticians or dieticians . . . or some clown or other, aren't they? Just trying to get their pious exercises down pat." And then he added, very sadly, as if getting off his subject, which he was not, "You have no idea what I have waiting for me at home tonight with Marcia . . . when and if I get there. I don't know whether I should face it sober . . . or drunker."

After some reflection, I said, "Maybe soberer, Mel. Let's go get some fried eggs and hashed brown potatoes."

He didn't answer, obviously considering the alternative, and while he considered, I said, "Mel, how come we almost never like the women we get involved with, I mean, personally?"

"What do you mean?"

"You know what I mean, Mel. Is it really because when we see pictures of our psyches, we're always embarrassed?"

"Oh, yes. The Anima Theory. I take it you didn't like the sight of your Anima friend, Norma there, dancing with Ralph."

"Did you like seeing Althea dancing with Long?" I countered.

"No . . . "

"What's the story with her, anyway? How does she go about giving you a pain in the ass? Same as all of them?"

"No," he said, very stiffly. "And what's more, if you hadn't just said that she was a picture of my soul, which flatters me greatly, I would have rapped you across the mouth for even mentioning her name in this conversation."

"Is that right?" I said, noting that now *he* was the defender of a lady.

"That's right."

Silence. The car tunneled along.

"You know, Mel," I said peaceably, "Long's theory of love isn't all that bad, the more I think about it. I mean, Norma wants something from me, but I don't know what I want from her, which means I don't know if I love her, by Long's definition."

More silence.

"Hey, Mel . . . what do you want from Althea? Is it any different than what Long wants? I mean, is it anything more than her undivided attention?"

"X.J., I wouldn't expect you to understand the difference by yourself, so I'll explain. Long is a predator, and I want to help Althea, which is *very* different."

"I see."

"No you don't see, you asshole! I want to help her *live*. Can you understand that? *Live!* And all Long wants is to get her number, devour it, and then he'll be licking his fingers and looking around for his next meal even before he's finished digesting. You see, what Long didn't elaborate on is that what the lover usually wants is nothing less than the other person's entire liver, just like that lady said, their very soul, all for himself. It's a real killer instinct, just like it is in Marcia, and in your pal Norma . . . and in you, for that matter."

"But not in you."

"Not," he said, "when it comes to Althea. Whether you can comprehend the difference or not, I don't want to devour Althea. I want to help her live, and it's not all that easy, because every once in a while she tries to kill herself. She has ever since she was a kid and I'm trying to prevent that."

"I see. So then . . . you are not like the rest of us low types."

"That is correct."

"And all women are a pain in the ass, but not Althea . . . I'm just trying to get it right, now."

"Let me put it this way. *All* is an exaggeration. There must be others who aren't, but I don't know them. So let me say that Marcia and Norma are a pain in the ass of the ordinary feminine, pious, protohuman kind, O.K.?"

"But not Althea. She's different . . . somehow?"

"Yes. You said that already."

"And, unlike Long, although you love her, if I may be permitted to use that word . . . "

"You may . . . you may . . . ," he sighed.

"You don't want to eat her liver, steal her soul, or anything like that, which makes you unique . . . and I notice superior . . . as a lover, too. So both of you are unique. Do I have it right?"

Silence.

Finally, "Look, X.J., I can't stand talking to a lowly type like yourself about this, so if you don't mind, let's drop it. Of *course* I think I'm superior to you. O.K.?"

More silence. Then, I asked more gently, "You didn't really answer my question, you know."

"Sure I did."

"Yeah, but I wasn't satisfied by your answer. Were you?"

"I don't know," he confessed. "I don't *think* I want to take her soul from her. And to make matters more confusing, sometimes I don't even mind Marcia so much. Maybe I even need it. No. No maybe. I do need it. You know, an ordinary home where we can tear each other apart. But Althea *is* something else, X.J. Something different for me. Believe me, she is. And I don't know if I can help her anymore . . . "

"Why not?"

"Because she won't *let* me. Not anymore."

"She doesn't trust you?"

"Hell no. She thinks I'm like Long. She thinks everybody's like Long."

"Then she agrees with his theory of love."

"That, I'm sorry to say, she does. And does she *ever*. She's convinced we're all cannibals when it comes to other people's souls."

I thought about that for a bit, and then I said, "Maybe . . . since he admits he's a cannibal . . . that's why she prefers Long."

Again silence, until finally shaking his head, Mel said, "Honest to God . . . one more word, X.J., and I'll brain you."

I laughed, as if we were playing, and he grimaced, as if he were grinning, and then he drove me straight home.

Where I would find little rest. Only a night's sleep.

NORMA

The next day, even though I woke up erotically aroused, as is my custom, and even though I expected a telephone call offering me sex, I lay in my bed dreading the phone. The way I figured it, Norma's voice was going to tell me in warmly liquid, promissory tones (equalled in intensity only by her hatred of Ralph) that she would be coming over sometime in the afternoon. That was the logical time. Therefore, I should stop everything and be available then for her, just like I was supposed to stay put, all day if need be, until my phone rang. And I was doing just that, of course.

Without any formal announcement, my subconscious had declared a moratorium on all work, and maybe on all motion, until I heard from her, and from the time I woke up all I seemed capable of doing was to lie there, multiplying my own body heat under my blankets, molested all morning long by the memory of our last (and only) sexual encounter, right in the room I was in. I wasn't exactly awake all the time, of course. Mostly I washed passively in and out of the shallows of tepid daydreams and naps where her warm-skinned limbs swirled around me. Paralyzed, I told myself I was conserving my spiritual and physical energies in preparation for the afternoon, remembering the last time, with her moaning and yelling and even her triumphant shouting of my name at the moment of climax, all within the hearing range of the small-eyed, domestic serenity of the Panskys, one floor away. I could almost see them, sitting at a table, not saying a word, hearing everything. No, I didn't expect our display was likely to move them to a similar action on their own.

And now that she'd told me, all by herself, that her sexual experience with me had been the most successful of her whole life, I understood I had become a terrific candidate to be her next husband, which I didn't like at all. I didn't like it any more than I liked being sexually used by her, vain as that might sound, because mostly it just made me feel pushed around and incapable of doing anything about it.

Which also meant, of course, that my attitude was not entirely negative, no matter how I grumbled to myself under my blankets, because I was wallowing around in thick erotic memories that I was also hoping would be the future. And my memories, washing in and mixing with my daydreams, kept getting more and more agitated with Norma's passionate noises, her imagined spasms and so forth, as in my fantasies—just like the last time—she obviously didn't care who heard what as she threw her head back and called for more force, bit me and clawed my back, never looking me in the eye as she smiled with an almost preternatural rictus as she got wilder and wilder. But with the presence of the Panskys always so near, the whole thing was like a dream where I found myself walking naked in a public place, with no idea where my clothes might be and with a long, long way to go.

But, as erotically appealing as it all was, her smile about herself and her passion celebrating itself in its own grandeur was managing to make me increasingly distant from her as a person. And the fact that she didn't care about my relationship with my neighbors didn't make me feel any closer, either. By which I mean, despite my being paralyzed from erotic fantasies about her, Norma was decidedly giving me, as Mel would say, a pain in the ass, which convinced me that when she finally came over and closed the door behind her that afternoon, took off her clothes and slipped into my bed under my covers (from which I might not have moved, except for the most pressing essentials), she was going to get beside herself with excitement, for sure. She was going to act as if she wanted to rip the ceiling apart with paroxysms of loud delight.

Of course, I also suspected that if we were alone in the middle of the Pacific Ocean, on a desert island, instead of in my room surrounded by people, she wouldn't make a sound. She'd be like one of those women with whom sex is like a cotton ball falling off a table, a notion which irritated me because I had to admit that I, too, just like her, was taken by the acoustical part of the show. All of which meant that I was so hamstrung by lust and resentment and other ambivalences that I didn't even get up to have my beloved daily escape from the world by reading the sports page for half an hour.

But she didn't call.

I lay in my bed until one in the afternoon before I admitted the possibility that she wasn't going to visit me that day. And then, I don't know why, I got it into my head that she wasn't even going to call me up to explain. And I was right.

So finally, at about two-thirty, I got up, got dressed and went out to buy the evening paper, and turned to the sports pages as if entering a friendly tavern.

But they no longer offered me an open door to a happier, trouble-free world, a land where I was never followed by my thesis or people that might hassle me. I couldn't even concentrate on them because I found myself infected by more worldly concerns, the kind that render the heart too impure for admission through those idyllic gates. My erotic impulses, freed from the possibility of her presence, now demanded her wildly, unequivocally, more than ever. They clouded my mind to the point I couldn't read, much less think straight for the rest of the day. It truly was like a fever, with her arms and legs and head flashing in a whirl through my mind like an Indian goddess. And it was painful for me, because normally I refuse to give in to erotic fantasies that don't seem likely to come off. But I didn't seem to have any choice in the matter. I was convinced she wasn't going to call, and yet, instead of being able to drive her out of my imagination for it, it seemed to help her take complete possession of it and become more desired than ever.

Not that I liked her any more as a person for it. That had nothing to do with it. But it was so intense I had to ask myself, am I in love?

And my suspended, erotic condition was not just for that day.

It was like that for a long, long time. Days and days. And weeks. And I was feeling increasingly wretched. Not so much from sexual

211

frustration (a negotiable issue with options), but because I was pretty sure I had been dropped.

I had to face up to the fact that maybe she didn't think I was such a terrific candidate for her next husband, after all, something which to my horror I suddenly found myself wanting to be.

But I started wondering why she'd dropped me that very first afternoon. Maybe she'd made up her differences with Ralph, which I could believe. Maybe she'd decided that even though she hated Ralph, and would forever, taking me on a full-time basis was a sure prelude to divorce, and maybe she thought divorce was bad. Maybe her concern for her kids had changed her mind.

Or maybe she just had come to the conclusion I was a jerk after our last meeting.

And maybe, just maybe, she had one of these little shows with somebody or other every few months. How the hell did *I* know? I really didn't, as I full well realized again and again that I didn't even know such basic things about her as whether she was a patient of Mel's, or not. Her stories showed she was, but they showed a lot of other things, too, which she claimed weren't true.

And, to make it worse, about two weeks later, I found out that though she had not called me, she had called Mel.

He took pleasure in telling me so.

I wasn't expecting it. We were sitting around his office, having a beer after squash, and he said to me, *a propos* of nothing, "You know, I'm feeling kind of bad, running off at the mouth the other night, knocking everybody."

"What are you talking about?"

"Oh," he said with a shrug and a little smile, "I guess you don't remember, but I was running on about women in general, after Norma's party . . . and all I meant was Marcia, of course. I included Norma very unjustly."

"Norma . . . ?" I said, uttering her name with difficulty.

"Yes. Your friend, and now mine, Norma. She really isn't a bad kid, you know. I've gotten to know her a lot better."

"Why? Is she a patient of yours now?"

"Goodness no!" Mel said, laughing. "I like her too much for that! No, she wanted to be but I insisted she talk with me as a friend, instead. Much more civilized! Naturally, she's told me all about you and Ralph."

"Swell," I said.

"Oh, it's not as bad as all that. Since she's not a patient, I guess I can let a few things out about our conversations. As you may already know, she's been thinking of leaving Ralph quite seriously for a couple of years now."

"She has?"

"Yes. And she still doesn't know exactly what she's going to do, except, of course, that she's about to do *something* instead of nothing . . . and the reason she hasn't been in touch with you is that she's trying to have a clear head . . . but" he added with a smile, "she wanted me to give you her best."

"Oh . . . ," I said. There was much to mull over, including how I was feeling about Mel being closer to her than I was.

"Yes," he said, "we have a nice relationship, Norma and I. We pour out our hearts to each other these days, and I can't wait for my turn, because she's a friend of Althea's."

"Oh," I said. "Althea."

"Yes. Even though I'm no longer Althea's doctor . . . I didn't admit that to you before, did I . . . ? Anyway, since I'm not allowed to be her doctor anymore, I'm still keeping up with her as best I can, through Norma. It seems that Norma has been attending the meetings of Althea's organization for the last few months, and is becoming rather serious about it."

"What organization?"

"Didn't Norma tell you? The Sisterhood of Sophia. It's a Feminist group Althea founded. All by herself. Bizarre, eh?"

"What *are* you talking about?"

"Well, you see, the Sisterhood, representing Sophia, the feminine aspect of the Godhead, is trying to liberate the human soul by 'rendering the Masculine Spirit mild'. That's how Althea puts it."

"So how do they do it?"

"Oh . . . they meet and grumble, I guess. They spend an awful lot of time hating men there. It's kind of like their bar, you know. Anyway, Norma first went there because she wanted to do research for a novel she wants to do, but it turns out that having come to laugh, she finds herself staying to pray . . . or at least to observe more respectfully."

"Wait a minute!" I said, putting my hands to my temples. Suddenly I was remembering her last story, about Eva and Althea, and just as suddenly I found myself struggling with a number of fusions of Eva/Althea, Norma/Eva and now Norma/Althea which were all

213

whirling in my mind at once.

"Yes . . . ?" Mel said. "I'm prepared to wait a minute. What is it I'm waiting for?"

"I don't know yet . . . What is this Feminist organization? What's *she* doing there? Is she a lesbian or something like that, too?"

"What do you mean, 'lesbian'?"

"I mean a female homosexual. What do you think I mean?"

"That, I doubt. And if you are implying it about Althea," he said, getting a little huffy and then pausing, " . . . I wish I could tell you. I don't know. If I were another hack in my profession, I would of course say that this was at the root of the Sisterhood's organizational tree. But I'm not sure. I even doubt it. But if they are, they certainly are not exclusively so."

"Yeah," I said, "you're right. After all, Norma did take me on, and then there's obviously the fact that Althea is screwing with Frank Long, so they couldn't be too sticky about it."

"Watch your mouth!" said Mel, pretending to joke.

I looked at him, and then looked away. Poor Mel seemed quite hurt by the painful reminder of Frank Long, but I was more concerned with myself. Finally, I said, "Mel . . . *is* Norma intending to get in touch with me?"

"I don't know . . . I have no idea what she intends to do."

"Do you think . . . she likes me . . . ?"

Mel smiled, not unkindly, thank God, before saying, "Well . . . does she know you? Are you a person, or an actor, or maybe just a hope for her? Do you know? How can she like you if she doesn't know you?"

Mel had a point.

"X.J.," he said, "if I may give you some advice. Why don't you wait a week or so, and if she hasn't called you, why don't you then call her."

"Call *her*?" I said, surprised by the notion.

"Sure. Take the chance, X.J. And I say a week because I'm pretty sure she is about to leave Ralph. Maybe she's done it today, from what she told me the other day. So why don't you give her a little time to move her belongings . . . surely you don't want to get involved in the physical side of that . . . and then call her."

"Gee . . . "

"What is it, my boy?"

"Well . . . I'm shy. I don't know. It doesn't seem right for me to

214

call her, unseemly somehow, do you know what I mean? I mean, I might lose my maidenly passivity and then she might lose respect for me for being too forward."

"True, and she also might refuse to see you."

"That hurt, Mel."

"Sorry. Just mentioning the possibility. I'll let you know the minute I have any news. Who knows? Maybe Norma will even *want* you to call her in a few days."

And in a few days, I did hear from Norma, but through Mel again.

"She's left Ralph," he said.

"And . . . ?" I inquired, feeling like Christian asking Cyrano about Roxanne about permission to mount the vine, up to the balcony where I hoped she waited for my kiss.

"She says, don't call her, she'll call you. *If* she calls you."

"That," I said, "is swell. Not that I give a shit, but where is she living now, anyway?"

"She is quartered at the Sisterhood of Sophia. The place seems to serve as a halfway house for ladies that leave their husbands. As Senator Joe McCarthy would say, it is a subversive organization."

"Is it . . . permanent . . . do you think?" I asked, meaning her leaving Ralph.

"Oh, no. I told you, it's a halfway house. She'll only stay there until she gets her own place. But please don't breathe a word, O.K.? Because Ralph doesn't know where she is. It's really very curious, you know, because the Sisterhood's main building is an old church from back in the Abolitionist days, with secret rooms to hide runaway slaves. And I can tell you, for sure, that the Sisterhood considers itself a modern continuation of that noble tradition. Amazing, isn't it?"

"Yeah . . . I guess so," I said, finding Mel gratuitously pedantic when I was suffering the pains of rejection. "Are they all crazy in that place, like Althea?"

"Crazy . . . ?" he said, and then laughed. "No. Not like Althea, anyway."

"You know, Mel, one thing I can't figure out, why is Althea chasing around after Frank Long if she's such a Feminist?"

"Some things, I'm sorry to say, are not matters of choice. But you've got a point, maybe. Norma tells me Althea hasn't been seen at the Sisterhood for a long time, not since she took up with Long. Maybe she's ashamed, and feels it has compromised her leadership position."

"Or," I said, "has better things to worry about," with a malice I was immediately ashamed of as Mel only replied with a wounded look.

ALTHEA

(Just as I was about to give up hope)

Just as I was about to give up hope, I heard from Norma. Directly for a change. But it wasn't very flattering. Just another of her women's magazine type of stories, this one titled "Althea", without so much as an explanatory note. Naturally, I accused myself of being over-sensitive, but I couldn't avoid the new suspicion that maybe Norma had always been primarily interested in an editorial relationship with me, with adultery being merely the front to make it seem respectable. So, for the first time, to my growing demoralization, I began thinking of Norma in a way I never had before; that is, not as a woman with mysterious wants, using me as she might, but as an aspiring writer, which in my experience is a separate gender altogether, like vampires are.

Therefore, very half-heartedly, I glanced at the first few pages of her story before putting the thing face down on my table. Not surprisingly maybe, I found that her style was starting to irritate me, and that I was in no mood to care about Norma's "unfulfilled femininity," nor about cold lunar Eva's troubles, either. I had my

217

own, and, unhappily remembering a theory of Mel's about what he called "Ego erections", I discovered I was most unwilling to serve as what he called a "Vaginal Ear" for Norma's presently "Tumescent Ego". Particularly so since I now figured Norma thought so little of me she was ingenuously expecting me to find *my* fulfillment in that function alone. I told myself I should not have been so surprised by her, though. After all, as Mel, the old Master himself, put it to me one day, "In their heart of hearts, people can't help hoping that you'll find ecstasy in simply serving *them*, and if not this time, well, maybe next time. Optimism in this area is unquenchable. People even treasure the touching illusion that somewhere on this planet there are not only individuals, but maybe even entire races just craving the chance at this happiness. You see, sex, at least as we know it, is only a sublimation of the Ego drive, no matter what they tell you . . . which has often made me think of changing McLeod's here into a bordello, incidentally. After all, McLeod's is an elitist institution which can only help a few, whereas the bordello I have in mind could serve great numbers from the general public, who would pay very modest sums to feel themselves . . . oh, licked all over by the applause of, say, one million grateful Indonesians who keep chanting and giggling, "Our joy is your joy!" in their native accents, with first names included at no extra charge. I really think I could bring it in, as they say in Hollywood, under the present McLeod's budget just by using drugs, mirrors, films, echo chambers and just two or three cynical but all-purpose Syrians of my acquaintance who might be willing to perform these succulent Ego jobs on my clients. What do you think . . . ?" he said grinning at me that day. "If I do it, I'll find a place for you, and you can get out of graduate school."

At the time, when Mel first told me about it, the idea hadn't sounded bad. But now, it sounded even better. Sounder. And I certainly wanted to change my life about now.

So, with Mel's smiling face filling my mind after having re-explained his plans for the Great Ego Bordello, I turned sourly away from Norma's typescript to let myself lapse completely into dark thoughts about human nature in general and Norma in particular.

And then, unexpectedly, a powerful Light began invading my mind. It was the Unseen and Mysterious Forces again, announcing Althea's luminous image, which began sifting up through the filter of Norma's sappy words, the very ones I'd just read before putting her story down. Mel's taunting, didn't-I-tell-you face vanished, and suddenly I was seeing Althea once more, sitting on the hill at the Hospital's abandoned golf course, her legs straight out, head tilted to one side, looking like a discarded rag doll—except for the strange jumpiness of her hands as she sliced apple after apple with febrile movements that seemed independent of the rest of her stilled body.

Now I realize the Unseen and Mysterious Forces were making their final preparations for my first full encounter with the Light, and, in the fullness of the daylight reality, at last.

It would happen the very next day, only hours after she had shot Frank Long in the right temple and mutilated his body. After she had returned from her ghastly visit to Long's mother in New Hampshire, at their summer place, having delivered there a strange package for which she would always be remembered as a thoroughly inhuman monster, to nearly everyone's horror.

But even though I couldn't possibly know that then, my heart nearly stopped because I immediately sensed there was something different, as again the Light was absent from her image. No more present than when I saw her at Norma's party, so completely absorbed by Frank Long that it seemed as if her soul were in suspended animation. But something else was different, something of which I was conscious. Before, she had always emerged in my mind as standing up somehow, obstinate and even darkly triumphant in her resistance. But not now, with her legs straight out and her head to one side. And yet, as unheroic and whipped as she looked, I still noticed a flickering sign of resistance in the strange, obsessive movements of those hands that kept cutting away at the apples, so out of keeping with her general inertness it was as if her soul were thrashing in her hands, as if fighting for a last breath.

And as she sliced and peeled away, practically dicing the apples before letting them drop, it seemed as if her hands were looking for something in those apples that wasn't there anymore, but once had been.

And then I noticed that the two gnarled trees above her had also changed. Very much. They didn't look anything like the peers of pre-Christian gods, as they had when welcoming Eva and Althea up onto the hill, into their number, with bristling upraised limbs, ecstatic in their apotheosis as the two striding women became transformed into just one: the Huntress that had made us howl like babies as she held up a palpitating red heart, and smiled. Instead, the trees now looked like cynical, even arthritic, dirty old men, gloating over the reduced mortal that sat beneath them on the hill, who now looked so very much more like a whipped rag doll than like any goddess of the hunt.

But Althea didn't even seem aware of their gloating as she kept obsessively slicing away with her jumpy hands. The knife blade reflected the whitening, swelling sun which multiplied its size, and whenever she cut into a new dark apple, it was as if the revealed white apple flesh had been infected by the sun-blade, always giving more and more naked whiteness, no matter how small she cut the pieces. And each new little sunny piece of apple was like an infantile smile, mocking her with its very existence.

And what was worse was that the whiteness of each apple was not only a defeat for her, but endlessly repetitive. I kept getting the sense that she was at a disadvantage because of the knife, which kept turning the apples white with its glinting blade. And the repetitive hopelessness of her activity made it look like Althea was engaged in her own Infernal punishment, which included mockery in the endless, smiling, infantile pieces of apple.

The knife in her hand made me nervous.

Defeated as she looked, she felt just as distant and opaque to me as she had the first time I saw her, from Mel's office window. I remembered how that first time the wind kept her heavy hair over her face, and how she stood so obstinately upright as the heavy sky sagged overhead, pregnant with endless quantities of icy water ready to drown the world. Then she'd looked as full of darkness ready to explode as the sky above her, while the round-backed patients busied themselves with trying to load her down with enough apples to make her bend. But now the Indian Summer sky was absolutely clear, and Althea was alone underneath it, except for the gloating, arthritic Trees. The sky was opening up in the distance, brilliant and swollen with light like the mainsail of a sailing ship crashing through the sonorous waves of an illuminated, foaming sea that had the sun in its guts.

And then I knew that, like the very first time I saw her, Althea was pregnant this time, too.

Althea's Infernal, repetitive punishment was happening in a merciless, shadowless world. Nothing had darkness, not even inside. Finally, I began to understand she was looking for darkness.

And the swollen noon sun above the gnarled dirty old man trees reclined in the middle of the sky like a sexually gratified, Solomonic

220

lion, waiting to be served. And then I realized that there wasn't any darkness inside Althea either, because I could feel she was swelling with some monstrous sunball, some golden cub that would eventually explode her and invert her. And all of it seemed to amuse the gloating trees, including the fact that the Solomonic lion was resting after having gotten its burning seeds into everywhere, including Althea, the swelling rag doll.

And then, the distance between me and Althea began to diminish as I read:

(. . . . .)
. . . he sees me sitting here, with this knife, Eva.
He doesn't want to say anything about the knife.
He's wondering why I'm back here again, sitting alone,
as I've sat on this hill a thousand times before.
As if I'd been born on this hill.
He hopes I've come back because I finally want him to
take care of me.
I've never wanted him to do it. Never. (But now I want what I don't want, Eva. My hands are jumping like frightened fish on the hard ground, and he's watching, wondering about the knife . . . and about my hands, frightened fish, lungs on fire inside, jumping.) I've never wanted him to take care of me, Eva, never, not even the first time, when I was sixteen and Mrs. Duffy came back a day early and found me in the attic, blue in the face and cold, when they pumped my stomach and then wound up scraping my womb (Eva! Everything I breathe is turning white and starting to burn again!). I'd never seen him before. Old Dr. Hough was away, and they sent him instead, young Dr. Fish, the intern. Just a pompous boy with glasses, pretending to be older by the way he stood, imitating some grave old doctor I'd never met, that maybe he'd never met, having just read my file, talked to my parents, talked to Dr. Hough on the phone and having decided to be angry with me for having gone up to the attic with a lot of pills full of whispering darkness. He kept his face grave, cast down behind his glasses, masked with the invisible old doctor that always walked the dreary corridors of his institutional mind, and he waited for me to say something, to dare to speak after my transgression (Eva! my raw, red wound is sucking up the white oxygen again, and I don't want this wanting I have now) and as he waited for me, posturing himself before my open eyes, I wasn't con-

cerned with him because one hundred feet beneath my stiff, cold body . . . I was starting to feel giddy . . . thinking now how unbelievable it was that only a few hours before, in abject terror, I'd swallowed all the pills and listened for the darkness whispering its sentence, and I'd waited for the explosion of silence, waited for my punishment, for being garroted in my dreams . . . and I did fall away into the blackness, Eva, though I couldn't remember when, and yet for all of that, there I was, with my eyes open, and happy! Incredibly, I hadn't been punished. I'd been rewarded! I knew I'd been rewarded, because suddenly I was stronger, as if in my sleep I'd been bathed in some miraculous black waters that had made me invincible! I knew it at once, even though I didn't feel I could move my cold stiff face yet, or any other part of me. And then, a hundred feet below my face, where I had fallen through and was now floating to my surprise, I felt like laughing!

He'd think it was at him, of course, if I did. But I was giddy because of the Darkness, which instead of choking me, now flushed me through and through, opened me out in a direction I'd never imagined, blowing strong and dark like a subterranean, no! like a heavenly wind, Eva! A fresh, whispering joyous Darkness was what I carried soaring inside me! And it was alive, Eva! Alive, playful and carrying on like invisible racing, living rivers of gossiping girls in a flood of secret tongues that I suddenly understood because I realized they were all just one, and it made me want to laugh and rush with them all! I wanted to stand up and run, Eva, sail, fly away filled with the incredible, funny secret breath of the rivers of girls that was blowing all through me with its amazing news! And when I closed my eyes (he must have thought I was resting), I could even taste the marvelous breath of that sweet, wild, million-voiced Darkness that sprang from somewhere inside me . . . and which was even saying my name! It was saying my name, Eva! I no longer cared about dying! To my great surprise, I understood for the first time that my life was mine. Absolutely mine! The Darkness was saying so with its wild rush, and my inner ears tickled with the foaming rivers of rampant girls that could race so fast that every few moments there were explosions, pandemonium, seas of marvelous, living dark air, all soaring with the same single incredible breath I could still taste . . . still taste in my mouth when I closed my eyes. How could I possibly care about the pompous boy glaring at me? . . . and then I realized he thought I was defying him with my silence. But I wasn't,

222

*Eva. I was simply drunk and reeling with the full sweet breath that
was telling me now the secret within all things, the same incredible,
simple, funny secret, which was even beginning to whisper and
giggle about him now as he puffed himself up, posturing the old doctor more fiercely than ever, enjoying the chance to get angry. I could
tell he was about to try to lash me into the daylight, into life, hoping
to make me cry, grateful to cry. He was still so much a boy (Just at
the sight of him, the blowing Darkness wickedly turned into nothing
but foam-headed rivers of laughing girls, Eva!), so much a boy he
thought that because of his daring, because he was he, the one and
only, he just might be able to overpower me with one magic blow
from his sword, succeed where the old had failed (The rampant
rivers were tossing their heads everywhere, getting hysterical, Eva!)
and tame the melancholy shrew! As I looked at him in his preposterous conceit, all the rivers now suddenly whirled even faster
and faster with a foaming hysteria I was sure would explode into an
uncontrollable laughter that would hurt my body.*

*But he surprised me. Even though he was pretending to be much
older, he started out by saying in a clear, young voice that our ages
were sufficiently close that we could talk the same language, and
that he wasn't like old Dr. Hough so he wasn't shocked by my
screwing with so many different people, but that he was revolted by
how selfish and stupid I'd been. And then he announced that I had
no more right to take my own life than I had to permanently maim
my parents, and that he found my behavior not only cold, but vicious
toward everyone, including the unfortunate unborn child that surely
couldn't yet deserve to have such a repellent, inhuman creature for a
mother. And furthermore, just to let me know that I wasn't quite the
gift to the world I might think I was, he'd heard from any number of
males at the Hospital that screwing with me was like screwing with a
dead seal . . . which distressed the younger boys and offended the
older ones esthetically if not morally . . . which again didn't surprise
him because I cared for nothing, loved nothing, and that was all
right as far as he was concerned, he repeated again, except that I was
destructive to other people who were alive and wanted to be alive,
and that I had no right whatsoever,* no right whatsoever! *to take my
own life because . . . whereupon I began to stand up, Eva, all purple-
faced, six feet of me as he looked at me with bug-eyed disbelief, and
I cranked up with all the strength I had left and slapped him across
the face, and passed out again.*

He never told me I had no right to take my life again, Eva. He even understood it had been that very notion that had offended me, and he was shocked when my parents were informed and agreed with me that he'd been insolent. He disapproved of me very much, at least at first. I knew he would have liked me to go through the pregnancy, and hopefully a difficult birth, and then worry wretched with guilt about the child . . . like a lot of other girls at the Hospital, who ended up putting the baby up for adoption, all on doctor's advice, to teach them a lesson about the reality of their acts. They could sound so much like lower-class Catholics, those doctors! . . . not that anybody really cared about the slimy little embryos. But he arranged for my abortion with very little conversation.

And he knew very well that I intended to take my life one day. The day I chose. That had not changed. But I think he was puzzled by my being so much "better" so soon, so much stronger in the light, among the things in his world. We met every day, and with an indifference that was joy, I was even becoming gay and forgiving, and he, after a while, even apologized about his anger, though never about having faked it for his own aggrandizement. "Just as long as you understand," I told him, "that my life is mine," and he laughed and put up his right palm as if turning down an offering. "Please! I don't want it," he said, and I smiled although I didn't believe him.

And he talked about my rashes of sexual incidents. "They're nothing," I said. "Believe me." "Oh, I believe you," he said. "I'm sure that's exactly what you're proving . . . and considering how cold you are, I'm beginning to think that promiscuity with you is a form of practicing your virginity." I didn't quite understand him then, but of course he was right. "Do be careful, though," he said, "because something might go wrong, and you could begin to feel something, and then you might start losing yourself." "I know that's what you'd like," I said, and he said, "Oh, I'm all for it! I only wish you could get yourself a real good screw, but I know you're going to be too crafty for anything like that." He didn't understand, Eva. Not the important things. How could I ever give anyone my Darkness, when that was only for me? But now that I had tasted it, and felt alive and mine as I never had before, I felt pleasant, and I said, "But I don't mind if they have a good time, doctor," and his eyes brightened as he slapped his forehead, mimicking me with, "Good time!" and he laughed and shook his head. "Sometimes you sound like a kindly whore . . . but it really doesn't fool me," he said good-naturedly. "I suppose, though, that few people understand the militant chastity of a whore, do they? . . . I mean, the real freedom, the arrogance of giving somebody a second helping of something you cook but don't eat . . . am I going too fast for you?" "No," I said, and smiled at him, "But you do make it all too important. All men do. Quite honestly, I don't mind at all if they have a good time," which made him laugh again and shake his head. "Gee! I only wish you wanted to have a good time! But that's just the trouble. You're so arrogant you always make sure you don't. We're all a little like that, of course, so it's a question of degree. But I would say that you are about the least sensual, pleasure-loving person I've ever come across. Actually it takes humility to be sensual, you know. I hope you don't mind my saying so, Althea, but your pride turns you into the dreariest kind of Puritan . . . ," and then he paused to smile reflectively, saying again, "Puritan . . . ," and he burst out with a felicitous-sounding, "Hey! . . . I've got an idea . . . do you think maybe . . . it's partially ethnic?"

"Ethnic?"

"Yes. I mean . . . maybe in one way you aren't too crazy, but just too . . . well, Brahmin? I mean, if you were Italian or a Jew I'd have to think of you completely differently. Maybe I might be able to consider you cured, if you'll forgive the expression, if I can convince you to have just a very little good time. After all, dear, no offense, but no one ever said your people were a fun people." He was clowning, of course, and I laughed (I found he could often make me laugh) and the boy with glasses who so often imitated the grave older doctor now laughed along with me, like a boy at play. When he laughed like that, so unselfconsciously, I rather liked him. But the moment he sensed I was liking him (Pale verb, nothing more than a beam of light glancing off an object before moving on. Why do people think it's related to love?), he'd begin hoping for something else. His soft brown eyes would begin to swell behind his glasses, with a plea he could never say—and then, I'd feel my Darkness again, its chill wind filling me, making me smile, defining me with distance, and the boy, wounded (again) would mask himself with the invisible older doctor once more. After such moments, Eva, he was amusingly patient. He would wait, perhaps even weeks, before finding an occasion to tell me very nicely (and as if it didn't have to do with him) that he knew I depended on hurting others for my sense of Self, especially when they offered their hearts to me on humbly

upraised palms. "And don't pretend," he said with his squinty smile, "that you do it just to teach people to keep their hearts to themselves, because . . . show you a heart and you skewer it, like shishkebab. Wolves are better sports than you, you know. If one of them loses in a fight, he just offers up his throat to the winner, and the winner never takes him up on it."

"Worse than a wolf . . . imagine," I said to his lament, and, feeling my Darkness, smiled. "Yes, I admit it. Now I know how I am to a lamb . . . I wonder how I'd be to another wolf?" and he grimaced pretending to smile, jealous of all wolves, and I said, "And I also wonder if you'd admit, doctor, that knowing what they know about what will happen never stops people from offering up their hearts again?"

From my unassailable distance I watched his hopeless, puppy-warm impulses struggling on his face against the stern old doctor's leash. The old doctor didn't want him to jump up and say bright-eyed, "I admit it," before breaking into a shamed grin and even wagging his tail low. The old doctor wanted to match my distance with his, wisely knowing it was his only protection, but the impulsive puppy couldn't help trying to get closer. Bravely, young Dr. Fish tried to harden his face like a shield behind his glasses, but it only turned pink in the struggle, Eva. He averted his eyes from mine as long as he could, but then, finally, he couldn't help stealing a peep, and then he knew that I knew, and he got redder as he broke into a new smile, as helpless and nude as a baby, and defeated, he lowered his head and shook it as I looked down on the top of his head. Then, he grinned at me and shrugged. And I liked him again, Eva. I liked him as I like a baby, a puppy, a warm cup of chocolate in the winter. We both knew that very soon, no matter what we said, he'd be betrayed again by those swelling brown eyes, hoping again, no matter what was learned, the eternal triumph of optimism over experience, and knowing its inevitability (and knowing I knew it too) made him laugh and shrug again, the way he always did at fate. (His face contorted into a clown's pained grin, Eva, and I never told him it was his finest grace, his clown's grace before a recognized fate which made him so much more amusing to me than other lambs, and so much better company.)

His hoping always made me smile, Eva. Seeing my hard-edged image floating in those swelling, incurably warm brown eyes like "la belle dame sans merci" always amused my sleeping Darkness into *gusts that tickled me with their marvelous, free chill, awake again. He was wrong to say I felt nothing, because I certainly did feel . . . that cold, hard girl I could see floating in his pained eyes. But he was quite right to say I used him. I did, I never denied it any more than I denied having used the pills, boys, girls, and even death itself . . . and anything else I could . . . to feel my life as mine. That was why I felt strong and could stay in the world of light for a while longer, chatting with him, apparently "better". I was there as a visitor from the Darkness now, from where I had emerged only for the pleasure of seeing the hard unmoving girl that his eyes returned to me, and once I'd enjoyed that enough, once there was no more point in staying or leaving, I would end by leaving, escaping with my Self. You see, Eva, I knew the most important thing now: I wasn't being kept up in the world of light by fear or by guilt or by ambition or by anything else he might want me to feel (and which could steal away that girl we both saw and wanted) because I had no other ambition than that Me I could simultaneously see and feel . . . and I lived for that feeling, Eva. That feeling was my life! It was like looking on the face of a black pond, seeing an icy moon and feeling its smile inside me. It was a double smile, Eva, a lovely irony that was me. And when I was that double smile, Eva, I was! I was! And the Darkness knew it, and soared! And spoke! And I understood!*

There are no true laws, Eva, that's what the serpentine Darkness told me, just as it told you, except for the ones that are meant to chain you and drag you behind the sun's chariot, chanted by the slaves who are themselves in bondage. Come feel the warmth, they say, come live! Taste the heat in the earth, give up your solitude and love! You are worth nothing as an end in yourself. Don't you see that if you don't love, you don't live? Love is the salt taste of the sun in the earth, they say, in the sea, in your own blood, and it makes the mud rise up and walk, open its eyes and see! You aren't living now, Althea. You're dying, growing cold, becoming the mouth of a black Nothing with no end. When you speak, death comes out of your mouth like the black dove head of an endless serpent. Find a way to let the sun's strong yellow fingers open inside you and make you bloom with salt and fire. You're the sun's daughter, too, Althea (Are we, Eva? Aren't we the moon's?) and the pulsating heat that's inside everything, wanting to flow, is inside you, too (and becoming a wide, infinite smile, Eva, as it freezes with a double joy they cannot understand) . . . only, they say, that heat is caught by the hard, coffin

227

walls of your pride. That is a true Hellish pride, Althea, that coldness of yours. It's making your soul a terrible well filled with still,
black water, and you're so enchanted by the ivory whiteness of your
own image floating there, suspended by some deathly moonbeams,
that the ice branches out through your spirit like gangrene, poison-
ing you, and you do nothing but smile and smile with your frozen
mouth and love the image more, the more the poison overtakes
you, and when you close your eyes you are tasting the passing ridges
of that frozen image with your still cooling tongue, loving its un-
bending shape for its own hardness, its eyes of cold silver for their
metallic blindness, with all the multiplying chill of your own icy soul.
But you are only savoring a dead thing, Althea. A proudly cold,
proudly dead girl that never changes her shape as only dead ideals
never change their shapes. They get stiff with pride, stiff with death.
Believe us, Althea, pride always drinks with death. And it's in-
tolerably bitter in the end, more than you ever thought.

That's what Dr. Fish was saying to me, too, Eva, in infinite ways,
but it always ended up making the living Darkness gust inside my
ears and make me laugh with its wild free breath. As if living could
really be anything but savoring the lunar coldness of that girl that
was the purest Me! If she'd been impure, I mean, still full of sun,
still pumping with its heat, wanting to move, change, make more
bread out of her dough, who . . . what would have been living? Not
that girl I could see and feel, Eva, anymore than a wave is what
wants to move on the sea.

Of course I tried to explain it to him, but he wanted to think it was
all because I was simply afraid of dying, just the way he might be
afraid, and so, to calm me (as if I needed it), he said, "In one way, we
never die, Althea, especially if we are resigned to be at the service of
Life. Then, you see, you never die because, being Life, you become
other shapes, don't you see? Future shapes which we might all do
well to learn to love better than ourselves, because we really aren't all
that much fun. Don't you see, Althea? Life is no more interested in
pride than water seeking to flow. It always goes along the course of
least resistance, just where it can, just like weeds or trees that take
root wherever they can, even changing forms to be able to take root.
The history of Life is the discarding of pride, I'm sure of it. It has
nothing to do with the history of Pride, which is the history of death.
Everything changes in order to live, Althea, because that's all that
Life is interested in, and to insist on keeping one shape is the only

sure way to die that I know of. Flowing and changing often hurts, I grant you, but it's also what gives relief because it always turns out that none of us is really so in love with our shapes, despite what we think, that we aren't finally quite glad to be rid of them in the end. Changing is both our punishment and our reward, don't you see, and we have to learn to ride it out with dignity, Althea, a different kind than the one you're cultivating. Frankly, there's no sense resisting with a childish arrogance that is always hopeless in the end, and only good for producing all the forms of feeling spite. Oh, I'm convinced that spite produces greatness, you know, but only an ugly kind. You see, Althea, I realize that you are oriented to becoming a monument, or you wouldn't have founded the Sisterhood of Sophia, which is precisely why I'm convinced that what worries you most is death. But when you think about it, don't you agree that all monuments are ugly? And even though they are such fierce protests against death, there's no question they're all as dead can be. Ugly and dead, their two distinguishing and identifying qualities, which is why I'm hoping for more for you. Don't become a monument . . . please. Not yet anyway. Your only faithful will be the pigeons . . . ."

His mentioning my wanting to be a monument made me smile. But I still told him, no, I'm not afraid of death. Not what people usually call death. I must have told him the same thing in a hundred ways, Eva, always the same: Can't you understand that you aren't really asking me to live, but to die? To lose myself to what you call living? And I do not intend to give myself up, not for anything so base, so ignoble, so invincibly cowardly as Life, nor for the sake of anyone's tears or the company of the rest of the slaves (because we are never alone with the Darkness, Eva), nor for whatever pleasures lie in feeling the heat of the sun. And certainly not for a good screw! Life cannot have me for such a small price. Above all, I'm not a whore, doctor. I shall not give myself over to the flow. My shape shall be mine! And I'm quite confident I shall not lose myself as long as you have nothing I want, and you never can, because I only want what is mine now! Understand me: I feel no guilt whatsoever, none whatsoever! Guilt is a weakness, and weakness makes for fear. And the only Right in the Universe is what I care about: the salvation of my mortal soul saved for me! I shall have it while it lasts, even though it can only be for a moment (but that moment will be mine alone), and then you can have all the rest, for your flow. Make dogfood out of it, or bridges or fertilizer or playing cards or the next race, but leave me *to me, and let no one come between my soul and me except to excite us and to make us embrace even tighter, and to make me laugh with joy and feel my freedom. I know you don't understand, but it really does all have to do with my soul, doctor, much more than with my body. My soul, and the Darkness which is my friend, and I'm cool and dark and blowing with Sophia's wind. I know what Sophia's wind is now, with serpents and fish the cold flutes for Her music, as I too am a cold flute for her Holy . . . Dark and Laughing Breath . . . which made Anne Hutchinson giggle and Jonathan Winthrop rage, which made Heloise wretched with shame and fury for having sold herself to Abelard. I know that this laughing Ghost, Sophia, animates me too, and I'm truly free of what you call desire, and glad I am!*

Shaking his head, "Sophia's wind, yet," he used to say, and he'd sigh philosophically, that is, as if accepting his impotence.

Perhaps he did accept it, secretly, but he never stopped trying, Eva, no matter how hopeless he felt knowing I was only there talking with him as a visitor from the Darkness, knowing that the time was coming when I would escape with my Self. My inevitable victory, his inevitable defeat, making his sensitive eyes swell, making my dark, bottomless breath fill me and blow chill . . .

But now he sees me sitting here with this knife, Eva.

He's hoping again. (Everything I breathe is turning white, Eva, and starting to burn again!) I know he's watching, hiding in his office, Eva. He doesn't like this knife, but he's smiling because he sees my hands are jumping out of me like terrified fish, thrashing, burning inside, going blind with fire, sucking up more white air which always turns into more fire. Going mad, even starting to thirst for the fire! He knows about Frank, and he's glad. No one can resist the excitement of seeing a wounded animal about to fall, dying because it isn't dying. It makes all eyes shine, Eva. They're all the hunter's dogs. He thinks I'm going to fall here, for him, because he's heard that Frank won't see me (he will*, Eva, just once more, but he doesn't know that). He thinks he'll walk out of his office to find me panting, glassy-eyed on this hill, when my hands stop jumping, looking up at his coming with gratitude, dying because I'm not dying.*

He can see into me, Eva, because I'm up on my surface now, beginning to burn beneath my skin. I'm out of the Darkness, Eva! It's almost as if I were glowing, humiliated, transparent. They see me at Frank's office, Eva, and they all smile because they can sense

230

the acid burning just under my skin, making me want what I don't want, and I see the acid white light come alive in their eyes the moment they see me come in the receptionist's door. Even the coarsest, stupidest people, people who've never seen me before, see into me now and they smile, Eva, and they savor the little acid tingle taste of the knife inside their lips when they say he's busy, or out of town, or will call me later, or make me wait in an empty room where I'll stay for hours after everyone is gone home. Eva, I want what I don't want so much now I almost don't care when I hear them tasting the white steel in their mouths, their acid pleasure, all from his knife, Eva. Frank's knife! They love the hunter, he makes their eyes dance with that white, cruel sunlight, and I can even hear its taste in his mother's voice when I call and she says, "Oh yes. Althea." I hear it there most of all. She's proudest of the white acid that her son got into me. I can hear it so well, "Franklin! It's the Stanton girl!" and I can even hear it in her steps as she walks away from the telephone, knowing I'll be holding it, waiting, dumb, without even being able to be furious . . . the acid tingle in her saliva as her eyes meet Frank's when he comes to take the phone.

He took me by surprise, Eva, just when I was finally going to take my pills, just when I was going to escape with my Self, when I was alone at Norma's house, after having walked around trembling softly, sickly warm inside for days and days. Everything I saw, people in the streets, cars, birds, had become putrid and warm inside, promising to blur at the edges, to rot and melt, when suddenly, I realized that the world had stopped spinning. Nothing could move by itself anymore, Eva! All motion was false, just like a newspaper flying briefly with a broken back on some fake street breeze—and then I knew that I was in the last season of the world . . . no more would come to repeat itself at me, because next Tuesday afternoon had disappeared up ahead as sharply as if it had rolled off a table. It was gone, absolutely, and the moment I knew that, my eyes became strong as two suns. I could see every edge with perfect clarity again, and I went to get my pills, moving through all the warm stillness of people and cars and birds that existed like a wavy forest of non sequiturs, as if having secretly conceded that Time had rolled off its table just ahead of us, without admitting it to themselves.

Eva, I was the only creature truly capable of moving on the whole earth! I could feel the stillness in everything I passed in that forest of dull-eyed non sequiturs . . . I hadn't felt the chill breath of my

Darkness for a long time, but at least now I wasn't trembling anymore, no longer so sickly warm inside. Because now with my pills, I knew the Darkness couldn't leave me behind, because I could move . . . and I went to Norma's house, which would be empty all weekend . . .

. . . And I sat on Norma's bed, with my pills on my lap, alone in the house . . . when I heard the front door open downstairs, and a man's voice say, "Norma?" I held still on Norma's bed, listening to him walk around downstairs, into the kitchen, out of it, saying again, "Norma?" and then I heard him coming up the stairs, toward the room I was in. The door was open. It was Frank, emerging up the stairwell like a sea monster, so big he looked as if he'd have to stoop to come through the door and when he saw me he stopped, puzzled to find me there, but then he smiled at me as if I were found money. Every time we'd met before, he'd looked at me, making me know what he wanted, and it had always quickened my chilly Darkness, Eva, made it move inside me, just like Dr. Fish's pleading, lamb's eyes . . . and I felt it again, Eva, for the first time in so long, very faintly . . . the chill, the beginning of the double smile . . .

I knew he'd come to find Norma alone, with her children and Ralph away at his mother's, and I knew, without her ever having told me, that she'd waited for him on other Saturdays. But for some reason, without telling him, not on this one.

And he looked at me sitting there, saw the dozens of pills on my lap.

He understood at once, and it amused him. And as he moved toward me he was so big, Eva, so confident and ruthless I stiffened, suddenly feeling as I hadn't felt in a long, long time! And he put himself in front of me, making me see him directly, showing himself, smirking at his own size and making me smirk with my cold mouth too, with a reflex imitation, mirroring him, the same smirk on both our faces, which amused me because I was sure he thought I was thinking just like he was, excited by the same thing, not knowing I was excited by the prospect of feeling the full, free, wild breath of my Darkness one more time! I held very still, my pulse quickening, Eva! Big as he was, smug as he was, I was going to use him, all of him, all his ruthlessness and strength, to feel my Self again! One more time, Eva, Sophia's secret, laughing wind in the stillness of the last weekend in the world . . . and I kept my head still, looking ahead as he sat down beside me on the bed, wanting me to realize the difference in our sizes, even though I wasn't looking at him . . . With a huge paw, he scooped the pills off my lap and tossed them on the bed behind me, always smirking, making me smirk too at the corners of my mouth, because I knew he wanted to make me roll on the pills, . . . and then he gently took off his glasses, put them on the bedside table, and he began, knowing I would let him pass his huge palms over my shoulders, under my arms, knowing I would let him turn me to him as he did and pass his hands down my ribs to my thighs and inside my legs . . . he was defining my shape under his smirk with his hands as if staking claim to his domain, making me feel where it was, as if teaching me where and what I was . . . and I didn't move, Eva, I only smiled with my cold mouth, letting him, as I waited for the coming of that mocking, whispering Darkness—the rivers of laughing girls, to give me my true definition again, to spring up from where he could never touch, and I closed my eyes . . . and I felt myself being lifted, Eva! He'd put his hands under my shoulders and was lifting me up to my feet on the floor, to take my clothes off, and I let him . . . he took them off very slowly, always smirking, always without a word, always supremely confident, and then he passed his hands slowly, always more slowly, all over my surface again, along my axis, as if I were a statue he were fashioning into life . . . and with his fingers he slowly drew my face, the circles of my eyes, my lips, always defining me, teaching me my perimeter and I knew he wanted to do all that before finally trying to invent my center, reduce me to one point and nothing more, and I started listening for the secret rivers of girls to come laughing and foaming . . . with my name bright in the Darkness when suddenly his hands were nowhere on me, and I felt air all around me, outlining my nakedness as I stood on the floor where he'd put me, my feet slightly apart . . . He'd stepped back to take off his own clothing, confident of my immobility . . . and as I looked at him, his arrogance made me smile again, irresistibly, Eva! I didn't move my head, or even my eyes once they were on him, I just smiled at the corners of my mouth as he stood up and then lay me down on the bed, on the pills, and he began to pass his mouth over my body . . . never saying a word, or touching my mouth . . . what arrogance, Eva! except his hands, parting my lips, moving down, parting me where he chose . . . and he began penetrating me everywhere with his hands, leaving nothing private now, possessing everything as if reminding me of its existence, and it all was beginning to make me smile and tremble with

233

excitement while I tried keeping still as I could before the coming of the promised wild, dark wind, and the more his hands tried to make me concrete, though he couldn't know it, the more I could feel myself opening wide inside for the bottomless, rimless Darkness where there is no center . . . and when I saw him studying my face, to see what effect he was having I said, "Try harder . . . ," and he stopped. For an instant, his cheeks hardened and I smiled the very same smile that had made other men want to slap my face, throw me down in their fury, shake me about if they could, try to thrash me into life if they dared, only to make me feel my cool, dark distance all the more the more they raged . . . and my breathing became quick and shallow, drying and chilling my throat in anticipation as I waited, confident now, for all his strength to throw itself against me, to lash the serpentine rivers of gossiping girls out of their hiding place and let me taste the secret laughing breath of my Self in their hysterical foam . . . and I closed my eyes, and felt the bravado of his enormous thing pressing against my thigh . . . but then it withdrew. He withdrew. I heard the bed groan as he stood up on the floor, and I turned to look at him to see if he was simply going to leave me there, when I found him smirking down at me again, confident as ever. He wasn't at all furious, Eva . . . it was odd . . . His distant little eyes, naked without his glasses, brightened like a knife edge, and he was grinning down at me, appraising and savoring the white acid taste of the knife in his own mouth. He looked genuinely excited now, different than before, as if suddenly come alive like a giant lizard flicking its tongue in the breeze, smelling prey . . . he was accepting my challenge, Eva! He understood it, and he was going to openly battle me with his distance and must have seen my eyes brighten though I tried to hide it, tried to hold stiff as I started breathing icy jets through my nose . . . because he laughed as he went off to his clothes.

Keeping my voice flat, I said, "Don't put on a condom," but he only turned, never saying anything, only looking at me over his shoulder as he did something or other to himself, putting something on he had taken out of a pocket. And then he came back to stand next to me, without a condom, and he turned my head with his hands making me see his enormous size again, his blind, remorselessly reptilian animal, as if trying to frighten me . . . ! Eva, if the rivers of girls could have seen him, they would have flooded over with laughter, and thinking of them, I began to tremble, cold again and

thrilling with promise, happy now, sure I was going to feel the chill
of my dark wind inside me again filling me infinitely. I closed my
eyes to feel it, Eva, as he spread my legs and held my hands over
my head as if I were his prey and as he penetrated me, for one in-
stant, I was almost sure I was beginning to feel the chill, Eva, very
faintly, but it was him . . . it was strange, Eva, warm only for an in-
stant, and then instantly cold, like ice, making me mistake it for the
chill at first . . . only I'd never felt it like that . . . and then I began to
feel I was being penetrated by a huge thick icicle, impaling me,
disorienting me and a shocked, hissing noise escaped out of my
mouth . . . it was as if the serpentine darkness itself were escaping,
Eva! I'd never made a noise with a man in me before, but I was so
surprised, so short of breath, and as he impaled me, hurting, jam-
ming me, I thought there was almost no room left for me! The ice
burned, Eva! And as he moved his huge, expanding ice animal in-
side me slowly, I began to feel myself swelling and chilling inside,
too . . . but not my chill, Eva, his! The acid burn of a white chill,
penetrating me, cramming my organs . . . and defining my center
with ice, and then slowly turning into fire, Eva! Fire, penetrating me,
licking my center, setting it on fire, freezing it and burning it as he
kept moving and I began to get numb and to feel the cold numbness
radiating . . . and then the numbness passed and I began to feel raw
and cold inside, and then raw and hot. He was irritating me and I
said, "Hurry up . . . ," but he kept on imposing the same rhythm,
smirking, and it started to feel like ropes running through me, Eva,
burning a path, and I began to feel the irritation burning white in-
side, and turning red, swelling, a red raw wound that started to
scream white, and I said, "Get off me!" but he held me down with
my hands over my head and kept at me as if trying to drive me out of
myself, and I tried to push him off but I couldn't move my hands un-
der his and I began to cry from the pain that was so raw, which sud-
denly turned liquid and hot as if my flesh inside were beginning to
melt. I didn't want to, Eva, but I started crying as suddenly my
wound hurt so much it started thirsting for more fire, more fire to
burn it and melt it as if now that there was no escape it could only
find relief in more fire, nothing but fire, disappearing in the fire,
becoming transformed into the fire that was killing it. I wanted to
explode, as if the only possible relief lay in dying, and I was dying
because I wasn't dying, but he kept penetrating me and with the
same implacable, burning rhythm, never letting me move my hands,

235

never saying a word, always smirking down at me, not about to stop,
and I realized he was going to go on forever, or until he'd killed me,
and I yelled "Get off!" and smirking he drew his thing back very
slowly, as if he really were finally going to get off, and I began crying
and sobbing uncontrollably again because my wound was screaming
for fire, freezing and burning at the same time, when suddenly I felt
him bang down on my pelvis, again and again and again and again
and I couldn't tell what I wanted anymore except to die, to burn, to
disappear, and I began writhing as if I were being fried and I
couldn't tell if it was happening to me or to a body beside me as I
heard myself screeching with a voice that wasn't mine anymore, that
I'd never heard before and I felt myself struggling with my body, in
and out, like a dying person fighting against giving up the ghost and
the two feelings would come together when I felt his hard, bristly
legs, his beast legs, and his stubble scraping my face, and his
hateful, hot breath that was becoming all I could breathe, filling my
mouth and my throat . . . until suddenly I felt myself explode,
crying, flooding hot and releasing, flowing completely like rivers
running fire, humiliatingly sweet, and I heard my hiss come out like
from a dying snake, long and defeated.

. . . smirking, he put on his clothes, with me lying on my pills,
pills sticking to the backs of my arms, my thighs, incrusted in my
back . . . and as he dressed he looked over at me, then looked down
at the floor beside the bed . . . he took a step and bent down, picking
up some pills that had fallen there and put them on the bed beside
me, letting them roll against me.

. . . and he left me without saying a word.

I didn't move, Eva, not until after I heard the front door close. Not
even then. And finally I took the pills that had rolled against me, saw
how small they were, and hated them for their smallness. I held them
for a long, long time, still not moving, until finally I threw them
across the room.

I already knew I wasn't going to take them, Eva! I couldn't, and he
knew it too, just as he knew I'd end walking through the last season
of the world—which would last forever now—looking for him, my in-
sides cut open to the air, burning with his white acid, seeing his
traces everywhere, mocking me, like the acid taste of the knife
playing in everyone's eyes when they saw me.

He's the one laughing now, Eva. I can't think of myself the same
way anymore. He ripped out that hard-edged girl I'd seen in Dr.

Fish's eyes, and he took her with him . . . and lying on Norma's bed, I began hating him while I still could. I began hoarding, husbanding my hatred, Eva, because it was all I had left of me.

He had me, Eva, folded and tucked away like a handkerchief, and as I began living, thinking of nothing but him, waiting to see him again, I never felt so small, so alone, because the Darkness had left me, Eva. It didn't know me anymore, because I'd changed. Nothing was secretly infinite anymore. No double, icy smile, ironic anymore. Everything was just itself, reduced, like me, and I began to be afraid that soon I'd burn so much, hate so much, I'd even lose my taste for the Darkness, forget the cool, bottomless breath of my soul . . . and lose it, Eva . . . lose it forever, just from thirsting for the sweetness of the liquid fire.

Eva, I'm not like you anymore, and the Darkness won't know me until I stop wanting what I don't want . . . He stole my Self, Eva, and he's even bored by me now . . . Sometimes he's even kind (I hate him so!) as if wishing he could give me back my Darkness, give back that hard-edged girl he ripped out of me . . . but he can't, Eva . . . I must take her back from him . . . I must rip the fire out of him . . . I must avenge myself, Eva, or the laughing Darkness in Sophia's night will leave me behind forever . . . The serpentine Darkness has no interest in charity for the weak, Eva . . . the weak, the burning slaves, . . . we used to laugh at them, Eva . . . as I know the Darkness now laughs about me, gossiping in those foaming rivers of girls that never forget . . .

And Dr. Fish is watching me from his window, hoping, knowing Frank has been avoiding me. Wondering if I'm back on this hill because I want him to take care of me, at last.

He doesn't know I'm hiding here, Eva, trying to keep myself from going looking for Frank again, from trying to meet him even before he said he would meet me (out of kindness, Eva! I hate him so . . . he's agreed to let me be near the girl he's got tucked and folded away, to tease me with her before he puts her back in his pocket, dead and white). Frank said he'd meet me tonight, Eva, but for the last time. I tried to promise him one last humiliation, an even greater one than any before . . . he smirked, he thought I was asking him to kill me, I think . . . he smirked as if he knew my secret, as if I could have no other than the one he burned into me . . . he burned his portrait into me, his smirk, his hateful, acid smirk . . . burning out the Darkness . . . but I do have one last secret, Eva . . . my belly *is swelling with fire, with his smirking face, growing until it parts me open to the skies and screams its fire like a rooster . . . but he doesn't know it. I won't tell him about that. He might think I'm begging, asking for his pity. He'd tell me to abort . . . and I will, Eva . . . I will, I'll abort his fire forever. I'll negate it absolutely, absolutely . . . and then the free Darkness will come fill me again . . . I'm going to avenge myself, Eva. I'm going to breathe my Darkness again, I'm going to get my soul back. I'm going to rip out his fire. I swear I will, I swear it by my soul, Eva, by our soul . . .*

As I said before, Althea killed Frank Long the very next day.

UNEARTHLY RUMORS.
ALL TRUE

(The Trial)

I will never forget how people reacted.

The first public announcement came over the two o'clock news: some socially prominent girl had killed her equally prominent, married lover. Odd, but only because people of that sort didn't settle their differences that way, not in Boston.

That was all that people heard at first.

But something else started flying, communicating itself through the air, because people's voices immediately took on a peculiar, faintly depressed, muffled quality, as if already sensing that some unfortunate disruption of the Natural Order had occurred. It was almost as if they were instantly and subconsciously preparing themselves for coping with the fact that now, behind the familiar face of Boston's reality, nothing was the same anymore. As if maybe, while they'd slept, there had been an invasion of bristly-legged night beasts that had come from their Underground to set up a new government on Beacon Hill.

Then, with the setting sun and the appearance of the first evening tabloids, it came: that first, crucial photograph fixing itself in everyone's mind.

People buying the papers stopped on the street and looked at it as if it were the first visual confirmation of that dreaded, dimly suspected night beast invasion.

It was of Althea. Giving herself up. Caught in profile, in stark black and white, as she walked into the Joy Street Police Station.

And God knows she *did* manage to seem like a member of another, inhuman species, making a rare appearance in the light of our photographable reality, after having been around us for who knows how long before this self-revelation. She looked unnaturally serene in her stride, faintly mannish in her tweed jacket, dark despite the unmistakably feminine lunar smoothness of her white face, and a good head and a half taller than either the nervous Mel Fish or her family lawyer as they trailed behind her up the station steps, a stride or two behind like her toadying human companions, already selling out to the blood-drinking night beasts.

That was all it took.

From that photograph's appearance, New England's collective imagination was off and running, fully launched into the process of mythifying her into the most inhuman of all our regional monsters. Canonizing her. Sending her up to take her place in a pantheon that included Lizzie Borden and had a spot waiting for the Boston Strangler.

But from the start, even Lizzie Borden, or for that matter, the eventual Boston Strangler (who did things to older women that tough civil servants close to the case would still rather not discuss) were more indulgently regarded than she.

Awful as they both were, they achieved a kind of popularity. They inspired ambivalence. Lizzie, after all, killed her parents, and gave her mother an extra whack of the ax to show the difference in her feelings, while the Strangler appealed as a sort of traditional Romantic. Whatever they did, ghastly as it was, also struck a dark but richly responsive chord within their audience which above all humanized them. But Althea never did strike that chord. And worse, never once seemed to be trying to do so. From the very beginning, she repelled like some alien, scaly creature caught feeding on the still warm bowels of a Little Leaguer in the dusk of some neighborhood playground. If anything, looking up, she seemed mildly surprised that there was such a thing as public reaction to her feeding. And people seized on that insensitivity, because to the politically sensitive world of Boston, it let them make her recognizably Brahmin. They saw it as a kind of inhumanity that was the most humanoid thing about her.

And as the tensions of those politically charged times began mixing in, with Senator Joe McCarthy making such capital of attacking Harvard and the fancy folk of the State Department for selling out the People, I began getting the helpless feeling that the alienating process would never reverse itself.

As for me, shocked as I was, when I heard the news, as I mentioned before, I wasn't surprised. Only surprised that I wasn't surprised. Which made me feel odd. Alone.

But then, how could I have been surprised after having been confronted by the outraged Light in the story I'd just read and couldn't get out of my mind. Frank Long had mocked her ruthlessly by diverting her from suicide. Worse. He'd diverted her from joining that interior living Darkness she called Sophia's Wind, making her roll in helpless erotic spasms right on top of her dozens of sleeping pills as he'd plundered her will with a small smile.

What I was expecting, now that she'd killed him, now that she probably felt autonomous again, was to hear that she'd finally gone to kill herself, at last. Triumphantly.

And she certainly looked autonomous in that first photograph as she walked into the Police Station. Quite unlike the strangely beautiful but possessed girl I'd seen dancing with Long at Norma's party, the one whose very soul seemed absent when he wasn't around.

Looking at that photograph, I kept thinking she was just savoring her triumph for now. By killing him, she'd more than avenged her pride. She'd purified herself. Regained her good standing with those rivers of laughing girls in her interior Darkness which she was sure had been laughing at her of late. Because of Frank, of course, and what he could do with her. Just like they'd always laughed with her before at all the other "slaves", as she called the rest of us life-bound sorts. Soon, I was sure, she was going to walk away from life, when she'd grown tired of savoring her triumph.

241

And as her black canonization progressed all around me, with more and more pictures of Althea striding across the front pages, day after day, it pained me to see that, just as I'd feared, she was progressively looking in everybody's eyes like the coldest and most distasteful night beast of them all.

Right in front of me, she was becoming the Monster of Beacon Hill, and there was nothing I could do about it.

And the more people mythified her, the more openly they resented her. She didn't even show the modesty of trying to hide her face from the cameras, like others accused, say hoods, or gangsters, or even politicians. She had an uncanny way of turning and looking directly and evenly at the cameras with her clear eyes that made people's reactions back off into grumbles about how the rich think they can get away with murder, and laugh in the common man's face. Worse, for Christ's sake. Not even to laugh. Like Althea there, that big, cold, black, night beast that looked so icy, so composed, she even seemed beyond arrogance. And beyond gender.

But galled as they were, their sociological complaints soon started sounding hollow to me. Forced. Like something they were seizing on to sound their notes of helpless bitterness about something else far more humiliating than mere sociology. Something which they dimly understood, but understood well enough to want to avoid understanding any further.

Only, the Unseen and Mysterious Forces were intent on not letting *anybody* avoid it now. That's what was happening.

With Long's killing and mutilation, the UMFs were trying to force everybody—not just me alone anymore—to confront the full and quickly hardening blackness of Althea's Light, right up in the plain light of waking consciousness. The moment I realized that, I confess I felt a strong and shameful flush of jealousy. Whether they liked it or not, it was now part of all their lives.

And they *didn't* like it, because the Light, that expression of her very soul, had instantly looked to them as black as the blackest of sins, somehow. From their first intuitions about her, long before the horrible evidence that would come out at her trial, confirming those intuitions.

So it was a battle. The UMFs were trying to force their consciousness, and the people, suddenly finding there was no turning away from it, unable to avoid its presence, fought back. Not wanting to see and feel her humanity (which made me feel alone again, pained me for her, but eased by jealousy), they mythified her. At once. To shield themselves from seeing full on that bottomless blackness they sensed in her. Because they also sensed she just might be, portrait of the human soul, the ultimate mirror that would absorb them all into the Void as the Light unveiled itself before them, showing off its nude, icy Darkness with a wanton, smiling pride that would violate all decorums.

That was why, when the first news came out, it was as if a faint shudder had rippled through the interior caverns of the town's dream life, as if responding to some dark, odd wind that had escaped from some unremembered season. Sophia's Wind, followed by fear, the beginning of self-protection. Which was immediately followed by that first, blind, mythifying reflex—blind and wanting to be blind, as everyone's chill, anticipatory horror began crystallizing itself around her visible black Light, covering it and turning her into a painfully brilliant but opaque apparition in their waking lives.

What was really happening was that, suddenly confronted, people counterattacked by glazing their eyes over at once. Instinctively, with the immemorial animal wisdom of the species, they were stupefying themselves, dressing the naked blackness of her Light with their militant incomprehension, eclipsing her humanity from their consciousness as much as possible.

That was why she was being turned so quickly into the Monster of Beacon Hill.

But actually, it was quite easy for them to associate her with the un-Natural. Leaving that first photograph aside, if nothing else, just from the way those unearthly rumors about her started up would have been enough. They'd started up as if by spontaneous generation. Or worse. Like unsuspected miniscule creatures that had been around all the time, lying in wait, as for a death, before breaking loose, which they did in nothing flat, with the usual lack of respect for the deceased.

And then, too, there was that disquieting, obvious difference between the mood of the people finding themselves somehow forced to utter the rumors (always with an odd sense of self-violation) and the mood of the rumors themselves.

The people talking were edgy, depressed, given to uncomfortable laughter, while the swirling rumors they found streaming out of their mouths and into the public air had a peculiarly gay, cruel and distinctly celebratory tone. Nobody could miss the malice and spite there. Not that they were celebrating Althea, either. Their champion. As if her victory (nobody knew *why* it was, except that it was) were their victory. And as they came pouring out they started multiplying, joining forces, mixing and sounding like a nastily teasing bunch of invisible schoolgirls holding hands and snake-dancing through the town, chanting, "Nyah-Nyah! Nyah-Nyah!"

I swear, Long's naked body couldn't have been drained of its blood for more than a few hours when those taunting, snake-dancing rumors were already running rampant all over town, multiplying faster and faster and cavorting all over the place. By the next noontime there were so many they were swamping the town, absolutely brazen, answering to no one, mocking and obviously impossible to restrain for ordinary mortals.

(To me, there was something familiar about them which continually made me remember Althea's invisible rivers of laughing girls, those overflowing, rampaging rushes of suddenly gossiping, giddy Darkness turned into thousands of crystalline voices by its energy, which Althea had felt foaming inside herself in her own few moments of triumph. Just like these rumors, they'd been gossiping and laughing about everything and everybody, too, themselves exempt, respecting no limits, accepting no laws, only made more wildly amused by such things now that they knew themselves as uncontrollable as a rising tidal wave of wild schoolgirls when the last bell has announced the freedom of a summer from which they shall never be recaptured. And when I was sure I recognized them, I felt more alone than ever. I knew I couldn't tell anyone, not even Mel.)

But what made them odder still was that the stories going around were unbelievable, one might say—if it weren't for the fact that they were believed. Completely. As if people just didn't have the energy to fight them. And they had a nasty way of suddenly appearing at any social gathering, just as people were starting to think that for once, the subject wouldn't come up—and then the rumors would flood the area, occupying all points of human contact, leaving no room for argument, before suddenly rushing off, snake-dancing and giddy as ever, leaving everybody silent and with a renewed sense that they'd been had, again, without anybody feeling capable of rationally explaining why.

But the very strangest, most un-Natural thing about them, something which made them unique among rumors, was their oppressive consistency with one another.

244

In every cycle, Althea (her clear profile, Librarian smooth, always still as a mask) bought the pistol exactly two weeks in advance of the killing, as undramatically as getting a volume from its proper shelf.

In every cycle, Frank Long was the same. Huge. Successful. Rather ugly. And a ladies' man . . . who obviously should have had the sense not to have sex with her in the first place. But who somehow, in every cycle, finding her alone on a bed at an empty friend's house, was never able to pass up the conquest. He was the rooster in his social circle, they said, "got their number right away", and moved right in for the kill where other, lesser men might pause. But this time, he always regretted it. A lot. In all the rumors. Because after having sex with him, she took to haunting his house, his office, even his mother's house up in New Hampshire. She even materialized uninvited at parties (silent as ever, dark, even despite the lunar whiteness of her smooth, still face) where he was, or was expected to be.

In all the rumors, early in the game, while Long still thought things were normal, when she'd show up like that at some party, almost out of thin air, he'd smile at her presence, because *of course* other women had chased him before, even a little crazily sometimes, like this one . . .

(. . . for example, everybody had heard now how last year a certain blond Mrs. Briggs had chased him all over town, too. Even down to New York. Leaving her husband. Not caring what anybody thought about it, either . . . until she finally stopped, and went back to her husband. She stopped because of what was left of her pride. Because she figured out that what Long *really* enjoyed, what he truly found satisfying, was her chasing him. She said it herself. And since he had what he wanted, she knew she'd never get what she wanted.)

So Frank Long hadn't really been alarmed when Althea showed up some place unexpectedly, looking for him. Not at first anyway. Because he confidently assumed that eventually their own pride stopped them. He counted on that. It was only human. The only question was how long they might keep after him . . . now, *that* was interesting.

But soon it appeared that this crazy, silent girl Althea didn't seem to have any pride at all, which was so surprising, especially after she seemed to everybody to have so much . . . which of course had been what had made her so appealing a quarry for Frank in the first place . . . not her looks, goodness knows. She'd hardly been the best looking, most alluring female around, by any means.

And what made her even stranger was that, once she'd been had, having been made to change, even in public, Althea didn't even look bitter about it. Not even after each of his escapes. She seemed most inhuman that way, as if a large section of her were missing. She was so set on him that when she showed up some place like that, she didn't even seem to notice how people looked at her. All her edges, even her severe black hair, seemed suddenly yielding, more rounded, softer. People who hadn't seen her coming in would instinctively turn to look, as if called by her new, even hammered, softness. And her unlined face was almost ghostlike in its unselfconsciousness. Looking with her eyes for Long she seemed nude. And naked. Both like a lost soul in search of its body, and like a child, as children never are, with an unearthly air about her of something like purity and docility, now that she'd lost something he had. And everyone thought, without having to say so, she looked beautiful now, as she had at Norma's party . . . as well as unfortunate. How strange. After looking at her, people had to turn away, embarrassed, and excited.

And God knows Long tested her. Like the time, in all the rumors, when she drifted into one particular party, when he said in a loud voice, "Really, Althea . . . the *way* you behave. Sometimes I think you are pre-Social Contract," and everyone laughed, like a sudden fusillade he'd triggered as he sat back and looked around with a little smile.

But her face didn't change. Not even then, except for a soft, surprising smile of her own, as if the sudden cutting laughter at her expense had been like a light, pleasant breeze. If anything, the laughter only seemed to smooth and round her face a bit more, for the moment it lasted.

And then she quietly waited where she stood, again showing no bitterness, as the disconcerted hostess began scuffling about, eventually producing a chair and some plates for her, too. She said, "Thank you," and sat down, and the conversation went on again, eventually as if she weren't there at all, so clear was the suspended animation of her soul as she waited for Frank.

. . . She was so insistent, so like water, like wind, that soon he took to hiding. Forced to escape. Warning systems were set up. Everyone was forced to collaborate with their silences.

. . . and then she took to coming out after him in the daylight, more and more often looking for him in his office. His staff was alerted, of course, like his hostesses. And when she'd come there, again it was like trying to keep the wind out. She would not leave, at least no further than outside the front door. So to keep her from under foot, she'd be ushered by the receptionist into a room out of the way, with a promise to keep her there . . . with Frank Long of the small smile (smiling a bit less now, beginning to show the strain) eventually slipping out without seeing her.

And more than once she came out of the room, usually a storage room, to find a janitor buffing the floor of an empty office corridor, himself surprised to see anyone there at that time, all the office doors locked, the street lights on outside, the traffic noises in a different mood . . .

And then, in all the rumors there was always the next to last time she called him. At his mother's house, having traced him there. Up in New Hampshire. When the elder Mrs. Long picked up the phone, recognized her voice, and told her stiffly—the way those people can be—that he was not in . . . but then he came to the phone anyway.

Again he told her he would not see her anymore. Which she seemed to finally believe as he hung up the phone without saying good-by, curt as his mother. And Althea went and bought the gun.

And then she gave him five days rest, always five days in every cycle of rumors, before she called him again, this time at his own house, and begged him to meet her one more time, for the last time. She said she understood that. No, she wouldn't change her mind. The last time, yes, she said, with that low, flat voice of hers, that Yankee monotone. And Long gave in, for the last time. The ladies' man. He would grant her this last favor. She said thank you. He hung up.

And that last time, in all the rumors, they always met in the apartment of a friend of hers, to make love . . .

(. . .make love . . . hearing it, nobody liked the word because . . . is *that* what they did? . . . can we really bear to use that same petaled word, even if sometimes, profaned, it has smelled of churches and other times of medicine, that word which we use to describe the secret energies of sentient life when it is blooming through our souls and up through our bodies, for what *they* did? Is *that* the word to describe what our horrified mind's eye could only see magnified—and then only in outline, mercifully, through the swirling screen of the giddily laughing rumors, laughing at our expense—as the violently titanized confusion of their tangling, reptilian shapes? In our mind's rumor-clouded eyes, their huge shapes

247

thrashed and twined like prehistoric beasts, roaring deafly and fighting to the death, until at last . . . suddenly . . . which one? it was hard in our horror to see through the screen . . . one of them was caught by its rearing, outstretched neck, shaken, toppled, slammed down to the ground, making the sad earth itself reverberate . . . And then, the toppled one moved less and less, as if its life were ebbing away into the other's jaws, growing limp at the neck, finally, as still as death, to be consumed by the victor . . . who was also slowly becoming still too, with a momentary peace too cruel for our eyes and hearts to accept as peace . . .) while the FM radio played a recording of Mozart's *Don Giovanni*.

. . . *Don Giovanni*. In all the rumors the chorus was *Don Giovanni*, amused by the spectacle of life. And it played as they tangled and thrashed because Frank loved opera.

His family name always appeared on the program among the patrons, and he loved this opera above all others. He was known to sing whole sections, and he insisted on hearing it even while he granted Althea her last meeting, not wanting to miss it under any circumstances. Having never missed by his own account any live performance of that opera in either Boston or New York.

And the absurd chorus of the rumors became an absurd, incontrovertible fact at the trial, when Ernest Minelli made much of the effect of the music of *Don Giovanni* on Althea in his opening remarks, presenting her as a woman scorned by a cold seducer, so cold he insisted on listening to his own celebration in the music, reveling in the solitary voluptuousness of irony. Even while thrashing.

The trial. People still talk about it, it was so offensive.

The court was jammed by the limited number that could get in, but it was as if it were held out in the Boston Common. Everybody was looking, their heads filled with all the rumors, wondering only how much of it would be made public.

And it fell on poor Ernie Minelli to defend her. I'm sure he didn't want it. Mel and I had known him at Boston Latin, and he went to Harvard Law. He played defensive tackle and offensive center at Bowdoin where he went on an athletic scholarship. A North End Italian. A Republican because the Irish had it locked up at the

248

Democratic Party. A deserving ethnic who once seemed born to bridge the gap between the Catholic urban vote and that of the swamp Wasps in the sticks. Photographed in his campaign literature with his wife and eight lovely daughters, which signified that though Republican, he was not a complete apostate. Everything going for him, maybe even a crack at being Lt. Governor soon. And then it happened to him. Althea's trial.

But Ernie didn't flinch. Broad-chested, he stood up to take the punishment just as he must have had to take the punishment in all that college line play, back when they called him "Two-way Minelli"—a name that was about to come back to haunt him. And with the whole world looking at him—a stoic, white-shirted, stripe-tied, blue-suited, two-hundred-pound block of clean, indefatigable careerism at a lonely crossroad—he started in slowly, saying she was only a poor, pathetic creature. Disturbed. In love. And hopelessly overmatched by a man he began referring to almost exclusively as "this ruthless, experienced Lothario." Indeed, he claimed, though she might not look it, "because of the advantages of birth and wealth", she was still "just a poor, lost little girl who had to endure the untimate humiliation" of being minimized by his "heartless insistence on hearing *Don Giovanni*, even at the moment, the very *last* moment she could ever hope to have his full attention . . . "

And with that, everybody started looking at big Ernie more closely. Particularly remembering he always ran for office as a hard-fisted Law-and-Order candidate, always volubly opposed to coddling criminals. "Yes, she was disturbed!" he protested loudly, his face stern as could be. "Yes, she could think of nothing in her obsession but of this ruthless, experienced Lothario! But don't forget . . . ," he paused, nodded, looked around the room slowly while nodding on, before resuming, "she *also* came from a cultured home, and even in her troubled mind, the irony of the music . . . was not lost on her . . .

"My question now is, was *he* so insensitive, so filled with himself, that the irony was lost on *him*? As a father of daughters myself, ladies and gentlemen, I shudder to think: can men be so cruel? I mean, couldn't he *see* that the music was salt rubbed in her open wounds? Was he so bestial that he did see, and didn't care? Or . . . that he did care, and it amused him? . . . I am sorry to say, ladies and gentlemen, that from what I've learned of this ruthless, experienced Lothario, the last alternative, the cruelest alternative,

249

seems the likeliest one. That is why I say, when violence welled up inside her like a scream, *can* we be surprised?"

And there it was. Right in front of everybody, Minelli shamelessly was going all out, trying the character of the victim in the great tradition of murder defenses. He was on "their" side, Minelli.

People at court shifted in their seats and exchanged glances. In Brighton, my cousin Tommy Muldoon (who *knew* I knew both Mel and Ernie and who never trusted me in the first place for going to Harvard), himself a postal employee, Veteran of Foreign Wars, a Catholic and anti-Communist, lowered his newspaper and rolled his eyes at me over Minelli, and said what he always said when something overstrained his capacity for belief, "Jeh-suss!"

Part of the problem in selling Althea as a poor little thing overmatched by an "experienced" Lothario was, of course, her much-rumored promiscuity, which no one doubted.

A newspaper cartoon appeared, with Law-and-Order Ernie wearing a mask like the Lone Ranger, with Mel as Tonto, his Indian companion, both gunning down the "decent folk" and helping the Bad Man escape, with the caption, "Are you sure this is our job, Keemosabe?"

Mel, of course, was in the cartoon right along with him because he was figured to be the star witness, as her doctor, for both the prosecution and the defense. Which didn't make him popular with the general public either.

And they all remembered him from that first photograph, too, trailing along behind Althea into the Police Station. So they knew damn well he was on "their" side. But Law-and-Order Minelli . . . that he should be doing "their" dirty work with such zeal shocked them so much, they still couldn't believe it.

It started a revival of World War II jokes about Italians.

But Minelli pressed on.

The coroner had said that Long's death had "occurred" somewhere around the time the opera was playing on the radio.

Minelli seized on it and carried it further. He decided to claim it happened at *exactly* the end of the performance.

And the times Mel took the stand, people were fascinated because everything Mel said coincided with every story everyone had heard. Perfectly. Their general disgust was momentarily stilled by the symmetry they saw before them. It was almost as if they could only be silent out of awe and admiration as it came out in court, *all* of it.

Just as in every rumor, after Frank and Althea had had sex for the last time (yes, Mr. Long was in the habit of applying cocaine to his member, making himself even more powerful through prosthesis and accounting in everyone's mind for his great reputation with the ladies), Long once more ended up laying beside her, next to the wall. For the last time. Dozing naked, smiling as his favorite opera applauded him even in his dreams . . . while she watched, and kept vigil, unfathomable, all blackness behind the impassive whiteness of her smooth face, her lunar forehead as unlined as always, her eyelids cast down, as always, while his rectangular, rimless glasses lay on the bedside table (and now everybody, not only me, could see his thin lipped grin, the little white spectacle marks at either side of his huge, Mt. Rushmore nose) . . . and as the music came to its cascading, laughing conclusion (for the last time) all the voices soaring and sinking and soaring like an explosion of rococo angels, she silently produced the cold black steel of her snub-nosed pistol, held it an inch from his temple so that the touch of the metal wouldn't wake him before she meant to, and then she pulled the trigger . . . and the bullet that leaped out, penetrating his skull, shattering and flying past his own startled dreams, kept on flying into all our dream lives, and kept on rising until finally it emerged in our waking lives, hard as fact, incontrovertible, only stopping its flight to have its dark shape held up at the trial, for everyone to see, by Ernie Minelli's right thumb and forefinger, and we all had to look, as Ernie called for compassion for a helpless, love-crazed girl.

One the public could *not* see in Althea.

Because when they looked over at her, sitting Sphinx-like at her desk, one forearm over the other, what they saw was somebody composed beyond all decency, as if she were reigning. They couldn't think of her as helplessly out of control. Not now, that was for sure. Nor when she'd bought the gun so far in advance, either, or when she'd so sensibly called her doctor and her lawyer before turning herself in with a ready plea of insanity. And most of all, which really stuck in their craws as they looked over at her, not when she was somebody with a history of abortions, who suddenly and most conveniently didn't want one, for once, in a state where no pregnant woman had ever received capital punishment.

And much of the time she didn't even look interested, much less contrite, while poor Ernie kept on straining in her behalf, shoving the bullet up in the air, exclaiming, "Hatred is dehumanizing, ladies and gentlemen! And it reduced this poor, already disturbed girl's whole being to nothing more than the bullet I hold before you. Obviously, ladies and gentlemen, we aren't looking at a responsible human being, accountable for its actions. Deadly, yes. But *only* because of the circumstances that impelled it. But in itself, innocent! We are looking at something we would not deign to punish!

"Because . . . when she pulled the trigger, that's all she was: a bullet! Impelled by circumstances. Completely out of touch with any sense of right or wrong!

"Imagine, if you can, *how* she must have felt, watching that ruthless, married man, sleeping smugly before her after having had his way with her, *again*, listening to that laughing and fiendishly refined music play . . . *knowing* she'd been discarded! She would have been inhuman indeed if she didn't think at such a time of all the other women who have been seduced and abandoned, laughed at, mocked, scorned . . . and even *more* inhuman if she didn't think about the child, *his* child, which she already knew she was carrying in her entrails. The child was being scorned, too!

"Then, it all came together. Her brows knit, her soul coagulated with total fury, and then, as the applause exploded in her ears at the conclusion of that sophisticated music, this wounded young girl, in a fit of mad, vengeful passion . . . perhaps even righteous passion in the eyes of some . . . herself scorned, her *child* scorned . . . *shot* the Lothario! . . . And then, her pent-up fury unleashed, carried away, she *mutilated* his body! *Mutilated*, ladies and gentlemen! We cannot turn our eyes away from that! Mutilation, ladies and gentlemen.

"Obviously, only the act of a desperately sick person, carrying out a self-destructive revenge while the enthusiastic applause rang in her ears . . . the applause of the very audience that had collaborated with the man she had loved and rejected her, which had even collaborated in the rejection of her, taking *his* side against hers!

"Because I am quite sure, ladies and gentlemen, that in her tortured mind, the audience applauding the music was made up *entirely* of those very people who had taken his side . . . and she felt herself inside that music, too. But as the butt of the comedy! With the Lothario as the popular favorite!

"No wonder she could take it no more. No wonder she struck and struck! Can't we see? She was striking at the whole world, ladies and gentlemen! No wonder she mutilated him."

And there it was. At last. The much-rumored mutilation. People had expected it would not be played up, because it was so distasteful, so awful. But now, to their amazement, it was becoming clear that the worse the things she did had been, the more they were going to be used in her favor by Minelli.

And as they looked over at her, even as the mutilation made people murmur, they saw her looking exactly the same as always, as if she were hearing nothing at all, her unlined face as ever in accord with the silence of a Library. Or if hearing, then ignoring, as easily as she might ignore the discreet steps and whispers of some people passing her by at her table at the Boston Public Library. "Wax museum smooth" that's how one newspaper writer had described her expression, and that's exactly what it was.

And now, looking at her, with the rumored mutilation an admitted fact, with her making no move to deny it, it was impossible not to wonder: had her face looked just like that, "wax museum smooth", had her eyelids been cast down, Librarian calm, even as she put the pistol one inch from his temple . . . even as she pulled the trigger? Had her face *ever* contorted, or struggled against tears, at least out of human nervousness, even as she got up and went to the kitchen, leaving Long bleeding from the head, eyes popped open, dead, as she got the huge carving knife? She couldn't have been dressed. Surely she was naked. But can a night beast ever be considered naked? Had she looked exactly as what they saw, coming back with the knife, when she castrated his body, put his private parts in a white towel, wrapped them in a brown S.S. Pierce bag and tied the package up with a white string? Did her face change, even for one moment, smiling, *anything*, as she drove those incredible three hours up to New Hampshire to his mother's house?

One thing was sure. She looked exactly as calm as what they were seeing (the Long maid reported it) when she stood at his mother's door, package in hand, and rang the doorbell. The maid saw her through the kitchen window when she handed the package to his mother, and then turned, . . . to drive three hours back to Boston . . . leaving the elder Mrs. Long collapsed in shock.

They could guess, too, how she'd looked as she'd dialed her doctor, and then her lawyer. But they didn't have to guess how she'd looked as she'd walked into the Police Station. They knew that first hand, from the first photograph. No one had forgotten that. Exactly like the monster they were looking at now.

And Mel took the stand.

He smiled nervously behind his glasses, aware of the general attitude toward him. Minelli approached him, looking most severe, as if determined to wring the truth out of him, as if he were an elusive witness but fooling no one by now.

"For the record, how long have you known Miss Stanton, doctor?"

"Since she was sixteen, when she first came under my care after an attempted suicide."

"Not her last attempt, I understand."

"No."

"I see. And does she not have an even longer psychiatric history than that?"

"Yes . . . since she was thirteen, when she first came to Mc-Leod's."

"I see. Now then, did she not also exhibit . . . and please excuse my poor command of your professional terminology, doctor . . . a distinctly morbid sexual psychopathology?"

Mel smiled, sighed. "Yes. And the word morbid is the most operational term here, I regret to say."

"Would you say she was . . . promiscuous?"

"At times, militantly. If you insist on these terms, I would say she was both promiscuous and what people call frigid."

"I take it that's not an unusual combination, doctor?"

"No. The only unusual thing here is the degree. Of both."

"So, you present us then with someone who is promiscuous, frigid, and a perennial suicide risk . . . and this is, of course, *not* her first pregnancy."

"Uh . . . no."

"How many before *this* one?"

" . . . four."

"All aborted, I understand, on your advice?"

"Uh . . . well, no. Last year, for example, it was too late, so the child was put up for adoption. Fortunately, we believe it is now in a loving home."

The principally Catholic public was not liking this any, and Ernie, Catholic father of eight was forced to publicly knit his brows at Mel: "Three aborted . . . on *your* advice," he said. "I believe you should tell *why*, doctor."

"Well, it seemed much the best course, on balance . . . her state of mind was not, well, promising, in terms of her relationship to the future child."

"Doctor . . . ," Minelli's voice deepened, "I can't help but ask, has she ever inquired . . . about her one surviving child?"

"I'm afraid not. She never showed any interest in it. Not even curiosity."

"But . . . don't you find that odd?"

"No. Not in Althea."

And with that, the disgust of the assembled Boston crowd became sufficiently audible for Judge Mott to look up and glare, reaching toward his gavel, which was enough for the moment.

Althea, immobile until now, as if sensing the jury was all looking at her, which it was, lifted up her head slowly and turned her clear, purple eyes on then, held their glance without expression, and then returned to looking at her forearms again, like a caged predator already long accustomed to the passing crowds.

In the pause, Minelli was making a show of shaking his head, until he finally said, "Now, doctor, about these abortions . . . and I warn you I am opposed to them personally, on religious grounds . . . though I try to respect other opinions . . . did she *ever* resist the idea? I mean, did she ever seem to be in any sort of moral quandary about them?"

Mel smiled modestly and shrugged, "I'm not a Catholic . . . but, we, well . . . our staff, would have been most encouraged . . . if . . .," and he shrugged again. "But no . . . I'm afraid not."

"Well . . . did she at least show signs of remorse afterwards, or at least, . . . I don't know, some *depression*?"

"Uh . . . no. Actually, her spirits always lifted visibly. I'd have to say that socially, she was at her best after her abortions. And she made splendid physical recoveries, too. I honestly believe that a layman might think, at such times, that she was normal and well-adjusted . . . for a shy person, of course, which is what she's always been. I'd even be tempted to say the abortions had a tonic effect on her," he concluded smilingly, but as he noticed the newly disagreeable silence in the room, he added quickly, "Uh . . . on the short term only, of course. Naturally."

But it was too late. Mel had been too enthusiastic about the "tonic effect" of the abortions. Sincerity had revealed itself, and Minelli put his right fist to his chin, crossed his arms, pretending to take in this medical estimate, but actually glaring angrily at the unhappy Mel, to whom it was just returning, apparently, that part of the defense was based on Althea's frustrated maternity.

The audience responded by exchanging cynical smiles behind Ernie, who looked as if he could have cheerfully strangled Mel right in the witness chair, for making things look even worse.

Then, Minelli said quietly, "That is very strange, doctor. By any standards. No sign of remorse, of loss . . . for a human female whose biological system has made a mother? I can't understand it."

"Well," Mel said, looking as serious as possible, "don't misunderstand me. You see, she didn't show those things, except *negatively*. I assure you, an unconscious defensive maneuver. Let me explain . . . you see, she *naturally* felt an irreparable loss . . . like any mother . . . which then, you see . . . translated itself into good cheer . . . ," and Mel smiled, but having said that, he must have felt terribly alone, because Minelli nodded and chose to turn away, heading for his table, while Judge Mott also chose this moment to neaten up and shuffle some papers.

Poor Mel, sitting there, trying to control the writhe in his smile. He must have sensed in that lonely moment that if the assembled people had then risen from their seats to come at him, neither Ernie nor Judge Mott would have done a thing to stop them.

. . . and damned if a newspaper caricaturist, of the "serious", naturalist variety, didn't choose to illustrate this moment, of *all* moments. With the caption of, " . . . the abortions had a tonic effect".

It was a pencil drawing, with Althea huge in the foreground, in half profile, looking on at a handwringing, bespectacled Mel talking to a stern, dark-suited Minelli beneath the aegis of the snow-haired, black-robed Judge Mott . . . whom rumor had now correctly identified as a distant relative of Althea's, on her mother's side.

Usually, in such caricatures, Althea had been looking down, one forearm over the other, enigmatic and immanent as ever. But in this one, she was looking right up, and there was the faint but unmistakable trace of her smile at Mel's words, and at the whole show. And to my amazement, the mediocre caricaturist caught the spirit of her singular smile perfectly. Thanks to him, everyone did. It was impossible not to. Her smile was now also part of the public domain.

It was the only time she was seen to smile during the whole trial. As far as I know, nobody but the caricaturist saw that smile. Maybe she never really did, just as she never did afterwards. But that drawing, that possible fiction, stayed in people's minds better than any words they heard or read. It was exhibit "A" in the people's case against Althea. The unspoken truth. The meaning of it all, as far as they were concerned. And quite enough, just in itself, aside from all the other evidence, for them to want her publicly stoned, to teach her her place. And all the more so because they were all sure now, in the futility of their furious hearts, that Althea would have smiled exactly the same way at the stone bearing mob, too, if she happened to choose, in her incomparable arrogance, to break through her usual immanent serenity to reveal her true contempt for them all. That is, if she really felt there was something about them important enough for her attention, which even the stones would not guarantee. Which made the public's blood boil even more.

The lower-middle-class public went wild, sending letters to newspapers calling her a "living insult", as well as everything else.

Now, with that portrait of her smile out in the open, if Ernie Minelli hadn't known it before, he must have known he'd better stop dreaming of running for Lt. Governor next time around. If ever. Now, his reward would have to be appointed office, next time the Republicans got in. If they didn't dump him.

And then came the final phase of the trial. The big finish. Mel was the brains behind this one.

By the time he got through, she was a monster to the middle class, too. Even out in the college graduate suburbs, the magazine-supported, pro-sexual-adjustment-to-the-woman's role Liberal opinion of the '50s couldn't possibly take her to its wall-to-wall bosom.

It made Mel famous as he never was, giving local anti-Semitism a whole new avenue of expression.

Everybody saw the pictures of Dr. Mel, with him walking up the white marble of the courthouse steps, holding dark Althea's left arm protectively (I always knew it was her Heart arm, though God knows I couldn't say so) as if he could give her more protection than the inner ring of blue, bulky Police Matrons and the outer ring of taller Policemen. Which he did. As everybody knew. To their mounting indignation. Because if any one of them did what she did, they'd sure as hell fry, or spend the rest of their lives in the can.

And the one picture that stayed in everybody's mind had him stopping halfway up those marble steps. Smiling. Never letting go of her Heart arm. With both Mel and Althea framed on that white marble hill by the Patrician sternness of two massive, twin pillars that waited up ahead for them, looking upstanding, Puritanical, and hypocritical as hell to the glowering mob that watched as Mel answered reporters' questions.

The crowd, forced most grudgingly to look at them, seemed to be squatting, and very much as if they would have loved to rush in and tear them both apart, flesh, hair, clothes and all, starting with him and ending with her. But holding back, they had to rechew the cud of knowing, which they certainly did, that once the smiling Dr. Mel had escorted Althea through those two Patrician pillars up ahead (which continued trying to suggest morality and equality before the Law), not only would she be out of their reach forever, but once again it would be demonstrated that they, the common folk of the Commonwealth, were very much the lower orders as far as the rich and well-connected were concerned. A point that the pro-McCarthy, anti-Harvard tabloids seized upon with a vengeance.

And no matter what Mel might have actually been saying to the reporters, the gist of it was the same in everybody's mind. Just as Althea's smile was imprinted in their memory, so was what Mel stood for, as her apologist. And his words were always some version of what he told Minelli from the witness stand.

"Now, doctor, you have described Miss Stanton as both promiscuous and frigid."

"Yes. Very much. Both."

"What do you mean by promiscuous . . . and forgive us for returning to this point, but it is important."

"Well . . . I don't like the term, really . . . but, I'd say . . . at one time or another she probably slept with nearly every willing male at our hospital. However, her own sensual pleasure from these activities was always negligible, by her own account."

"I see. Now, doctor, I am trying to determine . . . why she chose to kill Mr. Long out of all the men in her life." Mel nodded, and repressed a smile (maybe nobody else knew it, but I did. I could see he'd been waiting for this, the big finish) as Minelli continued, "We all know, don't we, doctor, that Mr. Long was an extremely experienced philanderer. But obviously this was not her first affair, either . . . or was it? You see, doctor, despite what you call her promiscuity . . . I still have a sense we all have, I think, which is that despite everything, Althea was really a very inexperienced girl."

"I couldn't agree with you more. Actually, I wouldn't call those other encounters affairs at all. I would say, if we insist on this word,

that this was perhaps her third . . . with the previous one having occurred perhaps two years before, with someone her age."

"Therefore, you *do* agree, do you not," said Ernie, as if beginning
to zero in (and Mel was just waiting, biding his time), "that she was,
despite her promiscuity, a *very* inexperienced girl?"

"Oh, absolutely, and very shy, too, as I explained. As a rule, she
hardly spoke to anyone, and at public gatherings she tended to with-
draw into herself completely, almost as if she hoped to disappear into the background."

(And as eyes turned to Althea, hardly surprised, they found she
didn't particularly look concerned one way or another about disappearing into the background, not any more than a crocodile on a
bank who knew the birds were cognizant of its presence.)

"Therefore, doctor, despite her promiscuity, you would have no
trouble agreeing that Mr. Long, older and worldly-wise, took advantage of her inexperienced and willing heart?"

"Hmmm . . . I don't know. Heart . . . "

"Excuse the unscientific term, doctor . . . but isn't it correct to say
she killed Mr. Long because she fell in love with him, and found herself vulnerable?"

"Well . . . kind of . . . " Mel, I knew from knowing for years, was
being coy, leading Minelli on, setting him up, better and better.

"Kind of?!" said Ernie. "You surprise me, doctor. Don't you
think, having been her long-time spiritual confidant, that this shy,
suicidal girl, so completely closed in on herself, killed Mr. Long
because . . . well, because . . . having completely given her heart to
this older man, having thought for *once* in her life, now that she was
in love, she had a chance at happiness at last . . . I mean, damnit,
doctor . . . wasn't she bitterly disappointed? Isn't it only natural optimism on her part, especially at her tender age, to think that with
love one can start living at last? Wasn't her violence in proportion to
her sudden, unexpected hopefulness at joining the . . . Human Community?"

"Well . . . ," Mel said, and Minelli was looking more flustered by
the minute, so convincingly that onlookers were beginning to
whisper, some in admiration of his performance, others not, forcing
Judge Mott to bang down his gavel.

"You don't agree?" said Ernie incredulously.

"I wish I could, but . . . well, I regret to say she was never in love
with Mr. Long, or optimistic in the pleasant way you describe. I have

259

it from the horse's mouth that she hated Mr. Long from the very beginning."

"But . . . why?"

"Well . . . Mr. Long was not a likeable man, as you have pointed out, and Althea has always been a magnificent judge of character. I wish I could say that she did feel, once upon a time, that she could start living because she was in love, even with Mr. Long. It would make her prognosis more hopeful. But she did not regard him any differently than she regarded all the other men with whom she'd had intercourse. The trouble was . . . well, in a way . . . I'm forced to say . . . technical."

"Technical . . . ? Could you . . . elaborate?"

"Yes . . . ," Mel smiled. It had come. The moment he had so patiently been waiting for. The crux of the defense. "Yes . . . you see, the real trouble started when she experienced her very first and I take it extraordinarily powerful . . . sexual climax . . . from Mr. Long's . . . uh, offices. Such a thing had never happened to her before. You see, her indifference to all other men before Mr. Long, her frigidity, you might say, had been a guarantee of her freedom. And this climax, this new dimension, was a most remarkable surprise for her to which we must now add the further surprise of finding herself aroused to the point of obsession. You see, Mr. Minelli, with other women, whose initial mood might be different, we could describe what happened to her as enthusiastically aroused. But this was not her case . . . well, anyway, she didn't like it. I mean, this considerable surprise . . . enraged her."

"And . . . she *killed* him for it?"

"Uh . . . yes. And mutilated him."

A great silence followed.

Mel smiled modestly, tilted his head and looked at Ernie's feet.

Finally, Minelli said in a quiet tone, "I'm only a layman, but . . . isn't this reaction . . . to what we might consider . . . a successful sexual experience . . . unusual?"

"Indeed, yes," said Mel, "I hope so." And then he added, gently pedagogical, "But if I might be permitted an analogy here, consider how a woman raped by a man she detests would feel if she is also brought to a climax."

"Raped? What do you mean . . . raped? I mean, really, doctor . . . I'm not unsympathetic, but she hardly seemed after that first experience . . . how shall I put it, *displeased* by Mr. Long. I mean, it *is* a fact, is it not, that she thereafter pursued Mr. Long for some time?"

"Yes. But not quite . . . in the spirit it would seem. You see, it was not a rape, as you say . . . *until* the orgasm. And then, in her mind, it was. Puzzling as it may seem, I think it's fair to say she didn't like it. We certainly have the proof of that."

This, apparently, was too much for Minelli, because he just stood there and scrutinized Mel for a few moments until his mind seemed to sail to something far, far away, as if he weren't seeing Mel before him anymore.

And then, finally, with a nod to Judge Mott, as if excusing himself, he turned and went to his desk, and as everyone watched, went through some papers. He seemed to be thinking, buying time, while Mel, his hands folded now, looked at his hands, then at his feet again, and occasionally peered over his glasses around at Judge Mott, smiling very modestly indeed.

Then, Ernie came back to him, as if regrouped at last, and said to the Judge, "Your honor, I am not a psychiatrist. If it please the court, I would like to ask Dr. Fish some general questions, with the hope of perhaps educating us all . . . because, very frankly, I find this extremely confusing."

Mel was looking up at Judge Mott, comfortably, almost fondly, to see what the reaction would be, and when Judge Mott nodded his permission, without looking at Mel, Minelli said, "Thank you, your honor. Now doctor. My psychology courses were few and far back in my college days, so please excuse me if I sound naïve. But is it not normal for *any* living organism to seek pleasure rather than displeasure? I mean, isn't the pursuit of happiness a fundamental instinct in *any* healthy living organism?"

"I would say . . . ," said Mel (whom I suddenly suspected of having trained Ernie in jargon for this very moment), "*that* is the rock on which my profession is founded, yes."

"And is it not true, according to psychoanalytic theory," now I was sure Mel had coached him, and cringed, hoping Ernie wouldn't slip, and make it obvious, "that the prototype of the experience of happiness we all are seeking is the *satisfactory* sexual experience?"

Mel smiled, nodding approvingly like a schoolmaster as Ernie kept his face straight, his eyes bravely unaverted. "Sigmund Freud would agree with you. Yes."

"And are you saying, doctor, that Miss Stanton was *not* seeking

261

happiness with Mr. Long?"

"Hmmm . . . Let me put it this way. In her state, what she found with Mr. Long was not happiness, but the sudden loss of her autonomy, which made her most unhappy. You see, one could describe Miss Stanton as not only suicidal, but also as being arrested in what we call a state of infantile organization, with a strong desire to return to early power-narcissism. So, you see, for her, in her mind, suicide had the effect of maintaining the ego rather than destroying it. In my opinion, it has always been a way of achieving omnipotence for her. Therefore, you see, Mr. Long was a clear challenge to her desired omnipotence, and in fact, a successful one, until she could remove him. You could say she felt he was killing her. And her act, uh, the mutilation included of course, was also . . . in my opinion . . . a great blow she wished to strike against her superego structure, by which I mean the rest of the world, me included, I'm afraid, because it had been trying to force her to live quite as devoid of omnipotence as the rest of us, all her life."

" . . . I don't understand . . . ," said Ernie, at last. "Not only intellectually, doctor. I don't understand emotionally, either."

"Oh, it's not so hard, really," said Mel, "and once you can, then you'll also be able to understand why Althea always showed sudden improvement from her depressive conditions after her abortions. To tell you the truth, I was always a little alarmed whenever I saw her looking cheerful, because it just might be a danger sign that she was about to try suicide again. The whole thing comes down to this, I think. Althea was, and still is, under the infantile delusion that she will live by killing herself."

"Doctor . . . I still don't understand. As a human being, I mean. I don't think many of us here today can understand how someone who has all the advantages this young girl has, wealth, position, an education . . . could want to avoid happiness, . . . or even not to live."

"But she *does*. She does want to live."

"Not the way we can understand it, doctor. From what you say, and I have no reason to doubt you, I can only conclude that Miss Stanton is far more ill than any of us ever thought. She simply cannot be considered, in any normal sense, a healthy life-oriented person . . . can she?"

"That was my point."

"Then, doctor, the accused is an even more pathetic creature than any of us imagined . . . and I think we must all, all of us who are more fortunate than she . . . by the grace of God . . . pity her and pray for her. I, personally, cannot censure her. How can we do anything *but* pity . . . somebody who reacts with such a ferocious violence against any glimmer of normal happiness when it presents itself? Really . . . I think I now speak for all of us, doctor, when I tell you that I am deeply moved by this poor, poor girl for whom both love and life are impossible."

Mel nodded, and said, "I understand . . . "

Ernie nodded back, and then said, after a reflective, melancholy pause, "Now, I suppose 'I have only one question left, doctor . . . and I want to thank you now for your patient and illuminating testimony . . . I think we all want to know . . . do you consider this suicidal girl, this poor creature who is her own worst enemy, who considers any happiness a violation of the terrible unhappiness she identifies herself with . . . well, I might as well say it, do you consider her . . . a hopeless case?"

And having said this, Minelli looked at Mel with large, intent eyes, as if already pained by the expected bad prognosis. No one else seemed quite as moved. Certainly not Althea, who now stretched her arms a bit on the table, and seemed like a Brahmin matron dutifully sitting through a public lecture, patiently awaiting its end.

"Well," said Mel, "as a matter of principle, I try not to consider any case hopeless. But I'd be lying to you if I didn't admit her case is very, very difficult."

"Of course . . . "

"Yes. You see, she loves nothing, has rejected love all her life . . . as a threat to her ego's freedom, of course. So far, she's even refused to love life itself, with great ease, I might add . . . which should explain her apparently unfeminine attitudes toward abortion."

"Of course . . . ," Minelli nodded.

"However . . . I do see a *very* faint glimmer of hope now that I never saw before, in the midst of all this tragedy. In fact, I'd even have to say I consider her far less hopeless now than at any time before her affair with Mr. Long."

"Really . . . ? Is it because of . . . well, sex? . . . I mean, because of that painful, but successful climax? I mean, is she thinking it over?"

"No," Mel smiled, "actually, it's her pregnancy. You see, for the very first time in her life, Mr. Minelli, Althea has not yet asked for an abortion. Not thus far anyway. And I cautiously . . . find it . . . *cautiously*, mind you . . . hopeful."

A thoughtful pause followed while Minelli continued looking intently at Mel.

Unfortunately, while that pause was going on at the stand between Ernie and Mel, people all around me were making disgusted eye contact with one another.

No one, I'm afraid, was willing to buy it. And it was because they too interpreted Althea's not asking for an abortion as evidence of interest in life. Her own. Nobody doubted that once the legal advantages weren't needed anymore, she would ask for an abortion, and get it, with Mel's smiling blessing.

But, Mel, to my amazement, at picking up the crowd's reaction, insisted on looking sincere, even irritated, because he said, right over Ernie's shoulder. "I *mean* it. There just *might* be something in Althea that is finally asking her to live, and in such a way that she is beginning to listen."

"Is it . . . *possible?*" asked Minelli, wanting to believe.

"Of *course* it's possible! After all, she is human, she is flesh and blood, you know. She is a woman, and pregnant, and anyway . . . ," he went on testily, "the sight of *anyone* not wanting to live diminishes us all, Mr. Minelli, and I, for one, assure you that *I* will not give up the fight until I absolutely must . . . and not only because of that innocent child in her womb, either . . . but because of her, too."

Minelli looked at Mel, shaking his head with admiration, and finally said, "Well . . . win or lose . . . God bless you, doctor. I'm glad she has you in her corner. Your compassion for your fellow man, your willingness to be your brother's keeper . . . is fine, Christian behavior, doctor. Really it is. I suppose we all doubt you'll succeed, doctor. We can't kid ourselves about that. But I, for one, salute your gallant Humanitarianism."

Very shortly after that, Judge Mott handed the pregnant Althea over to the custody of Dr. Fish.

She was to be put, under the strictest security, in a State Mental Hospital, with the full (and unstated) understanding that she was to spend the rest of her life institutionalized.

Which produced one last, unforgettable photograph. As the late afternoon light bathed the descending white marble steps of the courthouse, a hatted Mel Fish was caught escorting Althea's black figure into the open back door of a waiting black limousine, surrounded by scores of police. The crowd glared, sullen, not at all as impressed as Minelli by Mel's "gallant Humanitarianism".

In Mel's profile, one could see his all too human, nervous smile in the crowd's direction. Given without any real hope it would be returned.

And Althea, seen with her head turned toward the open door of the limousine appeared faceless against the whiteness of the marble steps, blacker and more mythically hermetic than ever. It was as if the camera had caught the subjective fact of the crowd's mind, because she truly looked black as sin in her unrepentant, pregnant, night beast's state. And then three quarters profile showed the outline of her black pregnancy very clearly. Arrogantly.

It was like a photograph of her black Light in all its purity, especially because her face was out of sight, eclipsed like her humanity. And there was even a sense of bodilessness about her, because she floated there against the whiteness indifferent to them all, as if nothing but Light, having now transcended such ordinary things as bodies. In their eyes, she was like an awful flaw in the solidities of our reality.

And nobody was really surprised, after a few months, when Althea was transferred out of the State Hospital back to McLeod's, still under the custody of Dr. Fish.

Not that it was played up in the papers, but everybody heard about it somehow. Everybody.

After that last photograph of Dr. Mel smiling nervously at the glaring crowd as he helped Althea into the waiting black limousine, they both vanished. Completely. As if that black limousine, once it had closed in on itself, had raced off for the secret opening of whatever Underground Althea had emerged from, taking Dr. Mel, her servant, right back with her, pursued from the courthouse steps by the ill-wishing stares of the offended Christian crowd until they were out of sight.

(Even I didn't see him for a couple of months. Somebody told me he grew a full beard and moustache so as not to be recognized on the street.)

And with that departing limousine, the battle was over. Everybody felt it in the ice-gray, Bostonian silence that descended, no matter what other noises could still be heard.

But even so, though the general fury slowly calmed down, it refused to dissipate and lift from the area.

Instead, it stayed on—and on—as if it were trapped within the whole town's temples, gradually turning into something like a massively cold, gray February cloud that seemed to squat from horizon to horizon behind everybody's eyes.

And there it stayed. Cold, silent, nasty and unmoving. Maybe Spring was due in not too long. It was, according to the calendar. But nobody seemed interested, making the notion of rebirth wait out in the wings like a stupid suggestion that might never be made now, for fear of derision.

But depressed as people were, there was something about their mood that gave me the growing, unhappy feeling that they'd won their war against her anyway, and that they knew it, because they seemed strangely gratified to be depressed. I kept getting the sense that no matter how much they grumbled about how she'd literally gotten away with murder, just because she was rich, they still felt they'd won because they never did acknowledge her humanity, no matter how hard the UMFs had tried to force her Light on them. As far as they were concerned, it was just as good as if they'd beaten back the night beast invasion all by themselves, just by hating it so much, at least for now. Because the known world was theirs again. They possessed it just like that huge, cold, February cloud that sat in our temples.

Wherever I went, I kept getting a new, overbearing sense of the triumphantly grimy MTA wires overhead, of the naked, smiling rails and the "that's tough, buddy" slush below, as the whole area became aggressively grayer, meaner and more meager than usual. And more pointless. As if swaggering about it. It was as if, now that the battle was over and her Light gone from sight, we were all condemned to breathing the spiritual atmosphere of an enormously expanded Registry of Motor Vehicles bureaucracy where it's always February. Where the neon office lighting is joyless and ever the same. Where the coffee is always bad and in paper cups and where one gets the sense that the Anti-christ reigns at last and forever over a dreary world not worth having, with silent, smirking spite. One elbow on the counter. Barely bothering to look directly at whatever new soul has entered its domain to ask some helpless question before

266

walking away to let a female assistant step forward to hear the same helpless question.

I've never hated the place more. Boston, I mean. Or me, because I felt so much a prisoner inside it. Leaving was impossible somehow. I just didn't have the hope or will necessary, and I just couldn't believe I'd feel any better anywhere else.

Everywhere I went, I felt exactly the same cold nastiness that had seeped into the marrow of everything. The same small hatred.

But feel it as I did, I still felt alone as ever because, for one thing, I continually had the feeling that *everything* was my fault.

Spring wasn't going to come, or it wasn't going to matter, and it was my fault.

Nobody had felt the humanity of her Light, and it was my fault. My fault, even though I couldn't do anything about anything as I wandered about Boston and its gray environs breathing in that small hatred that was now lording it everywhere, infinitely bored to the point of murderousness, and glad it was bored.

But much as I despised the small hatred and tried to separate myself from it, and much as that made me glad not to be like the rest, at least for that—that is, for my sadness about her—I guess it was too hard not to end up seeking the same solace it had for others, reductive as that was for me.

I had only one contact with Mel during that time, one telephone conversation. And that's where it showed up. In my own voice. The small hatred, seeping out, trying to bite on something as I heard myself say, "Hey, Mel . . . don't you think you put it on kind of heavy there at the end of the trial?" To my own helpless disgust, as I aggressed against Mel, I suddenly felt like Tommy Muldoon, as if his spirit had taken me over. I even felt his slanting smirk, the one that says, "You don't shit me, buddy," slanting across my own face.

"What are you talking about . . . ?" he said, sensing it. Maybe he didn't know yet what the specifics I had in mind were, but he knew I wasn't throwing him flowers. I wanted to drop it, but out came, "You know what I mean . . . that stuff about how all of a sudden she's supposed to have maternal inclinations. Just because she didn't ask for an abortion this time. I don't think it went over . . . especially when you said it was a reason to hope she might even get cured some day."

"Is that so . . . ?" he said very stiffly, which did surprise me. I had, after all, assumed he was conscious of having said those things for

267

the sake of the situation, which I didn't hold against him, of course. But evidently I now had to contend with the fact that he'd been serious, or wanted to believe he had been, because he said, "In other words, you don't think I really *do* have any hope of curing her, is that it? You think I was just lying, I take it."

"Hey . . . wait a minute. The way you say 'lying' . . . you make it sound like a pejorative of some kind. All I meant was that I didn't think you were doing it successfully, that's all. I mean . . . I'm sure you do think you can cure her and all that, but . . . "

"I'm not amused, Muldoon. So fuck off. And for your information, not that I have to give *you* any, I still find her not having asked for an abortion the most hopeful single thing I've seen in her . . . well, in years. And I mean it."

Which was followed by a pause, loaded with irritated indignation on his side, during which I felt quite awful, as well as a bit sorry for him for wanting to fool himself with his own propaganda. Because, if he really did believe what he'd claimed, he was probably the only person in Massachusetts who really bought it. But I didn't quite dare say a word, until finally he ended the pause with, "Look, I've got to go. I'll call you for squash when the dust settles."

And that was it, for over two months really.

The moment we hung up, I wondered if this might not be the end of our friendship, or at least the beginning of the end. I was still sure he'd been lying, of course, whether he currently thought so or not, for whatever defensive reasons. But that wasn't the point. The point was that I'd given him trouble only because I'd succumbed to the small hatred, and I was ashamed of that. I was tempted to call him right back and leave an apology with his secretary.

But the impulse passed when the small hatred came back and whispered in my ear, "Oh, fuck *him*." Its basic message. And I didn't dial.

Which didn't stop me from recriminating myself about the one thing that was bothering me most: how alone she was. I simply couldn't get that out of my mind. Althea was completely alone, and Mel, though he thought he was on her side, was no help. Not really. Because he didn't understand the Light.

She was absolutely alone, that was the real trouble. And the notion kept growing inside me like an awful black pit with continually inward crumbling walls that never filled it as it progressively deepened. And as it deepened, it kept bloating me with the helpless,

268

dark feeling that how alone she was, was *my* fault. Mine. Personally. For all Mankind. Somehow, for having been the one person to see the Light, I was to bear the guilt for all the rest of them, not that I was caring much about them at the time.

So now, like Althea, I had my own inner darkness too. But mine was no fun at all. No pride there. Just a loathsome, inflating blackness I carried around town with me like a secret, shameful pregnancy. One which, if it ever bore fruit, would only belch out sterility and hopelessness, not that it would have added anything very different to the world if it had.

And trying to be sensible was no help, because naturally I recognized that feeling everything was my fault was absurd, presumptuous and crazy. It even occurred to me that I probably felt as I did only because I'd had the bad luck to be the one person to see her Light clearly, which was also pretty crazy and presumptuous for me to think. Because, sure I saw her Light. I couldn't get away from that. But that did not necessarily mean that her Light was *really there*. Or that, even if it were, I could do anything about it.

And whenever I tried being sensible like that, the small hatred would come to my aid right away, the common man's friend, whispering in my ear, 'What is this shit? So nobody saw her Light but me. So nobody sees me, either. So welcome to the club, Althea, and if you're listening, go fuck yourself, like everybody else.'

But that never gave me any peace either. Only added to my feelings of smallness as the pit walls eroded and crumbled some more, no matter how much I told myself, pleading, 'Now wait a minute. I wish her well, really I do. But she has no right to expect anything from me. And she doesn't, for Christ's sake. I've never even met her. She doesn't even know I'm alive. I mean, it might be different if she did, or if I could do anything, but I can't, so why can't I learn to relax?'

But relaxing was impossible, particularly because a couple of weeks after the trial I started getting the distinct feeling that *something* was still pending. And also, unfortunately, that was all there was to it, just the feeling that something was pending, with nothing possibly forthcoming, which did nothing to chase away my constant expectations, which made me feel like an idiot. More than ever, as I carried all that unhappy jumble trapped inside me, I felt like the helpless custodian of an imbecile child (myself) whose aging never did a thing to alleviate either the compulsive childishness or imbecility.

So, as might be expected, I drank a lot those days, which helped. A little, anyway. Pregnant as I felt with that loathsome nothingness, and moan to myself as I did as to why had I been chosen from among all men to know myself as the bearer of this burden, when I drank enough, especially late at night and if I was in a crowd (for which I frequented the *Land of Odin*), I did find brief moments of relief.

It was funny, but during those occasional moments I started remembering things like being thirteen again, another difficult time, with a clarity and peacefulness I'd never had before. Certainly not at thirteen, when I'd walked around like a self-pitying fury with a bucket over my head.

And one of those times I even remembered a "proof of God" Father Cardoso, a Portuguese Jesuit, gave me back then, because I'd just admitted my doubts to him. Bragging, really. Now, without complication or any new shame, I could see how it had been an assertion of my manhood not to believe, even before not believing. It meant being tougher and hairier than those who did. More than announcing my loss of innocence, it trumpeted (mostly in my own ears, inside the bucket) my manly readiness to lose it. After all, the sexes were segregated in my school and we had to start somewhere. And I must have been dying to lock horns and be accepted by the menfolk as a peer, even if it could only be through being granted the respect accorded an enemy. Even at the price of tragedy.

I remembered—hadn't thought about it in years—kneeling on my side of the grill in the Confessional and getting up my nerve to tell Father Cardoso that I doubted because Science could not prove the existence of God. And remembering, I peacefully admitted what I couldn't then—that I might not have tried it with one of the Irish priests, afraid he just might reach around into my side, pull me out and let me have it. The truth was that Father Cardoso of the round glasses had looked soft, didn't speak English well, which I took as a sign of a lack of intelligence, and I'd wanted to start out slow. Father Cardoso didn't seem startled as he heard me out—I'd expected him to panic. But he kept saying, "Y-yess . . . y-yesss . . . ," every once in a while until I'd finished. Then, speaking gently, as if confident he was leading me with reason, he said, "I will prove it to you. Tell me, isn't there thirst?" "Yes" "And there is water to drink, isn't there?" "Yes" "And isn't there hunger?" "Yes" "And there is food, isn't there?" "Yes" "And isn't there the need for God, for His love and

His mercy?"

I didn't say anything. He thought he had me. He wasn't being nasty, or gloating, but then, he couldn't see me smiling, satanically proud of the complete triumph of Science over Superstition. My ego, swelling in the darkness, informed me that I should pity the ignorant and pathetically confident immigrant on the other side of the grill, and that I'd better not say anything or I might destroy the poor guy. My ego wanted to quit while ahead. "Now," he said, "when you go to the altar, say Ten Our Fathers and ten Hail Marys, and don't go worrying about things you don't understand anymore." "Yes, Father," I said, and when I finally pushed aside the curtain to let the next boy in, I knew I was not going to the altar. Unless somebody was watching—which happened to be the case. Father Droney, the hockey coach, was standing at the back of the pews supervising the traffic to the Confessionals, with his fists on his hips.

After that particular memory, my pending feeling came back with a vengeance, of course (it always did after moments of peace), as I assumed I had remembered that "proof of God", after all these years, because of my own troubles. And thinking about Father Cardoso, I had to admit that even two out of three wasn't so bad, especially if you thought it suggested the possibility of three out of three. If you believed in symmetry. Hell, I was batting 0 for 1, and without even the illusion of having a bat.

And then, unexpectedly, my impasse ended. When there was no reason at all to expect it.

It happened late one icy, rainy night, when I found myself at the corner of the bar at the *Land of Odin*, blankly looking at the TV, and drunk again. Drunker than usual, because it was so late, while my full bladder was gallantly straining against the crumbling darkness of my bloated emptiness, as if trying to contain it with the priority of its own possible demands.

The TV was showing Lugosi's *Dracula*, again.

Before my still eyes, the pale, tuxedoed Count, aristocratic as ever, undead as ever, once more confronted his arch-rival, the good Positivist Doktor, bearded in late-Victorian style as always, just like Sigmund Freud.

Once more, suddenly, the Doktor flashed a mirror at the Count (it was always a surprise), making him recoil and cover his pale face with a sudden raising of his winglike arm.

And though by then my poor bladder was desperately calling for

271

relief in its unequal battle against the blackness, instead of going off to the urinal, I found myself staying transfixed on my bar stool, and blissfully looking at the screen—because suddenly I was lost in admiration for Norma, of whom I hadn't thought in so long, and who now seemed as far away from me as being thirteen.

Norma.

The dear old horror movie was reminding me of her Dracula imitations, of her Viennese Herr Doktor imitations, and I was realizing how truly excellent they were.

And I gave myself over to enjoying her presence in my mind again. Norma. It didn't matter she never called me. That was some other person, anyway, not the one I was thinking about now. I was contemplating Norma the "potted plant", as she'd once called herself, the creature who felt so separated from the "inner cheese of life". And once again, watching the truly wax-museum pale Lugosi, who seemed to be imitating Norma, I remembered the appeal she'd had for me. How likeable she'd been. How alive, how admirably banal in her aspirations about "fulfilling her femininity". I even wondered how she was doing down in New York, where I'd heard she'd gone, and I wished her well, and loved Count Dracula with a generosity I'd hardly suspected myself capable of in those the days of the small hatred, because, of course, it was Norma in a black tuxedo I was looking at, and I found myself smiling.

And I was sufficiently deranged that, noticing how intently the few patrons there were watching the movie, as if discovering it for the first time, I was suddenly and enthusiastically on the verge of believing that they too were suddenly aware of how good Norma was. As if they could possibly have known her. It was odd, how intently they were looking up at the screen: sullen and grudging, of course—but then they usually looked at the screen that way. The amount of attention paid was unusual, though. Which made me drunkenly conclude it really was too bad that they could not appreciate how magnificent Norma was in her greatest role. No, in her *two* greatest roles, I suddenly realized. As Herr Doktor *and* as the Count! As both! Who could forget her Viennese accents!

Whereupon, watching their round, intent eyes set in their unusually sullen faces (I half wondered, why were they so sullen?), I was seized by the notion of rising up and lecturing them on the subject of Norma's dual role, imagining how they would look at me as I further explained how, you see, the Doctor with his Sigmund beard, championing the cause of the inner cheese of life, is fighting his exact opposite, our boy the Count, who looks down on everybody and who maybe isn't having such a good time being so totally separate from that inner cheese, granted, but who sure as hell doesn't want any bunch of turkeys getting in the way of his supremely refined misery, either! No sir! Which is precisely why, gentlemen, we're *all* on his side even though we aren't supposed to be. But then—I would assure them as they began exchanging glances—feel no shame! Even Milton, you can be sure, must have hated to see Satan go, especially when he realized that all he had to look forward to until Judgment Day was to see how Adam and his dull family made out. Gentlemen, now that I think of it (I imagined saying), surely Milton's lonely heroism consisted of having forced himself to pay attention to them for as long as he did, as bored as he was, and condemned to it by no longer permitting himself to follow what so obviously appealed to him and to us so much more—the career of somebody with distinction! Let's hear it for the Count, men, and for Norma, the modern woman who brings you this eternal drama!

But, of course, not having become that much of a drunk yet, I did no such thing. I merely stood up and prepared to go to the urinal because the movie was coming to its end.

We all continued watching.

The Doktor arrived with a wooden stake, the material of the True Cross, finding the Count vulnerable where he slept during the day in a box full of his native earth.

Then, Count Normacula was no more. As dawn broke and pious church bells rang, that aristocratically stubborn spirit that would not die—until the Doktor got to him—was finally sailing up to the lightening skies of dawning Transylvania, to benefit at last from what the good Positivist Doktor assured us was a great boon which we, the common folk, routinely enjoyed. Death.

Now all that was left was for the young lovers to go and populate the earth, protected by the Moses who had led them to this promised land—Norma in her Freudian beard and cravat, of course—and the movie ended.

I gritted my teeth, bracing myself for the crumbling of the pit walls again, as they did after each moment of peace, but I couldn't help smiling. I was very glad to have seen Norma again.

With the movie over, the *Land of Odin* remained completely silent, as if reflecting in the somber intimacy of that rainy night.

273

Then, as I maneuvered parallel to the bar, heading for the urinal, the silence was broken by a man behind me who said, his voice dripping with a tired hatred, "It burns my ass. Fuckin' creep, she is."

Suddenly, I couldn't take another step. Who's a creep? Norma? Could he have possibly meant Norma?

But my confusion was only momentary. Everybody else had heard him too, and they all knew immediately, just as I did now, that he'd meant Althea. There was no question about it. He'd meant: *their* vampire.

Unknown to me, word had reached them that she'd been transferred from the State Mental Hospital to McLeod's, which everyone knew was an institution for the well-to-do.

That was why they'd been looking so intently at the familiar movie. But I didn't need to know that fact to realize that whenever the Count had appeared on the screen, Althea had been on their minds while Norma had been on mine.

Almost with gratitude at having something to assault, I felt myself becoming hostile, ready to say something to the man who just spoke, anything which might lead to a brawl as the eroding pit inside me boiled and pulsated.

But fortunately for me, before I could think of anything, the man next to him said consolingly, to ease his bitterness, "Shit, Denny . . . what are you gonna do. She's not human, anyway . . . "

And with that, very slowly, the voices of the other few patrons there, as if themselves consoled by this thought, went about their own conversations.

I found myself standing there, looking around the room, furious, knowing if I did or said anything in defense of Althea, they'd merely turn and watch me froth away for a while—before throwing me out into the rainy night unceremoniously, denying me even the catharsis of equal combat.

Whereupon I stomped off to the urinal, knowing that after that I was not going to hang around.

And suddenly, I stopped feeling so empty and putrid. The pending feeling was still there, but now it glowed, burning with a positive fire.

Suddenly, I understood what was pending. I was going to see Althea. Alone. I didn't know how, where or when. But I knew it was ahead of me.

And I walked out into the icy rains, burning inside and protected by my fury, as all the way home I kept thinking about how they all

274

thought she wasn't human (not that I hadn't known it), and it got me madder and madder, and made me glad at being mad. Maybe I was furious because I was still so close to them, because I'd been infected for so long with the small hatred myself. But I understood all over again *why* they thought she wasn't human. Because she was a woman, plain and simple. Because people can't think of women without fantasy, and that includes women, too. Everybody knows that. And since she stepped out of the usual fantasies, like the grateful, fulfilled lover or the good old nurturing mother, they were covering her over with another one, making her some sort of Draculine Black Madonna.

Well, *I* was not. And it was good, it was important that I was not. For once, I knew it was.

All the way home through those icy rains I kept thinking about Mel's favorite Sicilian saying, "All women are whores, except for my mother, who's a virgin", and more than ever I was convinced we're all Sicilian men. All men, women and children among us and maybe our dogs and cats too, by now. Which means, I thought, that when women aren't even whores, but something else, like Althea, everybody's corny mandolin of a psyche explodes and pops strings all over the place, curling back in horror. What the hell *do* they think is human, anyway? Just biological urges, conditioned reflexes. Period. Right? Everything that isn't uniquely ours but something else's, so just live up to your parts in those things and you're a regular human. That's what they think. Just like everybody thinks their tribal prejudices are their own ideas. Just because they're sincerely felt, like hunger.

By the time I got home, cold, drenched and burning with my blissful righteousness, I was absolutely sure, it didn't matter *why* I was sure, that I lived only for seeing her. And that I couldn't die before I did.

I had to let Althea know that I, at least, understood.

And then, after thinking I couldn't die before I saw her, that I was invincible in my destiny, I started trembling, worried that I would die. Terrified that I would.

Suddenly I started trembling as if possessed by an interior electrical storm, sneezing and undergoing all the things a fragile mortal might after walking for three-quarters of an hour in an icy rain.

275

I was sick out of my head for a good week after that, ran spectacular fevers that drenched my bed, stank me up, and eventually had to be shot with wonder drugs. And when that was over, I slept where I lay for two days that disappeared from my life without a trace.

When I awoke, I must admit, I felt the optimistic freshness that comes after an illness lifts, and I did wonder, almost passingly, if I did happen to see Althea, alone, what I could possibly tell her that would satisfy us both.

And feeling sane, I wondered about my sanity again, especially about that hopeful sense of mission I'd had coming out of the *Land of Odin*, which seemed to have left me along with the fever, and I went back to sleep for another two days.

If Althea, by some miracle, had come to my room then, I would have looked up from my bed at her without being able to think of a thing to say. Which saddened me with its good sense. And many times, I dreamed that she did come, opened my door and looked in, and then, as if assuming she'd opened the wrong one, she closed it softly after stepping back without a word before moving on to try some other door.

Without me being able to utter a sound. With a stupid " . . . uh . . . " dying in my throat as I knew that there was no other door for her but mine.

That was in the first days of March, the month that enters New England like a lion, and, they say, leaves like a lamb.

BUT MY CHANCE COMES (APRIL)

Mel, just as he promised, called me up to play squash.

But his voice over the phone was formal, stiff, almost like a shove, as if he were being forced to call me against his better judgment.

Which was odd. Why was he doing it in the first place?

But I didn't comment, because I didn't care. I wasn't much concerned about either him or squash at the moment. I just said, "O.K.," and went anyway. Which was also odd.

And I even found myself going early. I'd never gone there so early before, ever. It would have made more sense to kill time in Cambridge. There was nothing for me to do at McLeod's, and Mel wouldn't be free until 6.

But I got on the 4:40 bus at Harvard Square faintly wondering why I was acting as if I couldn't get there fast enough, why I felt this might be the last bus out that way, when I knew damn well that they left every twenty minutes until late at night.

And the bus seemed to be taking longer than usual.

A couple of times I thought I didn't recognize the route. Maybe, I worried, I was on the wrong bus, or maybe just this once the bus was going to take me someplace else, and leave me there.

It was April, and there was still a lot of light left in the afternoon,

277

but for some reason I started worrying it was going to get dark soon. Too dark. For what, I didn't know. Worried (I shouldn't have been, the UMFs were in control), I kept looking out the bus window all the way, as if the driver might be trying to thwart me somehow, until I was finally deposited in front of McLeod's red brick gatehouse. And I felt relieved.

But only for a moment.

There I was, looking up the long, long driveway that goes from the gatehouse up a series of rises until it gets to the main buildings, and in that early April afternoon light, it suddenly looked endless. My stomach sank.

But suddenly I was on my way, walking almost before I knew I started, feeling like an anxious salmon going upstream, hurrying and not so sure it was good to hurry, but hurrying anyway, and as I looked at the main buildings from the top of each succeeding rise, I began realizing that the main buildings were not my destination.

I already knew I was going to keep on chugging past them.

McLeod's is like a park, at least around the main buildings and the abandoned golf course behind them. But beyond the abandoned golf course there's a very thick, very messy wood I've never liked, which eventually stops at a pond few people even know is there which McLeod's shares with a lot of other mysterious estates. And to get to the pond I'd have to cross the course and then go through some inchoate, highly uninteresting paths that were probably already bug-controlled territory. And I hate insects above most all other things, but damned if I didn't pass right through the main building area, start crossing the wet, muddy golf course, heading right for the wood with the full knowledge I was going in there toward the pond.

I tried telling myself this was absurd, but it didn't take. I was too worried suddenly about how wide the course was. Much wider than I'd ever seen it. And as I kept moving, or something kept moving me, I was surprised and quite relieved that I could cross it in such a short time, when I finally stepped off the course and into the first available path into the woods.

I pushed through, the afternoon light at my back now, and I headed for the pond, hurrying as best I could.

I feared the darkness coming too soon, now more than ever.

When I broke out of the woods, at the other side, at the edge of the pond, I stopped and turned to the right. Some fifty yards away, I saw

278

her. Althea.

She was very still. Sitting in a little gray rowboat that was tied to the dock by half a dozen yards of rope.

Her back was to me, away from the light, her shoulders curved forward, as if cradling some painful hollowness inside.

And the water was so still and dark it seemed unnaturally motionless.

I was very nervous, but nervous because I knew that that motionlessness (which had waited for me) couldn't last, as if the pond were pregnant with a secret black motion that could begin at any time.

She was alone. I couldn't see anybody else.

And then I began to get the sense she was sitting there—not moving, with the little boat still tied up, with the black water waiting for *her* to release its motion—because she was undecided as to whether to cast off yet . . . or to stay, just a little longer . . . maybe waiting.

I felt I *had* to look down at the pond again, to check to see that it hadn't changed, to see if it was still a small black pond, just as when I'd gotten there a moment ago, breaking through the woods. And it still was, thank God. The water was still motionless, but I didn't know for how much longer. Because I knew that any moment now, if she slipped the rope and let the boat go, even though nothing was moving yet, movement was going to start. Nothing would be able to stop it if she slipped the rope. The water was going to start sliding, expanding out, and the boat with Althea was going to start sliding away too, uncontainably . . . and then the pond was going to open out into a flat, widening lake on its other side, the far shore soon vanishing, and then it would go on, opening out mercilessly into a vast, dead sea, the distances always pushed out farther and farther by the sliding boat, sadder and sadder, until Althea's shape on the boat was going to disappear beyond the furthest point, like a ghostly sail. I knew it for sure, just as sure as I knew my head was beginning to flood with a blackness from somewhere in my chest. And then all outlines would disappear, and my brain would be completely flooded, drowning me, if she slipped the rope. She meant to. That was why she was on the boat. To cut it loose. That was why I'd hurried, even though I couldn't stop her, which I knew painfully well.

But she was delaying, her shoulders curved (I suddenly felt it) because she was mourning. And waiting. Without much hope, but waiting.

I still didn't know for what. Maybe, I thought, for me.

But I didn't dare move. I even held my breath. My head again started to fight the darkening flood that threatened to rise up from my chest, and I had to try very hard to keep her in sight—without moving—because the wrong motion might startle her . . . possibly, I didn't know why, kill her.

Sitting there in the boat, now she was nude to me of everything but her Light. And with her back to me, she didn't even have a face, a mask, to veil it. Inside my own emptiness—paining me—I began to feel what pained her, what made her shoulders curve down.

It wasn't being alone before she finally drifted off. She'd expected that, knowing it could not and should not be any other way.

It was, I realized, that her solitude was bitter now. And it was the bitterness that was keeping her there, because she still could not enter the Blackness fully and freely, with all her solitude pure. The way it was, she'd always leave something behind now, a part she wanted to take with her, or her freedom wouldn't be good. Wouldn't be free. Unless . . . somebody came from this shore to say good-by.

Which was why she waited. What she mourned.

Maybe somebody would still come and say simply, " . . . Althea," in such a clear, personal way her Light would feel kissed. And then she could finally, in peace, mortally blessed, slip the rope and begin to open out the far shores at last, released after not having been alone for one significant moment. Then it wouldn't be sad to go. She'd go as a member of the human race. Again. Slip away free as a free human, traveling out with our human understanding.

And I knew, then, watching her as she scarcely hoped anymore, that low as I was, the person to come was me. It had always been me.

And that I'd best come soon, before she was irrevocably out of reach, off in an eternal, inconsolable bitterness that would demonize her, dehumanize her forever.

It was up to me. That was what my life was for. And I felt paralyzed again by my smallness.

Then, incredibly, I found myself moving toward her, noisily, awkwardly, and, at my noise, not startled (strange), Althea began turning her head to see, having to squint into the light behind me. Three-quarters profiled, I could see how very pregnant she was (She hadn't aborted yet. Couldn't now.), and her turned face was very white, drawn, like a withered moon-flower, floating over her swollen body. Her tangled hair was blacker than ever and like the wood I'd just walked through.

With her eyes looking at me and my heart pumping blackness into my head faster and faster, I was suddenly afraid I'd fall down idiotized, lose my faith and die, but thank God I still kept moving as the light behind me made her squint . . . until she saw who it was, what stranger, now casting a long-reaching shadow that gave her face a shelter from the low sun. In a moment, her eyes stopped squinting. Then, protected, they opened up purple, large. And she smiled.

I kept moving toward her, amazed I dared, still afraid of falling yet not sure why I hadn't, and the light at my back kept moving back and forth across her face, as if caressing it as I kept coming closer and closer, on to the dock—and then I realized she was glad to see me! Althea was glad to see *me*!

Did she know who I was? Was that possible? Had she sensed me all this time, following her Light from the distance?

But then, another expression came across her face. I stopped. Was she wondering if perhaps I was *not*, after all, the person she'd been waiting for to come from this shore . . . to tell her, somehow, so she could understand and feel in her very soul, tell her all the things I wanted so badly to tell her?

Desperately, I wanted to be able to say, at least, " . . . Althea," so she could hear it, for once, not sounding as odious as it did in other people's mouths. But I still couldn't make a sound.

The more she watched me, the more taut her suspicious, drawn white face became, shrinking on her up-stretched neck, enlarging her unblinking eyes, serpentlike, as beneath, her smile was still a smile, but changing, saddening, withering.

I stood there, above her on the dock, stilled like a bird.

I couldn't pretend not to know . . . she knew I knew, I could feel it . . . why people thought of her as a monster.

And now, she was asking: . . . Well? Do you think I'm a monster that you've happened upon? Are you now going to skewer me on a pointed stick and watch me writhe, and then, when I'm done, go show me to all the people . . . and laugh and be cheered? . . . because if you are I . . . wouldn't be surprised.

Her resignation, her growing sadness, was so clear in her eyes that it made me want more desperately than ever to be able to say, no! . . . yes, I come from them, but no, not for that!

But I couldn't think how to make her trust me, how to make her know that I, for one, hadn't mythified her into a monster, not at all . . . that *I* could see her in all the purity of her Light. I'd have to say, somehow, well yes, a monster if you like, but a monster that is *human*, you see, monstrous for being *nothing* but human, and therefore not a monster, not really, Althea. Only monstrous for how human you are. I wanted to be able to say, really I can, yes I *can* see you without fantasy. That's why I'm here. To see you. Clearly. To see *you*, nothing *but* you and to let you know it . . . Althea, it's just that people confuse their biological impulses and their civic impulses, all those layers and layers of social toilet-training and all those millions of years of blood, with their true selves. I know that, and they think that all those borrowed, inherited and owed things in us, which are everything *but* our selves, our true selves, are their humanity. I know that, Althea, really I do. But it's because their humanity is only embryonic, like mine, Althea . . . and you frighten us because you are nothing but your Light. That unique and irreplaceable thing. That anti-thing so black and prideful, so loathsome and noble, maybe the worst and best thing about each of us, Althea. That thing that says above all: "No, I won't disappear," and which is only present (we only *feel* its presence) when it refuses to be absent—when it rebels even against pleasure, so much so it even seeks pain more often than pleasure, just so it can feel itself, so it won't lose itself.

I hoped she could feel me thinking, understand what I couldn't say. But Althea just looked on at me, standing where I was at the tip of the dock, where the rope began. And I knew she didn't understand, that she didn't know how I knew, how I could possibly know she'd refused *both* to be master and to be slave, refused everything, coldly and even cruelly, just to let her Light be free. Even from slaves. She just looked at me, and what was left of her first smile at seeing me now turned ironic.

In my head, I was yelling that I hadn't come to judge and sentence, but she kept asking me, *did* I think she was a monster? Well . . . did I?

And then, suddenly, her mouth contracted, her eyes hardened. And I became afraid. Was she suddenly considering the possibility that I might not be an accidental visitor, after all, but indeed, a messenger? Maybe I was another kind of messenger from the human race than the one she'd hoped for. Maybe I was sent to cut the rope

282

and send her off with a curse, just so she could never find rest, but instead drift out, stained by our hatred, pushed out into the bitter winds of a sour dawn, forever. Was that why I was so close to the rope?

I didn't dare move at all now, as her appraising eyes stayed on me, asking herself, not me anymore, which was I? . . . and then, I could feel her telling herself . . . really, which is most likely . . . ? And at that, her mouth contracted more, like a stubborn child's preparing never to be anything but stubborn ever again, if I did indeed turn out to be the kind of messenger she thought I'd probably be: the messenger with the curse.

Now more than ever I wanted to be able to say something, *anything* that might calm her, but I needed calming, too. I was terrified now, terrified I might say something she misunderstood, especially her name, because it might sound wrong, and then, in a last rage, as she glared at me, she'd begin to darken with hate. Suddenly, I was terrified she would crystallize before my eyes, looking directly into mine with pure hatred now, and turn into one piece of irredeemable, mute coal. Forever.

If she did, and she might, her curse for us all would be on me, and, knowing I'd deserve it, I would never live in anything but wretched misery. If I *could* go on living. Because I would have failed her. Her humanity. And my own. With my impotence.

But her face, thank God, began softening again.

I wasn't sure what she was thinking now, but I was relieved to see the softness return, and smile again as she looked up at me on the dock. The black Light of her soul floated in her dilating pupils, and I knew if I could only get closer, I'd see my own face in those round windows at last. Because that was where I was. The *only* place I really was. As she looked at me, she held me in those black pupils with the pure black strength of her Light, suspending me on that spot in the world much more than the wooden dock beneath my feet, because without her eyes sustaining me, I'd have already fallen over. I knew I would have. And drowned.

And then, incredibly, she began to pull the boat to the dock. To me. Smiling. Looking at me. And now I didn't know at all: was she still testing me? I still sensed her asking, but in a different tone now: did I think she was a monster? Was I frightened that she wanted me to come down into her boat? Because she did. And she smiled as she pulled toward the dock. My brain began flooding again because now the boat was near enough, and I was stepping down into it, absolutely sure that if it weren't for her eyes holding my balance, I would have already fallen into the water.

And now that I was in the boat, trembling, she kept on smiling, challenging, even though I answered only with my docility. She could see me tremble. I couldn't hide it. It even seemed to amuse her. And now as she looked at me, challenging, she was asking: did I think I'd been invited in, with the possibility of sex . . . was that it? . . . She smiled . . . Did I think I'd been invited for sex, only to have her long, thin arms suddenly unfold white and cruel and incredibly powerful from underneath her darkness, like swan's wings, to hold my head and drown me in the water? And she kept on smiling, aggressively enigmatic, as suddenly I didn't know if she was right, if I was there and shouldn't be, if I . . .

But then a new melancholy passed over her face, and her smile vanished.

Our faces were on the same level now. Hers became still as the pond. I kept trembling, and now my trembling didn't in any way amuse her, only made her sadder and sadder as I cursed and cursed myself for my smallness, my lack of faith, my lowness, but just the same, I couldn't help thinking: what the hell *was* I doing there? Was I trying to kill myself? Was she to have the sadness of the executioner? Did she think I'd come to drift off with her? (Had I?) Did she think I was a sacrificial offering, from me and all of us, to the endless Blackness, because I too was rejecting everything? . . . Because I wasn't. I couldn't. I didn't think I could.

Her drawn, naked face with her purple eyes was like a hopeless question pulling me with its void, and then I felt myself move to her and kiss her mouth, close my eyes, feel wetness on my cheeks, taste the salt of whose tears I simply couldn't tell. And the kiss was gentle, receiving, dark and deep in me and in Althea whose very Light I could feel in my own soul now. I could feel her feeling kissed, grateful, kissing me, knowing me too, no masters, no slaves, as up and down and North, South, East or West disappeared in the blackness of her Light, which could feel itself in my saying, "Althea," while she, without knowing my name, was saying my name too, as it had never been said before . . . and suddenly in the kiss my nose and throat began to fill with black water. I was thrashing, choking, going blind . . . I was dying . . . I know I was dying, in the Blackness . . . and I began to disappear in the

Blackness, knowing it was too late as whole armies ran through the water outside my blindness, ran over me, pulled at me, pulled me down, pulled at my arms, my legs . . .

The last sounds I heard were a man's hysterical voice yelling desperately: "Jesus Christ!"

When I came to, on the dock, Althea was standing over me, shivering and wet, looking down at me with a man's blue jacket over her shoulders. It was Mel's jacket, complete with its little red crest on the left breast pocket. Beneath that jacket she had a white one, obviously belonging to the large, undershirted and coplike man standing next to Mel, who, for his part, contemplated me lying there with a rage and contempt I'd never seen on his face before.

He wore a very fancy, pale blue shirt, and just as I'd heard, had indeed grown a full beard and moustache, trimmed with great precision.

Just like Althea, I was wet and shivering too, and, lying where I was, I looked up at them through barely opened eyes. My lungs, I noted gratefully, were clear with air now, and I breathed as if it were a new activity. Mel turned to the undershirted man next to him, who looked most apologetic, and said, "I told you not to take your eyes off her, goddamnit! This should teach you to try to sneak off into the woods. I'ts just lucky for you I spotted him from my office and followed him out here."

"Jesus, doc . . . I had to go. I really had to go. I figured she'd be O.K. out in the middle of the pond. I mean, I really had to go, and there was nobody around anyway, you know what I mean?"

"Well, next time, you'd better just go right in front of her. Don't ever take your eyes off her again."

"I know, doc. I know. But, Jesus, I was only gone a couple of minutes. Anyhow, she had him up on the dock all by herself by the time I got here . . . "

"It's lucky for you, that's all I have to say," Mel snapped at him.

"I dunno how she does it, doc . . . ," the man said, looking down at me and shaking his head. "I mean, it's fantastic how she comes up with them . . . and I guess you never know if she's gonna fuck 'em or drown 'em. I swear to God, doc, I was only gone two minutes, the first time *ever*, believe me, and then this guy shows up, out

285

of *nowhere!*"

My eyes were fully open now, there was no hiding it, and Mel bent down, looked right in my face and said, "You absolute fuckhead. You can thank Althea for pulling you out. If it had been me, I swear I'd have pushed your head down every time it came up. You capsized the boat, did you know that? And if Althea weren't a big strong girl, you would have drowned her, too, from what I hear."

I just looked at him. I must have been in some form of shock, of which Mel as a doctor was surely aware, but just as surely he didn't care what my condition was.

"You are henceforth," he said, practically trembling with rage, "Not to appear at McLeod's, do you hear me? *Not* to appear! And if I ever speak to you again, which I seriously doubt, it will not be here."

And with that he straightened up his back, still looking down at me, put his arm jealousy over her shoulder and started to lead Althea away, leaving the man to tend me.

Althea looked back at me once more, and then turned to let herself be led away. And as they went, I heard Mel say, wanting me to hear, "I *knew* I shouldn't have asked him out here today, goddamnit. Something told me I shouldn't have. He almost ruined everything . . . And you, Althea," he said dotingly, changing his tone, ". . . *you* were very good." At which she bowed her head and kept walking, permitting Mel to lead her as she trembled under his arm. I was sure she was crying, crying for reasons he'd never understand as she leaned against him.

And I was sure he loved it. The bastard. Acting protective. His fulfillment as Big Daddy.

BUT MEL SPEAKS TO ME
AGAIN, MONTHS LATER
(He Felt He Could Afford To)

I truly thought that it was all over between us.

The importance of our friendship had been completely eclipsed by Althea, for both of us, and we both knew it without ever having to say so.

As it turned out, however, Mel did speak to me again, on his own initiative, despite having said that he doubted he ever would. And that very year, too. 1953. Many months, of course, after having banished me so righteously from McLeod's, during which time about the only bond that remained between us was a hostile silence, of the unmistakably serious kind.

It happened at a very odd hour. Midnight, when I was not thinking of him at all. I was just walking into my apartment, having heard the phone ring and ring while I hurried to open my door, wondering who could possibly be calling at such a time, ringing for so long. I even had the peculiar suspicion that the phone had been ringing intermittently throughout the evening while I'd been out, especially as a tightly happy voice, delighted the phone had been picked up just as it was about to give up hope, cried out in the receiver, "Oh . . . ! Hiya! How's things with you?" without giving a name, as was his custom. I suppose it meant to give one a chance to exclaim, "Mel!" but I didn't. Instead, I limited myself to a contained and dignified, "Oh, hi . . . Mel." The truth was that, beneath our Cain and Abel enmity, I was glad to hear his voice again. But I didn't want to reveal that. After all, he *had* thrown me out of McLeod's quite ignominiously. Not, of course, that that was the real trouble between us. That was Althea. So, my rude treatment was just the problem we could admit to. The superficial offense through which we might relate if we were to make contact again. Therefore, I suppose my stand-offishness on this point was really my own way of making myself available to his reaching out.

"Listen, ol' buddy, been tryin' to get-cha!" he said. "How you been?" Despite his conciliatory tone, his voice was having trouble containing some triumph which I could just tell had made him hoot with joy before calling me up, and would again immediately after hanging up. He also sounded slightly drunk to me.

"I've been fine," I said, stiffly.

"Gee, that's great!" he said, and I countered with a punitive silence. However, his spirits remained undimmed, which I could practically feel through my fingers as I held the receiver, so after a bit I said, "Things going well with you?"

"Oh, yeah. Great. Just great. A lot of work, of course, but I really don't mind that."

"Good," I said, gathering he didn't really want to come right out and tell me what was making him so happy, preferring to cradle it within himself. And, instinctively, I didn't want to ask. Something in me guessed it had to do with Althea, though I tried to keep it from my conscious mind out of a distant sense of dread.

(That something in me was dead right. A couple of weeks later I'd find out, indirectly, that Althea had given birth to Frank Long's son early that very day. And that Mel, who'd witnessed the birth and been more responsible for its life than anybody, including Althea and Long, was acting like the proud father. But, mercifully, I didn't realize it while I was talking to him. Nor that he was crowing to himself about a lot of triumphs because of it, not only over Long and Althea, but over the likes of me and the Greater Boston public, too. Because—and here is the point—he had not gotten over our earlier telephone conversation, back when I'd made cynical noises about his having made so much of her not having asked for an abortion this

288

time, when he'd seriously tried to tell me what he'd told the jury—that this was an unconscious sign of regeneration. An affirmation of Life on her part. A hope for her cure, no less. And all because she was a woman after all, capable of maternal feelings and all that sort of thing.

In other words, when everybody had reasonably assumed that Mel was lying to the world and selling out the People for the sake of his fancy friends, it turned out that he really hadn't been. Lying, that is. Because crazy Mel had really and truly been clinging to those notions, and had been deeply resentful of people for not believing him. Therefore, feeling himself now vindicated, or at least on the way to it, no wonder he felt he could make the first move now, call me and be as self-humbling and conciliatory as need be. If I'd known why at the time, I'd probably have blown up at him, told him to go stuff it and hung up on him, refusing to be gloated over and condescended to, which I might have taken as the greatest offense of all. Or maybe—even more probably—said nothing, because I might also have found him pathetically self-deceiving for choosing to make so much over her giving birth. But I didn't know.)

"The thesis going O.K.?"he said, pretending innocence, and I answered, "Yup," still being stiff about his having thrown me out and not having called me sooner. However, he simply would not be put off by my defensive manner. He just relaxed his tone even further with, "Hey . . . listen . . . come on . . . ," as if opening up his chest to receive whatever pent-up hostilities I might still have against him, due to the demands of my *amour propre*, of course, and he said rather sloshily, "Please . . . we've been friends for too long for this kind of horseshit between us, right? I mean . . . who else will have us? . . . Listen, I agree with you. If we ran into each other for the first time now, now that we're so discriminating and all, we'd have nothing to do with cruds like us, right? But lucky for us it's too late, do you know what I mean? I mean, let's face it, we're past the kinds of standards we have for new people, so let's take advantage of it, O.K.? Can we let bygones be bygones . . . please?"

What could I say? The serpent under cover, calling me with the appealing voice of a child, was disarming me. Mel was prostrating himself so low, was being so distressingly mushy, that I felt if I stepped on him and ground my heel—which he certainly deserved, and even more than I knew—he'd just squish away forgivingly until I stopped, and smile up at me with his everloving, understanding brown eyes. Or worse. Maybe squoosh and emit a foul odor, bringing rain. He was plain embarrassing me into giving up the posture of the wounded party, so I said, "Sure . . . what the hell," as I experienced the reflex of wanting to help him up. "Now that you mention it, no wonder we can't make friends anymore. Nobody can live up to our standards."

"Egg—zzactly!" he said, cheered up and as bouncy as if I had indeed helped him up to his feet. "God bless you, X.J. You're a big man in my book, really . . . and hey, listen, I want to come right out and say it. I'm *sorry* I lost my temper the other day. I shouldn't have done that, O.K.?

"The other day! What do you mean, the other day? It was one hell of a long time ago!"

"Oh . . . yeah, well . . . you're right again. You see, it's just that Althea's case" (I cringed at his even mentioning her, wished he wouldn't) "is, well . . . so sensitive, so important to me. I just popped my cork. Couldn't help myself." And then he started forcing a laugh, as if making light of my mischief, letting me know all was forgiven by being turned into a harmless anecdote, saying, "Hey! You sure scared the piss out of the guy watching her, did you know that? The poor bastard didn't know *what* she was going to do to you when he spotted her hauling you out of the water. Maybe pull your pants down and then have to be pried off you as she mounted your unconscious form . . . or God knows what!" and he laughed some more. But I could not join him. The best I could manage was, "Let's forget it, O.K.?" and his laughing eased off as he said, tactfully pretending to be offhanded, "Sure . . . and hey! For Christ's sake, can we start playing squash again? I need the exercise."

"Sure."

"Let's do it at the Harvard Club, O.K.? It's more convenient for both of us."

"I don't belong."

"That's O.K. I'll be your host."

Which meant, of course, that the olive branch Mel bore in his beak for me did not signify I could return to McLeod's quite yet, even though all might be forgiven after our storm.

It didn't surprise me. After all, Althea was still out there, wandering around within the preserve.

But I didn't want to go back to McLeod's, anyway. Going there could never be the same, not after Althea, even if Mel and I magically managed to restore our friendship all the way to what it once was.

It was inevitable, of course, that I'd hear about Althea's baby, that I'd instantly think back to Mel's midnight call and put two and two together. Word about her always got around. This happened, as I said, a couple of weeks later.

But strangely enough, I didn't get mad at him, even though I half tried.

As a matter of fact, I even felt a surge of new warmth for him come out of the old ashes which surprised me as I thought, well, that sly son of a bitch . . . so all the time he'd been showing me that shit-eating, fake humility, that readiness to turn the other cheek, he'd been crowing and flapping his wings to himself all along. *Immer der schmuck*, like he used to say.

I might have been able to get mad at him when he called, I thought, but now, damn his sly ass, I just couldn't hold it against him. I mean, at least he'd had the decency to keep the specifics to himself, right? And God knows it must have taken all he had to hold them back from me. And frankly, I had to admit, keeping his mouth shut like that had showed a touching kind of consideration for my feelings. Not that Althea still wasn't more important to him, or to me. But it did show he still cared a little about the old bonds, despite the Cain and Abel developments over Althea, and I was appreciating it. Really, it was awfully nice of him, I kept thinking. Kind of like Abel getting a Valentine's card from Cain. Which led me to think that Cain probably didn't hate Abel, or vice versa. Not even when the war was discovered to be total. They probably liked each other, in their way, I thought, though they couldn't have been oblivious to each other's faults. It was just that they had bigger fish to fry, just like Mel and me.

Well, I decided, old Mel certainly was a schmuck, calling me like that with his little triumph. Of course he was. Never was anything but. A cursed, incurably competitive, me-first schmuck to the death. But it turned out, I thought, he was kind of a nice schmuck. Even if he was stiff-arming me out of the way where Althea was concerned. Probably had McLeod's security alerted for me. But what the hell, I thought, that part of it was just life, the tactful part was how far he

291

was going beyond his schmuckery, the measure of his class of schmuckery. Which was, I decided, something. Something I promised to myself to say in his behalf when his circle of Hell was being discussed.

How innocent I was about him. How stupid, really.

I should have remembered. Some friends, usually the very oldest, are only kept around for their potential for jealousy. To show them. To display trophies at them some day, hoping to see them curl their upper lips back, pretending to smile, forcing them to transform their resentment into admiration right there on their bared yellow fangs. I guess it makes the trophies shine more.

Only Mel, even though he was setting me up, was another innocent, and possibly even stupider than I.

He didn't understand about the Light, so he didn't know that Althea never would be an accessible trophy. That she was truly impossible that way. And that loving her, hungry or not, had to be done at a respectful distance. Respectful of her impossibility.

Because anything else would kill her. That is to say, put out the Light in her.

But the issue didn't come up for a long time.

When it did, three years later, I was totally unprepared.

It still pains me to think about it. Very much.

292

CHRISTMAS AT MCLEOD'S
(Three years later)

For one thing, I was unprepared because during those three years—so much like a bridge over a desert—our old friendship deteriorated. There were no fights. Or anything else of the passionate sort. Just what seemed like an interior erosion, growing like a negative river, hollowing out our relationship and carrying away the living substances as implacably as time itself might do it.

And as Mel and I saw each other less and less, trying our best to reestablish the old days, we failed. And I was unprepared for what was coming because I was sentimental about our failure.

We met at the Harvard Club, which he finally convinced me to join after I finished my thesis and got a job, and each time we saw each other it was instantly celebratory. And then, repetitive. Inevitably, a spirit of stale conservationism descended on our relationship which we tried to counteract by throwing ourselves into almost conscious caricatures of our old behavior patterns.

It got so I dreaded our meetings. They became accomplishments, usually ending with an unspoken, "Now, that wasn't so bad, was it?" It reached the point where I, at least, agreed to get together with him once in a while *only* to avoid any new strains, just to protect the surviving exterior so it wouldn't deteriorate any further.

It was Mel, of course, who kept pushing for us to get together. I assumed it was because he felt guiltier, having thrown me out of McLeod's three years before, and because, as life and all its busywork (to say nothing of Marcia) carried him further and further out into middle age, he felt he had precious few chances at old time camaraderies. By which I mean, I guessed he needed it more than I, or thought he did, anyway, and this made me feel consistently sorry for him.

So when, three years later, he made so much of inviting me back to McLeod's on Christmas Eve, on the pretext of playing squash, even though I did *not* want to go there, I said yes. But meaning to find some last minute excuse to get out of it, since I couldn't find it in me to say no.

This was not one of my standard ruses.

In fact, last minute excuses were most untypical of me, which I thought was to my advantage. But his unfortunately high sensibility picked up on it at once, even over the telephone, and he said relentless, "Hey . . . Come on now! It's Christmas Eve! You wouldn't let me down on Christmas Eve, would you? It's a time of new life! New hope!"

So I said, "O.K. I'll be there," suddenly finding myself pushed beyond my initial false consent, all because it seemed to be so very important to him that I come back to McLeod's, as if my ritual return could really make the difference in our friendship.

"That's the stuff!" he said. "We'll have a *great* time! I'll be a great host, X.J. Better than ever. You'll be showered with surprises. Women! Food! Booze! The best McLeod's has to offer the returning prodigal!"

"O.K.," I said. "But I'm expecting you to release at least one thousand doves and two thousand dangerous loonies to celebrate my triumphant return. And I'm talking about the ones you've got hidden way in back, too. None of your presentable storefront types."

"Oh, at least. At *least*! First, squash . . . and then, incomparable orgies!"

"Good enough," I said, gladdened that Mel was so pleased about the whole thing, and, upon hanging up, instantly depressed about going back there.

Because it wasn't just Mel and me going through our futile

gestures, of course. There was also Althea for me to consider. Or, I should say, her absence.

She'd been released from McLeod's about a year and a half before, which we both knew I knew, though we still had never talked about her.

Because Althea was more than a taboo subject. I knew (and more than ever now wished he would admit it to himself) that it was she who had caused the enormous and impassable chasm between us, and that no matter how hard we mugged and clowned at each other from either side, nothing could change that fact.

And I also knew that once I was out there again, the Christmas season notwithstanding, I wouldn't be able to avoid brooding about her, even if I could overcome my depression from my fixed dance with the gallantly smiling, insistent Mel.

In whom, it seemed to me, I had to recognize good will, if not good sense, which made our dance all the more depressing.

How wrong I was.

Maybe there *was* some good will there. There might have been since nothing is perfect. But the truth was that it wasn't because of me that he'd tried to salvage our old friendship all these years. It was because of her.

As I said, some old friends are kept around to display trophies at them, for their potential for jealousy. And all that time he'd kept in touch with me, waiting for the day when he could finally show her to me in triumph, making me take the brunt for the rest of the world. Which had laughed at him.

"*Immer der schmuck!*" to quote one of his own favorite sayings, which I would have done well to have kept in mind while feeling sorry for him all that time.

But there were other reasons why I was so unprepared. For one, the very highest Bostonian discretion with which her release from McLeod's was handled. There was no interest in reminding the offended Boston public about her, to say the least. So it had to be done that way. And no American city can execute discretion like Brahmin Boston, with its now centuries of devotional, daily, silent practice by its chosen people, for whom it's become like a racial reflex, often confused with Puritanism. Actually, they do it so well because it's been more than a survival mechanism. Boston was built and maintained on it, and grew enormously (and invisibly, of course) because of it. And it would die, become something else, without it. I suppose it's the true practice of Brahminism itself, based on the simple faith that failure to observe this one sacrament will surely be punished by the loss of their unique access to the powers of Brahma. Followed, to be sure, by a consequent take over by, say, the Indians, or the Irish, or the Jews, or any of the other groups from Mayor Curley's "newer races". Or, when it comes to the national Republican party, by Westerners of all types, and Californians especially, from whom the Brahmins are discreetly convinced the world must be saved.

And I'm not saying they're wrong.

But that was why it wasn't really surprising that, for once, the local papers tastefully refrained from reporting her release, interesting as their readers would have found it. Of course, as usual with Althea, the word got out anyway. But after a while, and only as a confused rumor. One not always believed, which people treated as one more irritating possibility about her.

The stories going around were that she was not only out, but legally free and living in Australia, or some such, with Frank Long's kid. Maybe married. Maybe not. Or maybe in New Zealand. Or maybe she was out there, but in one of their institutions. But not married, and with no kid.

Then, when her release finally did get press coverage, we all knew for sure.

It never did come from Boston, though. It showed up in a lurid, out-of-town weekly called the *Twilight Inquirer* which catered to a reading public more interested in grotesque sex murders than show biz gossip. Show folk only appeared in those pages if blood and gore was involved.

And I saw it myself, about a year, at least, before Mel invited me back to McLeod's.

I was between classes at my new job, having my beer and sandwich for lunch, disregarding the copy of the *Inquirer* that lay open beside me, right to its "Where Are They Now?" page. But pretty soon it seemed that everybody who came in the place eventually came over, pointed to it by those already there, and looked in the paper, only to turn away after reading with the look of having bitten on a bad peanut. So I looked at it myself, and found, right in among a lot of customary information about the whereabouts of Nazi war criminals

296

and the like, an item with the lead: "Castrating Female Starts New Life!"

It referred to "Althea Stanton, the legendary Bitch of Boston."

Like everybody else, the minute I spotted the item, I was revolted, too. But not for the same reasons. What immediately made me furious was that two-bit "Bitch of Boston" tag which the *Inquirer* editors had put on her. Obviously, the editors, accustomed to dealing with Nazis, had made it up out of their own empty heads, answering the demands of some alliterative echo about the Death Camp lady, the Bitch of Belsen. So, with contempt, I noted to myself how obvious it was that this rag wasn't from Boston. Probably from New York. Or worse, L.A.

Nevertheless, disgusted or not, like everybody else, I read it, and carefully. Very carefully.

According to the *Inquirer's* special investigative team, "Althea Stanton, the legendary Bitch of Boston, one-time slayer and castrator who rocked staid old Boston a few seasons ago," had married, given birth to the child of the man she'd castrated, had recently given birth to a second child by her husband, and was now what the *Inquirer* termed, "a successful mother of two" and what's more, "a modern Pioneer raising sheep out around Brisbane".

The piece concluded with a clearly fraternal, well-wishing gush of: "Lotsa luck to Althea on her new start!" A sentiment the Boston bar clientele did not share with the *Inquirer's* editors. And I could hear them grumbling about it, too, as now more than ever, with the *Inquirer* staring them right in the face if they cared to look at it again at the bar, the whole cabal between the courts and the doctors intent on kissing the asses of the rich was insultingly clear. And even if they didn't look at it in print, and tried to turn their backs on it, the whole thing stood out in three-dimensional relief, anyway, rising out of the open page like the statuette of some evil god that smirked at them. But what really got them now was how well they saw what a set-up the whole deal had been, even more than they'd thought, for Christ's sake. Because at least they'd expected her to spend the rest of her days locked up, even if it was at fancy places like McLeod's ("Not where they'd send you or me, Charlie"). That would have shown at least *some* respect for the public, but Jesus, can't you see it? Can'tcha see it? They'd been planning to let her go free as a bird all along. Hell, all the courts had had to do was to hand her jurisdiction over to the doctors, being enlightened and all, and then all *those* slimy bastards had to do (by which I knew even better than they that they meant mostly Mel) was to wait a while, declare the bitch cured, and then, when nobody was looking, get her the hell out of the country. For Christ's sake!—the point was raised behind me—who did those fucking doctors have to answer to, anyhow! Just a lot of people like her, right? The trustees, right? People like Judge Mott, you remember him? You better believe it, Charlie, they always take care of their own. You can bet your rosy red ass on it. And so forth.

About the only solace they could find was that "they" hadn't let "that creep" out back here. Because that would have been *too* much, they said. Maybe enough, as one emboldened man put it, "enough for some shit to fly!" which, with the rolling eyes of those around him, was immediately treated as a particularly sad piece of bravado, since everybody there really knew that even that wouldn't have been "enough". In fact, a moment later the utterance only brought hostility to the utterer, such as, "What are you talkin' about . . . go piss up a rope, will ya?" because it had only served to remind this proletariat of how hopelessly domesticated they were, and they didn't like that reminder any.

But as I sat on my stool among them, something else was taking shape in my mind, cancerously, sitting there growing strangely like some nasty little demon smiling smugly from a cathedral cornice. Goading me on. Making me look up and down the article over and over again. Looking for something that just was not visible, as if looking hard enough might suddenly part the print, reveal the unrevealed.

And the reason I was looking so hard was that, frankly, I'd heard other rumors about her. Rumors which wouldn't have interested the people around me at all, but which certainly were interesting me now, and morbidly.

For example, I'd heard that she'd married a fellow patient. And now it was his name I was looking for. But no matter how hard I looked, the *Twilight Inquirer* kept withholding it from me as I cursed them for having chosen to be decorous, for once. Why on *that* point, the bastards?

To tell the truth, I was looking for her husband's name because one story I'd heard was that she'd married, of all people, Brownell, the despicable librarian I'd met at Norma's party.

True, this nauseating possibility did seem unlikely, considering

Althea. But I had, I had to admit, heard the rumor. Once, though. Only once. A long time ago. So maybe it wasn't true. But I did want to be sure.

Because it *was* a fact that he'd been at McLeod's at the same time she had. They'd even coincided there a couple of times that I knew of, firsthand.

And suddenly as I sat there, much as I wanted to avoid it, I couldn't help remembering all the times through the years I'd found myself standing at Mel's window, accidentally contemplating the sight of one persistent, trim male figure in an Exeter Academy sweat suit, running in and out of the woods, around the edge of the golf course, and back into the woods, and then, suddenly, like a cannon shot, out of the woods again. Running frenetically, always looking for all the world as if he were escaping some cruelly smiling pursuer he alone saw in those woods, which was after his little, red, palpitating heart—though God knows why anybody would want the miserable thing, except for him.

Back in those days, I hadn't particularly cared to know who this was. He'd seemed inconsequential.

Only eventually did I find out this desperately hurrying, hunted figure belonged to the same Brownell who painted Aztec pyramids, whose fagotty gargoyle of a signature had misled me into pity before I bumped into Althea, who'd been sitting under her own strange picture at Mel's loony art show.

He'd still seemed inconsequential, so I'd dismissed him from my mind.

And then I found out this was also the false Angel Brownell, who liked to think of Heaven as some eternal Broadway musical grand finale, from the Norma story where Althea's Light had suddenly appeared. And, later, also the same Anglophilic Catholic Monarchist, despicable Librarian and practicing Aztec I'd seen act as Long's toady, at that Norma party where Althea had drifted in like a lost soul. In fact, the more I thought about it, the more I realized he was always, somehow, in the vicinity of Althea's Light. *Much* too near, time after time, damn him.

I'd never really linked Brownell to Althea before. But now, frankly, I had to fight against it.

That was why I kept looking and looking into that article, eventually standing up as if ready to put my head into it. Until I overcame my apprehension sufficiently to straighten up, turn around, and walk out of the bar, pretending to myself I was irritated with the *Twilight Inquirer* because no husband's name had been given whatsoever. The truth, of course, being that once the first flush of fearful loathing came to nothing, I was positively glad. Relieved, as if given a reprieve, because at least *his* name wasn't there. Not yet, anyway.

And, as I went walking down the street, I found myself rechewing bits of information from the article with the purpose of dismissing such an odious possibility as Brownell as her husband from my mind forever. So I decided that, come to think of it, there was much there to reassure me. Because the article did say she'd had a second child by her husband, right? Well, that in itself should let him out, Brownell being, I noted to myself, a fag. Of *course* he was a fag, I told myself. Not to be vulgar or anything (and I was being vulgar, of course, out of jealousy), but the guy absolutely *has* to be one. Because, I mean, I'll grant I never saw him in the act. But given that the guy looks like one, talks like one and acts like one, maybe, just maybe, he is one, right? Because, let's face it, if Brownell is *not* a fag, then there aren't any. Anywhere.

Whereupon I started telling myself that actually I shouldn't have been so alarmed in the first place, because all the evidence pointed away from Brownell. After all, fags can and do father children, but does a Brownell, indefatigable snob and creature of the salon, go to No-Place, Australia, to raise *sheep*? Brownell? Living the solitary, rugged outdoor life, clutching his rifle by the campfire, ready to protect his flock from killer kangaroos and cackling dingoes and hundreds of hungry and misinformed Aborigines lurking in the shadows? Or *whatever* it is they do? No sir. Brownell out there, I decided, was completely unimaginable. And indeed, he was.

But then, as I tried imagining Althea, maybe to purify myself, suddenly I couldn't do that either. I tried again: Althea, out in . . . Brisbane? All I could come up with was a faceless husband and two faceless children. And I couldn't imagine what they'd be like any more than I could now possibly think of Althea as what the *Inquirer* called "a successful mother of two" and a "modern Pioneer". Suddenly, I couldn't even imagine Brisbane. It was all a blank, which gave me a sinking feeling. I mean . . . Althea . . . domesticated? Maybe churning butter with big red hands and long sinewy arms? Serving supper first to her God-fearing husband (he was coming into possible focus) with him sitting at the head of the table, maybe with an Old Testament, Patriarchial beard? Could she

300

really now be the kind of darkly obedient, mule-silent woman who called her husband "Husband" and answered to "Wife", having built her life on hard work, a rifle and the Bible, as I assumed all pioneers did? When she'd hated the Bible as much as I knew she had?

And yet, I did have to accept that she was out there, with a husband and two kids, though I still couldn't really imagine it. And logically, it did make more sense that she'd be out there in unimaginable Australia with some tall, skinny Hill Billy type with a long, thin, crooked nose, little eyes close together, and a temper like Jehovah's . . . than with Brownell. That was for sure. Which was also reassuring, in its way.

Because if there was one thing that I could neither imagine nor accept logically—for which I thanked God—it was Brownell as an Althea-tamer. Not that I believed in my heart she had been tamed in the first place. But if she had been, he surely couldn't have done it, fag or not. Which wasn't the issue. The issue was, with what authority, moral or physical, might that tyrannical and terrified little rodent carry it off, right, Muldoon? Because God knows that if Brownell were to suddenly find himself confronted by big Althea, all alone and in *Australia Deserta* no less, completely unprotected by Frank Long as he had been back at Norma's party (when he'd sniped at people from behind Long's back), and with the late Mr. Long's fate clearly portrayed in his anxious mind, I couldn't imagine that nasty little gargoyle doing anything else but cupping his hands instantly over his groin and running like Hell. Just like he'd run in and out of the McLeod's woods. Only faster. Much faster. And chattering all the way, like a fugitive squirrel. Like he always did.

After all, better men than he had been made to feel that way by Althea. So who could blame him if he acted like that, right, Muldoon? Not when she'd made all New England cup its hands in apprehension not that long ago.

Of course, he was. Brownell *was* her husband.

That's what I found out on Christmas Eve, 1957, when I arrived at McLeod's so unprepared, so lulled.

And Mel, the bastard, set me up for it. He was even pleased about it. I know he was.

After all his previous, pathetic gestures of friendship, he had me set up perfectly, of course. When I grudgingly accepted his invitation for squash and supper, I never expected such a vicious act of hostility from him. Such putrid perversity.

But Brownell's being her husband was not the worst of it. He was merely serving as one detail in Master Mel's Grand Design.

I should have known things weren't right.

We played squash in the twilight. His patients were already wandering everywhere, through the buildings, over the grounds, in groups singing Christmas carols.

Mel, apparently because I was back at McLeod's at last, seemed too happy to concentrate on the game, as if his cup were running over.

When he lost several points in a row, instead of slamming his racket down to the floor the way he used to in the old days, or complaining of some injury that was affecting his game, he just said, "Son of a gun! Got me again!" and then smiled, adding, "But I'll get you this time", or some such.

And we even played with a group of carolers singing outside the little glass window in the door that was the only way to peer into the four-sided court. The carolers annoyed me intensely with all those soupy eyes clustered together in the window like so many grapes as they sang away. Trying to get concentration back into our game, I ignored them, but he beamed at them over his shoulder and even waved between points, and smiled at me as he lost point after point while they sang. "I do hope they won't lose respect for me," he said. "It probably isn't good for them to see me defeated . . . or maybe it is. I don't know. What's the score, anyway?"

"Six-nothing, mine," I said, whereupon he shook his head and replied, "Son of a gun!"

The carolers eventually moved on down the hall, their voices becoming paler and paler, and then, just as I prepared to serve he started in himself with, "Tis the season to be jolly! Trala-lala-la, la-la, la-lah!" until finally I put my racket down, forced to say, "Mel! We *cannot* play squash this way."

"Why not?"

"Because it simply is not in the spirit of the game."

302

To which he lowered his racket and smiled, conceding, "I guess you're right, old friend. Now that you mention it, the fierce competitive spirit that squash is meant to foster in men is indeed irreconciliable with the spirit of Christmas. Shall we simply *not* finish our game . . . no winners, no losers? Shall we just go to my office and shower and change?"

"Might as well," I said, giving up, and followed him out of the court, finding the whole experience most unsatisfactory.

In his office, having been encouraged to change first, I waited while he showered and sang some more carols, going along with the singers we heard every once in a while drifting by.

It was very dark and cold outside now, and I began to feel an unexplainable apprehension. It was so dark outside his window that I couldn't even make out the hill or the big old apple trees. And I began hearing a little, unsettling clicking, and couldn't locate its source as it kept going on and off. Then, looking in back of me (I sat on the edge of his desk), I found where the clicking was coming from: some sort of large toy dog. A kind of melancholy, Snoopy-like beagle he had on his desk, proudly displayed. The toy dog had a battery inside which permitted it to blink its eyes alternately and apparently infinitely over its pathetic little pink tongue that stuck out, asking for our putrescent, Disneyfied sympathy.

"Ah-hah!" said Mel, sticking out his head from inside the bathroom, "You have noticed my trophy. It's got a three-year guarantee. A present to me from some of my people." And he came out to dress himself, saying, "I got it because the family of one of my patients owns the company. Unusual, isn't it?"

"I suppose it is," I said, picking it up. It was quite heavy. "It just blinks on and off, huh? That's *it*?"

"That's *it*!" he repeated cheerfully. "For three years!" and he rubbed his hair with the towel again. "We should turn the lights out to get its full effect."

"Jesus," I said, putting it down. "How can you take it? After a while I think I'd want to bust it, just to make it stop blinking."

And he laughed, "You old cynic, you," and shook his head. "A grinch, that's what you are. You know the story about the grinch who stole Christmas, don't you?"

"No, but spare me," I said, and at precisely that moment the near total blackness outside Mel's window was interrupted by a silent and not very strong blink of Christmas lights, coming on all in a triangle, decking a little Christmas tree that suddenly appeared out there on the hill as a complete surprise, and then disappeared again, just as suddenly, leaving the night just as black as before, before blinking on again.

Only the blinking of colored lights between black pauses made the huge old trees visible at all. And even then, they had to be almost completely reconstructed from memory, each time, as in the darkness they were completely erased. And in the moments of light, they only seemed to exist in contrast, no longer dominating the hill, like the bad old days remembered against the pleasant present of the cheerful and insistent little triangular tree, whose colored lights always managed to come back on after each black pause.

Mel, hushed, had been looking on beside me, until he finally said, very quietly, "Ah . . . good. It works . . . ," perhaps more to himself than to me, before adding just as quietly, and this time more clearly for me, "I was afraid it wouldn't."

The colored lights, blinking at precisely the same rhythm as the alternating eyes of Mel's desk Snoopy dog, were the usual five-and-ten cent store commercial reds and greens and yellows, with a few dots of purples and blues thrown in.

And both of us kept standing there, watching the fragile triangle of commercial lights, mesmerized by their almost miraculous, tepid reappearances out of the blackness, until we began hearing new groups of carolers outside, coming from everywhere it seemed, chanting away a variety of carols as they moved toward the lights as if drawn there like invisible moths. And as they came closer to the hill—which was something we could hear rather than see—their carols conflicted like so many different languages until they began blending together into one agreed-upon song which suddenly rose up like a tower as it became quite loud and strong. And then they too became visible, intermittently, around the little Christmas tree. Now even when the lights blinked off, the moments of darkness were sustained by their singing, which made a bridge for the moments of light, creating the soothing illusion that the lights were always on because their singing was always there.

As Mel and I kept looking on, he with a deep gratification, my mind began sailing away from the present. I remembered—or the memory presented itself—how Mel and I, long ago on summer evenings, had watched the fireflies around the apple trees on the hill, blinking on and off in the darkness too, back when I first saw

Althea's Light.

My thoughts wanted to stay there, in the past (they must have known why they wanted to avoid the present), but Mel brought me back with, "That tree, I'll have you know, comes to us courtesy of the same kindly corporation that makes the Ever-Blink dogs, like the one on my desk. By special arrangement. What wonders science can produce, eh, X.J.? It's good to know that it isn't all Atomic Bombs."

"Yes indeed," I said, and then heard come tumbling out of my own mouth, "The miracle of prosthesis. The great human achievement."

With an odd look of surprise at me, Mel let out a short laugh and said, "Why, I suppose it *is* prosthesis, isn't it? Well, it may not be a living one, but it sure is a *functioning* symbol of Universal Love, you know . . . blinking its sweet message of something for everybody, telling each and every little ego that no one is forsaken, that there *is* hope. Really, don't you think it's kind of lovely?"

"Yeah . . . ," I said, "in a tinny, Howard Johnson kind of way."

"All right, you purist, you," he said, and sighed with a smile. "But hokey as it is, I'm afraid it will simply have to do, as the old song goes, until the real thing comes along . . . which I understand," he added, "is expected, with luck, shortly after Judgment Day."

After a bit, outside, the singing stopped.

It simply left off, leaving the cold dark air suddenly vacant except for the palely blinking lights. But only for a moment, because soft chattering and laughing began to be heard as a new mood of partyish expectation took over on the hill. Now most of the carolers seemed to have decided to sit themselves down on the cold ground around the tree, which they did as good-humoredly as if it were a pleasantly sunny, summer afternoon on a lawn.

Then, someone stepped forward into their center, moving through them, and the chattering eased off as they began to pay attention.

The figure was as tall as the Christmas tree, and now nothing else seemed to exist out there but the figure, the vague shapes of the carolers, and the blinking colored lights, all floating in a hushed, comfortably expectant world where the giant, morose old apple trees had all but disappeared, almost completely absorbed by the cheerful mood imposed on the night.

And now Mel too seemed infected by the partyish attitude as he gave me a little glance, holding back a puckering smile. I kept looking straight ahead, concentrating on the person who'd stepped forward, which was what everyone else seemed to be doing, too. About all I could make out was that it was a woman, and that now a man was standing a step or two beside her, also having stepped forward. They were the only ones standing, and they looked like part of a set somehow, relating to each other Giacometti-like due to his balancing satellite position.

Mel, his smile puckering more and more by the moment, said to me, "Let's open the window so we can hear better, shall we? I didn't tell you we have a guest speaker. A practiced preacher, no less," and with that he pushed his window open, adding, "I understand Dr. Johnson said some unpleasant things about women preachers. Do you remember what they were? We were trying to remember them today."

"Uh . . . no . . . , " I said, puzzled a bit. "I don't remember, exactly. But . . . , " but I went no further because, covering his eyes for a moment as if to hear better, he also raised his right index finger to his lips, to shush me.

At first, as the cold air rushed in, I couldn't hear her very clearly at all. But then her voice seemed to get stronger, sailing on the icy air as she said, " . . . Thank you *all* for giving me this chance to prattle at you tonight . . . ," sounding quite cheerful. I thought the voice was in its Christmas cups because it was not only gay but more than a touch flutey in its Yankee accents as it added, "And we most certainly *must* not forget to thank our good and dear Dr. Fish!" which was greeted with, "Hear! Hear!" and some light, good-natured applause. Mel, like a good king, gave a little wave, knowing they were looking up at his window.

"I speak in the dark, and you don't know me, most of you, but first I *must* tell you," she said warmly in her flutey voice, almost laughing, "that I haven't *always* been here at McLeod's as a visitor," which was instantly greeted with laughter and more cheerful applause, to which she responded with, "Thank you . . . No indeed," (her amused voice, like the singing of the carolers before, also made for a continuum through the black pauses between the blinks of colored lights), "many are the Christmases I've spent here. Therefore I should certainly know, firsthand, that special sadness . . . ," she went on, not sounding a bit sad, "of being here at such a time, or feeling abandoned by family and friends . . . not that I had that many, being a difficult sort with what they call . . . personality problems," which occasioned a comradely, playful cheer. "I'd even say that Christmas is the very worst time here," she went on almost casually, "because it's almost impossible not to imagine the rest of the world having a marvelous time without us, as we sink into bitterness and self-pity . . . ," which was met with, "Hear! Hear!" and the most enthusiastic burst of schoolboyish applause so far, which made her stop for a moment before going on with, "Thank you again. . . . Yes, we feel, I think, that life is going on without us, which we tend not to like one *bit*. And that is why, tonight, my Christmas message is based on some reflections I've had about what a very, very snooty French aristocrat once said about life. As I understand it, he said, 'Living? Why, the servants can do that for us.' And you know, I *quite* agree with him," and she laughed. "That is basically what I want to tell you. I have discovered, not *too* late in the game, I hope, that it is *only* the servants that truly live. That is why, on this Christmas Eve when I am so very happy, I urge you, one and all, to become servants. Yes, servants! Your brother's keepers. Or anybody else's who'll let you. You see, I'm very lucky. Through great good fortune I find that I don't have to hunt. I find myself with a captive husband and children for me to serve. And I assure you, I give them *no* choice in the matter. None! And speaking as a servant, I want to tell you our secret. Just what it is that permits us to serve. I think I can let it out tonight. We submit to our masters *most* gratefully indeed because we owe them *more* than our lives. We owe them the very life in our lives,you see. The *meaning* in our lives."

"But the plain truth is that you don't really need to have a family. Oh, it makes it easier sometimes, though not always. The truth is there are always other masters for us. All around us!" and she laughed her flutey laugh.

"Of course, I quite agree with those who claim that love is always unfair, that the lovers are those who willingly submit to the tyranny of those they love. That it can't be any other way. Therefore, people, *do* take advantage of this unfairness, *do* hurry, and after supper tonight, or even *during* supper, *find* your tyrants! Pursue them! Be implacable! They are your quarry! And for *heaven's* sake, don't be snobs. *All* masters are worthy. They become our rightful rulers, you see, because their legitimacy is based on giving us our lives, as only our true lords can.

"Of course, I must admit to you, I myself did not always believe in the possibility of love. And then I met a man. The most terrible man

I *ever* knew. Perhaps the most unrelenting, cruel snob I ever came across, my younger, unenlightened self excepted, of course. And he told me that I was wrong. That love *did* exist. That he felt it. That it was an appetite of the soul. But according to him, that appetite was simply wanting what someone else had. And he made no bones about it. And me . . . ," she said with the small laugh taking shape in her throat again, "why, I thought him *such* a cruel predator, *such* an unremitting beast . . . which he certainly was, poor man, that I immediately became infatuated with him . . . ," and she laughed, "hoping, of course, that what he said wasn't true, though rather convinced it was. But now, looking back, I see he was indeed quite correct. And do you know? I don't mind at all! Indeed, I find him to be, fortunately, so absolutely correct that on this Christmas Eve, I happily urge you all the more to become relentless predators and pursue your brothers, because they *do* have *one* thing, at the very least, that *you* don't have. And that is, dear friends, their otherness, their merciful and sacred otherness, which will nurture us through this life, as nothing else can.

"You see, woman that I am, I also have to confess my vanity to you, as unnecessary as that might seem. Long ago I found I couldn't possibly live only for myself. Without those I can serve, I am not at all interesting. Not even attractive. But now, because of . . . well, my tyrants . . . I can tell you very candidly that there are even times when I feel rather beautiful . . . ," at which point, one enthusiastic male tenor voice rose up, all alone with, "Hear! Hear!" which made everyone laugh. It came from the man standing next to her, whose right arm had jerked up in excitement, and there was more laughter as she said to him, in a personal aside, "Thank you, dear . . . ," before going on with, "So you see, I'm still appealing to your selfishness! Make a self, a beautiful self, out of the servant you can be, out of the grateful and submissive woman in us all, and I hasten to add, incorrigible Christian that I am, out of the *Jesus* in us all . . . whom I'm sure you all recall became divinely beautiful . . . by feeding all his—I really should say her—hungry brothers with his mother's flesh," and she laughed. "*All* flesh is maternal, you know. *Can't* be anything else, and certainly not in his case. And I'm sure you all know, too, that Jesus didn't come to serve the grand. So let our womanly hearts . . . and *all* hearts are womanly, thank God . . . be *too* wise for that, because if the grand really are grand, then they don't need us. But there is no problem. Because, as it happens, my dear friends, if properly looked at, the happy truth is that *everyone* is grander than we are, simply because they are *not* us! We are in luck!

"So, now, *do* do as I say. No matter how unloving you feel . . . , " and she laughed, adding, "at *first*, that is. Acted love is the only interesting kind anyway. So, love your quarry in spite of your first, nasty instincts. Really, it's as they say abut prayer. Pray enough and you'll end believing. Act your love, and I guarantee you that your love will be at the very *least* as sincere as my new vanity . . . And if you do as I say, people, the day will come when you might possibly relent, briefly of course, and let your brother keep you . . . but then, if you didn't know it already, you'll find out he'd been doing *just* that, all along."

At that point, she stopped talking, though everyone kept listening.

Now there was a silent pause on the hill as the red and green and blue lights of the Christmas tree kept blinking softly on and off, like the wake of her voice. Everyone continued still, as if hypnotized by the lights, contemplating them as if they were carrying on her voice, underscoring it, repeating it. The intermittently illuminated stillness was so complete that all the shadowy figures seemed part of a tableau. An inanimate representation where the huge old trees in the background, tilted slightly to either side, made the hill like a great bull's head, with the old trees the horns of a monstrous beast that could, once upon a time, wound and destroy, but which now, in the colors of the new light, was tamed, like a castrated ox made to bear them all.

Then, quite suddenly, shattering the stillness, she clapped her hands and said, "Off to supper!" and the whole group came alive, everyone springing to their feet, instantly chattering away, and they began scattering off as she called after them, "And be good, every one of you!" And she laughed, "Even if you aren't! I must go and get ready myself!"

In seconds the cheerful, chattering group had disappeared, leaving only the Christmas tree blinking on and off, and all the small lights were like the afterglow of their presence. The hill didn't seem at all naked now, even though no one was there.

Mel turned to me, and with a small smile said, "Surprised . . . I bet . . . "

"By what . . . ?"

"Come off it. You mean to tell me you don't know who that is?"

And I looked at him for another moment before I heard myself say,
"... Do I ... ?" as a pleased Mel closed the window, nodding that
indeed I did.

"I wanted you to see her," he said. "She's back here for a very
short time, to settle some property matters, and I was sure you
wouldn't want to miss her. Incredible, isn't it? I mean, she's cured."

"... Cured ... ?"

"Yes. Still mad, of course, in her own marvelous way. But then, all
the best people are. Nevertheless, by ordinary standards, cured.
Functioning. All that stuff."

"It ... didn't sound like her ... ," I said, trying not to sound as if
I were pleading, but Mel smiled at me. That was his only comment.

Then, looking up at the clock on his wall, he announced, "We can
meet her and her husband down in the courtyard in fifteen minutes,
and then we'll go on to supper from there. You assumed, of course,
you were having supper with me, didn't you?"

"I guess ... so," I said as I felt all my strength drain away from
my limbs.

"Well, you are! You *are!*" said Mel, mercilessly good-humored. "I
have a whole group of guests, including ex-patients like Althea, and
we're having a fancy supper in her honor down in my conference
room. And incidentally, in case you were wondering, liquor *will* be
served, since no patients are involved ... at least, none from what I
call the 'active' roster."

"Oh ... and what will they drink, the patients?" I said
mechanically as I thought: Althea. Here. Althea. In the flesh. I felt
like a dead tree.

"Why, cider, my good man! The best cider in the world, so don't
feel any pity for them. Frankly, I'd rather have some of that great
cider than mediocre wine, any time. *Any* time!"

I was afraid I was going to topple. I had to sit down.

Althea, in a few minutes, was going to emerge out of that hospital
night to confront me, in three dimensions. Real. Talking. Breathing.
I was near Mel's desk, and I sat on the edge, next to his Ever-Blink
dog. Mel looked at me and asked, "What's the matter?" as if he
didn't know.

I didn't say anything. I felt too weak even to glare at him for taking
me so viciously by surprise this way.

He just kept watching me with fake uncomprehending concern until I finally said, "I want to know one thing, Mel ... do you mind?"

"Probably not. Ask me, then we'll both know."

But for another moment, I still didn't dare ask. And then, out came, "Is Brownell . . . her husband?"

His eyes twinkled, and he said, "Yup! . . . and it may surprise you to know that he's turned into a pret-tty acceptable guy himself. For which, if I may say so, I'd like some credit, although most of it, I have to admit, has to go to Althea. And maybe," he grinned, "a little to him, too."

" . . . Acceptable . . . ?" I said weakly. I still couldn't believe it. Any of it. It was as if there were a pane of glass between me and Mel. Between me and everything.

"Yes, acceptable. As a man, I mean. And I'm not just talking about the guy's homosexuality, either, which is pretty much a thing of the past, by the way, in my opinion. Not that I'm prejudiced against homosexuals, you understand, just because they're homosexuals."

And my voice sounded weak and resistant to me as I asked, "What do you mean . . . ?" I didn't care about Brownell's homosexuality. I was just asking to get more time to recover, and to resist believing.

"*You* know what I mean, don't you? Sure. Don't you remember? The guy, being queer to one side, was one of the worst little shits in the world! Frankly, he was just a sneaky, cynical, selfish little boy. That was his real trouble. You could see it all over his face, couldn't you? Don't you remember that sinister, goody-goody choirboy look he had, the pale waxy face, the twisted little pink smile, and that highly cultivated ability as a hypocrite? Just revolting, wasn't it? Well, believe you me, he's grown up an awful lot, X.J. He really has, and I'm proud of him."

I heard myself say, "That's good."

"Well, come on!" he said, "Let's get on down to the courtyard and wait for them!"

Seeing as how I hadn't budged from the edge of his desk, he helped me up, saying, "I've sat you down in between them for dinner, just so you can see for yourself how far they've both progressed." And he began escorting me across the floor, adding, "You know, as a doctor, I'm supposed to overcome negative feelings toward my patients, but it really was practically impossible with Brownell. God, what a sneaky little shit he was. Do you remember Jerry Foley, the guy who went to B.C.?"

"Foley . . . ?" He continued to disorient me.

"Sure! Foley. Back in high school. The creep, Foley. Of course you do. We all said he was going to be a priest, remember? He wound up in insurance. Actuarial tables. Anyway, this Brownell was just like Foley, if you know what I mean. The kind of pupil the teachers love, eviler than the worst hood in the class, moist little smile and all. They practically had the same face, to tell you the truth. For a while I thought I couldn't see Brownell because of Foley. Exactly the same expression, I swear. But let me tell you, they don't have the same face now, by God. I tell you, Brownell even looks different, almost. He really does. You won't recognize him."

As we left his office, I produced a cigarette and lit it without even knowing I'd done it, and he continued herding me down the hall, uncontainable in his chatter, as I began feeling as if I were going to my own execution. He was forcing me to go. I could feel it, resent it, yet not resist it as he was going on with, "And it's a *beautiful* relationship. You'll see. I want you to see it, because it's so fine, it rekindles the faith. Thanks to her, he's become a man. I mean it. Of course, without her, I'm sure he'd crumble. But with her, he's been able to face up to life in Australia. He's even faced up to fatherhood. To thinking of something other than himself first, like a little kid, for a change. I mean, he's *generous*, . . . *brave* . . . you name it! And by his becoming a man, damned if she hasn't grown up into a fine woman. Really. The kind of woman any man would be lucky to have at his side. And they're both so humble, so *nice* to each other! Honest to God, X.J., *that's* the part that's so beautiful. Their support of each other, their gentle dignity . . . you'll see it written all over them. Shit! Maybe I won't put you between them. Maybe I'll sit there myself," he laughed. "Just to enjoy their apprehension, if you know what I mean. Nah, I won't do it. I hate to separate them, really. They're so important to each other, still, especially with strangers . . . not that they'd go to pieces, either. They're getting too strong for that, too self-sure, because they trust each other so much," and he laughed, "Jesus! Can you imagine *anybody* trusting that little fink Brownell in the old days?"

We stood waiting for them in the white pebbled courtyard, wearing just our suits in the icy, clear night, with me smoking cigarette after cigarette, throwing the butts down onto the white pebbles as, in the cold, my initial shock was gradually displaced by nervousness. And while I smoked away, Mel, his hands deep in his pants pockets, bobbed up and down every once in a while, exhaling steam and apparently needing nothing more than his happiness to keep him warm.

The more nervous I got, the more I dreaded her appearance, but I said testily, "She certainly is taking her time, isn't she?" and Mel laughed. Even though he wasn't wishing she wouldn't ever come, as I was, he obviously gloried in the fact she was taking so long, saying, "See what I mean? A real change, right there! She's a real woman now, which cuts two ways. In the old days, no matter what her faults, she was always punctual. Of course, maybe you didn't know that about her, but she was . . . because she didn't really care *what* she looked like. And she usually looked like a spook, too. A real Medusa, half the time," and he laughed and trembled a little, both from the cold and his joy. "Not *now* though! She's taking a long time because she's fixing herself up. I'm sure of it. Isn't that a big change, right there? Admit it, isn't it?"

"How do you know it's her?" I said, lighting up another cigarette. "Maybe it's him."

"Nah. It's her, all right. I know it's her. Now that she's become socialized, she wants to look presentable for everybody, including him. Believe me, they've talked about it a lot with me. See, Brownell, being a male, naturally wanted her decked out all the time, and she resisted that for a while. As a matter of principle, as you can imagine. But then, when she finally decided to look nice, she did it for him, so he wouldn't be ashamed of her, or of himself, for that matter, Isn't that *incredibly* sweet of her? Can you imagine, Althea . . . of *all* women, making herself presentable so people wouldn't interpret it as contempt for her husband?"

"Is that why she does it?"

"It's part of it, that's for sure. I know, because he used to complain so much about it, back when she looked like such a Medusa. He said that women who look like hell do it to tell everybody they don't give a shit about anybody, starting with their husbands. And he's right. It's not the whole story of course, because now she does it for herself, too. I mean, she's got her own vanity, and she really is pretty socialized now. For her, I mean."

And as I puffed away, I remembered a story . . . was it a Norma story? . . . where, at a dinner party intruded upon by Althea, Frank Long had said, in front of everyone, "Really, Althea, the way you behave . . . sometimes I think you are pre-Social Contract". And I thought about Althea the rebel, whose black Light I'd seen, who had above all refused to serve anything but her freedom, and I couldn't possibly imagine the woman Mel was describing to me.

Maybe, I thought, what would appear would be some pathetic, tamed, over-painted female nut, not belligerent anymore, not dangerous, and therefore someone Mel could consider a successful cure. I dreaded seeing that. Suddenly, I wanted to see the Medusa again. I threw down another butt and said, "Jesus, Mel. She's taking so damn long, maybe she's going to come looking like Marilyn Monroe. She's sure taking long enough for it."

Which made him laugh. "That's pushing it, X.J. After all, she *is* a Boston Yankee, you know. However, I wouldn't be at *all* surprised if . . . in the privacy of their nuptial quarters, she didn't produce some kind of Song of Songs allure she won't be showing the public," and he laughed again at his own idea, very pleased by his vision of a wanton, sex-wise, harem Althea, which made me squint at him. It was very peculiar indeed, this attitude of his, yet, there he was, bouncing up and down, giggly and delighted about her sexual behavior with another man.

Suddenly, he started becoming alien to me. Mel, whom I'd known forever. Could this be the same Mel I'd seen so jealous, to the point of becoming pugnacious, the night of Norma's party, so wretchedly jealous, in fact, that he'd blanched in pain at the sight of Althea dancing with Frank Long as he kissed her neck?

But he smiled twinkly eyed at me, obviously about Althea's new boudoir life. Absolutely untroubled. I was sure he knew what I was thinking because he seemed to be displaying his new attitude for me.

Now he was making me wonder, was it possible that the miracle of psychoanalysis had helped him transcend sexual possessiveness? Was he now *that* mature? Maybe . . . but . . . even to the point of openly relishing what she did in private with another male? I thought maybe I should start regarding him as some kind of superior creature, even admire him. But I couldn't. Because suddenly Mel was not only alien to me. He was disgusting. Suddenly I couldn't help but find him more than slightly putrid, enjoying his own redolence. Perverted. Downright unmanly. I couldn't help it at all, and surprised as I was by him and his putrescent cheerfulness, I had to wonder what godawful vistas of inversion this new attitude opened up for him.

And then, as if intent on making it worse, he reached into his jacket, trembling happily, and produced his wallet, saying, "Hey!

Listen! Let me show you pictures of the kids!" I tried to restrain a grimace, since one of the kids was by Long and the other by Brownell, something he was now treating like the culmination of an apparently joyous cuckoldry.

And with insistent pride, he shoved the pictures up in my face. There was no avoiding them. A boy and a girl. I looked for traces of Frank Long on the boy's face, but I couldn't see any. However, around the corners of the girl's tight mouth, I could certainly see the afterglow of Brownell.

"Aren't they terrific?" said Mel, jumping up and down more and more in the cold. "I mean, I know I'm prejudiced and all that, but you have to admit they look great."

I nodded as he happily put his wallet away. To me they'd looked dreary, but Mel obviously didn't pick this up, maybe because he couldn't imagine anybody not seeing what he saw in them.

And then, as I tried to be compassionate, it occurred to me that maybe Mel might not really be a militant cuckold, but was just doing the only thing he could, under the circumstances. Maybe it was a defensive posture before the world and himself which was not only pathetic and good sportsmanship, but some kind of secret to survival from which I might well learn something.

And Althea still didn't show. I threw another butt down on the white pebbles. The area around my feet was becoming thoroughly littered. I was feeling very cold now, so I started bobbing up and down with Mel, whose eyes suddenly became shiny as he said, "Hey! Do you think . . . ?"

"What?"

"Maybe . . . well, maybe they're knocking off a quick screw before dinner?" and his face became illuminated with mischief as he snickered, obviously not minding waiting around in the cold for that, which nauseated me all over again, as all compassion vanished.

The whole thing was getting too much for me, no matter how hard I tried to think kind thoughts about him. As I hopped up and down with him, I turned away so as not to have to look at him, so loathsome a spectacle was he becoming, when—just then—my nausea at Mel began to dissipate because, simultaneously with a sense of how stupid I'd been, it began to dawn on me *why* Mel could be so cheerful. Suddenly, I understood: *he's* not the cuckold! Everybody else is! Sure, Althea's made Brownell "a man", but only because Mel made her "a woman". Through his craft. Through his

315

potency, for Christ's sake. No matter what he says about Brownell being "a pretty acceptable guy", he *still* looks down on him. That's why Brownell is "acceptable". And that reconstituted creep is perfect for the part. Mel is still the most important male in her life. He thinks she's *his*, for Christ's sake! And Brownell helps keep it that way. Of course! He's just the front man. And anyhow, Brownell's potency is just Mel's. And they *all* know it. Mel is having the supreme Macho pleasure of cuckolding everybody.

Now, as I watched him continuously bob up and down ever so lightly on his toes, fueled by his secret joy, happy, patient, with that damned ever-ready smile on his face, I thought: Jesus, that sly son of a bitch. I should have known. How *could* I have thought he was different from me. How could I *ever* have thought he wasn't just as much of a competitive male and as possessive as ever? He *is* superior to me, goddamn it, but because he's so much cleverer, that's why.

Hadn't it been Mel, after all, who'd told me that the most poignantly lyrical statement of what the male psyche is *always* about—can't *help* but be about—is the old Sicilian saying, "All women are whores, except for my mother, who is a virgin"?

Well, by God, Mel was actually turning that incurably childish demand of a fantasy into his existential reality. He was actually pulling it off! That's what I was beginning to perceive through the stupefying steam that clouds my psyche when women are concerned. And I was perceiving it with a cold and distant lucidity that was starting to make me feel both sad and olympian.

Inescapably, it all began arranging itself before me, like a military formation. Those photographs he'd shoved in my face. No wonder he was so proud. He was the true progenitor of those kids. But he was more than their real father. Without him, there'd be nothing, not even Althea, whom he'd captured and kept from vanishing into the Blackness.

What Mel had done, it was getting clearer and clearer, was the closest thing to keeping Althea a Virgin Mother. As well as keeping her his. Practically speaking, he'd brought off two immaculate conceptions, all through his infinite wisdom and guidance as Holy Ghost. The Djiin. He's playing God. She's his Mary. And Brownell, the obedient front man proud to tend to the donkey work of childrearing, he's his Joseph, that's all. The obligatory first cuckold at the service of his smiling Master. And just as in the mystery of the Trinity, God here has all the advantages that any red-blooded, glassy-eyed little boy could want: he's the father *and* the son. And above all, he's enjoying the whole thing as the son, the most enjoyable position . . . which he forever retains by virtue of the ever-burning purity of his impossible and jungle-steaming love for her. Which can be felt so purely *only* for the one unattainable woman in the universe, loved as only can be by a son and charter member of the primeval horde, and who can never be both the *one* impossible woman, and *possible* . . . and who Mel in his genius had managed to both attain and keep unattainable. Because if he didn't, he'd lose *HER*—his ultimate HER—destroy her basic virtue and identity the very moment he had her the way Long would want to.

I understood so well now. No wonder he didn't envy Brownell. For Christ's sake, Mother can't be Wife. It violates all the rules of Amor. Ask any Knight. Ask any infant who, like all other infants, wants to be the *only* one in the world. For Christ's sake, if he had her as wife, it would end both the game and her divinity, the *only* thing that makes her a worthy consort of such an Omniscient and Supreme infant as a God.

I couldn't get over it. Mel, *immer der schmuck*, was a genius. He had even managed to maintain, in the very teeth of having to grow up, the full, ideal purity of his own infantilism, as well as achieving his beloved role of Big Daddy. And, I thought, he never makes a mistake!

I had to admit, he'd done what Freudian legend has it every would-be father-killing little boy would like to do, but can't, because he'd blow his cool.

Only a mature man, I realized sadly, could carry it off.

At which point, reduced as I was to watching Mel snort his streams of steam as he hopped cheerfully—and smile at me as he noticed my watching him, not bobbing with him anymore—I felt two things: admiration, and the sinking sense that now she would never be, in any way, mine. Just his. Always his.

It was a strangely lucid moment. In my defeated condition I might have felt envy and spite. But I didn't. I couldn't.

I knew the fault was in me. Even if I'd had all his advantages, I could never have done it. All because I wasn't practical. That was the sad, inescapable truth. And Mel, unlike me, *was* practical. I'd always known it. He was committed to Life, wasn't he? To the possible? To adjustment and maturity? Well, that was why he was the one who had Althea, why he'd managed to take such lordly possession of her and keep her inviolable, even from his lower, short-sighted and grabby self, a creature who surely was just like me. A creature who, wanting everything, could have nothing. A creature eternally denied simply because of its unenlightened, self-defeating infantilism. Which his mature infantilism had transcended.

Watching me watch him, and as if he knew it all, which I was almost ready to believe, Mel gave a wink. I could do nothing but bow my head.

Finally a door opened before us emptying out into the white peb-bled courtyard, and out came a striding Althea, followed by Brownell.

No, she didn't look like Marilyn Monroe, or some pathetically over-painted female patient trying to conform to a childish notion of Mommy in heels and earrings. Just lean and very healthy, well-combed, in a tweed jacket and skirt.

It was Brownell who'd changed much more. He was gray at the temples now, thin in a sinewy way—they both were—and taller than I remembered. And now, at first glance, his older, tight-skinned, slightly weatherworn face struck me as austerely handsome. He stood very straight. Only the trace of nervousness at the lip line of his tight, reconstituted mouth as he watched me—another male—reduced the masterly, nearly military aura of his general bearing.

"Althea!" said Mel, "You remember Mr. Muldoon, don't you?"

"Oh . . . of course," she said as she turned toward me, raised her face to produce a rather horsey, patrician smile and simultaneously put her right hand straight out at me. "How do you do, Mr. Muldoon."

Unbelievingly, I reached out to take her hand in mine, her mortal hand which, even though its owner had pronounced my name, gave me no indication of truly recognizing me through the veils of our flesh.

Brownell, who'd been watching me furtively over her shoulder, made me wonder if he measured himself against every male he met, routinely trembling within his inner, fragile tightness. God knows I don't usually produce that response, but now I almost felt like big Frank Long, capable of freezing a bird in flight with terror simply by

318

a smirking, python stare. But she, placing her hand on his out-stretched forearm as he came forward to shake my hand, put him at ease with, "Dear, this is Mr. Muldoon. A friend of Dr. Fish's."

"Goodness!" Mel, to my surprise, protested, "he's much more than that, Althea. Why, he's the fellow you saved from death by water!" and he laughed.

Althea looked at me again. I nodded, wondering, hadn't she known that? Had Mel been cueing her from the beginning, because she had no idea *who* I was? And Brownell, more confident now, apparently reassured by her attitude that I was merely a formal occasion of some innocuous sort, not very important in her past and certainly not in her present, said, "Now that I think of it, didn't we meet once before, Mr. Muldoon? I forget where, but I'm quite sure we have."

"Uh . . . yes," I said. "We met. At a party at Norma's."

"Oh, of *course*! Norma . . . ," said Brownell. "How *is* she? I haven't heard from her in ages." And at the mention of Norma, Althea looked in my face with more interest, waiting for news about Norma.

Not one of the three seemed to remember, or if they did remember, to care, that at that very Norma party Brownell had spent his time ruthlessly baiting an obviously jealous Mel, sniping at him from behind Long's enormous reclining form on the rug, or that Mel had retaliated by publicly calling him a cocksucker, as I recalled.

I watched them watching me. Both Althea and Brownell kept smiling interestedly, waiting for news of Norma, until I said, "Well . . . I'm afraid I can't really tell you how she is. I haven't seen her in a long time, either." I didn't add the further specification that I hadn't seen her since shortly before Althea had killed Frank Long.

"As a matter of fact," Mel put in cheerfully, "*I* can help us a little more than Mr. Muldoon, because I saw a lot of her after her divorce, and I can report that she has moved to New York where she is *quite* successful as a free-lance writer. Last I heard, last year I think it was, she had an apartment of her own in the Village and felt well enough established and sporting enough to give up her alimony, on her own!"

"Wonderful!" said Brownell. "She must be doing very well then," and his eyes lit up with a touch of admiration over his smile, I thought, at the joint mention of success and New York. "You know, I've always thought she was an exceptionally talented girl. At anything she tried. She was an absolute whiz in grad school, you know. Well, *good* for her!" And then he asked Mel, "By the way, have you *read* any of her stuff?"

"Uh . . . yes," he said with a smile and an unconvincingly apologetic shrug. "Not my kind of thing, I'm afraid." Whereupon Brownell laughed and said it for both of them, "Thank *heavens*! I don't think I could stand it if she were actually *good* as *well* as successful. The most I can tolerate is one or the other, because frankly, I've always reserved those two possibilities together for myself, just in case I should ever try my own hand at writing."

And Althea (I kept glancing over at her every time I dared, unbelieving, as she still gave no sign of regarding me as anything other than "Dr. Fish's friend") holding herself in a way that indicated she had decided it was time for us all to move along, smiled at Brownell and said, "Dear, of *course* you'd combine those two very things, if you ever put your mind to it." And a pleased Mel looked over at me, pleased, I gathered, about how supportive she was of her spouse, as she added, "Shall we go to dinner?"

"Good idea!" said Mel, rubbing his hands together. "I'm famished."

Hanging back for another moment, I took my last nervous puff and threw down the cigarette I'd been smoking, and as I did, I also happened to smile nervously up at Althea, who saw me do it—throw down the cigarette, I mean—and instantly pursed her lips, annoyed.

Without looking at me any further, she bent down to pick up the butt herself. Brownell also looked down, and together they saw—to my grief—the nearly dozen or so butts I had dropped and even ground down among the white pebbles. From over her bent back, Brownell gave me an irritated glance before bending down himself to join Althea, who was already busy taking charge of the messy butts around my feet.

I stepped back. I could do nothing else.

Watching them I felt numbed to my very soul. Mortally separate from what I was looking at. Though it was happening before my eyes, I could only see their motions, especially hers, as part of some other reality than the one I lived in.

Together they were a team, taking possession of the world. Reclaiming it. Driving me off. And I, I was less than an uncouth barbarian. I was the lowly, innately depraved sinner who didn't even deserve civility, but only to be cast forth from the garden implacably (which, if I weren't dear Dr. Fish's friend, they would have done), polluting snake that I was in the form of a Brighton Irishman (who suddenly knew he would go to his death before ever daring to break through to her, already too far out in outer darkness to be heard crying out, "Althea, it's *me!*"). And they, the reformed Adam and Eve, they were God's righteous groundskeepers who did not stop their policing until all the butts had been gathered up from among the white pebbles, placed in Brownell's cupped hands, and then deposited in a suitable cement urn at the corner of the courtyard, the little cemetery where unworthy, rejected trash belonged.

As I continued watching, helpless, my numbness spread as if my blood had stopped flowing. And I began to feel deadly still, cold through and through, and progressively more alien from everything and everybody, including my own body, as I thought: she's changed. Mel's right. She's changed. And unable to do anything else, I kept looking at Althea, now turned into just another Yankee matriarch, the kind that is ever ready to lead the way to assuming the burdens of public service, who now vigilantly watched to see that Brownell slapped his hands free of dirt, before nodding.

I also became aware, even through my numbness, that my numbness was only the prelude to an inconsolable sadness that would surely come, once my blood, in its inconquerable obtuseness, not knowing what else to do, had begun flowing and feeding my body again. I kept trying hard as I could to deny the evidence before my eyes that Mel was right. That she'd changed. But she *had* changed.

But even while the butts were being picked up, as I think I managed to smile weakly at Mel (I saw him in a blur, did he glare at me too, picking up her lead?), I also started trying to take refuge in thinking that none of this was so because this woman was not really Althea. Not the Althea whose Light I'd seen. And it almost seemed possible she wasn't, just as much as it seemed impossible that the Light I'd seen could ever have come from this woman (who now, strangely, made me think of a tall, dark version of the Little Red Hen) who was giving one last look at the ground around my feet—as if they didn't exist, or deserve to exist—to see if any butts had been missed and who bent over once more to come up with a few matches and a tiny piece of silver foil paper.

Now I know why it seemed so possible she wasn't really Althea.

The Light was totally absent from her. It was gone.

321

After dinner Mel drove me home through the poverty of that empty, rainless night.

His happiness hardly bothered me, and his ultimate defeat, of which he was not aware, didn't make me feel any better. Either way, the Light was gone from Althea.

As he drove, I felt more than ever that there was no place for me to go anymore, that it would all be the same.

And I could see him misinterpreting my depressed silence, taking it for the mood of a bested lover. But to his credit, he drove a good five minutes before he came out with, "Well? What did you think?"

I didn't want to talk. But I knew I would eventually, especially since it no longer made much sense to make a scene with Mel, of any kind. I wasn't interested in him, or in me, or in us. I had transcended the old rivalry, having discovered I'd also gone beyond being interested in Althea. The Lightless Althea. So I said, "You were right. She has changed."

"Oh . . . ? How do you mean? I'd love to hear your views on the subject," he said, leaning over just a little but keeping his eyes on the road. His head was tilted slightly to catch what he'd take as a compliment.

"Brownell hasn't changed, though," I said, feebly trying to veer away from discussing her directly.

"Why?" he laughed. "Do you think he's still homosexual?"

"Who cares . . . He's still the same finky creep he always was. Just oriented to Big Momma now, that's all."

And he smiled, not at all distressed to have Brownell run down. "In other words, you don't care whether he's queer or not, you still don't like him. Well, that is advanced of you, in a way, I suppose."

"He reminds me of a guy I knew in graduate school," I said, "whom I accused of being a closet straight, just spreading the rumor he was queer so people would think he had a superior literary sensibility. I'm even prepared to accept the fact that Brownell never was queer in the first place, for all the difference it makes, 'cause, to quote you, *immer der schmuck*, no matter how you slice it."

"Brownell, you mean."

"Him too."

And he grinned, "You're trying to evade the important things, you devil, going on like that about your lower-middle-class prejudices. How has *she* changed? That's what I want to know."

I heard myself sigh, "I don't know . . . she used to be such a rebel,

Mel . . . But now . . . she's just going to wind up being the head of the local Audubon chapter, or some such . . . "

But Mel laughed, "Oh, you don't *know!* She's still a rebel, believe me. Delightfully so! And as much of a Feminist as ever, too. Right now, for example, she wants to come back to live here, just so she can be in the swim of things at the Society of Sophia . . . She can't do that, of course."

"*She's* a Feminist . . . ?"

"You bet she is. That's one thing I've never been able to talk her out of. And she won't take any teasing on *that* subject, believe me. For God's sake, X.J.! Didn't you hear her speech about how Jesus was a woman, with maternal flesh and all that stuff? Or about women ruling the world? Right at the supper table? Some things never change in people, and that rebellious Feminist streak is there in Althea for keeps, believe me. But I quite agree with you, it's part of her charm, as far as I'm concerned."

I didn't comment. Her ideological consistency, even if true, changed nothing for me. Her Light was still gone. And Mel, not that there was any sense now in being angry with him for it, had helped put it out, in the name of Life. I was sure he had.

Smiling, he drove silently for a while, and I was more persuaded of his obtuseness than ever, making me think I'd overestimated his intelligence and sensibility all my life, when unexpectedly he said to me, very gently, so gently he disarmed me, "But . . . you still think she's changed . . . for the worse, don't you?"

I didn't say anything, but, as if reading my mind, still very gently, he went on with, "X.J. . . . have you ever considered the possibility that . . . you might have been wrong about her? That you might have seen something in her that . . . wasn't ever there?"

"It sure isn't there now, Mel," I said sadly.

He continued driving quietly for a few moments, as if pondering whether to come out with something or not, and then, finally, he did, saying, "I wonder, X.J., how well you *really* knew her?"

"What do you mean?"

"I mean . . . how well you knew her personally. Because . . . well, I have, you see, for a million years . . . and you really couldn't have . . . not very well."

"Yeah? So . . . ?"

"So . . . I'm humbly suggesting that . . . and this is from knowing for a fact that she's changed for the better . . . well . . . that what you think you saw in her was . . . well . . . a deflected light as it were . . . a beautiful vision, no doubt, originating from you. You see, I think you saw her as some sort of romantic heroine, and . . . well, I wouldn't wish that sort of thing on a dog, old boy. Not even a dog that bit me."

I nodded. Said nothing for a while. Then, finally, "I take it . . . you haven't noticed yet . . . how deeply I resent your moronic condescension?"

"Of course I have!" he said cheerfully. "But what are friends for?"

"And so what if you're right?" I said, not that I believed he was. "I never told you I wasn't crazy, did I?"

"True . . . true," he said, nodding, and let the matter drop, which was what I'd hoped for.

We let a lot of other things drop after that Christmas Eve, 1957, including each other, pretty much.

For one thing, he stopped urging we get together, the way he used to. Which didn't surprise me. After all, he had kept me around until he could finally show me the Althea he believed justified him. Therefore, he might well have felt he'd finished his business with me.

As for myself, I found it too demoralizing to call him on my own.

Because, as it happened, for a long time after that night, my whole life became predicated on my feeling the absence of that Light which I'd seen so clearly in all its pained and quintessential humanity.

At first, like most mourners, I suppose, I was too numbed to begin grieving. And I tried to take advantage of it, to escape through reason.

That's why I tried telling myself, while I still could, that Mel might have been right to claim I made up the whole thing in the first place. After all, the woman I met at his dinner party was a most unlikely source for the Light. And there *was* the fact that while I'd had very little social contact with the historical Althea—to say the least—the Light I'd experienced as Althea had come to me from a variety of sources, not the least important of which was a group of short stories by Norma.

I even told myself that even if I hadn't projected my imagination on her, and especially if I hadn't, maybe I shouldn't mourn the passing of the Light at all. Because Mel was unquestionably right to say that being a romantic heroine was a wretched thing to be in real life, and not to be wished on anyone. So, if anything, I ought to have been glad for her adjustment.

But I wasn't. And what's worse, when I finally did lapse into a full, deep melancholia, I found I was even a touch glad, perversely, I suppose, to mourn at last. As if it were a kind of last gesture of defense of a Light I had to admit had no place among us. Eventually, of course, I adjusted to a life without that Light. Maybe hardened, or dulled, or both. And though this absence did remain a central fact of my existence, it became so central that eventually I hardly noticed it anymore, though I believe I built upon it.

As for Althea and her family, I heard they went back to Brisbane a couple of weeks after the Christmas Eve party. I also heard, through a mutual friend, that Mel—after a terrible fight with Marcia, I suppose—seriously considered moving out there himself and setting up a practice. About a year, or maybe two, later. But he didn't do it.

He stayed on repeating himself, which he claimed was the curse of the professional man, right in darkest Newton, Mass. right into the '60s.

So, as the gray, conformist Eisenhower years came to an end, Mel and I entered into middle age isolated from one another. Never expecting, I'm sure, to find somewhere up ahead in the '60s that the world, double-crossing us, had suddenly decided to become young just as we were beginning to settle into getting old. For which we had been dutifully rehearsing during our entire, unexciting youths.

325

THE BIG APPLE. 1965

One very cold January night in 1965—a good eight years later, when I was considerably deeper into my middle age—I unexpectedly found myself standing around the edge of a crowded Greenwich Village party.

I'd been down to New York before, of course. Many times. That night, however, I had cause to observe the goings on with new curiosity because, not only had my enthusiastic host urged me to move down ("It's the Future, Baby!" he'd assured me. "Believe me, Boston's just the Past!"), but there was now the distinct possibility that I might just do that, though I still wasn't sure.

So, having taken a position up against a wall where my plastic cup could most easily be refilled, I placidly occupied myself with watching the noisy rooms before me that had been transformed, for the evening at least, into a bright and smoky forest of people. And birdless and flowerless though they were, I could easily sense it was a world teeming with its own dangers and possibilities, its own ecology of prey and predators, as I let myself wonder about how I might make out in there.

Pretty soon, however, I stopped thinking about that because, still thawing from the cold outside and having ingested a little alcohol to

327

help me warm up, I had achieved an even more placid, rather cloudlike state. One of most comfortable disengagement. And my released attention began floating all the way across the room, to somewhere near the opposite wall which seemed worlds away, to settle around a hefty, fortyish white woman with tinted glasses, an Army jacket and slacks, and a drab, pale brown version of the Afro hair style.

There was a small group around her, openly lionizing her, smiling around her with angular deference, which she, her Afroed head up, received as her due. As if accustomed to it. With what seemed a faint irony permanently etched on the corners of the wry smile visible beneath her tinted glasses.

To me, she looked like one of the more successful local predators, and from the safety of my position across the forest, I began to let myself speculate about what the source of her importance might be—when suddenly, wracking my cloudlike state like lightning cracks through a vase, came the electrically unhappy, heart-stopping feeling that all this had happened before.

For excellent reasons.

The Light was back. Signalling. After eight long years.

But I didn't realize it because, I'm sure, I didn't really want to. In my subconscious, I desperately resisted acknowledging its presence. Associating it with grief.

Then, mercifully, the moment passed, and I was breathing easily again, as my mind began to yield once more, and quite effortlessly now, to the impulse to fantasize, which soon catapulted me far beyond anxiety. Made me feel even more cloudlike as I dreamily started wondering again why the people around the woman were lionizing her like that. Must be, I thought, because of how leonine she looks, drink in one paw, marijuana joint in the other (which she didn't pass around), with her whole imposing presence culminated by that leonine Afro.

And her entire lionhood, it struck me, was re-enforced in its regality by the uncomplaining way that the lesser, two-legged types around her (why did they seem two-legged, I half wondered, and she not?) had of sharing one single joint among them. Of smiling tightly and looking up at her—as if for permission to inhale—before passing it on. Their attitude, which gave her personality such a wide berth in the crowded room, began making me imagine that what I could see of her actually only the front part—not of an important 165 lb. woman standing—but of really a much greater creature, in fact, a mythic creature now reclining Sphinx-like on its forequarters in their two-legged midst. She must be, I thought, an avatar of the Powers, whose greater magnitude the two-legged devotees around her can see plain as day (while I had to guess at it), no doubt because of their religious training in the local Manichean faiths, which was why they were paying homage.

But then, in my warming, dreamy state, she stopped looking to me quite so much like a successful local predator of the oppressive variety. Her aura began changing, became increasingly heroic, taking off in my mind from the cut of her Army field jacket, from her militant Afro. And I started liking her better as I thought: no question she's military. That's why she's important here. But look at that bearing. That dashing informality. That out-of-uniform panache she's got. *Must* be one of the Good Guys.

And then, it came to me: A guerrilla! *That's* what she is. Of course! From the National People's Gang. Cleaned up, though, for the sake of socializing with these decked out, foppish New Yorkers here, above whom she so obviously towers, physically and morally. Normally there'd be a grenade or two hanging from the lapel. But not tonight. Don't want to scare the folks.

And even the tinted, droopy-lensed glasses evoked a military echo. Had their unquestionable romance. Made me think of the lonely heroism of Amelia Earhart, smiling wryly in her cockpit. Just as this guerrilla is smiling, I thought, the same kind of permanent looking, ironic smile as she stands before these admiring, lily-livered Liberals gathered around to see a real hero. No question, that must have been exactly how Amelia smiled, I thought, the day she knowingly soared up into the sky to go off to her doom. I could practically see Amelia, smiling, the same smile, even when she was alone in the cockpit, framed against the vast Pacific skies. The skies may be vast. True. And Destiny implacable. But, funny thing, there's something about the smile of the truly brass-balled that can make it look like an even fight, almost, can't it?

Then, as my dreamy admiration continued to increase, suddenly, an anxious thought came to me: Hey! Wait a minute. Why is this guerrilla here? It's dangerous! Couldn't one of these fancy types, suffering from who knows what slight, sneak off and call . . . the *Authorities*? She's got to know it. Of *course* she does. But Jesus, *there* she is, just the same. Risking everything by coming down from the Sierras to tolerate these toadies and phonies, flattering them with the presence of a real fighter. And smiling! What *sang froid*! No question about it, it's a real feat of bravery just to stand there (the Federales could show up any minute!) surrounded by these chic types, making small talk. It's much safer in the hills. Much. This is *real* bravery, that's what I'm looking at. And just as much a testimony to real guts as it is to the cowardice of these lesser, sweet-smelling types to be here, ogling the hero, jock-sniffing, instead of being up in the hills themselves, for Christ's sake. Up where the *real* brave ones go, to live clean with the filth and the grime of the Good Fight.

So, why come here? Why waste so much bravery? And then, it came to me. The obvious reason: Fund raising. Of course. That's it. Because unfortunately, in the reality of Revolution (the wry smiling guerrilla knows, you can see it on the corners of the mouth), bravery and true hearts are not enough. A steady supply of money is required.

Then, suddenly, from all the way across the room, the hefty woman with the Afro spotted me smiling (I didn't realize I was until that very instant), whereupon she pushed aside the man in front of her in no uncertain terms and started striding for me, making me think: my God! Am I about to be pummeled . . . in front of all these people? Jesus, she must have thought I'd been finding her funny all along!

And as the hefty woman kept lurching across the room, un-mistakably at me, I thought: this is ridiculous. I'm not really about to be physically attacked, am I? Because I don't believe it, but it sure looks that way!

But I couldn't bring myself to move.

And as the woman kept shoving decisively through the crowd, only a few yards from me now, with everyone around beginning to look at her, she opened her mouth to say something, when a smile showed up on her cheeks.

(In the meantime, the voicelike Light I still hadn't officially recognized was flooding my brain, increasing its force the closer the open-mouthed woman came. After all those years of me following it, it had turned around, reversed its field, and as it came at me, somewhere inside I began getting the sense that at long last, the voicelike Light was finally going to speak directly to me. Making me tremble.

There was a good reason for this overpowering notion, of course, since so often before, what I'd thought had been Althea's Light, and Althea's alone, had actually been emitted by the same person who now stood no more than four feet from me and said: "Jerome!")

"Norma . . . ," is all I said. She laughed and shook her head. "Jesus . . . if I'd only known you were coming, I'd have dropped thirty pounds. At *least!*" and she pulled me toward her, gave my cheek a resounding kiss, and then stepped back to say, "Aren't I a fright?"

"Oh . . . no . . . ," I said, and shocked as I was at her being so changed, so heavy featured now, I would have said more, but she cut me off with a good-natured, "Don't even try. But, God! God almighty! Tell me, how in the world did you wind up here?"

"Well . . . an old friend from graduate school, . . . Ben Vartoonian, brought me," I said, and she broke out with a much less good-natured laugh, one that splintered with a mirthless harshness I'd never heard in her voice before. "Ah. yes. Ben. Our genial host. Did he tell you . . . ," she inquired, taking a sip from her plastic glass, "I'm the biggest bitch in New York?"

Yes. He had. Though I couldn't possibly have guessed he'd meant Norma. And as I stood there, trying to cope with her familiar voice coming out of this bulky, middle-aged, para-military looking stranger (whose thickened features had made me think of a cheerful Eskimo, especially when she'd smiled at me a moment ago), I still didn't know he had.

But if I'd thought about her other question, that is, about how in the world had I wound up there, to run into her again after all these years at a party of strangers, I might have realized there had been nothing accidental about it at all.

Now that I think about it, just the sight of Ben should have warned me that the UMFs were back. Because, as a matter of fact, I hadn't seen him in twelve years, either. Not since the last time he'd guided

331

me to Norma, at the service of the UMFs. Which was on that fateful day back in '53 when he'd disappeared over my protests into the bowels of Widener Library, claiming to be in sudden need of the men's room. But with his usual sly smile on his face, and therefore possibly up to no good.

His maneuver, as I well recalled, had left me neurotically paralyzed on the street, waiting for him and terrified my thesis advisor might see me. But, more to the point as far as the UMFs were concerned, it had placed me directly in Norma's path as she emerged out of the cyclopic Widener mouth, looking for some new hope of existential fulfillment through her femininity, having thoroughly had it with her husband Ralph.

The true reason I hadn't seen Ben all this time was that the UMFs hadn't needed him.

About all I heard about him during those twelve years was that he'd been seen for half a minute in a reportedly loathsome underground movie called "Wall," set in a NYC movie house men's room. The word was that Ben, playing himself, passed through to give his distinctive smile at the star of the film, a muscular young fellow, also playing himself, who was on camera throughout the hour and a half, leaning against the title source. I missed the movie, myself, but everyone who saw it told me it was unmistakably our Ben, "making it down in the Big Apple".

But, recognizable as he might have been filmed in that men's room in the late '50s, he was so transformed when he surfaced in my life again on that strange night in '65 that I didn't recognize him at first, either. No more than I'd recognized the transformed Norma later that same night.

Of course, I wasn't thinking about him. Hadn't in years.

Actually, I was thinking about me, wondering about myself, because I was a little surprised I was down there in the first place. In New York, I mean. And actually considering the possibility of living down there. Because, as I mentioned before, maybe I was going to do that. Which meant to me I might have been a little transformed myself.

Practically until that night, such a migration had never seemed to me anything more than a grisly possibility. True, I'd always regarded myself as a marginal Bostonian, but even that had been enough to let me assume as my birthright a feeling of cultural and spiritual superiority over all New Yorkers, the Rockefellers included. And, mass man that I am, I was also convinced—more than is flattering to admit in sophisticated company—that this superiority was occasionally manifested athletically by Boston's professional teams over the detested New York entries, to my deeply chauvinistic gratification. In other words, and to be very candid, my willingly becoming a New Yorker had always seemed as likely as my willingly undergoing a sex change operation.

And yet.

There I was. Mr. X.J. Muldoon, sitting in a Greenwich Village coffehouse, and thinking it over, without horror, or even shame. Even though the only other people in the place were doing nothing but confirming my worst prejudices about New York City's quality of mind. (I didn't understand, of course, that they too were part of my preparation.)

They were a couple of youngish looking men dressed in what once would have been called bohemian garbs, sitting around a table presided over by an old, red-haired woman who seemed to own the place. For a while, all they'd done, the three of them, was to complain about how bad business was "all over the Village", which had the soft quality of a ritual wail, worn smooth with repetition, like prayer, persuading me that despite their Counter Culture clothing (no pun intended), I'd stumbled into nothing more than a spiritually representative pocket of petit bourgeois shopkeepers and minor New York promoters. Not that I minded, nor expected otherwise.

Then, when they were done with their commercial laments, the conversation was taken over by the imperious, nasal monologuing of the old red-haired woman, who took to saying a lot of daffy things with her trumpet voice about how she'd known most of the greats. past and present, mostly from show biz, it seemed. Apparently they had all not only been her customers, but her intimate friends, who had all turned to her for advice at critical times in their careers. And from the way the two young men sat there, listening and smiling without really paying attention to what she said, I began getting the sense that they were now involved in another ritual, one which consisted of indulging her as a cult figure. Maybe for being some sort of genuine link with the "true" Village of the past—as opposed to the "commercial" one of the present—where the bohemianism had been more legitimately that of artists than of shopkeepers.

Listening to them, I was vaguely on the point of wondering what in the world had happened to the Village's rich artistic traditions, and where had the old-time bohemian, anti-bourgeois spirit of rebellion gone, when, as if to answer me, the door opened—the bell rang—and a man rushed past me, heading excitedly for their table, with the door and bell slamming behind him.

His movements were quick, but not so quick that as he passed me I didn't notice he was shaven-headed, dressed in buckskins, and that he wore one round golden earring, which was the only piece out of keeping with the great quantities of other jewelry hanging from all over him, all of it suggesting the American Indian.

"Hey!" he said, "I don't know why I'm here. I must have forgotten something for the party. Did I leave anything, Irma?"

"No," said the red-haired old woman. "I don't think so."

"Good!" he said, appreciating her kindness. "Thanks, Irma!" and just as excitedly his footsteps started toward me, to be expected since he had to pass my table to get out the door.

But then, unexpectedly, they slowed, and as they did, I began to feel the back of my head scrutinized with greater and greater intensity as the steps came to a halt.

Instinctively, I turned around, and in one motion, as if pulled up by invisible strings, I was on my feet as he started moving again, faster and faster, his arms (as mine were) spread out to embrace me, continually crying out, "Hey! Hey! hey! HEY!" and stopping only by giving me a resounding kiss on one cheek, and then another, on the other, as I, while not kissing him back, found myself embracing him just as vigorously as he embraced me, and also crying out, "Hey! Hey!" myself, because the shaven-headed Indian in my arms, earring and all, had once been Ben Vartoonian, my fellow graduate student from Watertown, Mass.

"Ben!" I said, "Ben!"

"Yeh, baby! My God! You haven't changed at all! Shit, you changed so little I had trouble recognizing you," he said, laughing, and then withdrew somewhat from our embrace to better look me up and down. What he saw, of course, was my tweed jacket, my narrow tie, my button-down shirt, and all the other things that contrasted so sharply with his own triumphantly liberated, Rousseaunian Natural Man outfit.

"Man . . . ," he said finally, "I can't believe how *much* you haven't

changed. Like . . . you're out of the Time Machine! I mean . . .
you're exactly the same . . . only worse!" At which he laughed
quite happily, as if it had reassured him of all being right with
the world in some way, while continuing to look me over, which
only succeeded in making me feel increasingly like Mr. Up-Tight
Western Man as I held still for his inspection. And then he asked,
not unkindly, almost hopefully, "Hey . . . is that . . . possibly . . .
the same old jacket you used to wear all the time . . . ten years
ago?"

"Nah . . . ," I said, a bit embarrassed. "It's just like it though."
And as I spoke, he beamed at me with such open affection that he
embarrassed me further. "See, Ben, I found another one just like it,
so I snapped it up." At which he clapped his hands, laughing, and
cried out, "You're beautiful! Beautiful! Man, don't let the Smith-
sonian Institute get you, cause I want you for *me*!"

Then, taking a further step back now to permit me to focus on
him, he said, "But don't tell *me* I haven't changed!"

"Can't do that," I said. "You sure didn't dress like that back in
'53," and he laughed. The greatest change I'd noticed, however,
even more radical than his shaven head, was how infinitely more ex-
troverted he seemed now than in his sly and conformist graduate
student past, which was a difference that frankly became him.

"Well?" he demanded, "Aren't I beautiful!" and with that he
began turning around in display, looking at me over his shoulder,
with his buckskinned arms raised up like wings as all the flecks hung
out in the full American Eagle glory. Indian, not Federalist edition.

"You are, Ben," I said, "no question about it," which he received
with a huge grin. His shaven head, especially when he grinned like
that, made his muscular face look mischievously simian, which in no
way detracted from his general Eagle-Indian aura. "Jesus," I said,
"I remember you when you were just an ordinary Armenian."

"Well, I escaped my fate, baby! I *outsoared* it!" he said, stretching
out his winglike arms and turning around once more. "Now I fly
openly through the night! You can do it too, man!"

"Thanks, Ben, I'd love to, but if I started flying openly through the
night myself, I don't think I'd keep my job very long."

A new, quizzical light showed in his eyes, making him look even
more monkeylike and mischievous than before, as I instantly
guessed that Ben was now wondering about me—if maybe I might
not have become *his* kind of night flyer myself, after all these years,

though of the secret kind. "Oh, yeah . . . ?" he said, a knowing smile waiting to form itself at the corners of his mouth. "Well, baby, don't worry. You sure look like a dull school teacher. I'll give you that."

"Really? Oh, good . . . Glad to hear it, Ben. See, I belong to Boston's educated poor, and this is my caste uniform . . . See, my mission is to inspire respect in the established order, by imitating it . . . on a modest scale, of course. I mean, nobody likes a pushy Irish school teacher."

"Yeah . . . ?" he said, still waiting, watching for a further revelation.

"Sure!" I said. "Otherwise . . . Jesus! I'd dress up like a Japanese colonel *all* the time," to which I added, "I mean, like I do in private."

He looked at me for only another second, taking it in, and then, suddenly, he shook his head and clapped his hands again as his eyes became absolutely bright with joy and he repeated, "Japanese *Colonel*! That's *beautiful*! I dig you, man! Masculine protest!" and having picked up my not so oblique message that I was not, after all, his kind of night flyer (and having embarrassed me by remarking on it), he burst out laughing. But not derisively at all. Very pleased, actually, which both surprised and relaxed me as he said again, "Christ, you haven't changed at all, man. Not-at-all . . . Still the wisecracks when you get up-tight, the same old stiff, deadpan face when you're trying to hang in there. Same ol' Muldoon. Honest to God I love it. *Love* it!!! Hey . . . I bet you haven't smoked pot even," and, peering into my face—which I instinctively lowered—he was now making me feel as if he were fondly chucking me under the chin, particularly as he added, "Hey? Have you? Am I right or am I right?"

"Yeh . . . I'm still a virgin," I said, quite self-conscious of my stiff face and my lame wisecracks as I tried to "hang in there", as he'd put it.

"I *knew* it! You're too much!" And then, taking a resolute breath, he announced, "Hey, listen, I can't stay here all night. I gotta go home, like right *now*, 'cause I'm giving a party. Wanna come? You're not doing anything, are you?"

"Uh . . . no," I said, to which he replied, laughing, "Of course not! Why should you start now, right? So put on that disgusting rag you've got there," he said, pointing to my overcoat, "and let's split! Who knows, maybe you can take some memories back to Boston!"

And in no time we were both hurrying along the icy, black and vacated Village streets, where all human traffic seemed to have disappeared as if absorbed by the buildings' dark foundations, to stay there until the spring.

"What are you doing here, anyway?" he asked me, snorting steam.

"I don't know," I said. "Maybe I'll move down."

"Oh, do it! Do it!" he enthused, congratulating me for the notion. "Move down to the Big Apple, man, 'cause it's the Future! Believe me, Boston's just the Past!"

"Yeah, well . . . ," I hedged, and then I asked, "Were you really in a movie?"

"Man, I was in *tons* of movies. I'm out of that scene now, though. You never saw me?"

"No," I said, and he laughed, "Jesus, you never smoked pot and you never saw any of Andy's movies. I can't believe it. You're like an aborigine, for Christ's sake. This is 1965, Muldoon, 1965!"

"Well, I'll try to catch up," I said. "What are you up to now?"

"Contributing editor, baby! That's my title. I'm starting a new magazine with a lot of people, see, and between you and me, I think it's got national possibilities."

"Great!" I said.

"That's what we're hoping. Wanna hear the title?"

"Sure."

"*Custer's Enemies*! Great, huh? See, it's gonna be a forum for gays and spades and women and all kinds of enemies of the white sexist oppressor."

"Well, that's a big following if you can get it together. Who's the editor? Not that I'd know . . . "

"Oh . . . yeah, well, that's Evie," he said, contorting his mouth, which made him look momentarily like an old, unhappy monkey. "Man, she's the problem. See, she's this real ball buster of a bitch with a lot of connections, and what makes it worse is that she's raised most of the dough. Maybe you heard of her, Evie Moon?"

"Can't say I have."

"Well, she's been writing for all the big women's mags for a million years. Stories, mostly. And now she wants her own book. She's coming out Radical, dig, right out front. But she's radical like a fox, if you know what I mean."

"I guess I don't."

"Well, the way she figures it, if she can make her move first, and

337

have the magazine *her* way, she just might beat the rush and have the new *Ladies' Home Journal* on her hands. Maybe the new *Cosmo*. She doesn't put it that way, but that's where it's at."

"Really . . . ?" I said, a bit surprised.

"You bet your life. You know, like telling all the little girls what they can like, what to wear, what to talk about, all that stuff. That's what all those mags are like, anyhow, right? Catechism, man. You can dig it. And the whole shtik depends on their insecurities, right? So Evie figures she can clue them on the new styles . . . but for *everything*, man! I mean, from clothes, to food to fucking, believe me . . . like the old mags can't, 'cause they've all got fixed positions and a committed constituency, right? Like, what self-respecting young chick wants to be clued on how to screw by her grandmother's mag, right?"

"But . . . I thought . . . ," I said, a bit disoriented.

"Yeah?" said Ben, suddenly defensive, "What *did* you think?"

"Well . . . nothing, I mean . . . I didn't think from what you said . . . it was going to be . . . so . . . commercial. I thought what you had in mind was more of a . . . uh . . . ," but as I struggled to come up with an inoffensive word (I was about to say 'more ideological'), Ben looked at me out of the corner of an eye which instantly grew colder. I could tell, to my discomfort, that he wasn't appreciating my efforts one bit, particularly as he said, "That's right. You heard me right. I want it to be . . . *something* else."

"Yes, well, I thought so," I said, nodding with serious respectfulness, and I thought he was going to let it pass, only to have him stop short and turn on me, announcing, "Lookit, Muldoon, I'm Gay and I'm not ashamed of it, O.K.?"

"Oh . . . sure!" I said, smiling a permission I thought he took for granted, unhappily aware now that the possibilities of offense were multiplying around me.

"Like back in school," he said, continuing to look me right in the eye (his shaved head made his contentious face look even more unforgiving), "I had to hide it, so maybe you didn't know I was Gay."

I did. But I still found myself trying to look surprised. As a matter of fact, he'd told me so himself, one long ago night in graduate school. And then gone on to tell me hundreds of stories about that particular Boston netherworld, amazing me with all the people he said it included, making me think for a while that I could suddenly see society with something like Proustian X-ray eyes. But evidently he'd forgotten.

And I didn't want to tell him that we'd all rather guessed, anyway, because I was afraid he'd think I was implying he was obviously effeminate, or some such, which he was not, and I was sure I'd offend him with that, too.

"Lookit, Muldoon," he said, "I'm not telling you this to make you up-tight, or anything . . . but don't worry about being "tolerant" with me, O.K.?"

Maybe he wasn't trying to be nasty, but the way the word "tolerant" came out rang with barely contained disdain.

"It's fine with me," I said, trying to smile and shrugging. "And, really . . . that's what I thought your magazine was supposed to be about, from what I heard listening to you . . . back there . . . you know . . . a forum."

He looked at me for another moment, making me wonder if he was about to attack some more, but his tone eased off a bit, though only a bit, as he said, "Yeah, well . . . you heard right. Like, I want this thing to be part of the Resistance. Like, I'm against sexism, 'cause it's just another way to oppress the individual with a lot of bullshit roles, if you know what I mean."

"I can see that, Ben," I said, but he replied unconvinced, "Yeah, well . . . Maybe I better tell you something else before we get to my place."

"Sure . . . "

"Like down here in the Big Apple, man, it's not like back in Boston, O.K.? 'Cause as far as I'm concerned, down here there's just one gender, man. And that gender is *you*. I mean, *You-Making-It*, dig?" he went on rather grimly, apparently unable to avoid becoming more exercised about the whole thing the more he explained it to me. "See, down here, man, it doesn't matter if you do the boy bit or the girl bit or the albino turkey bit, dig? And *that's* why I like it. 'Cause the way I figure it, there's *nothing* more important than you fulfilling yourself. 'Cause . . . everything else is *rheetoric*, O.K.? And you better not let anybody stop you, either, 'cause you only go around once."

I nodded, humbly showing him I acknowledged his admonishment, and then tried to smile a kind of white flag to him, but he shot back at me with, "So don't worry about walking into some fairy orgy over at my place, 'cause there's going to be all *kinds* of individuals there, man. I mean, we're people, just like everybody else, man, so don't sweat it."

Actually, until moments ago, I hadn't.

But now, with Ben obviously long past his initial enthusiasm at having run into me after all these years, I began to dread the evening ahead. In a matter of minutes, I had changed in his mind from a pleasant reminder of old friendships into a living symbol of the worst kind of cultural oppression. And though I badly wanted to reverse the process, I couldn't imagine how.

We started walking again. Ben was silent. I was still trying to think of something friendly to say, but dreading that anything might start him off again. I even began getting the sense that Ben had managed to feel offended by me to the point of triumph, and therefore would be impossible to placate. Consequently, only a few yards later I was wondering how I would be able to escape gracefully as soon as possible.

Then, to my surprise, I was the one to stop short to make an announcement. "Hey, Ben. Jesus, I just remembered. I forgot something back at the coffee house. Why don't you give me your address, and I'll show up later."

I'd said it smilingly, unaggressively, I'd thought, but he looked at me quite surprised and said, "What's the matter?"

"Oh, nothing . . . I just left some papers behind, and I know you have to get going, so I'll just show up in a little while, O.K.?"

But he was looking at me with wounded eyes now, and glumly said, "Yeah . . . O.K."

He didn't believe me, of course. And it was obvious from his attitude that he couldn't imagine why in the world he was being victimized so. In fact, I half expected him to rally at any moment and start accusing me of dropping him because of my sexist prejudices.

Had he done that, he would have made my escape easier. But instead, to my surprise, just as I was about to fake taking his address from him and before disappearing into the night, he came out with a sad little, "Hey, man . . . did I *say* something?" and a thoroughly disoriented look had come over his face.

"No, nothing," I said. "Really, I forgot something back there." But he kept right on looking at me with his now enlarged, wounded eyes, and said, "What, man? Please?" adding a very penitent sounding, " 'cause whatever it was, I take it back. Honest, I'm real glad to see you, and I didn't want to make you up-tight or anything."

"For Christ's sake, Ben!" I said, laughing now, "I can't believe it!

What the hell *did* you expect? Like . . . ," and as soon as I said "like" I knew I'd been infected by his rhetorical devices, but I plunged ahead, "Like, what *else* could I do *but* get up-tight? I mean, if you're going to give me a hard time all night at your party, I don't need it. Believe me."

"But . . . ," he said, totally incredulous, "*who's* giving you a hard time?"

"*You* are, you crazy bastard," I said, shaking my head. "I mean, so you're Gay. Terrific. But I sure as hell don't want to spend an evening being the hick foil for you emancipated types. You can see my point, can't you?"

Understanding at last, he bowed his shaven head, scraped the ground with his right foot, and conceded quietly, "Yeah . . . I can dig it, man. I guess I was working something out. I just got paranoid. Honest, man, I was real happy to see you. I still am. I don't want to give you a hard time."

"So don't, and let's forget about it. Give me your address and I'll catch up with you later, O.K.?"

But he wasn't buying. "No, man. I can't let you go. I'm sorry I crapped it up, man. I want you to know that. You must have been making me up-tight without my realizing it."

"But, Ben!" I protested against his confession, fearing he might be the impossible kind of person that can only see himself as victimized, "I didn't *do* anything."

"I know, man. Not you, personally. What I mean is, you must have made me paranoid because you're from my hometown and all that, maybe looking down on me, you know what I mean?"

"Sure . . . ," I said.

"See, man, that's why I can't let you go now. Like, I *have* to make my peace with the old days . . . you're not going to deny me that, are you? Honest to God, man, I really *am* happy to see you . . . so, please don't reject me, O.K.?"

What could I say to that? My escape route was blocked. I found I could only shrug and smile, before announcing, "O.K. I'm yours, Ben. How could I reject you?"

"You'll come with me?"

"Sure . . . ," I said, lowering my eyes, and finding he'd put out his right hand, which I took, saying, "But try to remember, Ben, you're not the *only* paranoid in the world," at which he laughed disproportionately, relieved, and he squeezed my hand with happy gratitude,

341

saying, "Oh, man, I'm *so* glad. 'Cause, I'd feel like shit forever if you didn't come with me now. I mean it, I've always dug you, Muldoon. Always!"

"Well . . . ," I said, fearing a blush, "likewise." As a matter of fact, I'd always had a fondness for Ben, myself.

"Oh, hey! This is great! And man, there's gonna be straights at my place, too, lots of them, so maybe something will shake loose for you!"

"That's good," I said, to which he countered, "You bet!" And with that off we went again, with Ben keeping his arm around my shoulder, making physically sure I didn't get away. "I just *gotta* tell you this, Muldoon. Like I'm into this total honesty trip, see, and I want you to *know* I think you're beautiful. I'm not gonna be defensive about it, man. I really do. In your own ugly, up-tight, Boston Irish way, man," he declared, his eyes round with sincerity. "To me, you're absolutely beautiful, and I appreciate you."

"Thanks, Ben."

"No, man. I mean it. You're the most beautiful flower you can get out of the old hometown. Honest."

"Yeah, well. I want to be honest too, Ben," I said, to which he replied, his eyes bright, "Yeh? Yeh?" "Well, you're O.K., but I've met better Armenians."

"Oh," he said happily, looking at me and squeezing my shoulders again. "You're *so* up-tight, I love it! You can't tell me right out that you dig me, man, but I *know* you do." And he laughed, "so *please* . . . for me, get plastered tonight. Smoke pot, even, O.K.? Have a blast!"

"I'll give it my best, Ben."

Soon we were standing before the small and deceptively quiet looking door to his basement apartment.

He gave me one more look, smiled sentimentally at the sight of old, up-tight me, and we both sensed our visit with the past was about to be over.

Then he opened his door, and it was like an explosion of noise bursting out onto the cold, dark street, revealing the low-ceilinged, bright and noisy forest of people that had been waiting there for him.

And for me. Because this was where the UMFs had wanted him to deliver me. Which he had done.

We both contemplated it for a moment.

To me, there was nothing charitable looking about that forest, maybe because of the way people held themselves, as if already having appraised the values, virtues and weaknesses of everything around them, and remained ever unimpressed, which assured me this was not a gathering of friends, but of potential options.

Ben winked at me, "Come on in, man. The water's fine, if you can swim in it."

"I don't know if I can," I said.

"Sure you can! Make it!" he urged me. "Remember, this is the Big Apple, that's what it's for!" I nodded, and he said, "Lookit, you're gonna be on your own now, like the rest of us, O.K.?" I nodded again, understanding he had to go on his rounds.

Then, as if already knowing we'd never meet again because he'd concluded his mission he turned and looked at me, shook his head and pursed his lips at the sight of me (was it, I wondered, at how little I'd changed, at how much I'd necessarily have to change?) and then embraced me very tightly, slapping my back, and said unconvincingly, "I'll catch you later, O.K.?"

I nodded, quite moved, frankly, and said, "Yup . . . ," and we disengaged from our embrace.

Then, with a last wave of the fingers from his right hand, and one last monkey grin, he turned and disappeared into his natural habitat, to make it.

I deposited my coat on a pile, got myself a plastic cup, and went to lean against a wall, to let myself thaw and to contemplate a world I might possibly be disappearing into, myself, someday.

Until I lost myself in fantasies about the bulky, Afroed white woman in para-military garb, the guerrilla hero across the room. The leader of the Resistance who incredibly spotted me, detached herself from that mélange of strangers, and came charging across the room, to stand only a few feet from me and say, in a voice very much like Norma's: "Jerome! Jerome! I can't believe it!"

_____

"Ben. Our genial host." Norma's voice had just said, coming out of the Afroed woman masked by tinted glasses. "Did he tell you I'm the biggest bitch in New York?"

And before I could counter with my reflex, gentlemanly "of course

343

not", I knew he had, indeed. Because from across the room, a man called out, "Evie!" and the woman in front of me turned around. "Evie!" the man called out, "There's some people here I want you to meet . . . when you get the chance!"

She nodded, grinning beneath her tinted aviator glasses, and craned her neck to see who they were. Then she waved to them, like a politician to a constituent he's supposed to know before turning back to me, saying, "It's all right. They're nobody. I met them already, anyway . . . but, for God's sake, what I demand to know is . . . is this really you, right here, right out of my sordid past?"

"Guess so . . . ," I said, and then asked, incredulously, "But . . . are *you* Evie?"

She didn't like the way it came out. Her mouth stiffened (now she was certain Ben had told me), but only for a brief instant, because then her wry smile took over, on the offensive again. She sipped her drink and then said, "Yes I am, sweetie. You look so shocked . . . Is it . . . too much for you to handle?"

"Uh . . . no, no . . . ," I said. "I'm not shocked . . . I mean, not what you call shocked. See, Ben was telling me what a big deal Evie was . . . actually . . . and I guess I'm surprised to find out it's you," and I smiled, beginning to feel depressed. It wasn't so much her hefty, mannish appearance now, which was a contributing factor, but the brief glimmer I'd just caught of her new personality, if that's what it was, which had affected my mood so negatively. Because the Norma I remembered best, that benignly ironic creature who'd called herself a "potted plant", had been, above all else, nice.

And I really didn't think Evie Moon was. Certainly not above all else.

"Yes, Jerome," she said. "You just never know about people, do you? I'm afraid I really have changed a lot. An awful lot. To be expected, I suppose."

"Well," I said, "You certainly do seem to be blooming," and Norma-Evie, or Evie-Norma smirked at this. "Watch your language!" she said, and took another sip. "But . . . I guess I am, now that you mention it. In lots of ways. I do believe I am closer to being myself than ever before, though . . . certainly more than when I was doing my stupid best to live up to being a male literary fantasy about women. Trouble is, I never expected the real me to emerge so plump. That *was* a surprise," and grinning, and shrugging philosophically, she added, "However . . . ."

"Is that what you were . . . a male literary fantasy?"

And she laughed, more easily now, "Of course. Aren't we all? Mere literature, as the French like to say? And that's what we're fighting to change, you know." And I must have looked a bit puzzled to her (which I was) because she knitted her brows and declared in a pedagogical baritone, "I tell you, Muldoon, too *much* literature! *That's* the trouble with women, and always has been. Why, haven't you read Madame Bovary, for example?" and then, taking a further glance at me, she added, "Or . . . don't you know nothin'?" and back came a softer version of that new laugh of hers, the one with a deadened and, in fact, rather punitive harshness in it that I didn't remember from the old days.

(Now, watching her smile at me, not sure of quite how I was being teased, I couldn't help remembering how this was not the first time she had shown me how, indeed, you never do know people. How Norma the Nice, the one I moronically kept looking for in Evie—was that why she smiled?—had turned out to be only a mirage of mine in the first place. Evaporating instantly, burnt out of every place but my imagination the moment I'd found myself sexually involved with a surprising Cantabridgian wife I'd never imagined as a reality before. Whom, of course, I'd instantly liked a lot less than the fictional Norma the Nice. Because I could never imagine my old, sweet mirage, mere literature that she was, ever oppressing me, not the way that melodramatic married lady with all her theories about "giving" gave every indication of being ready to do.

But the truth was that somehow, from the beginning, the ideologically pat, romantic, Cantabridgian wife hadn't seemed solidly real to me, either. As a matter of fact, she'd always been the one to strike me as the most likely to be "mere literature", and a male literary fantasy, at that. Because, throughout our making love, I really hadn't been at all sure that the space called Norma wasn't really occupied by someone called Eva, the cold-mouthed creature from the stories I'd taken to be autobiographical who believed that nothing mattered, beginning with who slept with whom.

Of course, when she found out, she'd laughed fondly at me and told me most femininely that Eva, her fictional creation, was, if anything, her very opposite. And just a pathetic thing, really, because she couldn't love, and therefore, of course, couldn't live. And what's more, the literary married lady told me, smiling happily and stroking my hair, the poor thing was further to be pitied because

345

she hadn't had the marvelous good fortune of running into somebody like me, capable of making her become truly alive and real in the world by the sheer force of his warm virility. To which I'd nodded, under many smiling kisses and tried to agree.

But despite everything, Eva had rung terribly true to me in the secret corridors of my soul. At the very least as true as the improbable, disaffected, married lady who showed up naked on my couch one afternoon to firmly deny the existence of Norma the Nice, a contented wife and mother I'd known for years.

And there, in those secret corridors, Eva stayed, wandering around incorporeally, confusing me about the person I was involved with, possessed as she was by her godlike knowledge that nothing really matters, that the value attributed to anything was only the hysterical invention of the weak, who cannot face her Truth. And, of course, turning Norma into a bewildering female Cubist monster for me.

That was when, in my heart of hearts, I think I wondered if, whether she knew it or not, the basic form out of which that female Cubist monster confronting me had evolved its two Norma wings wouldn't one day turn out to be Eva, after all. Because maybe, for the time being, Eva only existed below the Norma surfaces. But maybe it was precisely Eva's reality that made the other two Normas, pious aspirations both, whirl hysterically around her, desperately asserting their existences while trying to avoid being devoured by central Eva, the matrix vortex that waited. Smiling her ultimate serpent smile. Calmly prepared for the day when the other two Normas finally owned up to their irreality and collapsed into nothing. Which would leave me Eva nakedly lunar in my arms for good.

That never did happen, of course. I never did find myself with Eva in my arms because the Cubist monster lost interest in me.

But now, here she was, twelve years later, and calling herself Evie Moon by choice. And smiling at me from behind her tinted aviator glasses, with a touch of challenge about what I saw, as if knowingly answering an old question I must have had about her. And surely, surely aware I was trying to perceive her all over again, trying hard to understand both what she was now and what she had been, in the light of each other.

Frankly, whether it meant anything that she'd changed her name to Evie or not, I still didn't know, but as I kept looking at her, doing my best to retain a social smile, I admit it made me instinctively grateful that the Cubist monster had lost interest in me.)

346

"Hey!" she said, "That's one sickly smile on your face, friend! I mean, I know I've changed but . . . *that* much?"

"Oh . . . I . . . ," I stuttered, self-consciously adjusting my smile. "I was just remembering something. You know, those stories you had me read a million years ago. About somebody called Eva, right? You know, back when you were just an aspiring . . . ?"

"Yes!!" she interrupted me, suddenly delighted, and then she good-humoredly completed my sentence for me, "Sure! Back when I was just an aspiring rat, of *course*! No kidding. You *actually* remember them?"

"Sure . . . "

"You know, Jerome," she said, "I *knew* there was something I liked about you. I mean . . . if you remember them favorably, of course. Because otherwise, forget it."

"I'm trying to think . . . I *guess* I do," I said, but she cut me off with mock severity. "Don't get honest with *me*, buster!"

"No, no . . . I mean, just remembering them after all these years is a tribute, isn't it?"

"Yeah . . . ," she conceded, "I guess it is. I finally sold those things, you know."

"No kidding?"

"Oh, indeed. For years!" she added, laughing quite easily now. "In *various* forms!" And after looking at me for another moment, she added, "God, what a memory you have. You even remember Eva. Wow!"

"That part's not so hard," I said, "because you spent a lot of time telling me how completely different she was from you, do you remember that?"

"No, did I *really*?" she said, amazed. "God only knows what I was talking about. But you know, as a matter of fact, I have taken my *nom de guerre* from those stories. And I use the term advisedly, by the way, since these are Revolutionary times. Yes sir! Times of combat, not of personal indulgence . . . did you know that, Jerome?"

"Uh . . . no."

And she laughed, "God, you *are* behind the times!" Then, knitting her brows again in what looked like a caricature of masculine seriousness, she announced, "My boy, we might not look like it to you, but we're making war *all* the time . . . which is why my *nom de guerre* has taken over my full identity . . . now ask me against whom."

"O.K. . . . against whom?"

"Why, the Establishment!" and she laughed again. "God, Jerome, you've *got* to come to New York more often. I bet you haven't even figured out who the Establishment is yet."

"Oh, yes I have. I figured that out last year! It's Them-that-runs-the-world, right?"

"Right!"

"There!" I said. "But, was there some reason, I mean, some special one, for your choosing Eva for a name?"

"Well, I didn't exactly *choose* it . . . but," she shrugged and grinned, "what happened was very strange, really. I wrote a couple articles for the *Voice*, not for the money, God knows, because they hardly pay. My women's group put me up to it, actually. You know, it was time to say a lot of things that weren't being said, guerrilla criticism, I believe we called it. Sniping away at the Establishment in hit and run raids. Everything was guerrilla this and guerrilla that for us that year. Year before last, as a matter of fact. We liked it better than consciousness raising. Anyway, my mission was to howl away about how you bastards treat us, how unsatisfactory you are in bed . . . not all of you, love . . . and in those days we did a lot of name changing. It was a regular routine. Kind of like the Black Muslims. Personally, I favored Norma X, of course, but my group vetoed it, so I finally opted for Eva, from one of my very favorite oppressed characters. The Moon part I made up fresh. Not that I agonized over the choice, mind you, because I really didn't. But then, the damnedest thing happened . . . and believe me, I expected nothing . . . but those little articles I tossed off for the ratty old *Voice* suddenly got me more damned attention than I ever got out of *ten* years of writing stories for the big slicks. I mean, I got money for those things, but no notoriety . . . so, I stuck with it. I mean, I had to, almost, didn't I?"

"But why?"

"For heaven's sake, Jerome! That's what people knew me as, and I *did* want to be known, you know. I've *always* craved notoriety! I mean, suddenly there I was, recognizable as a minor somebody, at least in the Village. I *stood* for something, don't you see? Why, people even started asking me how I differed from the other feminists. It was terrific."

"I guess it must have been. And now, I take it, you are a prisoner of success."

"Ah, yes. Of success . . . *and* of the demands of the Revolution!"
she said raising her glass. "But how can I mind? It beats hell out of
Norma Brown, don't you think?" and from beneath her tinted
glasses she smiled her friendlier version of her old wry smile and
shrugged. "So . . . there you have it. *That* is how I became Evie
Moon to the world . . . but you, my dear, may still address me as Mr.
Norma."

"Thanks," I said. "It would be my pleasure."

"Think nothing of it. I never did get around to changing my legal
name, you know . . . but don't tell."

"Oh, I won't . . . but I'm most impressed. I mean, here you are, a
spokesman for the Sexual Revolution. Imagine!"

"Plisss!" she said, raising up her right palm and looking away
for a moment, reminding me more and more of the clowning and
modest female "potted plant" I'd known in Cambridge, "Not . . .
zzz-sspockzs(!)man," and then clarified, "Zzzz-ssspockzs—puhrzon,
Puhr-r-rzzon!"

"Oh. Excuse me . . . I stand corrected . . . And by the way, Ben
already told me about the magazine. Really, I'm most impressed."

"Yeah . . . ?" she said, looking sidelong at me as I kept on trying
to look impressed, and smiling. "You are . . . huh?"

"Sure! You've made good, right? Right here in the Big Apple,
right? And Ben tells me he thinks the magazine could make
millions, on top of everything."

She laughed, "That would be nice . . . ," and then she looked right
at me for a moment pausing before saying with a melancholy
seriousness, "But let me tell you, the more I look at you and think
back . . . you, with your obscene memory and all . . . the more I
realize I should have you assassinated."

"But why? I thought we were friends?"

"Oh, Jerome . . . ," she said, dropping her shoulders and looking
wistfully at me, "when I think of . . . all the crap I must have told
you . . . God, how it embarrasses me now."

"I don't know what you mean," I said, but she gave another unconvinced, sideways glance and said, "Come off it . . . or are you
trying to tell me, you bastard, that there I was, pouring my heart out,
and you weren't even *listening?*"

"Oh, no. Sure, of course I was listening."

"That's better! Well . . . ," she said, and gave out a sigh of the
sort that is more in sorrow than in anger, "I was afraid of that. Like

349

I said, I should have you assassinated. One of these nights, much as it grieves me, I'll have to send somebody from my cell, and then they'll find you one morning, dead, probably with a vibrator between your eyes."

"But Norma," I said, "I swear you didn't say anything all *that* embarrassing. At least, not that *I* remember."

"Oh, please, don't pretend you've forgotten. Jesus, how awful. I mean, *Me*, the future Evie Moon yet, talking as if I believed that childbirth would be my greatest orgasm which I looked forward to undergoing with a blissful smile, provided I was having the son of the man I loved, presumably Captain Potent. It's *too* humiliating for words. How can I possibly let you live?"

"You *are* exaggerating, you know that, don't you?"

"Only a little. And the worst part is that I was sincere, which you know perfectly well. Not honest, mind you. Just sincere. I wanted to believe that stuff. Ugh."

"And now . . . ," I said, "you don't."

"God, no!" she looked up, blurting out a laugh. "And furthermore, Jerome, you better get it through your head I don't, if we're going to be friends." And then, easing her tone a bit, she added, "That's really why I owned up, you know . . . so we can leave it behind." But then suddenly, she launched into, "My *God*, man! What do you take me for? The person you *knew*?"

"Of course not," I said.

"Damned straight. I'm a new woman. *The* New Woman!"

"And you really didn't talk like that, anyway."

"If you say so," she said, evenly now. "Just as long as you know I don't now."

I nodded. And then an odd comparison came into my head: this was a little bit like running into a girl who said she'd once been promiscuous but now practiced chastity, just to warn one to keep one's hands off.

"Oh, well," I said, "so what if you did? After all, you weren't Evie Moon back then, right? So, how can there be any shame?"

"I suppose," she conceded. "Theoretically no shame, anyway. But I am also convinced that the world should be damned grateful that I'm Evie Moon now. . . . I mean, Ralph was a bastard. Still is, by the way. Do you ever see him? I do, about once a year. The kids stayed with him, you know. All grown up now, and I'm afraid they like him better. Much better. For which I can't blame them. After all, I didn't exactly stick around to devote my life to them, did I?"

"Oh . . . I didn't know about that . . . "

"No need to drop your voice, Jerome. I know it's customary, but no need. Actually, they sized things up correctly. I *didn't* want to be saddled with them, and that's the truth. Naturally, I wanted their adoration . . . but that's all. At first, when I took off, I was afraid of the guilt I'd feel, being a mother and all. But you know, it's really quite surprising how much we overestimate the powers of guilt," and she smiled, "I mean, usually anyway. Most of the time, the best I could do was to feel guilty about not feeling guilty."

"But . . . you get along with them now."

"Not really. It's hard, because they do resent me. Which I can understand, of course, the selfish little wretches . . . But the worst part is that I'd have to say I don't find them particularly interesting as people. Now, isn't *that* a discouraging thing for a mother to say? . . . Oh, Garth shows a little promise, maybe . . . but not Timmy, I'm afraid."

"But . . . you like them," I said, I'm afraid, hopefully.

And she smiled at me. "What can I say . . . would I, if they weren't my own? The word *is* awfully strong . . . if I'm going to be honest about it. Let me tell you something I can live with, though. Hope it doesn't make you think I'm a total monster. But if somebody told me I had to spend eternity with Ralph or either or both of them, bastard that he is, and he is . . . I'm afraid there'd be no contest. At least he's brighter than they are . . . which, of course, is why he finally understood why I took off and left him with the kids. He finally did understand it was either them or me, on top of which, I really knew they'd survive anyhow, whereas I knew I wouldn't have, if I'd stuck around. I mean, not survive the way I wanted to, that is. He's fairly happy now, by the way. Married a little girl who thinks her entire importance radiates from him, as life from the sun, my dear, so she treats him like a living god, which he seems to enjoy . . . Who wouldn't, right?"

There was a pause, as I didn't quite know how to react to what she was telling me about herself, which she was managing to do without shame or guilt, it seemed, not even with vindictiveness or self-congratulation, until she asked me, finally, "Do you think I'm awful, old chum?"

"No," I said, truthfully, but looking down nevertheless, as if I had made a terrible admission of my own.

351

"Don't you think . . . just put yourself in my place . . . that you'd have run for your life, too, especially if you could have left the kids safe enough with somebody else?"

The first reply that came to mind was, yes, but I'm not a woman. Instead, I said, "I don't know. I guess somebody has to stay, right?"

"Yup. So we think, anyway. In the end, you see, it becomes a test of wills. Sort of, well, . . . the person who cares least, wins. And Ralph, well . . . lost. Maybe. And until I took off, you see, I was the one always losing, always the one to hold the bag. No need to worry about Ralph, of course. He's a master bag passer."

There was another pause now, until, to end it, I said, "You . . . uh, still haven't told me why the world should be grateful you've become Evie Moon." And she half laughed at how it came out—but so gently, so refusing to take advantage of the opening and pounce on my *faux pas*, that now I couldn't possibly believe that she was anything close to being the biggest bitch in New York. Despite all the things she'd said, however unmotherly, and not that I doubted them, it was Norma the Nice that I kept seeing once again. Older. Heavier. But still, Nice.

"It does seem to call for an explanation, doesn't it?" she shrugged a bit ruefully. "Well, at least now, I don't blame the world for my lack of bliss. Not that I didn't spend years doing that, just like my kids. But honestly, as big a bitch as I might be today . . . "

"You don't seem like one," I interrupted, and she smiled and said, "But I am one, and with pride, by the way. Only I'm on my good behavior in your honor, and . . . I have a gently modulated voice, for which you dumb men always fall . . . anyway, as I was trying to tell you, I no longer blame the world, and you'll be especially glad to hear, I particularly don't blame the men in my life, either. Not even for being rats. Because I *always* understand, from the inside, Jerome." And she smiled, but I must have looked puzzled to her because she added quickly, "Oh, don't get me wrong, I sure do in my writing. I bitch away like *crazy* there. But that's Evie Moon biz. The Revolution and all. I mean, my public, not my private life."

"Oh . . . ," I said. "I guess . . . well, I thought in Revolutionary times, we didn't have private lives."

"Now, I didn't say I was perfect, Jerome, did I?"

"Guess not. Well, anyway, glad to hear that in spite of everything, there are still men in your life," I said, and that didn't come out felicitously either. However, this time, she laughed quite harshly at

352

me, "Why, Jerome! What *were* you thinking?" and I'm sure I blushed miserably, but I kept my face up nevertheless as she went on, "For Christ's sake, of *course* there's men in my life. I can't *stand* women!" she declared emphatically, and with that laughed some more, not so nicely this time, though obviously at the idea of women rather than at me.

"You can't?" I said. "But I would have thought . . . "

"Lookit, Jerome," she said, patient as someone pulling cattle by the nose, "currently I'm fiction editor for this magazine, right? Well, let me tell you, just try reading all that self-pitying bilge coming in every day, and you, me or anybody would come out raving like Nietzsche, championing whips for the ladies. Really, they're incredibly tiresome. And after a while, it all sounds like it was written by one person, too, one tiny wheedling voice complaining away about how nobody listens when she talks, how the big beast doesn't appreciate sacrifices, only sees things from his point of view, never giving any consideration, and so forth and so on, while the tears get swallowed with the snot. That's why I'm trying to get rid of reading the fiction, by the way. Or I'm going to go crazy. But they all tell me it would be elitist and unfair, so I can't. Yet."

"Boy, you really *aren't* perfect as a feminist, are you?"

"You don't understand. It's not that I don't agree with them. Really I do. But I *know* all that stuff already! And I get so much of it, I guess my feeling tends to be, who cares? I mean, who cares about millions of Norma Browns and their Doll House routine, for Christ's sake? Especially if they don't do anything but whine about it. God knows I can't respect them for it, *not* being the Evie Moon I am today, right?"

"Well . . . ," I said, "I sure hope you don't make a practice of talking like this in public, Norma. They'll lynch you one day."

"Oh, but I'm afraid I do. And especially to the womenfolk. I believe it's part of my charm to castigate them, which I must say, I usually do with gusto. Don't you see, I *do* care . . . well, I *think* I do, anyway. But Jesus, they've *got* to *develop* a little bit! My God, Jerome, *I* know why they all sound alike. Of course I do. It's because finding our own, genuine, human voices is one of our first problems. Just think about it. Just think of all those thousands of years of practice we've had at being unreal! It's going to be a while, I'm afraid, before many of us come out sounding like human beings . . . which . . . are you ready for this?"

"I hope so."

"Which most of us are not. Not yet, you see, that's what the battle is all about. *Battle* . . . listen to me."

"I am very glad," I said, "that it's you saying all this stuff and not me."

"And well you might be," she said, smiling at me. "Because if you did, my dear, I'd strike you dead where you stand. But really, it's all true. Which is what justifies the movement, as far as I'm concerned, and which is also why I can't stand them. My God, Jerome, most of them don't even have their own *faces*, did you ever realize that? Think about it. Most of them invent those damned cliches they face the world with every morning . . . invent, hell, I take it back. They don't invent much of anything, most of them. They just take dictation on their faces. As far as I'm concerned, that make-up business represents the most obscene oppression imaginable. Far more soul destroying than anything men have to go through . . . and that's just in the *developed* countries. Think what women are like in most of the rest of the world!"

I nodded at that, looking thoughtful, I suppose, and kept on nodding thoughtfully, without quite knowing I was, until she asked me, "Hey, what's the matter? Are you lost in thought about the plight of women all over the world? Honest, I didn't mean to make you do that."

"Oh . . . No," I said.

"Well, what were you thinking about?"

"Oh . . . well, I guess I was just remembering . . . how much I like painted women," and she laughed at that, and shook her head, "I should have known! Of *course* you do, you swine!" And as I shrugged apologetically and grinned, she laughed some more.

Then, very easily, we found ourselves sinking into our own private pocket of silence within the noise made by the strangers around us, and she kept on watching me, smiling pleasantly, even indulgently now, from behind her tinted glasses.

And, as I smiled back at her, her new bulk, her military costume, her Afro and even her tinted glasses had all but vanished for me. Because now my mind became flooded with remembering her amused, intelligent gray eyes, which had just successfully filtered themselves up through the years and through all other obstacles, so much so I thought I was seeing them again as they once had been.

They'd always done the same thing to me, Norma's eyes. After the first few moments of each time we met, they'd always ended up by making the rest of her disappear unimportantly behind them, and I was left thinking of her as beautiful. Unquestionably and limpidly, smilingly beautiful. Norma. And so she'd remain in my mind, until I saw her again (especially from afar, moving with what she called her "Radcliffe Forward Lurch") when I'd realize I'd been wrong. Until, after only moments of being face to face with her again, smiling at me, any such objectivity disappeared once more with the rest of her behind her clear, gray eyes. Because of that uniquely live, perceptive quality that came out of her black pupils, I think. Always gently ironic, it seemed, principally about herself, which also always managed to make me feel seen, too, and therefore momentarily more freshly alive on this earth than usual.

And through my memory, they were taking me over again.

Which she almost seemed to know, from the way she was standing there. Smiling.

And then it happened.

There, behind the remembered clarity of her amused gray eyes, I began to see the black and secret Light, the one I'd always thought came from Althea alone. Looking at me.

There was no question at all. I could see it watching me, black, naked and absolutely alive. The very same Light she'd emanated in her stories years ago without knowing, without either of us knowing it came from her.

Something must have shown on my face, because instantly she seemed to feel discovered, sensing I was seeing her as I never had before, exactly as if I'd happened upon her most forbidden nudity in her most private chambers, where no man should ever enter without fearing blindness or madness.

But, making a gesture of her stillness, she chose not to cover up. Rather, to smile. And suddenly, all I could think of was: *Norma!* as the Light simply kept on watching, waiting now, letting me see.

And then, she broadened her smile, almost as if she could hear me thinking *Norma, Norma, Norma,* and then she deepened its intimacy.

We were standing perhaps four feet apart, just looking, but I felt as if our souls would easily step out of our bodies at any moment, embrace and kiss desperately, disregarding everyone around, not that they would have cared or understood. And our silence, and our distance, seemed to be made for leaving our souls enough room to do so, in our sudden, secret understanding.

Neither of us dared move. We both held our breath, as if knowing that nothing should be allowed to prevent it now, that anything might be fatal.

We were frozen in silence. Our eyes were fixed on each other's. She no longer smiled, nor did it matter, because in that moment we were beyond faces, breathing another air. More than amazed now, beyond astonishment.

"Evie! *There* you are!" said a long-haired, bespectacled thirtyish woman. She was standing next to Norma, annoyed, but trying to mask it—badly—with her smile.

Norma turned to her. Smiled. And said simply, "Yes. I'd like you to meet an old friend of mine, Mr. Muldoon, a big financial wizard in Maine these days. Mr. Muldoon, this is Ruth Edd, our advertising person."

I nodded. So did Ruth, though obviously not buying Norma's story about me. I guess I just didn't look like a financial wizard, from anywhere. Then, rather quickly, she said to Norma, "Listen, as soon as you get the chance, there's some people who've been waiting all night to meet you, O.K.? I'll be with them over there."

"Right . . . ," said Norma. Only not Norma, but Evie now. "I'll be with you in a second," and Ruth Edd moved away.

We were left to face each other again, but now we couldn't quite do it. We lapsed into looking off at the floor, in separate directions, until finally she said, "Vell . . . zee Revolution calls, you know."

"I can appreciate that."

"Good," she said, with a half grin now, "becauss vee zzimply *cannot* vaist a moment . . . Varr iss Varr."

"I know. Go ahead." I said. "And by the way, it's nice to hear your old crock Viennese accent again."

"Oh . . . zzattt!" she laughed, "Vell, now zzatt you mention it . . . I guess I alvvays used it vvenn I felt zzee need for a voice with rreal auzzorrity."

"But now," I said, "you've got one of your own, right?"

"Pree-zicely! Zzo I don't know vvy I'm talking to you zziss vay . . . Egg-zept, of course, I *do* like zee bossy part." And then, she concluded with, "Zee you later, O.K.?"

I nodded, and after giving me a stiff, doctoral bow, off she went to Evie.

I hung around the party, drinking and smoking, until one in the morning. Waiting for Norma. Increasingly nervous. Because, from the beginning, though I didn't admit it to myself, I suspected the worst. Which was why I kept myself stationed near the front door, so I wouldn't miss her.

Then, one time, as I came out of the bathroom, I caught sight of her, putting on her topcoat, ready to go out.

She was again in the company of the long-haired, bespectacled Ruth Edd, who already had her heavy coat on.

I called out, "Norma!" and she, turning and raising her eyebrows as if recognizing a casual acquaintance, gave me a cordial little finger wave, and, to my amazement, finished putting on her coat with a shoulder shake and started walking out.

Suddenly I was in a fury. I didn't want to make a scene, but I was afraid I might.

As I went to get my coat, having to go through a pile on the floor to get it, the door had already closed behind her.

I tried putting it on as casually as I could, so as not to make it so obvious that I was about to chase after her, and then I hurried out.

It was very cold. The street was black and empty, and I looked around, finding that she and her friend were already a block away, both of them bent over with their hands deep inside their pockets, walking fast.

"Norma!" I yelled, and she slowed her step, turned to look over her shoulder, and then stopped. She said something to her friend, who stood still, holding her ground. And then she, head down, still huddled over, walked back to meet me.

"Norma . . . ," I said. "You left . . . without saying good-by, or anything . . . "

She shrugged apologetically, "Sorry about that," she said, her breath, and mine too, both very visible as we spoke, exploding and vanishing. It was so cold my face would hurt soon. "Well," she said, "it *was* nice to see you. I mean that."

"But . . . can't I see you again, Norma?"

"I'm afraid, Jerome, it really *isn't* Norma now. Believe me, Evie is much more like it." And as she said that she looked me firmly in the eyes.

"Nobody's perfect, Norma," I said. "*Can* I see you again, please?"

"Sure . . . but if I understand your attitude correctly, love, I think I better tell you now that you won't like it."

"How do you *know* I won't?" I demanded, before bowing my head.

She contemplated me silently for a moment, then, finally, she said, "Aww . . . did you think you'd found a soul mate? I'm so-rryy."

I looked at her, momentarily unable to say a word after that. I simply couldn't believe how rotten she was being, or that she really meant it. Though I didn't doubt she wanted to get rid of me.

Then finally, looking down, I said, "I'm hurt."

"Oh, hey . . . please, that's not fair! I don't want to do that, Jerome," she said. "Listen, really, it *was* nice to see you."

"Well, I'm still hurt, I'm hurt anyway, because all the time we talked, you never asked me about *me*," I said, which made her peer into my face, to see if I were joking, which I half was, and she smiled.

"See what I mean?" she said, "That's just the trouble with me. I guess I've gotten downright masculine that way. You can see already how you wouldn't like it, can't you? I'd always come first, be untrue, all that stuff. I guess I'm saying I'm never going to love anything better than me, which you couldn't possibly enjoy . . . and still have my respect, that is . . . but thanks a bunch for the gesture. Really. I'm more than flattered."

And I nodded, didn't say anything to that, and then looked down, so she said, "You know, if I were still Norma, it could easily be a possibility. But the trouble is, Jerome, I really *am* Evie now. Evie, the professional New Woman. Every day, twenty-four hours a day."

And I nodded to that too, until finally I said, "Can I see you anyhow, sometime? Even if you won't be my sex object?"

"O.K.," she laughed. "You can get my address through Ben. Listen, it's cold as hell, and my friend back there isn't getting propositioned, so I really better go."

"O.K.," I said.

But she still didn't leave. She stayed there, hesitating, until she said, "Hey, will you forgive me for being such a shit and skipping out back there?"

"Sure . . . "

"It's just that . . . I guess . . . I didn't want to ruin a nice experience by having any more to do with you. No faith in people, I guess."

"I can understand that," I said.

But then, as she smiled at me, I caught sight of something like a cloud passing over her expression, as if precisely at that moment she

358

was just thinking to herself, what *would* she do with me if I did come into her life again? There was really no room. And she said, "Remember Evie Moon, professional New Woman, twenty-four hours a day. We understand that, don't we?"

"Yup."

And then she turned and hurried up the street to join her friend, who would soon no doubt be rewarded for her patience with an explanation from Evie about her undistinguished-looking old friend.

THE END

I never did get her address from Ben.

That was eight years ago. More, now.

I went back to Boston, and stayed there.

However, I still think of her very often. Probably every day. And now I can never think of her, I swear to God, without the Light I saw coming out of her eyes at Ben's party.

All the other Normas are gone. They are like characters in old stories now and don't confuse me about reality anymore. They aren't the ones I think of each day.

That's why I'm convinced that everything in my life, Althea included, was a preparation for finally letting me see the Light coming from her. That is, for finally letting me see her.

And sometimes I think that feeling about her as I do was implanted in me like, if I may say so, original sin, that maybe I was always in love with her, though most of my life as ignorant of it as she was of the Light she emitted.

But more than that.

Because whenever I think back to the last time I saw her and remember her walking away as Evie Moon, cold and huddled over, hurrying to catch up with her waiting friend, the same thing happens to me. Again and again. I get the same awful, vertigo-like feeling that the Unseen and Mysterious Forces fated me not *only* to be in love with her, but worse: to be among the first humans to experience the full sadness of an event no less important in the history of the Western Psyche (and no less depressing) than the crucifixion of Jesus.

I am talking (and it still affects me) about the divorce of Adam and Eve, of which, by now, I think we have all gotten wind.

And, in my orphaned mind, along with that visual memory of her walking away, something else happens. Invariably, the figure of the new Eve emerges, transformed, irreconcilable. No longer young, of course. No longer pretty. But determined during what might be the sunset years of our species to earn her new reality through the sweat of her brow (convinced that Adam's ancient punishment was really a privilege denied her) by making a go of it on her own, in New York publishing circles to begin with.

She must, of course. The world may be cooling. The sands are certainly running. This is hardly the time for her to spend her life incarnating male literary fantasies. Really, for the sake of us all, she must manage to escape from the labyrinthine prison of masculine dreams, or we'll all stay inside. And she must manage to succeed where Althea could not by being able to live, as herself. She must cease to be what she called "mere literature".

True, to do this she began by incarnating a female literary fantasy.

But I do believe it was only the beginning. I do believe, because I trust her integrity, that she does mean to find the way to avoid becoming ideal, at last. Which I recognize as a Promethean task.

And that is one reason why I didn't try to get in touch with her. I didn't want to get in her way.

I decided she was quite right: in the end, feeling about her as I did (and do), I wouldn't have liked it. She really was, even if I deserved it, in no position to love me, having so much else to do.

And I have privately thanked her in her absence many times for having had the decency to say so. Speaking as she did from her new knowledge of herself, I am sure she was relieved I never did come around again.

I have had the occasion to thank her this way very often, of course, living as I am in my own new Adam's solitude, which I haven't liked much, either.

Now and then, I admit I have blamed her for it. But only in my weakest moments, when self-pity overcomes both memory and reason.

By and large, however, I am grateful to her even as it is, because through her turning into the new Eve, I think I have already learned to give up certain illusions it is much the best to give up. Again, for the sake of our humanity, which we have so often sacrificed to dreams.

Some things, though, I never have given up, and probably never will now. Such as thinking about her every day, about her kind of honesty and new and perhaps final inaccessibility, and about her eyes, and the incurable effect they have had on my spiritual metabolism. Always.

And thinking about other worlds, too, of course. Like the ones orbiting in the daily sports pages, where I'll rest. As always.

FICTION COLLECTIVE

books in print: